F
WOOD

Wood, Bari,
1936-

The basement.

$17.95

DATE			
9/90			

THE BASEMENT.

Also by Bari Wood

THE

BASEMENT

Bari Wood

WILLIAM MORROW & COMPANY, INC.
NEW YORK

Copyright © 1995 by Bari Wood

Material on pages 110–112 is reprinted by permission
of The Putnam Publishing Group from *The Black Arts*
by Richard Cavendish. Copyright © 1967 by
Richard Cavendish.

Library of Congress Cataloging-in-Publication Data
Wood, Bari
The basement / by Bari Wood.
ISBN 0-688-13351-7
p.   cm.
I. Title.
PS3573.0588B37   1995
813'.54—dc20   94-21657
CIP

Printed in the United States of America

First Edition

1 2 3 4 5 6 7 8 9 10

BOOK DESIGN BY BRIAN MULLIGAN

To Dan Lustig, super cousin

ACKNOWLEDGMENTS

*Thanks to Chris Malachowski
for suggesting what I think is the best scene in
this book, and to the Ridgefield branch of the TSSG.*

THE BASEMENT

CHAPTER 1

Barbara Potter drained her teacup. Honey thickened the dregs and she thought she felt an immediate lift from the glucose.

"Where'd you get the honey?" she asked Myra Ludens.

Myra broke into a smile and blushed. She had the kind of moist, smooth skin that blushes easily. She must have been very, very pretty when she was young, maybe beautiful; but she was in her forties now and carried an extra thirty or so pounds that smeared her features and made her nose too small for her face. But her eyes were wonderful anyway. They were bright, clear blue, fringed with thick, pale lashes, and her hair was a corn-gold you'd never get from a bottle. It would have been lovely, too, but was permed into a frizzy halo that made her face look even rounder.

"It's my husband's honey," she said proudly. "I mean, he keeps the bees that make it. You can see the hives from here."

They went to the bow window that looked out on a couple of acres of brown meadow ringed with trees. In the distance were a couple of grayish-white boxes on stilts, under an old oak.

"Those white boxes?" Barbara asked.

Myra nodded and her smile widened, showing small, even teeth. "Why don't I give you a jar before you leave."

"I'd love it!" Barbara meant it. The honey *was* delicious.

Myra said, "The meadow's full of wildflowers, that's what gives it that rich taste."

"Mmmm." Barbara tried to sound interested.

Myra turned away from the window.

"I guess we should get started," she said.

"I guess we should." Barbara looked at the clock on the breakfast room wall. It had an expensive porcelain face with hand-painted flowers. Everything in the house was expensive and had that look of having collected over generations, not bought in the space of a couple of months from decorating catalogs. It was the look Barbara tried to emulate in the homes she "did," but this was the real thing.

The breakfast room table on which they'd just had tea, for instance, was a Connecticut Valley piece, circa 1830, worth about fifty thousand if you could even find one.

Barbara suddenly felt good.

Myra Ludens was pink-faced, overweight, maybe a little silly, and her clothes were abysmal: Her sweater was a fuchsia that only added to her damp, pink look; her slacks pulled across her rear and were too short, so the cuffs flapped around her bobby socks.

Bobby socks!

But her taste was good when it came to the house; she seemed shy, uncertain, and malleable, and she was rich.

"Ready?" Barbara asked, picking up her pad and marker.

"Ready."

Myra led her through a large, sunny, state-of-the-art kitchen, to an old slatted wood door. "The stairs look terrible," she said with her hand on the knob, "but they're sound. We've had them checked." Then she opened the door, and Barbara smelled mold and sour dirt mixed with a heavy, sickish-sweet odor of rot that should have been hot but came up the stairs on a draft of cold air.

"Holy . . ." *Shit,* Barbara almost said. But it was the wrong word to use with Myra Ludens, who'd been Myra Fox of the Quaker Foxes, with a Colonial Wars lineage and trust funds.

"Cow," Barbara finished lamely and Myra turned the color of new brick.

"Mice," she said miserably. "They get in and die no matter what we do to stop them. Maybe you know a way...."

"I might, Mrs. Ludens."

"Oh, dear, call me Myra...." She flicked the switch next to the door and bulbs in old metal cups came on, making pools of light down a rickety-looking flight of stairs.

Myra's eyelids fluttered like the wings of a nervous moth and Barbara thought, *She hates it down there,* and felt a tug of pity for the plump, pink woman next to her.

"Don't worry, Myra," she said gently. "We can fix it so you'll look forward to doing the laundry down there."

"Oh ... no one does laundry *down there.*" Myra sounded horrified. "The washer and dryer are up here in the mudroom."

Not that Myra Fox Ludens did laundry anywhere, Barbara thought.

"Well ... I guess we'd better," Myra said.

"Let's." Barbara tried to sound like she was looking forward to it, and they went down the wooden stairs. Barbara stepped down onto a dirt floor that she knew, from the look and thickness of the stone foundation, had been tamped down centuries ago. The smell of mold, sour dirt, and carrion became a reek, and she suddenly thought, *This is vile!*

"Don't forget your honey," Myra said. She held out a jar topped with a square of calico, tied with red ribbon. The golden honey swam thickly behind the glass as Barbara took it.

"I'll get back to you in a couple of days with prices," she said.

"Oh ... yes. But I'm sure it'll be okay. Your ideas are just the sort I was hoping for." Myra was blushing again. Her blood pressure must be stratospheric, Barbara thought, as she made her way along the stone path across the lawn. She climbed into the 7-series BMW that she was already two payments behind on and waved to Myra Ludens, who waved back from the open front door.

*   *   *

Vile, Barbara thought as she laid out the measurements and notes she'd made. She brewed herself another cup of tea, added some of that amazing honey that turned the tea silky and gave it a wild kind of sweetness.

She started her diagram of the basement and a sudden sense-memory of the chill and reek attacked her.

"Vile," she whispered, looking up over her drafting table at the shelves of catalogs and design books in her clean, light, airy home office. "Vile..."

She'd give a lot not to go down there again. But car payments were overdue, she was a week late with Richie's tuition, and the first of the month, with the mortgage payment and Visa bill, was closing in. She'd net eight thousand on the job, enough to keep her solvent through the summer with a little planning; plus get her primo references from the likes of Myra Fox Ludens, which could mean as much as the money.

She was stuck.

"How much?" Don Forbes asked. It would be superpractical, flat-footed Don asking that particular question, Myra thought. The others leaned closer to hear the answer, and she mumbled, "Thirty thousand," then blushed.

"Good God," cried Helen Dumott.

"I know it sounds like a lot..."

"It *is* a lot!" That was Irene, Don's wife. Worth even more than he was, giving them a combined fortune of maybe eighty million, Myra thought. Thirty thousand was *not* a lot to them.

"But"—Myra pushed on with all the firmness she could muster— "they've got to lay new floor, put up new walls, plumbing, windows ... everything from scratch. It'll be lovely when they get done."

"Lovely?" Arlen Pinchot asked wryly.

The basement was a joke among the club members. The black hole, they called it, and Arlen teased that he'd instructed in his will that he be buried down there. In honor of his ancestors. Pinchots had once owned the house and land still called Redman Farm, though there were no Redmans extant in Fallsbridge, and none of them remembered when the last one had left.

Something fell downstairs with a thud, and they all jumped, and giggled. Then a buzz saw burred.

"They started?" Helen asked.

"This morning, eight sharp," Myra told her.

"How long will it take?" asked Angie Withers. Angie was not wearing sunglasses today. The bruises had faded, her skin was smooth and fair, and she looked as lovely as ever. Bill had started AA and Myra knew it would take this time; this spring would be a new beginning for them, and Angie would never wear sunglasses again except to shade the sun.

"Eight weeks," Myra said.

"It *could* be lovely," Reed Lerner said. "Stranger things have happened. We'll have an unveiling when it's done, maybe eat lunch down there."

Lambie Folger shivered and Myra said quickly, "Oh, no! It'll still be a basement, after all...."

Lambie shuffled the cards at her table, Reed at his; the buzz stopped and the Pastoris' dog howled, then started yapping.

"Damn dog," Myra muttered.

"Call the dog warden." Lambie said the same thing every week.

"I did," Myra announced. Everyone at both tables looked at her.

"I really did. Finally got up the gumption and called."

"And?" Arlen asked.

"And he said I should talk to the Pastoris, one neighbor to another."

"And?" Helen asked.

"I haven't gotten up *that* much gumption yet."

"Want me to do it?" Arlen asked.

Arlen Pinchot was respected, handsome, educated, not like Myra, who had never finished high school for all her father's money. They'd listen to Arlen, but Myra shook her head. "Bob says I should do it myself. And he's right. I should ... I will...."

But weeks passed while they worked on the basement; the Pastoris' dog yapped from early morning until after dark, and Myra could not bring herself to cross the road and complain.

*　*　*

On April 27, when trees were budding out and lawns starting to green up, they finished the basement. The cleaning crew washed the windows and floor, hung the drapes, laid the rugs, and took away the debris.

"Okay, My," Barbara called up the stairs. "Come look."

Myra had made a promise not to look until it was done, and she'd kept it. Now she went down the stairs, head bowed so she wouldn't see until she got to the bottom and could get the full effect.

She stepped down on pale gray quarry tile and raised her head for her first look at the new basement.

"Oh, Barb!"

"Like it?"

"Like it! It wonderful." She'd never imagined the dank, grim, moldy basement could look like this. The floor had been cemented over and tiled in light gray; the new windows were larger than the old, and draped in light yellow, with yellow and green chintz-upholstered furniture on a green rug. Tongue-in-groove paneling pickled a color as light as the floor covered the rugged, ugly stone walls and everything looked light and airy, as if the ancient basement was filled with sunlight. An alcove with sliding shutter doors had been built for the washer and dryer and the furnace and hot water heater. Barbara hadn't stinted on tile, and it covered the floor even in there, so not an inch of the sour old dirt was left.

Myra inhaled, nostrils flaring. "The smell's gone!"

Barbara laughed. "I told you it would be. The contractor caulked the stone outside and in, then coated it. An ant would have trouble getting through, much less a mouse. They also put in the blower system I told you about."

Myra looked up, expecting ducts in the ceiling, but saw a smooth pale expanse of light gray acoustic tile with a couple of small vents.

Barbara said, "The tile'll keep it warm and dry and blanket any noise. You can have wild parties down here while your husband's asleep upstairs and he'll never know."

"Oh, Barbara . . . oh, my. . . . " Myra's eyes filled with tears and Barbara looked away, embarrassed for the plump, desperately shy woman she'd come to like over the past eight weeks.

Myra walked slowly around looking at perfectly matched boards of paneling, the drapes that were weighted at the hem so they wouldn't billow when the new double-paned windows were open. She took in the perfect join of wall and ceiling, and the tile floor that was the softest gray she had ever seen on a hard surface.

She came back to the middle of the floor, turned a full circle. Then, trying to ignore that hair-raising prickle she'd always gotten down here, that she'd prayed would go away when the basement was finished, she said,

"It's perfect."

She wrote Barbara a check for the ten thousand, the last payment on the job, and handed it over. Barbara thanked her, folded the check smartly, and tucked it in her purse, wondering what it would be like to write checks in multiples of thousands without thinking about it.

"And tell anyone who asks to call me for a rave recommendation," Myra said.

"Thanks. Believe it or not, that means almost as much as the money."

"And . . . this is for you." Myra handed her another calico-topped jar of the honey.

"Oh, thank you," Barbara said with true gratitude. She'd finished the last jar weeks ago, and would hoard this one.

The workmen left in their pickups. The job was over and the women hugged awkwardly, not sure exactly how to say good-bye.

"We'll keep in touch," Myra said, turning an alarming cerise.

"Of course." Barbara did her best to sound as if she meant it.

"We'll meet for lunch, and you'll come back to admire your work, and take those pictures you talked about?"

"Sure," Barbara lied. She was never going down those stairs again if she could help it.

She left a little later, climbed into her BMW, on which payments were now current, and set the jar of honey on the seat next to her, like a tiny passenger. She waved good-bye to Myra, who waved back from the door-way, then she put the car in gear and pulled away.

She drove to the end of Old Redman, turned left toward town to keep a four o'clock with a potential client. She'd gone about half a mile from the turn and suddenly realized she could barely see the road through the tears in her eyes.

It was over ... really, finally, and forever over. She was never going back to that house, down to that basement again. She pulled over because the tears blinded her, let her head drop to the steering wheel, and shocked herself by sobbing with relief.

Myra watched until the BMW was out of sight, then she went inside, crossed the kitchen to the basement, and tried the door. It was a little sticky; she'd have to soap it or get it planed before the spring damp really swelled the wood.

She yanked it open, turned on the new lights, and went down the solid new stairs with the strip of carpeting the same shade of gray as the tile.

Halfway down, that prickle started racing across her neck, up her arms, making all the fine hairs stand up and press against the sleeves of her blouse.

She stopped on the third step from the bottom and looked at her old enemy: the basement.

It was new and pretty, clean and smell-less, without a hint of rotting mice or moldy dirt; nothing like it had been. But the old stone was still there behind the paneling, the sour dirt under the tile floor . . . and she knew whatever had been down here all these years still was.

"Today, the unveiling," Arlen said.

"If you want," Myra mumbled.

"Of course we want. We've been waiting eight weeks to see this wonder."

"Oh . . . I bet you did a few other things," Myra said gently, and they laughed.

She stood up. "Okay, but don't expect too much."

Angie was late, but only a few minutes. Not enough to worry about yet, and Myra left the door unlatched for her. The seven of them trooped across the kitchen and down the new stairs to the new basement.

Myra hung back at the foot of the stairs, watching them. Hoping against hope that the sensation starting its run across her neck and up her arms was a relic of the old basement, the way they said you could still feel an amputated limb.

They ranged around, oohing and aahing at one feature or another. Lambie went into the alcove with the washer-dryer and furnace, ducked right back out. Irene and Don opened the door to the washroom; Don flushed the toilet. To make sure it worked? Probably, knowing Don, Myra thought. Reed ran his hands down the join of paneling and said, "Gorgeous work."

Helen tried out the couch, then called to Myra, pointing at the new "entertainment center" with the thirty-two-inch Sony. "Bet you have a mob down here for the Series."

"Think so?" Myra said.

No one answered. A few minutes later, less than five, Myra thought, they were back at the foot of the stairs.

Reed looked up at the ceiling. "Nice tile," he said, then looked down at his feet.

"It's the same, isn't it?" Myra asked softly.

"Of course not. I mean it's just so new, it'll take time. . . . " Helen didn't know how to finish and trailed off.

Silence again. Then Reed, who had less patience with baloney than the rest of them, said, "Fuck it. Let's get out of here."

It was almost twelve-thirty and still no Angie.

No one mentioned the basement. Myra served the sandwich loaf with cream cheese frosting, saving some for Angie, who still hadn't shown up.

Traffic through town must be bad or there'd been some harmless domestic crisis, Lambie thought. Bill couldn't have backslid so soon, he couldn't.

He'd joined AA at Christmas, hadn't laid a hand on Angie since, and she'd finally stopped jumping at unexpected noises; her face smoothed out, and she had not had to wear the huge, mirror-lens sunglasses in months.

"I bet it's her car," Helen said brightly. "Lots of people have trouble with those Range Rovers."

"It's not her car," Arlen muttered.

Arlen had been Angie's champion since they were kids. He hated Bill Withers for what he'd done to her, and Bill returned the hatred.

Lots of tangled relationships in Fallsbridge, Lambie thought, but not around this table.

They'd known each other all their lives, knew each other's darkest secrets, and had long since gotten used to and forgiven each other's faults. If *forgive* was the right word.

Quarter of, no Angie. Conversation died.

Don and Reed cleared the table, and Myra trailed them into the kitchen. The men came back, and a moment later Myra brought out a tray with a pear tart and the coffeepot.

She served the tart . . . Lambie took a bite. Myra was a stupendous cook, and Lambie thought it was the best pastry she'd ever tasted.

The French carriage clock out on the hall table bonged one. Myra started to pour coffee, and the bell rang.

"Angie!" She slammed the pot down and raced out, the pot teetered, and Arlen grabbed it, burning himself. "Goddamn!" He yanked a handkerchief out of his pocket and wound it around his hand. Helen jumped up. "I'll get some salve for that."

Spilled coffee soaked into Myra's good tea-cloth. Lambie said, "Better get something before the stain sets," and *she* got up. They must look like jack-in-the-boxes, she thought.

She went into the kitchen, and heard Myra's voice in the hall . . . then Angie's. She wanted to rush back, but made herself open the refrigerator and look for club soda. She didn't see any and wet a dish towel with cold water.

Last time Bill fell off the wagon he'd given Angie a concussion, and the intern at Fallsbridge General wanted to call the cops, but Angie wouldn't let him. Time before that, Bill broke a couple of her ribs and raped her on the kitchen table.

"I know he's my husband," she'd said, "but it *felt* like rape."

She'd also told them he'd done it on the table in the huge, spare, stainless-steel kitchen of Brooks House, Angie's house, with all the lights on and the dimity curtains, the only softness in the room, open.

"I didn't give a shit about anyone seeing. No one *could* see from twenty acres away. But I was terrified the kid would pick that moment to come downstairs for peanut butter crackers . . . and get a down-and-dirty introduction to the birds and bees." She had laughed, actually laughed! Angie's sense of humor could be her worst enemy, Lambie thought, but it was fraying—had frayed. Lambie had not heard Angie laugh for a long, long time.

Lambie and Helen arrived back in the breakfast room at the same time. Helen had found a tube of something in one of the downstairs bathrooms and handed it to Arlen, who thanked her, eyes on the door they all fixed on. Lambie had to remind herself to breathe.

Then Myra and Angie appeared, with Myra a blotchy crimson, and Angie wearing the aviator-sized, mirror-lensed sunglasses.

Arlen made a strangled noise; Lambie sank down hard in the chair so it squeaked slightly under her. Reed groaned.

"Shit."

"Shit," Angie echoed softly, and took the glasses off.

She didn't whip them off—there was nothing remotely dramatic about the gesture. She simply removed them because they were large and heavy and she'd be more comfortable without them.

They knew what they'd see, but Irene gasped anyway, and a couple of them looked away, including Lambie, who stared down at the damp dishtowel wadded up in her hand. Too late to do anything about the stain now; Myra would have to take the cloth to the dry cleaners.

Lambie looked up.

You expected a black eye to be . . . black, and Lambie knew from other times that it would be in a day or two. But now it was red, swollen, and shiny, like a scald about to become a blister. The swelling and discoloration reached up into Angie's temple and down to her cheekbone, and Lambie saw her bottom lip had a deep split in it, probably from a backhand delivered by William T. Withers.

There'd be other marks, too, hidden by her clothes.

The silence was long and terrible, then Reed said gently, "Tell us, Angie."

"Yes." Irene patted the empty chair next to her, Angie's usual place. "Tell us."

"Tell you for the millionth time that my rat's ass, son-of-a-bitch husband got stinko and kicked the shit outta me? You want to hear it again? Are you all nuts? Are you sick . . . "

Angie's anger had once been real, but now had the forced, tinny quality of an emotion she knew she should have.

"No," Reed said quietly. "We know what happened, but maybe talking will help."

Angie sat down and put the sunglasses on the table in front of her. Myra went to the sideboard and came back with a liqueur glass, probably filled with the outrageously wonderful cognac her father had brought back from somewhere in aughty-aught, and which she hoarded for special occasions. It was the only thing Lambie had ever known Myra to be the least bit stingy about.

Angie took a sip, then jerked her hand up to her lip.

"Burns."

Reed said, "Drink it anyway. One gulp, down the hatch."

She nodded, picked up the glass, and tossed down the liquor. She shivered; her good eye watered. The other had been leaking (although she didn't seem to be crying) and she dabbed at it with her tea napkin.

Lambie had forgotten the damp dish towel in her hand. She started to put it on the table, then thought it might soak through, ruin the pad underneath, and she kept it balled in her hand.

"It's the same story," Angie said softly.

The dog started yapping again, but the sound was muted in the breakfast room.

"Go on any way," Don urged.

Angie looked at them with her good eye; the other appeared too swollen to see out of.

"I got overconfident."

"Don't blame yourself!" Reed said sharply.

"Shit, no!" Don cried.

"But I should have known." She bowed her head over the table. "Only it'd been since before Christmas . . . and I didn't think anything when he didn't show up for dinner or call. Oh, I must've *thought* a little something, but kept it buried. You know. Anyway, Nanny Peg had put the kid to bed, Cook and the dailies were gone, and the house was quiet. I . . . I went into the kitchen. I know it's kind of . . . institutional . . . but it's peaceful. I had a book with me, thought I'd have milk and cookies . . . like we always had at sleepovers late at night, remember?"

The women nodded.

"Then I heard his car . . . heard him come across the court from the garage. It was so late by then, I knew what state he'd be in. But I just stayed put. Like I was drugged. Or like . . . I wanted it to happen." She looked at Reed. "Did I, Reed? Is that why I didn't do anything?"

"No," Reed said solidly, "it is not."

"I knew I was in for it the second I saw him, and I was.

"He did the *rich bitch* number. You know the one: rich bitch wife with all the trust funds and how he was going to fuck her on the kitchen table. Get her spread-eagled in the awkwardest, ugliest . . . Christ . . . you know."

A few nodded. No one said anything.

"Only first we had to have a couple of good hard punches. I think he wasn't as drunk as he thought he was, and he gave it more than he meant to. Planted one on me from the ankle, like the guys used to say in high school. Remember?"

Another couple of nods around the table.

"I lost my balance, fell back against the counter, and hit the knife rack. Knives flew all over with this clatter . . . and he grabbed one. First time he ever had a weapon, and I don't mind admitting it scared the shit outta me. He's gonna kill me, I thought . . . I'm dead. Surprising that it didn't make me feel much . . . except scared. Only scared"—she frowned, apparently intent on explaining herself—"not panicked or sorry."

As if she didn't care if she died. Lambie squeezed the damp dish towel hard in her hand; a few drops of moisture leaked onto her skirt.

Angie went on, "He picked the chef's knife—biggest one of the bunch—and held it up to catch the light on its blade. The light reflected back into his eyes, and he looked happy . . . exalted. He held on to it and dragged me across the room to the table. I went like a lamb . . . a little dopey from the punch I guess."

Or too beaten to care what he did to her, Lambie thought.

Angie said, "He got me positioned on the table, got his pants open . . . without letting go of the knife. Amazing how dexterous a drunk can be.

"Then came this little squeal from the doorway, like a slightly rusty hinge—or a tiny hurt animal—and I looked over . . . we both looked over . . . and there was our son. Little Billy Junior, in his brand new PJ's with the dinosaurs on them."

She gave a short, convulsive sob and Arlen put his arm around her. She pulled away and glared at him out of her good eye. "What am I crying about, for God's sake? What the hell did I think was going to happen?"

No one answered; she went on. "Anyway, there he was. Our little kid, our sweet-faced boy. And you know what William T. Withers Senior did when he saw him . . . when he saw his son with his eyes bulging at the sight of his mother staked out on the table and his father with his pants open, and a knife in his hand? You know what that prick did?"

"What?" Reed asked with total gentleness unmixed with pity. Must have taken him years to perfect that tone, Lambie thought.

Angie looked at Reed, seeming to shut the others out; her voice dropped as if for his ears only, and Lambie had to lean forward slightly to hear.

"He put the knife point to my neck so it just barely made an indentation, and he glared at his son and snarled, 'Get the fuck outta here, you little shit . . . or I'll slit her fuckin' throat.'"

Lambie glared at the wadded-up damp dishcloth in her hand, trying desperately not to see little Billy in his PJ's with the dinosaurs on them, staring in mute horror at his father and mother . . . and the glittering blade of the knife in his father's hand. But of course she saw the kid vividly, with his knobby knees, pitcher-handle ears, and a thatch of white-blond hair. Homely kid, which was odd, since Angie and Bill were two of the best-looking people she'd ever seen off the movie screen.

In her moment of reverie, Lambie missed the denouement of the scene in the kitchen. Just as well, since she would have hated hearing it. It must have ended like the others, with the rape followed by another couple of

punches, followed by Bill stalking out of the house to the old carriage
court to chop wood. He did it often, as if to cool down after the exertion of
beating his wife, or to blow off extra steam to keep from killing her. She
picked up the tale again with Angie telling them that she found Billy Junior upstairs in his room under the covers, and no amount of cajoling from
Angie or Peg could get him to come out. That night, Angie slept in the
other bed in Peg's room, next to Billy's, and this morning it had taken
them an hour to get Billy to even uncover his face.

"He wouldn't go to school," Angie was saying, "and I couldn't bear to
force him. So we played with him all morning . . . four solid hours of Junior
Clue and Ninja Turtles. He's eight . . . thought he'd be too old for Ninja
Turtles by now.

"He finally whacked himself out and fell asleep and I left him with Peg
to come here. I'd've only been about ten minutes late, but I decided to stop
at Doc Moffet's to see if he could make this"—she touched the eye—"look
a little better. Poor Moffet forced himself to swallow my usual story about
running into something—he probably can't bear to contemplate what really happened and how often he's ignored it—and he gave me an ice
pack." She gave a leering grin, made crooked by the split, swollen lip. "It's
nineteen ninety-five, they're building a space station and mapping the
genome, and an ice pack is still the best they can do for a shiner."

Silence, then Myra mumbled, "Maybe you should eat something."

"Can't. Lip's split inside, eating hurts. Couldn't get down anything but
juice . . . and that fabulous cognac. Thanks, My."

Tears brimmed in Myra's eyes, and Angie put her hand over Myra's,
which was resting on the table. "My . . . My . . . you must be a little used to
it by now. I am."

"No one could get used to that," Myra said.

"You'd be amazed. Bet there were people who got used to Auschwitz, if
they let them live long enough."

Silence again.

Angie said, "C'mon . . . it's not a funeral. Lighten up."

No one spoke.

Then, with a false brightness that made Lambie want to slap her, Angie
said, "What about the basement? Wasn't today the unveiling?"

Wrong subject, Lambie thought.

"The veil has fallen," Irene said.

"And?"

"It's a showplace," Don said grimly, "a veritable showplace."

"That bad?" Angie asked.

"Of course not. It's very nice. . . . " Helen was defending the basement and, by extension, Myra, Lambie thought.

Reed pushed back his chair and stood up. "C'mon, I'll show it to you."

"She doesn't want to see," Myra muttered.

"She doesn't want to sit here being mourned over and pitied and smelling food she can't eat either," Reed said firmly.

Downstairs Angie sank into the new chintz sofa without even looking around.

Reed crouched on his heels in front of her.

"Angie . . ."

"Don't, Reed." She looked at him. The eye was swollen to a slit; the flesh around it looked ready to burst. She looked so young and hurt he felt a lump in his throat. But crying over her wouldn't help. He didn't know what would.

"I can't let it go," he said.

"You have to. You're just going to say what you've said a thousand times. Leave him . . . toss him out . . . get him to talk to you."

Reed Lerner was the only M.D. shrink in Fallsbridge.

"Not to me," he said. "I hate the son of a bitch too much to even look at him by now. But I know other shrinks, Angie. . . . "

"No."

"Christ, why not."

"Because even suggesting it will get me another beating, and leaving him—or trying to throw him out—will get me maimed . . . or killed."

"Angie, he could . . . do that . . . anyway."

She looked past him at the newly paneled wall. "I don't think so," she said quietly. "He's got me and my money; he's got my house, and the kid, and the fun of getting loaded and kicking me around. Bill Withers is a happy man."

No one wanted to believe that, especially Reed, who'd built his career on the ultimate ascendancy of reason and decency; the truth will make you free and all that bullshit. But of course, Angie was right. Most of the abusive bastards in the world did it because it made them happy.

Stalemate as always, Reed thought. They had talked about it behind Angie's back; agonized over it; discussed and rejected a hundred plans for helping Angie, including confronting Withers. But he was a brutal, violent shit; they were spoiled, superrich, nonconfrontational nerds who'd never knowingly hurt anyone in their lives.

They had nothing to threaten him with, and confronting him *would* get Angie beaten up again.

"Angie . . ."

"Please, Reed. Be sympathetic as you always are, listen as you always do. Don't humor me, as you never have, and leave it alone. I wasn't lying to Myra, you really do sort of get used to it."

Wrong, Reed thought. Angie was not getting used to it; she was building a rage that would tear her apart one of these days and Withers with her. Bill Withers was walking a very high rope without a net and some day Angie would break, and . . .

Reed didn't know what she'd do. Kill him before he killed her, maybe, and more power to her, he thought. It was happening a lot these days, and maybe all the assholes who beat their women as their fathers had, and *their* fathers, even unto the dawn of time, would finally get it through their thick skulls that times were a'changing. That some night, the little *woman* would pick up the old deer rifle, the buck knife . . . or pour gasoline on him in his drunken stupor and light him up like a Fourth of July bonfire. But that had already happened; Reed had seen it on a TV movie of the week. He should send a tape of it to Withers, with the quote over the National Archives portal: THOSE WHO DO NOT KNOW THE PAST ARE CONDEMNED TO REPEAT IT, or words to that effect.

Angie finally looked around the basement.

"My really did it to death, didn't she."

"To death," Reed said.

"Still weird as shit down here, though, isn't it."

"Weirder than shit," he said, and they laughed. She stopped suddenly and shivered. "Jesus, Reed, let's get out of here."

"Hilary, oh, Hilary . . . " The old lady's voice floated out the open door. "Hilary . . ."

Only her mother-in-law, Joan Scott Folger, called Lambie Hilary. Lamb was her maiden name . . . hence the Lambie. But she hated Hilary, and when she and Angie were at Radcliffe, Angie had dubbed her Lambie and it stuck. Except with Joan Folger.

"Hilary . . ."

Lambie went into the sitting room of her mother-in-law's suite.

"I thought I saw your car," Joan Folger said. She was sitting in a recliner next to a window that looked out on the courtyard, so of course she'd seen Lambie's car. She was wearing a loose, flowing garment that would have been called a hostess gown back in the forties, and her feet, resting on an embroidered footstool, were encased in soft leather slippers.

"Yes, Joan." Lambie could never call this woman Mother and Mrs. Folger would have been insulting after being married to her son for twenty-three years.

"Larkin said there will be dinner guests tonight. The Adamses and Lerners."

"Yes . . ."

"I will not be joining you. I have never broken bread with a Jew that I know of, and never will if I can help it."

The old bitch meant Reed and Riva. Lambie felt the usual burst of rage, but forced herself to answer calmly.

"Okay. I'll have Mrs. Larkin fix a tray for you. We're having rolled rib, but there's chicken salad if you want something lighter."

"The beef will do. Only it must be well done. I insist on well done."

Everyone knew that. The last time she'd been served pink meat, she'd pitched the tray at poor Mary Dodd, the downstairs maid . . . and missed, thank God.

"Of course," Lambie said.

Joan Folger had moved in after she'd had a heart attack, followed by a triple bypass last year. She claimed her servants weren't equal to caring for her and refused to have a nurse (bound to be black, she'd said). The retirement community of spacious condos that rambled over acres of Westchester with a golf course, restaurant, maid and nurse service, would not do. Nothing would do but that she live with her son.

After she moved in, Lambie's beloved mother, whose house this was, who had lived here all her life, moved out. And the girls stopped coming home from school for weekends, and only spent a day or two at holidays and breaks.

So the old bitch had cost Lambie her last few years with her children, and maybe with her mother.

Joan gave her a severe look.

"You are very late. Today's bridge must have been immensely enthralling."

"Myra redid her basement. We spent time admiring it and didn't start until late."

"Her *basement?*"

"Yes. It's very nice."

"Basement and *nice* is a contradiction."

Lambie didn't say anything.

"And while you were admiring a basement, Larkin was making free with tonight's menu. It won't do. The mistress of the house should plan the menu."

The menu had been decided before Lambie left and she said so.

"But changes were made—" Joan said.

"Asparagus for artichoke. Mrs. Larkin said the asparagus looked nicer."

"Not that it matters what you feed the Jew."

Lambie looked away.

"I'll tell Mrs. Larkin about the tray," she said, and left the room. She went down the hall, crossed the gallery, and grabbed and clung to the banister across it. She had to get hold of herself or she'd fight with Evan. Amazing that gentle Evan had been born to that Nazi bitch. If Lambie fought with him, he'd look miserable and murmur, "Lamb, Lamb . . . what

can I do? She's my *mother.*" And Lambie would think snappy, vicious re-
torts: *Hire a hit man. Spike her granola with cyanide.* If she said them, Evan
would look even more miserable and Lambie would hate herself. Evan and
the girls were all that mattered; she had to keep thinking of them and remember that the girls would come home again when the old bitch died.
She was seventy-nine and had a bad heart, arthritis, osteoporosis, and residual kidney damage from the heart attack. How much longer could she
go on?

Years, whined a nasty little voice in Lambie's mind. *Years and years.*

It had turned chilly by dinner time, but the Pastoris left the dog out anyway. It had been yapping for hours.

Myra put her fork down. "I can't stand it," she said almost conversation-
ally.

Bob Ludens looked up from his plate.

"Tell *them,* not me. It's their dog."

Myra blushed; her bottom lip trembled shamefully, but she swallowed
hard. She was not going to cry; she was not going to cry over that rotten
dog. Bob hated when she cried, especially over little things; and the Pastoris' yapping dog was annoying, upsetting ... nerve-racking ... but it *was* a
little thing. She should take it in stride, turn it off the way Bob seemed to,
but the yipping felt like needles in her ears. It stopped for a second and she
tensed, waiting for it to start again. It did.

Her husband watched her.

"I have pear tart for dessert. . . . " she said quickly.

"You're going over there now, Myra."

"No. Please, Bob. I'll call Mrs. Pastori in the morning."

"You've been saying that for months. You're going over there."

"You'll come with me. . . . "

"I'll do no such thing. You've bitched and moaned to me for months.
Now you're going to bitch and moan to them."

"No. . . . " She *was* going to cry. "I'll call the dog warden ... I'll lodge a
formal—"

"The dog warden won't do shit and you know it."

He pushed his plate away and stood up. She'd really annoyed him this time; he'd left most of the veal stew he usually had seconds on.

He stalked out of the room and came back with her shell jacket.

Bob wouldn't do this if he knew how bad her blood pressure was. Slightly elevated, she had told him, and made Moffet swear to do the same. It was *her* blood pressure, her secret, except from the seven club members.

Her heart hammered in her ears, sweat beaded itchily at her hairline, and her underarms felt swampy.

She couldn't face those people. What if they set the dog on her. . . .

"What if they set the dog on me?"

"It's a Jack Russell terrier, for Christ's sake. About the size of your foot. Kick it."

He held out the jacket. If she dug in, they'd fight; rather Bob would fight and Myra would feel her pressure soar until the blood literally roared in her ears and everything got a pink aureole around it.

"You've got to take it easy," Dr. Moffet had told her when he prescribed the Inderal. "Nothing's worth having a stroke over." Taking it easy seemed possible in Moffet's office with its lovely mauve carpeting and nice prints of Degas pastels. Life should be pastel . . . like her new basement.

Bob had given the basement a cursory look when he got home, then came right back upstairs, and she knew he would not watch games down there with his buddies on the new TV. He wouldn't go down there at all; neither would she or anyone else.

It was a failure, in spite of all Barbara's work. Poor Barbara. Tears burned Myra's eyes; her blood started its song in her ears, a high, sweeping moan, like the wind through a mountain pass; and her husband gave a groan of utter disgust.

"You don't like me very much, do you?" she said softly. He blinked in surprise, then that irresistible look of tenderness filled his eyes.

"You're wrong, Myra. I love you. Always have and always will. It's just really hard when you act like a dishrag."

But I *am* a dishrag, she thought.

He held the jacket out. It was her new shell jacket in bright blue, with a teal-green lining. She'd ordered it from a catalog only to find that the color looked execrable on her.

"Please, honey," he said. "Stand up for yourself, just this once. . . . "

She looked down at his plate with the veal stew getting cold, skinning over, starting to look nasty. He couldn't even enjoy his dinner in peace.

She stood up and took the jacket from him.

"That's my baby," he said. "That's my little soldier. Go get 'em, My."

At the same instant, Joan Folger sliced into the meat, saw it was well done, and nodded. The maid ducked out of the room, and Joan cut and chewed the meat thoroughly. They no longer taught children to masticate their food. They no longer taught them anything.

She left enough on the plate to show Larkin it wasn't good (though it had been delicious), and she pushed the tray table away, then left the suite. With her long silk skirt whispering around her legs, she went down the hall to the gallery to look over the banister at the center hall below.

The dining room doors were shut, but a muffled burst of laughter came through them. The Jews were in there, battening on Evan's food. But something much worse was going on than having the wrong people to dinner. Joan had known it from the day she'd moved into this house six months ago, and today she'd almost had her daughter-in-law dead to rights. Hilary had come in late and disheveled, looking as if she'd been doing exactly what Joan had known she'd been doing all along.

Seeing a man.

Certainly one of the male members of that "club" that met every Wednesday. But which one? Maybe Don Forbes, who was nice-enough-looking, but had acquired the coarse manner that came to many middle-aged men too rich to care any longer what people thought of them. He was not downright vulgar, she thought, staring down at the closed double dining-room doors without seeing them, just what he probably thought of as rough and ready. A manner he'd no doubt picked up from some safari movie. And he watched birds! Hardly the romantic type. Besides, his wife, Irene, who had added her own considerable fortune to his (making them the richest pair in Fallsbridge) appeared far too savvy to let a dalliance with Hilary or anyone else go on under her nose.

It could be Arlen Pinchot. He was single and reckless enough, far too handsome for his own good, and there was much delicious gossip about his sex life.

Or it could be the Jew.

The thought was sickening and compelling, and she let herself imagine exposing Hilary Lamb *inflagrante* with Reed Lerner. Evan would be hurt, furious, beside himself . . . Joan would comfort him.

It was close to happening, ready to happen. She could feel it.

That fabrication about a remodeled basement was an insult to one's intelligence, and tomorrow Joan would confront Myra Ludens with it. Myra would lie to protect Hilary, of course, but turn every shade of red under the sun when she did. She was a weak, silly woman with a mind like loose pudding, and sooner or later she'd break down and tell Joan where Hilary had really been this afternoon, and with whom.

First thing tomorrow, Joan would go to Myra's.

Myra should have worn her heavier jacket, but Bob had brought her this one. It was almost dark, she should have taken a flashlight. She picked her way down the drive to the road and looked both ways; no headlights in sight and she crossed the road to the Pastoris' land. The dog heard or smelled her, and yapped madly. Dull thuds made her think it was throwing itself against something in the backyard. It was too cold to leave a little dog out, and she pitied it almost as much as she hated it.

She rang the bell. The dog went wild.

The poor little thing was going to break a rib or leg. If she couldn't get anywhere with the Pastoris, she'd call the Humane Society.

The lights were on, but the Pastoris might be in back and not hear the bell over the TV and the dog. Then she could tell Bob she'd tried, but no one answered and she'd be off the hook for tonight.

Let me go tonight, she prayed silently. *Let me go. . . .*

Then she heard, or rather felt, feet padding to the door.

The door started to open; her legs shook helplessly, her ankles felt like cooked cereal. The door swung in, and Mr. Pastori stood backlit from the foyer and surrounded by that pink halo her soaring blood pressure painted around everything.

He peered at her; she peered back.

He was short, sallow, and bald, with a fringe of black, oily-looking hair around his skull.

His eyes were dark with permanent bags under them, like the ex-governor of New York, and the whites were a little yellow. He could be liverish, or the color might be a trick of the light.

"Mrs. Ludens?"

"Yes, Mr. Pastori. I'm so sorry to bother you, but it's about the dog."

"Dog?" He sounded as if he didn't know what she was talking about, although they had to yell over the yapping.

"Your dog in the backyard?"

"What about it?"

"The yapping . . . "

Her throat was so tight, talking hurt. Why was she like this? She'd never been abused as a child or wife, her mother and father had loved her, so did her husband and grown son; her granddaughters had inherited her fairness, but were like their mother otherwise—strong, gutsy, noisy little girls Myra adored and who adored her back.

"Yapping?" Pastori said coldly. "I prefer to think of it as barking."

"Barking. Of course . . . " She tried to sound grateful for his correcting her. "Barking . . . " she yelled over the yapping.

"What about it?" he snarled and the aura around him went from pale pink to red. She was going to drop dead right here on his doorstep, because of a dog. Goddamn fucking rat's-ass dog, Angie would say. But Angie's guts were hot air.

Myra cleared her throat hard. "The barking's very . . . disturbing and I was wondering, I mean . . . it's so cold and damp . . . I was wondering if you couldn't let him into the house more than you do, so he wouldn't, uh . . . bark . . . quite so much."

"It's an outdoor dog."

"Yes. I see, of course, but the noise . . . "

"A watchdog . . . " Pastori bit the words.

"Yes . . . of course . . . but he barks all the time, so no one would pay any attention to him if someone did try to break in. . . . "

"He doesn't bark all the time."

"But he does. From noon until night and you see . . . the thing is . . . I have hypertension. Very serious hypertension . . . and the doctor says I must have a certain amount of quiet."

He grinned; you couldn't call the spasm that stretched his mouth a smile. His yellow-whited eyes glittered at her and he said,

"Hypertension?"

"Very serious hypertension."

The grin widened, showing long teeth as yellow as his eyeballs, and he said, "Tough shit, lady," and slammed the door in her face.

She stood in the pool of light from the front window with blood raging in her ears like a forest fire and the brass eagle knocker smeared in a haze of red.

Tough shit, lady.

He might as well have said, *Die, lady,* because that's what he really meant. My leaving my dog penned up in my backyard is more important than your life.

Die, lady.

Her rage almost got away from her. She almost pounded on the door with her fists, kicked the smooth white paint until it scuffed.

You die, you sallow little bastard, she wanted to scream.

She took a deep, slow breath, compressed her lips, and the raging in her ears softened a little. Her legs shook wildly, but they carried her down the drive and across the road to her house.

The dog had shut up by the time she got back to the kitchen, and Bob congratulated her. She couldn't bear to tell him that they always let the dog in about this time, and out again in the morning.

He went to watch TV while she rinsed dishes for the washer and dealt with the pots and pans. Then she brewed herself a cup of decaf tea with some of Bob's honey (the *bees'* honey) and sat down at the table with the book she'd bought yesterday, but something kept drawing her eyes to the basement door. She couldn't look away from it for more than a minute at a time.

CHAPTER 2

The weather changed; wind shifted from north to south and it was sunny and in the fifties when Sandy, Myra's daily, arrived at eight-thirty.

Myra looked out the breakfast room window at the field behind the house. The dog was yapping again, but with Sandy here, and water running it was not as intrusive. Wind blew the heads of the daffodils in the field; they bobbed in clumps around the beehive stilts. Soon a new queen would make her wedding flight with winged consorts; they'd mate, the males would die, and the new queen would return to the hive to take the place of the old. By July, Bob could start collecting the honey.

Not a minute too soon, since they were halfway through the second-to-last jar. Giving Barbara Potter two jars had been prodigal, but Myra had been so grateful to her.

Barbara would never call to have lunch or come by to take pictures of the new basement. And Myra had a feeling Barbara would be otherwise engaged if Myra called her.

Myra dragged her eyes away from the flowers' mesmerizing dance and went upstairs to bring the hamper down, since it was laundry day and

Sandy'd been having trouble with her back again. Sandy looked at the hamper, then at the basement door.

"I suppose I gotta do the laundry down *there?*"

"Well, that's where the washer is now," Myra said. Sandy stared at the door.

"Oh, for heaven's sake, Sandy. The smell's gone, it's dry, and pretty . . . you'll see. You'll like it."

Sandy gave her a look that said *never,* then went back to polishing the counter tile.

At nine-thirty, Myra drove to Playthings in Fallsbridge Center. Her older granddaughter would be seven next Friday and Myra had to send something today to be sure it got there in time. Playthings had just opened for the day; she was the only customer and could look around without bumping into anyone. There was so much more for kids these days than when her son, Dave, was young, before video and computer games . . . before Nintendo.

She passed battery toys and game cassettes and came to the Playmobil display. She picked out a huge box, with a picture of a castle and knights on it. It even had a little white plastic ghost that reminded her of Caspar in the comics. It was really cute and came with its own miniature chain to rattle. She thought of buying just the ghost for herself, but that was really silly.

She pulled the box down and looked at the price tag. It would be over ninety with tax and postage, but you were only seven once, she thought with a smile, and took it up to the counter.

Birdie Rudkin, the owner, totaled it up along with the mailing to Boston.

"Will it get there by next Friday?" Myra asked.

"No sweat. It'll go out today, and UPS guarantees three-business-day delivery. It'll be there in plenty of time. You want the gift paper with the clown or teddy bears?"

"Teddy bears."

The castle was more than she'd expected to spend and she wrote a check.

"Gift card," Birdie said, handing her one with a picture of a fluffy puppy on it.

Myra wrote, "To Ellie on her birthday. From Grandma and Grandpa Ludens, with all the love in our hearts."

She looked up to ask the date and noticed a box with Ouija on it on a shelf behind the counter.

Does Pres like me or Nancy best? she'd asked the Ouija board when she was thirteen. *Will my mother let me buy the new blue dress and wear heels for the Harvest Dance? Will I pass Biology?* And much, much later: *Am I pregnant? Will I have to marry Bob Ludens?*

She and the other girls were kind to each other and pushed the planchette around to the answers they knew their partners wanted. *Yes... Pres likes you best. No, you're not pregnant.* But she had been pregnant, did have to marry Bob. She didn't know then (or now) why she'd let him do *that* to her in the back of his father's new Caddy except impulse, maybe. Or finally just having to know what all the fuss was about. It wasn't fair. One time with Bob Ludens, who'd actually smelled like Luden's cough drops, and there went her life. No high school diploma, no college, no other men, or job or apartment of her own in the city with Helen. (Helen never got the apartment in Boston either.) All down the drain, because Bob had insisted and her folks had backed him up. No abortion in those days, anyway . . . no choices . . . no way out.

So she'd married him and gotten . . .

And gotten a man who adored her, even if he didn't like or admire her very much, and David, her son, and her daughter-in-law, Melissa, and the two girls.

It was worth it.

"Myra? Earth calling Myra!" Birdie said.

Myra's vision cleared; she was staring at the Ouija board box, which looked drab compared with the other game boxes.

"How much is the Ouija board?" she asked.

Birdie levered it down from the shelf and looked at the tag on the side. "Twenty-two. You want it too?"

"No . . . no, that's okay."

* * *

The dog was yapping when Myra got home, and Joan Folger's black Lincoln limousine was pulled up in the driveway with the chauffeur leaning against the fender, cap pushed back, his face turned to the sun.

She pulled up next to the limo.

"Morning, Miz Ludens," the chauffeur (Gary? she thought) said and politely touched the rim of his black cap.

"Morning." They had to raise their voices because of the dog.

She didn't know what else to say to him and she smiled foolishly and went in the side door.

Joan Folger was in the breakfast room. Sandy had given her a cup of tea and, Myra saw with a sinking heart, the honeypot, with the remains of the second-to-last jar. Joan had taken almost all of it.

"Joan, how nice."

Joan Folger smiled up at her from the chair inside the bow window. Her face accordioned back as her lips spread. Someone famous had said that God gives us our faces till forty; after that we buy and pay for how we look (or words to the effect).

Joan Folger had bought and paid for her coarse, cruel, furrowed face, with eyes like wet stone and skin like raw dough.

Myra sat down across from her.

"Your maid was kind enough to give me some tea with that delicious honey."

The dog stopped for a second, then started up again.

"Heavens! That dog's been at it since I got here. How do you stand it?"

"It's a problem," Myra said. "They keep it penned up in the backyard."

"*Someone* should call the dog warden."

Myra started to tell her she had, had even confronted Mr. Pastori. But it wasn't worth the breath because Joan wouldn't listen.

"You're right," she said wearily. There was just a thin coating of honey left in the jar.

They talked back and forth about the spring dance at the country club; the tulip festival on the Congregational church grounds; the garden club flower show just two weeks away and how none of the women knew how to display flowers except Joan and the others refused to listen to her.

Finally, Joan got to the point.

"I was just passing by and decided to stop and see the new basement," Joan said, slyly.

"Basement?"

Joan looked down at the bright yellow flowers on the table cloth. "Hilary mentioned it when she got home last night."

It took Myra a second to realize Joan meant Lambie.

"She said she was late because all of you were looking at your lovely new basement. And I thought . . . well . . . we've been thinking of redoing the basement at Old Oak. . . ."

The basement of Old Oak was the size of a football field and Myra knew this wasn't about basements. The turmoil about Angie had made Lambie late getting home yesterday, and Joan was checking up on her.

"I see," Myra said. "We did spend more time down there than we meant to."

That was a lie. They'd gone down, looked around, and rushed back up as fast as they could. And Sandy hated having to do the laundry down there.

Suddenly Myra wondered how Joan Folger would react to the basement.

"Everyone liked it very much," Myra said. She leaned closer to Joan Folger, who smelled of dry hair, lily of the valley, and the rich, yellow scent of the honey she had devoured.

"Would you like to see it?" Myra asked softly.

"Of course, assuming there's anything to see," Joan Folger snapped.

Myra leaned back and smiled. "Oh, there is. Finish your tea, then we'll take a look."

Joan glared at her, drank off the tea, and struggled to her feet. She was old and had arthritis, rheumatism, bursitis—one or all of the miseries that attacked the old at every change of season—and Myra almost felt sorry for her. Almost.

Myra led the way. Upstairs, Sandy turned on the vacuum; the whine of the motor mixed with the dog's yapping, and the furrows in Joan Folger's face deepened as she glared at Myra as if it were all her doing. It was, Myra thought. She didn't know how to run her house or get the Pastoris to shut their dog up. A million things she didn't know how to do, but she could sure commission the shit out of having a basement done, she thought.

Now, they'd see how Mrs. L. Evan Folger, Senior, liked it.

Myra opened the old slatted wood door and flicked the switch next to it. Lights came on and she politely motioned Joan to precede her.

Joan Folger stepped into the light at the top of the stairs.

"Right behind you . . . " Myra said.

Down through soft light they descended to the basement floor. The centuries-old stone foundation covered by paneling and the acoustic tile in the ceiling muffled dog and vacuum and the basement was silent.

"It was just stone walls and dirt floor before," Myra explained. "With dinky little windows up near the ceiling."

Joan Folger stood in the middle and looked around as Myra pointed out the tongue-in-groove paneling, the blowers in the ceiling that kept the air warm and dry and had finally gotten rid of the smells.

"Very nice, very nice," Joan kept saying but her voice got fainter and her eyes darted around, not looking at what Myra was showing her. At one point her head whirled as if she felt something come up behind her and her voice started to quaver. "Yes, I'm sure she did an excellent job. Yes . . . it's rather chilly down here. . . . "

"Oh, do you think so?" Myra looked pointedly at the thermostat on the wall. "It's seventy-two, exactly what it's set for. . . . "

"I tell you it's chilly," Joan cried, her eyes blinking here and there, trying to see into corners the recessed lights didn't quite illuminate. She'd jump a mile if Myra yelled *boo*.

Myra went to the alcove with the washer and dryer. "The designer had the entire floor tiled, so none of that old dirt's left." She turned on the light in the alcove; the washer and dryer looked glossy, square, mundane, but the furnace loomed in shadow, a strange, boxy, featureless presence.

Joan backed away.

"I think we'd better . . . "

"There's a light right over the furnace," Myra explained. "So repairmen can see what they're doing. The designer thought of everything. . . . Oh, and there's a little powder room." Myra opened the door and turned on the light to reveal the tiled washroom.

"No way to get a window in there," Myra explained. "But Barbara put in a vent and fan that comes on with the light . . . hear it?" Myra cocked her head. The fan sounded like breathing and Joan backed into the stair rail, gave a short, sharp yelp, and started up the stairs.

"Got to turn the lights out," Myra called. She would be as glad to get out as Joan.

Joan reached the door to the kitchen and tried to open it, but it must have swelled too much from the spring dampness, and it stuck.

"It's stuck!" she cried. "It's stuck. . . . " She pounded on it and Myra called, "Hang on, Joan, I'll be right there." She turned out the washroom light and Joan yelled, "I can't get the door open . . . it's stuck. . . . Myra, help me. . . . "

Myra rushed to the foot of the stairs as Joan banged her shoulder against the door and cried out in pain. The door didn't budge.

"Help, Myra, please help me. . . . " She was gray with fear and Myra felt terrible about bringing her down here. She ran up the stairs, Joan moved aside to give her room, and Myra shoved the door. It didn't move. "It really is stuck, isn't it." Myra's heart started to flutter at the thought of being trapped down here. "It's the spring damp, Joan. Damp swells the wood. . . . " Myra realized her breath was hitching and she probably didn't look much better than Joan. She twisted the knob hard, laid her shoulder against the old wood slats, and shoved with all her might. The door gave a squeal and flew open; sun streamed in from the kitchen and Joan moaned, "Thank God."

Sandy came in lugging the vacuum. "What's all the thumping about?"

After Joan Folger hobbled double-time out the front door to the Lincoln, Myra drove back to Playthings in Fallsbridge Center and bought the Ouija board, then came home and called Lambie.

* * *

"Let me get this straight." Lambie said. "You want me to be your partner while you ask a Ouija board what's going on in your basement?"

"We did it in high school, Lamb."

"I know, My," Lambie said as gently as she could. "But we were kids. Do you know how nuts that sounds at forty-whatever?"

"I know how nuts it *is*. But she was terrified, Lamb. Joan Folger, the bitch of Fallsbridge, whom mothers probably invoke to scare their kids, was terrified! Why?"

"I don't know."

"Everyone went down there yesterday and couldn't wait to get back up. Why?"

"I don't know," Lambie said again.

"Me either. And I don't know anyone who does. So why not ask the Ouija board?"

"Because . . . because . . . "

"Because it's crazy, right. But what could be crazier than the fact that I've just spent thirty thousand dollars making that basement warm, dry, pretty, and odorless and everyone still hates it? Even Sandy, who's about as sensitive to 'atmospheres' as a squash. Even Bob, who'd rather cut off his right testicle than admit he's scared even to himself. Something's wrong down there, Lambie, and it's not going to show up on the gas gauge or radon meter. So I want to ask the Ouija board. Why not?"

It did have a bizarre kind of logic, Lambie thought, and a vision of the basement rose in her mind. It had been a dungeon before, was a photo spread from *House and Garden* now, but still a dungeon in some way Lambie couldn't explain.

Lambie looked at the board.

"Why me?" she asked.

"It works better with a partner."

"But why *me?*"

Myra smiled. "Actually, Reed was my first choice, but he'll be at the office now. I can't very well drag a shrink away from his patients to help me consult a Ouija board, and you're the only other one of us who's not going over the edge."

"Myra!"

"It's true, Lamb. I'm on the verge of a stroke over a barking dog. I don't have to tell you what shape Angie's in. Arlen's the male equivalent of a slut and can't keep his pants zipped in spite of AIDS; Helen's been playing Donna Reed so long, she's sure she'll go up in smoke now that the kids have left; and Don and Irene watch birds and whales past all possible interest and endurance and have created a life that's about as challenging and rewarding as a Tide commercial."

"And me?" Lambie asked, half afraid of the answer.

"You put up with the mother-in-law from hell. But you *do* put up with her. You're not letting it numb you out or tear you apart that I can see. So I figure you have the guts not to push the planchette in another direction if you didn't like the answer it was heading for. At least you used to."

"I guess that's a compliment," Lambie said.

"Oh, it is. Maybe a little backhanded . . . but it is."

They looked at each other. Myra was pink and moist as usual, but she didn't have that sick red glow she got when she was upset. In fact, for once she seemed calm, in control of the situation, and suddenly Lambie remembered Myra at fifteen when she'd been the prettiest girl in town, with skin like blushed porcelain and hair like spun gold. She'd been lush, not fat, and every man she'd passed had turned to look at her. The remnants of that lovely girl were still there and Lambie ached for her old friend.

The dog shut up suddenly; the silence was blessed, like a stuck horn stopping. Lambie looked down at the board with its YES and NO, letters of the alphabet for more complicated answers, and a sad GOOD-BYE at the bottom as if the spirit reluctantly bid farewell when you were done with it.

The dog started again. Lambie's head jerked up and she thought, *Someone should put strychnine in that mutt's Kibble*; then she said, "Okay, Myra, you're on."

Myra beamed at her. "We both hold the planchette, remember? Very gently, fingertips only, and whatever you do, don't push. Okay?"

"Okay."

They put their fingertips on the little device, which had felt-tipped feet and a magnifying lens in the middle, like a monocle . . . or the eye of a miniature, cyclopean, pagan god, Lambie thought.

"Ask a question," Myra said.

"Such as what the fuck's going on in the basement?"

"Exactly."

But they started with neutral questions to get into it. Lambie asked if her daughter, Kathy, who was fourth in her class at Brown, would get into Yale, University of Michigan, or University of Chicago Law School. The planchette didn't move. She asked if her youngest, Emily, would get engaged to the jerk with the ponytail she'd brought home from UConn. Then Myra asked if her son, Dave, would get the law firm partnership in Boston he'd been angling for; if Bob would need that hemorrhoid operation. They giggled a little; the planchette didn't move.

"Maybe we should ask what we really want to know," Lambie said.

"Okay." Myra took a deep breath, stretched her fingers, then put the tips lightly back on the planchette and asked, "What's in the basement?"

Nothing happened.

"What's going on in my basement?" she asked. "Why's everyone afraid to go down there?"

The planchette stayed put; the thick, unmoving lens mocked them.

"Try who," Lambie said, and Myra asked, *Who's in the basement?*

The dog shut up suddenly; the planchette vibrated, then slid slowly, inexorably across the smooth board on its felt-tipped feet until the eye was over the letter *E*. It paused, then slid away and stopped on the *R*.

Bernie Samms's office was a cubbyhole back of the main counter at the Fallsbridge Public Library. He smoked, the air was foul, and Myra and Lambie involuntarily wrinkled their noses.

"Sorry, ladies." He wheeled back in his chair to the small window and yanked it open. It was warm and breezy out, the smoke started to clear.

"Sit, sit," he said pleasantly, indicating two molded plastic chairs across his desk. They sat; he cleared away a stack of *Library Journals* from the desk to the floor so he could see them.

"What can I do for you?"

Lambie remembered him working in the library when she was a kid. He'd been middle-aged then, must be in his seventies by now, but had the kind of smooth, ruddy skin that didn't wrinkle, and his beard was still dark. He could pass for fifty.

He was considered the last word on Fallsbridge past and present and had written a book on its history that the town published for its tricentennial.

Lambie said, "I'm Lambie Folger and this is—"

"Oh, I know who you are. Hilary, right? Hilary Lamb, whose ancestor Milo Lamb was killed on Valcour Island during one of the Indian Wars and whose bones, if any are left, are washed by the waters of Lake Champlain. Your great-great-grandpa was in the Tenth Connecticut Regiment. He lost an arm at Gettysburg and I dressed his grave with a Grand Army of the Republic plaque on some long past Memorial Day. And you're Myra Fox, of the Quaker Foxes of Fox Hill, Fox Valley, Fox River fame. Family almost as old in Fallsbridge as Lambie's here. Once owned half the town, you know, Mrs. Ludens. Sold it back in the eighteen forties, to buy Manhattan real estate.

"And I'm Bernard Samms, of the Dublin Sammses who came to these shores in the eighteen eighties to work in the mills of Massachusetts; family moved to Connecticut when the mills shut down after World War Two." He settled back in the chair.

"Now that we've been properly introduced, what can I do for you? If you're here to bitch about the choice for the book club discussion, I'm the wrong one to talk to."

"Oh, no," Myra cried, afraid they'd offended him somehow. "It's about a set of initials I found in my basement. I mean a worker found them . . . scratched in stone he was about to panel over, and he called me down to see if I wanted to leave them exposed."

What a cool liar, Lambie thought admiringly. Myra was blushing, but she always blushed.

"Initials?" Bernie asked.

"Yes. *ER*. I thought the *R* must be Redman since the house is on Old Redman Road. . . . "

His expression darkened.

"Oh, dear," Myra cried. "Did I say something wrong?"

"No. Go on."

"Anyway, it seemed logical the *R* was for Redman, but I don't know what *E* stands for, and I thought . . . we thought . . . since you know so much about the town . . . "

"In your basement?" he said.

"Yes. Scratched in the stone. *ER.*"

Lambie doubted she could have come up with such a plausible spur-of-the-moment tale.

"Do you know?" Myra asked.

"Oh yes. *ER* is Elizabeth Redman; she was accused of witchcraft, tried, convicted, and hanged not far from where we sit."

"I've heard of her, but I thought her name was Goody," Myra cried.

"Most Puritan women were called Goody, for Goodwife. Sort of like Comrade for Commies. A way of stifling individuality, I imagine. Puritans prized individuality even less than Communists, especially in women."

Lambie and Myra looked at each other, then back at Bernie. "When was she hanged?" Lambie asked.

"June sixteen ninety-five. No one knows the exact date. Shortly thereafter, John Redman sold the place to Edward Pinchot, forebear of Arlen. Then John Redman took his kids and left."

"Where did he go?"

"No one knows."

"But why?"

"Why? His wife was hanged as a witch, and maybe he was afraid her 'crime' would reflect on him or his kids. Or maybe he hated the folks of Fallsbridge for the ignorant, vicious, murderous bastards they were and wasn't too crazy about having his wife's executioners for neighbors. Sounds like a good reason to leave town."

"What happened to him?" Myra asked.

"No one knows."

"And to her?"

"I just told you. . . . "

"I mean why did they hang her . . . what did she do that made them think she was a witch?"

"The trial records are gone; earlier records are extant, so the Redman records must have been destroyed on purpose." Suddenly his voice roughened. "No one even knows where she was buried. They wouldn't want to pollute their churchyard with her remains, so her husband probably buried her on the farm . . . your place."

"Oh, God . . . " Myra whispered.

He looked disgusted. "What's the big deal, Mrs. Ludens. She was *not* a witch; they hanged her because she was epileptic and had fits, or because she pissed someone off, or they wanted something of hers, like her land or even her husband. So they accused her of consorting with demons and/or putting a hex on their cattle or their persons.

"Then, maybe the shits stripped her before the elders to look for the mark of the devil, which of course they found since no human body is without blemish. Or maybe they tossed her in the river to see if the devil kept her afloat. Or tortured a confession out of her. Subtle torture, of course . . . they were Christians." His mouth twisted. "Maybe they even sent in the big guns—Willard of Groton, or Cotton Mather himself—and they interrogated her day and night, without sleep or food, until she couldn't remember who or where she was, until maybe she began to wonder if she *was* a witch.

"They were degenerate, not dumb, Mrs. Ludens. They had their methods and maybe she gave up in the end and said whatever they wanted her to. We'll never know because, as I said, the trial records are gone. But they *did* hang her. . . . "

He jumped up, his thigh hit the edge of the desk, jarring a Styrofoam cup, and coffee splattered the faded, already stained blotter. He ignored the spilled coffee and looked out the window.

"They'd've hanged her up there . . . at the crest of Hillgate."

Hillgate was the highest point in town.

"Right at the peak," he said, softly. "Maybe from the oak that used to be there."

Lambie remembered the oak; there'd been some protest when they cut it down in the seventies, but not enough to stop the DaSilvas, the biggest local developers, and they built condos on the land.

Bernie went on, softly, "They tied her skirts down out of modesty, waited for the sun to start setting, then strung her up. They wouldn't build a special gallows for one woman, so she didn't fall through a trap and break her neck. She strangled. . . . "

Lambie paled and looked at Myra to see how she was faring. Her color was indescribable. Scarlet or vermillion was close, but still below the mark. Lambie had seen paler boiled lobsters.

Bernie kept on, "Her husband would have been made to watch, then to take the body away afterwards. I hope they at least had the decency to help him cut her down and lay her in the cart. Then he took her home through the June evening. How far is it from Hillgate to your house, Mrs. Ludens? Four, five miles?"

"Four." Myra choked.

"Four miles. He must have had a horse, I pray he had a horse. But the cart probably had no driver's seat, and he'd've walked beside it, urging the horse along a road that was only a track then. For four miles in the June twilight, he walked with the cart heaving over the ruts and hillocks and his wife's body lolling and flopping in back. Farm carts weren't much in those days, just slats and a flatbed. And he must've had to stop every now and then and resettle the corpse, so it wouldn't fall out. Some four miles that must have been, ladies. Some four miles. At last he'd arrive home where the children were waiting; even in those days—the good old days—they wouldn't make children watch their mother hang. So the kids'd be waiting at home, watching from the open door as the man and the horse and cart carrying their dead mother turned in at the gate."

Myra sobbed violently, and Bernie jerked around. "Oh, Jesus . . . I'm sorry," he cried. "I get carried away. I'm really sorry." He yanked open one of the desk drawers, pulled out a box of Kleenex, and handed it across to her. "Please," he said. "Oh dear. . . . Would you like some water, or a soda?"

She shook her head, grabbed a wad of tissues and wiped her face and eyes, then clenched her hands in her lap, with the crumpled tissues in them.

"Look, I'm really sorry," he said.

"It's all right," she murmured, but the tears wouldn't stop and she had to take more Kleenex.

They were quiet for what seemed like a long time; then Bernie said, gently, "You didn't find *ER* scratched on the stone foundation, did you, Mrs. Ludens?"

"Of course she did!" Lambie tried to sound insulted for Myra's sake. But Myra said:

"No, Mr. Samms, I didn't."

"I thought not." He looked at Lambie. "Graffiti's old as humankind, Mrs. Folger. There're initials scratched on Edward the Confessor's chair. But it's an act of will and defiance that would be extremely unusual for a Puritan woman. Why don't you tell me what this is really about."

Myra started to, but her voice was a breathy whisper that choked, wheezed, and finally shut down in a gasp. Bernie ran out of the room, while Lambie rubbed Myra's back to help her get her breath back. Bernie was back in half a minute with a Dixie cup of water. He gave it to Myra and she drank, watching him over the cup with grateful eyes. She finished it and stopped wheezing. "Better?" he asked.

"Much." She looked around helplessly. Lambie didn't know what she wanted, but Bernie did and he pulled over a dented metal wastebasket.

"In there," he said, and Myra crumpled the cup and dropped it in the can. She looked better, but shook her head that she couldn't go on with the story. Bernie looked at Lambie, and she took up the tale of the basement. She expected him to laugh in her face, but he listened intently and she found herself wishing he *would* laugh. She finished and he was quiet for a moment; then he came around the desk and propped himself on the edge, with one foot planted on the floor, the other dangling. He wore penny loafers, Lambie noticed, and argyle socks. His slacks needed pressing, his shirt collar needed stays, and there was a big oily blotch on his wrinkled tie. His wife had died three years ago, and he looked a little more bedraggled every time Lambie saw him.

"Mrs. Ludens?" he asked gently.

Myra dragged her eyes away from the Kleenex in her hand and focused on him.

He said, "You think your basement is haunted, is that it? And you came to me to find out by whom or what."

"No!"

"No?"

"I mean . . . I don't know what I mean! But something's down there, Mr. Samms."

"Get rid of it," he said softly, and Lambie felt every hair on her stir.

"What?" Myra whispered.

"You heard me. Get rid of it. I don't believe or *not* believe in ghosts, but one thing I can tell you with total certainty: The spirit of Goody Redman, if it exists, will not be benign."

"Get rid of it?" Arlen asked.

"Yes," Myra mumbled.

"Get rid of *it?*"

"That's right." Myra couldn't look at him; she kept her eyes on her hands in her lap. They were in the library of Pinchot House, one of those perfect rooms you knew shouldn't be an inch higher, wider, or longer than it was. It was paneled in mahogany, lined with shelves of mostly leather-bound books. A fireplace between the shelves was faced in the same mahogany. It would have been a gloomy room, with all that dark wood and deep-colored book spines, except for the sun streaming through windows and French doors that took up two walls.

"Because it's 'not benign'?" Arlen persisted.

"Yes . . . " Myra's voice was barely a whisper. Lambie sat stiffly on the big couch next to her, staring into space.

"And what do you suppose Mr. Samms meant by 'not benign'?" Arlen sounded exasperated. "That it's going to start stinking down there again? Or maybe this famous *it* will come creeping up the stairs some night—"

"Stop it," Myra gasped.

"I'm sorry, My. But you must realize how absurd this sounds."

"We know exactly how it sounds," Lambie said tightly. "But you weren't there, Arl. You didn't hear him. Samms meant it, and I swear, every inch of me shriveled when he said it."

"Okay . . . okay . . . " He raised his hands, palms out in a gesture of sur-render. "There's an *it* in the basement, and it's not benign. Sounds like you should be talking to Reverend Bodgett or Father Thomas. What're you doing here?"

"Mr. Samms said your father had a collection of books on the occult and ... another word I didn't understand," Myra said.

"Incunabula?"

"Yes."

"That's medieval arcana, Myra. In other words, bullshit!"

Myra clenched her hands tightly in her lap.

"I don't doubt it's ... what you said." She had trouble swearing, unlike the rest of them. The gang of eight, she thought. Old, old friends. Best friends who'd once had grand hopes for themselves and each other, and wound up a bunch of born-rich, bored, middle-aged bridge players.

She went on, "But he *did* mean it, and he said that maybe there was something in one of the books. A rite or ritual, a spell, that would ... get rid of it."

"Get rid of *it*," Arlen said tonelessly.

"Yes."

"The ghost."

"Yes," Myra said, very firmly.

Arlen sat in the big, softly worn leather chair across from them, leaned his forearms on his thighs, and clasped his hands between his knees. "My ... Lamb ... do you honestly expect me to buy a word of this?"

"We don't expect you to 'buy' anything. Just look in some old books for something we need," Lambie said. "Is that too much to ask?"

"Don't get angry," he said gently.

"She's not. Neither am I," said Myra. "But it's important to me, Arl. It's my house ... my basement. ... "

"Your ghost." He grinned at her.

"Don't laugh at me." She spoke with all the dignity she could muster. "He really did scare me."

"And he's an asshole for doing it," Arlen said. The women didn't respond, and after a moment he sighed and got to his feet. "Okay, if it's what you want. ... " He went to a section of books next to the French doors that opened onto the terrace and back gardens. They must have had a thousand parties out there through the years, Myra thought. Including their high school graduation party. She hadn't graduated, having had the baby by then. But she'd come anyway, without Bob, who'd graduated years before, and with Dave, who'd been a fat, adorable baby with hair like gold spider web, and huge, saucer eyes of the purest, sweetest blue, and who was now thirty, and a father himself. Impossible to believe.

Arlen gestured at a section of shelves. "Here they are, ladies. Gardiner Hale Pinchot's seven hundred years of Twilight Zone bullshit."

The section was eight feet high and about as wide, and was crammed with books of every color, size, type of binding.

"Too many," Myra said hopelessly.

"A lot," Arlen agreed. "But they're cataloged."

"By subject?" Lambie asked. Bless her, she always knew the right question, Myra thought.

"By subject." Arlen looked at them. "Only what subject do I look under?"

"There must be master cards."

"Yes."

"So . . . flip through them, see what fits."

He went to the big partner's desk in front of the doors and opened a deep bottom drawer, from which he dredged up a swing-topped wooden box and set it on the desk top. He hesitated, as if to build suspense, then swung open the lid to reveal four-by-six cards, divided by buff tabbed dividers, with the subjects in neat, fading manual type.

Old man Pinchot had been tall and skinny, with flyaway white hair and a distracted air, as if he heard distant music or couldn't remember zipping his fly. It was hard to imagine him doing this precise job.

Arlen slid the tabs forward, half chanting. "We've got abjuring and astrology, black magic, black mass, and the ineffable Cabala. . . . "

"Try abjuring," Lambie said.

"What's it mean?" Myra asked.

"To deny or renounce," Arlen answered, and Myra murmured, "I don't want to renounce her, I just want to get her out of my basement."

It was one of those funny lines that sometimes dropped out of her mouth to the others' delight, and Arlen and Lambie laughed, but not Myra, because she'd said *her*, not *it*, and with the change of pronoun,

Goody Redman became real. A wife and mother whose neighbors, people she must have known all her life—trusted—hanged her on the crest of Hillgate for a crime that didn't even exist.

Hillgate made no sense, Myra thought suddenly. Hills didn't have gates, and she knew in a flash the name had been softened from *Hellgate,* and the gate to hell for those citizens of Fallsbridge had been the deed they'd done that June afternoon three hundred years ago.

All at once, Myra saw it, was in the crowd, as some of her forebears must have been in their Quaker gray. She saw Goody Redman on a stool, with the noose already around her neck, drooping from the weight of a sloppy-looking knot. The rope was looped over a low, thick limb of the old oak and tied to a stake driven in the ground a few feet beyond the tree.

Goody Redman had on gray homespun, with a long skirt, and fine white cotton collar. Her best collar to be hanged in. And over her head was a coarse white sack, like flour sacking, making her head round, featureless, balloonlike.

The day was ending, and the long, slow, soft June twilight had begun. Shadows of other, long gone trees crawled across the ground toward the crowd's feet. The sky was turning a splendid orange. A man in black clothes like a Thanksgiving Day pageant costume, with high hat, breeches, and white, pointed collar, detached himself from the crowd and went up to the woman on the stool. He had long scraggly black hair, long pointed nose and chin, and eyes the color of a glacial crevasse. If he felt any pity for Goody Redman, or the smallest stab of doubt about what they were going to do to her, it didn't show in those eyes.

He bent over and grabbed the stool by the legs, while the crowd held its breath. Then he yanked the stool out from under her, backpedaling to keep from being hit by the body . . . and Goody Redman swung. She thrashed and twisted, bent her bound legs in a vain attempt to loosen the cord around her neck, while from under the sack came horrible, mortal-sounding grunts, groans, snorts, and gags. The front of the sack turned dark with saliva, then red. The rope must have torn something in her throat and she was drooling blood. . . .

Myra reeled and started to fall. She reached for the desk for support, missed, and hit the back of the couch. Hanging on, she inched her way blindly around it and collapsed on the cushions as everything heaved and turned gray, and the couch rocked under her.

Lambie called from far away, then Arlen put his large, strong hand flat on Myra's back and said, "Put your head down." With his help, she got her forehead pressed against the couch cushions between her legs. Blood seeped back to her head, the couch stopped swaying, and the roaring that sounded like waves on rocks receded. Carefully she raised her head, which felt huge and fragile, and opened her eyes.

Lambie crouched in front of her, looking frightened; Arlen sat tensely on the couch next to her, his hand still resting on her back. She managed a shaky grin and croaked, "We skipped lunch."

George brought the huge carved-silver coffee service with a platter of assorted sandwiches on whole wheat bread. Myra gobbled a sandwich, drank the coffee black and hot, burning the roof of her mouth. She probably wouldn't taste anything for the rest of the day. But the food and coffee helped immeasurably; the last vestige of dizziness passed.

"Let me take you home," Lambie said shakily. Lambie had one of those rocketing metabolisms that had to be fed four or five times a day just to stay even, and she was looking very pale. She'd probably lost a pound just from the strain of the day Myra had put her through.

"You okay?" Myra asked anxiously.

"Fine."

"Then why don't we get this over with."

Lambie nodded, and a look of understanding passed between them. They'd made Arlen a victim of their wild insistence and couldn't just say *thanks but no thanks*, then walk out on him, though they both wanted to, Myra thought.

Besides, Arlen now seemed to have gotten sucked in and was back at the desk, flipping through the cards with a little frown of concentration on his face.

So they'd play it out, she thought, until he got bored or she and Lambie got up the gumption to leave.

* * *

Nothing under *abjuring* fit after all, but Arlen said a title under *Black Mass* seemed to, and he took down a large, impressive-looking volume bound in morocco leather. He scanned a couple of pages, then turned as red as Myra at her worst, and looked up at them.

"Jesus . . . they strapped rubber genitals on holy statues and . . . uh . . . copulated with them. Then skinned cats alive . . . and boiled them. . . ." His lips twitched madly; he choked, "Doesn't exactly sound like our style. . . ." and they broke into a fit of helpless laughter that went on until Myra's sides ached and her eyes burned. They got hold of themselves, drank a little more coffee, and Arlen put the book back, then returned to the box on the desk.

It was getting dark, even though it was barely four. Must be clouding up, Myra thought; it looked more like November than May.

"Here's something. . . ." Arlen held up a card; Myra felt a feather-touch premonition of dread, and thought,

No, Arl, let it go.

But he was back at the shelves, taking down another book, that was much thinner and meaner-looking than the first, with a tattered blue-green cloth binding. Myra sat frozen as he opened it, praying the phone would ring or George would come flying in with a telegram, even one with bad news. Anything to stop what was about to happen, even though Myra had no idea what it was.

Arlen read a little, then looked up and grinned hugely. "Well, now, seems we've found just what you need, My! The mother lode of rites to get rid of all nonbenign whatevers in the basement. Only you'll need a few things that might be a little hard to come by, such as"—still grinning, he looked back at the book—"brain of a cat that's fed on human flesh, a parricide's skull . . . and some dragon blood. . . ."

At the same time, four miles downstream from the Pinchot estate, in Riverside, the only mean section of rich, pretty, manicured Fallsbridge, the section where the Fox River turned wide and shallow, and the marshy banks smelled like tidal mud—Reed Lerner finally admitted defeat.

He was exhausted. Belle Lambert must be too, although it was impossible to tell since she hadn't spoken for weeks, and her face was utterly without expression. Her lips were slack; a little strand of drool ran down the crease from the side of her mouth. She looked like a cartoon of a crazy woman, but she was real and suffering inside the mound of flesh she'd turned herself into, even if she couldn't show it.

He closed his notepad on the empty page and stood up.

"That's it, Belle. You need more than what I can give you once a week. Can you understand at all? Can you?"

Nothing.

"Ah, Belle, it's just gotten worse, hasn't it?"

No answer.

"Belle, I'm going to try to get a court order to have you committed. You'll go to a clean place, with decent food and professionals to look after you. Maybe that'll help, my dear. Maybe it will."

He felt stupid tears sting his eyes and blinked quickly. He was admitting defeat out of pity and true helplessness, not because he was lazy or incompetent. But it hurt anyway.

He moved away from the rocker she sat in, and around the table that hadn't been cleared for a couple of days. He took some dirty plates to the sink, but it was already full, and the smell of spoiling food bubbled up from milky water. He put the plates on the drainboard, then went down a narrow hall with a rough wood floor that would dig splinters into your feet if you walked on it barefoot. A strip of crusted carpet ran down the center of it.

He stopped at the first door.

Behind it, a TV blasted. "GE, we bring good things to life." He knocked hard to be sure he was heard.

The volume went down, the door opened, and Larry Lambert looked out at him. Larry was as thin as his mother was fat; his face was elongated, with deep lines running down his cheeks and around his mouth. Loose, sagging pouches under his eyes added to his hangdog look.

"Come in, Doc," he said. Reed entered the room; Larry sat on the edge of a bed that was no more than a cot, with dirty, crumpled sheets on it.

"Wanna sit down?" Larry nodded at two chairs, one upholstered and gray with dust, the other scarred wood. Reed took the wood chair.

Larry leaned over and clicked off the TV, but the big, blank screen still dominated the room.

"So, what's the story?" Larry said.

"Larry . . . I hate to say this. . . . You know I've tried, but it's no use. If you won't sign committal forms, I'm going to get another doctor to look at her, and if he agrees with me, and I'm pretty sure he will, I'm going to get a court order to institutionalize your mother." Reed leaned forward. "Larry, I'm sorry. I don't want to do it. But she can't go on like this. She sits in a full diaper most of the day, probably has abscesses all over her. I saw one on her leg today. Her color's abysmal."

"What's abysmal mean, Doc?"

"Uh . . . terrible. Her color's terrible. She needs a better diet, she needs drugs she can't take here, even with you to watch over her, because the effects can be untow— uh . . . unexpected. Could kill her without people around who know how to help her. Do you understand?"

Larry nodded; the loose skin around the indents in his face flopped. He was about forty; Reed knew Belle was fifty-seven (although she looked like a beaten-up seventy). So she'd had him at seventeen, maybe younger. Belle's mother probably had her when *she* was seventeen or younger.

Larry clasped his hands and looked down at them. "She's my ma. . . . " he said.

"I know that. And I know you want to look after her, and you've tried. I know you have, Larry. . . . " He *had* tried, but was not in much better shape psychologically than his mother. Had the energy level of a dying slug, Reed thought. It was a mean thought, he hated having it, but it was true.

"But it's too much for you, Larry, and I can't take responsibility for what'll happen to her if she stays here."

"You mean she'll die." It wasn't even a question.

"I guess that's what I mean," Reed said.

The door to the room opened and Larry's son, Belle's grandson, stood in the doorway.

He was nineteen and ran to fat like his grandmother. He was pasty-faced like the others, but his eyes weren't vague or blank; they snapped with life, cunning, and, most of all, spite, Reed thought.

He was tall, carried his weight pretty well; his clothes were clean, his boots polished. His hair was clipped so short you could see scalp through it; the sleeves of his crisp denim shirt were rolled up and exposed a tattoo of the German imperial eagle on his forearm.

"We was just talking about Ma," Larry told his son.

The kid leaned against the doorjamb and folded his arms. "What about her?"

"Doc here says she gotta go to the loony bin."

"It's not a loony bin," Reed said. "It's a hospital."

The kid glared at him, but didn't say anything. Larry ran a hand with black-rimmed nails down his face, dragging flesh with it, and Reed could've sworn the flesh wasn't resilient enough to come back up on its own, but stayed dragged, making him look even droopier.

The kid gave his father a look of disgust, Reed a look of pure hate, and said, "She ain't goin'."

Reed felt his temper stir.

"Don't think you've got much choice, Dick. I was just telling your dad here—"

"Don't tell him; he won't remember what you say two seconds after you're done saying it. Tell me."

"Okay." He told Dick what he'd just told Larry.

"You mean you'll just come in here and take her without anyone's by-your-leave?" the kid asked.

"Yes."

"That sucks."

Reed didn't say anything.

"Get out," the kid said quietly.

Reed stood up. "Look, I've got the papers with me. Why don't you let your dad sign them. It's for three weeks' observation; that's all, and I swear she'll be in much better shape after those three weeks. Then we can see. Maybe she can come—"

"Get out, you Jew bastard."

Reed was used to this. Calmly he said, "Calling me names isn't going to change anything."

"No, but it makes me feel a lot better." The kid had muscles big enough to bulge out his sleeves and pant legs, his arms hung at his sides, his hands curled into fists, and the eagle writhed as his forearms bulged.

Reed picked up the small black bag he carried, mostly for show, though he'd had to use the prefilled syringes in it a few times. He went to the door; the kid blocked his way, giving him that teenage look compounded of hate, snot, and a kind of dogged arrogance.

Reed said quietly, "If you want me to leave, you've got to let me pass, Dick."

The kid waited the requisite macho moment, then stepped aside. Reed crossed the threshold into the hall, then turned back. "Larry, think about what I've said. I know how you feel about her and I know how much you need the checks she gets." Belle's disability checks were the mainstay of their income. "But maybe we can work something out," Reed said.

"Such as?" the kid asked.

"I don't know. I'll talk to social services and see. It'll be a lot easier to work out without the court getting into it." He looked at the kid and thought he'd never seen such pure, hot hate in anyone's eyes.

"But either way, she's got to go," Reed said steadily.

"Fuck you, Jew," the kid hissed. Reed looked at the father, but Larry was staring off into space.

It was hopeless.

" 'Bye, Larry," Reed called. The other man didn't react, and Reed nodded at the kid and went down the hall to the front door. On his way, he looked in on Belle.

She hadn't moved from the frozen, classically catatonic position he'd left her in. On one of the wretched streets of this miserable part of town, a siren wailed. She didn't look up. He doubted she'd react if he set her on fire. Belle Lambert was gone, to someplace better than the filthy kitchen, he hoped.

He went out the front door and down the broken cement walk to the beat-up Honda Civic he usually drove on his visits to Riverside, knowing that, behind him, through the window of his father's bedroom, Dick Lambert was watching him.

* * *

A̲s Reed drove away from the Lambert bungalow, Lambie pulled into
Myra's driveway and killed the motor. The women looked at each other,
then at *the* book jutting out of Myra's purse.

Arlen had wrapped it in brown paper, tied it with twine, and presented
it to Myra. "Uh ... keep it for as long as ... uh ... you want. ... " he'd said.

By then she hadn't wanted it or anything, except to forget what a fool
she'd made of herself.

"I don't know what got into me," she said to Lambie.

"Into me, either."

"How do you feel now?"

Lambie laughed. "Like I farted at the ball."

"Oh, Lamb ... I'm so sorry. I just can't believe the trouble I've caused. I
sort of started to see how insane it was when Arlen read those subject
headings from the cards, but then he got to cannibal cats and skulls and
dragon blood ... and I wanted to die."

"So did I."

"Of course there's no ... ghost. ... And we're not going to do any of the
crazy things in there. ... " She glared at the book.

"You mean dance around burning bat brain?"

They giggled and hugged each other quickly across the book and purse,
then drew apart. Myra looked out at the side of her big, pretty house, with
its perfectly trained shrubs, and lawn just starting to put out spring growth.
It would be ragged soon; she'd have to call Mr. Abel to come and mow.

"I feel like two different people, like I had a sort of minibreakdown the
last two days. But it's over now—at least it feels over. Oh, Lambie, I
must've moved the Ouija board planchette without even knowing it."

"Or I did."

"Of course you didn't. It was me. I must've heard about *her* when I was a
kid, and forgot until today. And poor Mr. Samms is getting senile. ... "

"Or playing us for a donation."

"We should give him one for that performance," Myra said. They
laughed again, glad to have everything back to normal. Myra looked at the

book again. "I didn't want to take it, you know. I truly didn't. But I couldn't tell Arlen to just . . . stuff it . . . after all the trouble I'd put him to."

"Can't imagine you telling anyone to stuff it," Lambie said fondly.

Myra pushed the book deeper into her purse, then took the purse and put her hand on the door handle.

"Thank you," she said solemnly, not looking at Lambie.

"For what?"

"Not laughing at me."

"I got sucked in too, don't forget."

"Did you?" Myra looked at her, and Lambie grinned. "You know, My, I really did."

"That makes me feel better."

Myra climbed out of the car. "Talk to you tomorrow," Lambie called, putting the car in gear. Myra waved, Lambie pulled down the drive, and the dog, which had been quiet until now, started yapping. As if it had been waiting for Myra to get home.

But that was exactly the kind of thinking she had to stop.

She did feel more like herself and must build on that, not backslide into thinking things were stranger or more terrible than they were.

The dog was just a yappy dog, not the hound of hell. Pastori was your ordinary, run-of-the-mill, totally vanilla son of a bitch, no more or less, *and there was no ghost in her basement.*

Now the very notion made her grin.

She let herself in the side door, left her purse on the kitchen counter, and went to the front closet, scooping the Ouija board box off the breakfast room table on her way. She hung her coat up, pushing the ugly shell jacket out of sight in the dark reaches of the closet. Next week, she'd ask Lambie or Helen or Irene (if she could stop watching birds for a day) to shop with her for a new one so she wouldn't make the same mistake.

She took the Ouija board into the den and slid it under the Scrabble set. She'd put it up in the attic eventually or give it to the thrift shop.

She went back to the kitchen and quickly put together a chicken casserole for dinner. The dog was still at it.

She set the timer, started the salad, and had just finished it when she heard Bob pull into the garage. She took his chilled mug and a bottle of Labatt's out of the refrigerator.

He came in with his jacket slung over his shoulder and the paper rolled up under his arm. He gave her his usual quick but tender kiss, then raised his head like a wolf smelling blood.

"Dog's at it," he said as if she couldn't hear it herself.

"Uh . . . I guess Mr. Pastori didn't take me too seriously," she mumbled.

"So you called the dog warden. . . ."

"I was too busy today."

"Doing what?" His tone was inquisitorial and she felt her blood pressure kick in. But she knew exactly how to shut him up, and she prattled, "I went to Playthings in town. To get a birthday present for little Ellie? It's next Friday, remember? And I found this adorable Playmobil castle, with turrets and a drawbridge and knights in armor. . . ."

His eyes glazed.

"And it had this adorable little white plastic ghost," she babbled. "Reminded me of Caspar in the comics . . . remember Caspar? It even had its own little chain to rattle and it was *so* precious. . . ."

"Think I'll catch the early news," he said. He took the mug and paper and headed for the door. She started to relax, then saw he was about to pass her purse with the book sticking out of it. If he asked about it, she'd have to lie or try to explain why she was carrying around a book on black magic wrapped in brown paper like pornography. But he passed the book without noticing it, left the room, and she sagged against the sink, waiting for her heart to slow down. She'd give the book back to Arlen tomorrow, thank him for his trouble, and explain that she'd finally gotten hold of herself and realized how crazy she was being. Then she'd buy him lunch at the club to thank him for being so nice about it.

In the meantime, she had to hide the book.

Bob or Sandy might come across it anywhere in the house she could think of . . . except the basement.

She looked at the humble wood-slat door.

She'd never been down there alone at night, but six-fifteen on a late April evening was hardly night. Besides, her phobia about the basement was one of the things she must get over if she was going to get hold of herself.

She took the book out of her purse, went to the door, and listened. The dog was going full blast; Bob had the TV on in the den, so he wouldn't hear the door latch.

She opened it, automatically bracing herself against the chill and smell. But the air was warm, dry, fresh. She flicked the switch, stepped out on the landing, and looked down at the tile below that was a gray so soft it almost looked like cloth. Bless Barbara Potter, she thought, and started down the stairs, clutching the book in one hand, the stair rail in the other.

Halfway down, at the turn and landing the builder had added to keep the stairs from looking cellarlike, that prickle started dancing across the back of her neck, and she stopped.

Get rid of it, Bernie Samms had said; she could actually hear his voice. She clutched the book harder. Her hands were sweating; the paper wrapper was getting damp.

She was not going to give in to this. She was going to *get hold of herself,* go down the rest of the stairs, tuck the book in the shelf under the TV where it would stay until Wednesday.

Get rid of it, Bernie had said, but there was nothing to get rid of. The basement was just a basement, the Ouija board a game for silly, lovesick teenagers.

She took another step, the prickling got worse, the first itchy drops of sweat popped out along her hairline, and she saw something move. It was just a flick at the edge of her vision that started and stopped so suddenly she knew it wasn't there. It was a trick of her overactive imagination, her perennial panic, her blood pressure, which spiked enough to start that roaring in her ears.

Or a mouse had gotten in, in spite of the new caulking, or one of those humongous wolf spiders that gave even Bob the willies.

That's all it was, and she turned to look. It was one of the hardest things she'd ever done, because all her nerve endings screamed at her to shut her eyes and freeze, like a kid waking from a nightmare who knows if he moves, breathes, looks, the dream monster will see him . . . come after him.

But she wasn't a kid, this wasn't a dream, and there were no monsters.

She turned her head, which felt like a balloon full of gas, looked, and saw . . . nothing: a block of shadow on the floor cast by the wall of the new alcove. A shadow deep enough to hide a terrified little mouse or startled spider. She peered into the dark patch until she saw the outline of the tiles.

There was nothing there.

A half giggle, half whimper that sounded like a rusty hinge came out of her mouth, and she decided she'd tortured herself enough for one day. She'd go back upstairs and find someplace else to hide the book. Maybe under the pile of washed cleaning rags that Sandy never got to the bottom of, or in the garage, in the paint cabinet, or—best of all—in the trunk of her car. No one would look there.

Good. She didn't have to go the rest of the way after all. Of course she should conquer this mindless dread, but she had time. A lifetime to get over all her silly terrors, and she whirled around to rush back . . . and hit her head on a sloping plasterboarded beam next to the stairs. It connected with a sound like wood cracking. Dots of light danced in her head, the beam swam before her eyes, and she dropped the book. It hit the rail, bounced, and hit the floor below with a thwack.

She shook her head to clear it, then looked over the rail at the brown-wrapped parcel on the tile floor. She should go down and get it, but her legs shook, her head pounded from the blow, and everything had gotten that sickish pink halo around it.

She'd leave the book. No one would come down here before Wednesday; then Lambie or Reed would help her get it.

Myra started up the stairs to the door. It shimmered in that pink haze and seemed a mile away. Her feet felt like wet clay, her legs wobbled, but she kept going, hauling herself up the new, wide, carpeted stairs using the heavy new banister they'd installed.

She made progress, but it was amazing how long it took for the door to get any closer. At last she was in front of it, with the slats of wood pulsing in and out of focus with the beat of her heart.

She grabbed the knob, turned, and pushed . . . and the door stuck.

"Not now," she begged. "Please, not now. . . ."

She pushed again, but it was stuck solid. She put her shoulder to it with her weight behind it and shoved. It didn't budge, and she heard a soft, sly sound below her in the basement. It was a half scrape, half tinkle, unlike anything she'd ever heard before. But she knew what it was, knew the sound as surely as she did the doorbell, Bob's voice, the thud of her own heart. It was the sound of bone on tile, and she also knew that if she looked, she would see the marionette of a skeleton clicking across the floor with its grinning, yellowish skull patched with moss, eye sockets filled with dirt, and a few shreds of the Puritan cap still clinging to it after three hundred years.

CHAPTER 3

Reed was dancing with Belle Lambert, a spirited dance he thought was called a gavotte. She had on the same cotton housedress she'd worn today, last week, week before, only it was miraculously clean. Her hair shone, her body was slim as a girl's and vibrated with life, though her face had its usual death-mask blankness with eyes as empty as air.

He ignored her eyes, concentrated on her body mashed against his.

"Reed . . ." It was Riva, but he refused to let her intrude, sure that if he and Belle danced hard enough to the hectic music, held each other close enough, he'd uncover the secret of her sickness.

"Reed . . ." Riva spoke sharply, and he opened his eyes. She was pale and clutched her cardigan across her chest in an old-lady gesture that was totally unlike her.

The boys, he thought sickly. Something's happened to the boys. He struggled to sit up; the *Archives of Psychiatry* he'd fallen asleep over slid off his lap to the floor, and Riva said,

"It's Myra, Reed."

"Myra . . ."

"Bob is on the phone. He says something happened to Myra."

Stroke. The word screamed through Reed's mind. Followed by that

57

mad, but on-target medicalism that always made him want to laugh and say oops: *Cerebral Vascular Accident.*

He leaped up, skidded his stocking feet on the slick journal cover on the floor, and grabbed the table. The lamp and brandy glass on it rocked madly, then righted themselves, and he saw that the big balloon snifter, which had been half full, was empty.

No wonder he'd dozed; passed out was more like it.

He got his balance and raced to the phone with Riva watching, still clutching that sweater.

"Bob . . ."

"Reed? It's My, Reed. Something's happened to My."

"Listen to me. Call nine one one, not Moffet. Let *them* call Moffet. And don't waste any more time with me. Okay? Nine one one. . . . "

"I can't. . . . She won't let me." Bob Ludens's voice broke.

"Won't let you? She can talk. . . . " A good sign. A stupendous sign.

"Sure she can talk." Bob sounded startled by the notion she might not be able to. "Look, I know it's a lousy night . . . "

Reed became aware of rain splatting on the windows. It must've started while he was asleep.

"But I need you," Bob said.

The rain had an icy sound, the pavement felt slick, and Reed kept the Porsche at thirty. Main Street was an empty shining black strip, with its lone stoplight thrashing in the wind on its cable.

Myra, Myra, he thought as he traversed the two blocks of posh shops that made up Fallsbridge Center. *Be okay, My, honey, Myra, please, please be okay.*

Lambie had had a bad delivery with her second daughter; Reed had had a bout of viral meningitis; and a nasty ski accident had left Arlen in a leg cast for six months. Don gave them a scare when he'd been tested for throat cancer that turned out to be vocal cord polyps, and hanging over them was the knowledge that Withers could give Angie much worse than a busted rib one day; but that was the ghost of Christmas yet to come,

Reed thought. Until tonight, everything that had gone wrong with any of them had been temporary and reparable. Maybe this was . . . maybe not.

"Myra," he whispered with an ache in his throat. "Oh, My . . ."

He left the town center behind and entered the maze of roads that led to Redman Farm. "Please, My honey . . . please be okay."

"In the den," Bob said. "She won't eat, drink, or speak. Just sits there shivering."

She was in a wing chair, three quarters back to the door, and had to lean out of the chair to see him when he said her name. The TV was playing softly; she had her feet up on a hassock, her body covered by a green-and-gold afghan under which her clenched fists made small lumps.

Reed turned off the TV, moved her feet aside, and sat on the hassock to look at her at eye level. Her skin was moist and very pale, except for hot red spots on her cheeks and between her eyebrows. Her eyes were glassy, the skin around them looked bruised, and there was a pink welt on her forehead.

"Bump your head?" he asked gently.

Gingerly, she touched the spot. "I almost forgot."

"How'd it happen?"

"Later." Her lips barely moved. "Talk to Bob first."

"I just talked to him."

"Talk to him some more, tell him I'm okay. He's in worse shape than I am."

"I'll tell him you're okay when I'm sure you are."

He opened his bag, aware of how meager were his equipment and knowledge. She needed Moffet and/or the Coronary Care Unit at Fallsbridge General.

He said as much, but she shook her head and her eyes got a flat look he'd only seen a few times: Myra digging in, he thought. But he'd call Moffet and the paramedics no matter what she said if he saw the slightest reason.

He went to work.

Her pressure was up, but nowhere near blowout level. Her eye grounds were clear, skin turgor good, and her pulse fast but steady and strong in both wrist and ankle.

He asked if she'd blacked out or gotten dizzy when she'd banged her head. She said she'd seen little light dots, and everything had gotten pink. "But it's done that before," she said.

She had mentioned it before and Moffet had confirmed it was a common concomitant of labile hypertension. Nothing to worry about.

"What day is it, Myra?" Reed snapped out the question and she gave a faint smile.

"You really are worried about me, aren't you?"

"Just answer the question."

"It's Thursday, my name's Myra Louise Ludens, maiden name Fox. Mrs. Haft, who had blue hair in waves, I think they used to call it marcelled, was our second-grade teacher. I'm as compos mentis as I ever am, Reed. You've got to believe that, it's crucial you believe that."

"Why?"

"Because you've got to believe what I'm going to tell you."

"About . . . ?"

"What happened in the basement."

"I'm listening, Myra."

"Talk to Bob first, then come back. Alone, Reed. I can't say this in front of him. . . ."

Bob was at the kitchen table staring into a mug of flat-looking beer.

"She's okay," Reed said quickly. "At least I'm pretty sure she is."

"Pretty sure?" Bob snarled, not looking at him. "What kind'a medical science is pretty sure?"

"The only kind I have," Reed said gently. "The only kind there is."

Bob hunched his shoulders up around his ears, and started to cry. He was a big man, almost as tall as Reed. He had bulbous forearms, an eighteen-inch neck, and gray-brown hair in a fifties, macho buzz cut. Seeing him cry was awful, but Reed forced himself not to look away because Bob would take that for disgust. He'd also hate any show of pity, and Reed let him cry a moment, then said roughly, "Can it, Bob . . . I said she's okay."

"I know . . . I know . . . " Bob pulled out a gigantic, snowy, perfectly ironed handkerchief and wiped his eyes. No hired help had done that handkerchief, Reed thought, nor had Fallsbridge Laundry and Dry Cleaner, with which he had some experience. That handkerchief was a Myra special, and he saw her at the ironing board . . . then saw his mother in the same position in his mind's eye. Ironing in the kitchen back in the Bronx, before the old man started his chain of fat-lady dress shops that netted him fifty million, give or take.

Reed dropped his bag on the floor and sat down across from Bob. Bob stuffed the handkerchief back in his pocket, and looked at Reed. The tears had stuck his lashes together, giving his eyes a starry look.

"I thought she'd had a stroke," he said.

"Me too; we're apparently wrong. But something happened, Bob. What?"

"Dinner was late." Bob managed a shaky grin. "Doesn't exactly sound like the end of the world, does it? But in this house it's a fuckin' tsunami. We eat at six-thirty, no matter what. You've heard me bitch about it for twenty-five years. Six-thirty, every night, every season, all year, every year . . . unless we go out. So when it hit ten to seven and no dinner, I got worried and came out here to see what was wrong. Figured she'd spilled or broken something and was rushing to clean it up before I saw it and went into my ogre act. I do it, Reed; I hate it, she hates it, but it happens. Doesn't change the fact that I love her. . . . " He forced the words out and Reed thought, *No contest.* Bob Ludens had fallen for Myra Fox when she was a sophomore at Fallsbridge High and looked like a Renoir on porcelain. Reed doubted that love had ever wavered.

"But she wasn't cleaning up broken dishes," Bob was saying. "She wasn't *here.* I looked outside. It'd started raining by then, but Myra's a real spaz when it comes to messes, and I thought she'd be taking out the garbage. But she wasn't out there . . . she wasn't in here, and I called a couple of times . . . then heard this . . . scratching . . . like a cat scratching at the basement door. . . . " He shot a look of hate at the humble door with wood slats smoked almost black through the ages.

"I hate that fuckin' basement," he said.

"Everyone does."

"It was not a cat at the door, we don't have a cat. And I wasn't opening the door until I knew what it *was*. . . . " Bob laughed bitterly. "Limp-dick city, right? But that's the effect that fuckin' basement has on me." He gave the door another glare. "Then came this groan or moan . . . some kind of noise, and I knew it was My back there and something had to be wrong or she'd just open the fuckin' door and walk out, right? I ran to save her. Her hero and all that shit . . . grabbed the knob and yanked . . . and the fucker stuck. Can you believe it? That fuckin' decorator spent thirty thousand bucks on every piece of pussy crap in every pussy catalog in the Western world and can't find two lousy bits to get the fuckin' door planed. I mean it *stuck*. I yanked on it 'til my balls ached. Even thought of getting the sledge out of the garage and bashing the fucker in, antique or no antique. Would've, but Myra was quiet behind the door, too quiet, and I was a little scared to leave her. So I gave it a last shot. You know, wiped my hands on my pants, grabbed the knob in both hands, and gave it my all. . . ."

Reed heard satisfaction in his voice. Bob Ludens was strong and wanted people to know it. He captained the bank's soccer team, bragged that he took care of his bees without a head net, and could still fit into his ROTC uniform. Some considered him a braggart and a fool, but Reed knew him to be a devoted man who'd loved one woman all his life. An ardent man, and a welcome contrast to the clutch of cold-hearted shits who came to Reed because they knew they were supposed to love their husbands, wives, kids . . . dogs . . . and couldn't seem to get the hang of it. Stone people, numbed by ego, greed, control mania.

Bob Ludens was a prince compared with them.

"That did it," Bob said proudly. "Fucker screeched open, and out Myra spilled. She must've been plastered right up against it, and she fell out smack on her knees on the tile. I heard the knees hit and thought, Uh-oh . . . we'll need a hot bath here, and maybe some liniment . . . and then, then . . . Reed, I saw her face. She wasn't pale or wan, she was fuckin' gray. I mean the color of the counter." He gestured at the countertop of polished granite, on which a casserole faintly steamed.

"She had blotches on her cheeks that looked like paint," Bob ground on.

"And she couldn't seem to see me. Or like she wouldn't know it was me if she could, and I thought, *Stroke.*

"I know Moffet says her blood pressure's not that bad. . . . "

Moffet according to Myra, Reed thought.

"But neither was my old man's until it killed him," Bob said. "I managed not to panic, and I hauled her up and over to the table. Got her sitting, staring at nothing I could see, and ran to the phone to call nine one one. I knew what to do. Call nine one one . . . only then the damnedest fuckin' thing happened. . . . " His cheeks reddened; he stared down at his hands, clutching the mug.

"What, Bob?"

"I . . . I'd left the door open . . . and I could feel the basement behind me. Yawning behind me, Reed. I couldn't call nine one one or do anything. Not to save her life or mine or anyone's, until I shut that fuckin' door . . . " Another glare of hatred at the door. "I shut it, ran back to the phone, and punched in the nine, and then Myra, who I thought was out in cloud-cuck-oo-land, says . . . *Don't.* Just as calm and clear as that . . . *Don't.* I was going to anyway, punched the first *one,* and she says, *Please, please, Bob . . . don't.* She was begging me, and I could not go against her, Reed. Could not. Besides, she spoke to me, knew who I was. Suddenly seemed much better when I looked at her. I hung up and raced back to the table to her. Told her I was scared she was sick, that I needed help here, because I didn't know what to do. She took pity on me and said I could call you. Only you.

"I figured she wanted you because you're an M.D., and you're one of the eight. . . . "

Eight rich kids who'd started public-school kindergarten together when other rich kids were "sent away" and refused to be separated after that. Had not been, except for the years of college, and med school in Reed's case.

The gang of eight, he thought, like a cell of Chinese Commies.

"Figured you were better than nothing." Bob managed a sickly smile. "At least you'd know if she'd had a stroke."

Reed looked at the basement door.

"Why'd she go down there in the first place?"

"To see how pretty it was, she says. Then, apparently satisfied as to its loveliness, a view I'll never share no matter how much money she spends on it, she turned to come back up and banged her head on this beam they couldn't move 'cause it's structural. Some construction glitch left over from the seventeenth century. She said she saw stars, and got dizzy when she tried to get out and the door wouldn't open. That's her story."

Reed leaned on the table. "Story? Don't you believe her?"

"No. But that's nuts, right? I mean what the fuck else could've happened?"

"I don't know." Reed looked at the basement door and remembered them at the foot of the stairs, wanting to get out too much to be polite about it.

Very rare for them to want anything that much.

Reed shook some Xanax from the large bottle he carried into a meds envelope and gave it to Bob. "Both of you eat something, then give her one of these. You take one, too. At least you'll get a good night's sleep out of it, which ain't too shabby if you think about it. Also—and I mean this—if she has any slurring speech, complains of blurred vision, staggers . . . anything. Call nine one one, no matter what she says. Got it?"

"Got it."

Reed left him donning mitts to put the casserole back in the oven and went back through the house, past the forlorn-looking, fully set table in the breakfast room, to the den where Myra waited—alone—to tell him what had happened in the basement.

Ten minutes later, Reed stepped out into a tornado of sleet, shuffled down the ice-coated path to the Porsche, and slid into the front seat, drawing his long legs in soaked, icy trousers into the car.

He started the motor, put on defrost and wipers, and waited for the windshield to clear. He needed time anyway to get hold of himself and figure out what to do next.

Get help for Myra, obviously. But what kind, and from whom?

It was a cardinal rule with shrinks, as with surgeons, that you don't treat people you love. Too easy to care too much and screw up. He'd already screwed up, had listened to her tale of the visitation in the basement, and realized that Myra—their good, dear and decent, gentle-as-a-fawn Myra—had lost it.

He'd always known she was too shy, obsessive about crap no one should spend forty seconds on. But he'd also thought that under the compulsiveness and timorousness was steel. In fact, he would have bet Myra Fox Ludens would be the last of them to lose it . . . and he would have been wrong.

Not just wrong, but wrong for months . . . years . . . because this didn't just happen. Little by little, over a span of time he couldn't guess at, Myra had come to the brink of a breakdown, and he—big-time Yale shrink who had seen her at least four times a month, much more most months—never noticed.

In a spasm of self-loathing, he twisted in the low-slung leather seat, rocking the car.

He should be a Xerox spare-parts cataloger, sell ladies' shoes, slice salami in a deli . . . anything but go on trying to unravel the maze of the mind.

And on top of the immense screwup of missing one of his best friends' mental disintegration, he'd been so floored by what he'd heard from her, so poleaxed, he'd taken the worst possible course and *humored* her. Made a mad promise he didn't think he had a chance of keeping or even should keep if he could.

But he'd made it, made it to *Myra,* and he owed her the good will, the bare-knuckle love and respect, to try to keep it.

It was the least he could do, and the second the defroster had cleared a slice of glass large enough to see through, he jammed the car in gear, slid down the driveway to the road, and headed for Arlen's.

Sleet pelted Reed as he raced up the steps to the front door of Pinchot House, coated his hair and shoulders, melted down his neck in streams.

George let him in, helped him strip off the sodden jacket, and held it at arm's length to drip on the Delft tile floor brought from the old country by some eighteenth-century Pinchot.

"He's in the library," George said. "I'll get you a towel."

Arlen was wearing a blanket robe, shearling slippers, and looking obscenely warm and comfortable by the fire with a book. He stood when Reed came in, and closed the book on his finger.

"Jesus, what happened to you?"

"Look out the window," Reed grumbled.

George brought a thick towel, fresh from the warmer, and Reed rubbed his hair and the back of his neck. His trouser cuffs flapped icily around his ankles; he was starting to shiver.

"Take your shoes off, warm your feet," George said. His faded brown eyes twinkled. "According to that eminent medical journal *Reader's Digest*, colds start in the feet."

He took the used towel from Reed, offered tea, coffee, or cocoa. Reed refused with thanks, and George left them alone. Arlen poured large tots of the same Armagnac Reed kept at home and handed him a snifter. Reed sipped, and pried off his loafers with his toes. The fire touched his freezing feet and ankles and sent a shudder through his body. Maybe *Reader's Digest* had something, he thought.

He took a couple of more sips of the Armagnac, felt the shakes ease up, and the certainty that he'd never be warm again faded.

He sank back in the chair and, fighting the sudden, draining feeling that succeeded the shakes, he haltingly, with a feeling of embarrassment for Myra . . . and for himself for some reason . . . told Arlen what she thought had happened to her in the basement.

When he finished, Arlen was silent, with a series of emotions sliding across his face, chief among them incredulity.

At last, in an overcontrolled-sounding voice, Arlen said, "What you're telling me is that Myra saw a ghost."

"No. I'm telling you she saw what she said she saw—a flicker of movement—followed by her hearing whatever it was clink up behind her. She did not see the thing itself."

The *ding on sicht* as the more pompous in freshman philosophy would have called it.

"Jesus Christ, Reed. All she had to do was turn and look, and there it'd be . . . or not be."

"Ah, but that's the one thing she could not do, Arl, because she really did hear it. That's what having a hallucination means. And having heard it, she could no more turn to look at it than you or I or any of us could have."

"What's that supposed to mean?" Arlen snapped.

"Think about it, about us . . . what we're like, have always been like."

"Is this a test?"

"No."

"So say it."

"It'll mean more if you do. If it's something you come up with on your own." Reed grinned. "I think we've just reached one of the basic tenets of psychoanalysis."

"Well, bully for us."

"Don't get annoyed, Arl. You know what I'm saying. We don't look at things that scare us or might hurt us, and we never have."

"You mean like that old zombie flick all the other kids loved, and we sat through with our jackets over our faces."

A perfect for-instance; it had been about the dead rising to roam the countryside, devouring the living. Shot in grainy black-and-white, with no name actors and a budget of maybe fifty bucks . . . it was then, and to this day, the most terrifying thing Reed had ever seen—even in the snatches he'd caught over the collar of his jacket.

They'd all covered their faces, only wanting it to end so they could have their ice cream treat and rush home to Upper Fallsbridge, where they were safe and rich and there were no monsters.

Years later the movie showed up on TV. Reed's sons predictably adored it, rented it for sleepovers, and Reed was unable to enter the room while it was on.

He said, "That's exactly what I mean."

"And now I'm supposed to understand what happened to Myra?"

"Don't you?"

"I know why she didn't turn to look. But something more important still escapes me."

"What?"

"I took Psych one-oh-one on the assumption it was a snap and multiple-choice tests were easy. I was wrong on both counts, squeezed by with a C. Point is, I remember that hallucinations, while fantastical by definition, have their own logic, and that logic is in keeping with the personality of whoever's having them."

"More or less," Reed said, wondering where this was heading, "unless they're drug-induced."

Arlen grinned. "Like my seeing unlogical purple halos around the green snakes slithering out of the walls on my only acid trip."

"Like that," Reed said.

"But Myra wasn't zoned, was she? I doubt she's ever even smoked a joint. Yet she hallucinated she was trapped in the basement with a ghost she saw and heard and couldn't get away from because the door stuck. She yanked on it until she was sick and dizzy and literally seeing red, and all the while, *it* is getting closer. Tinkling up behind her, getting so close she can feel the draft it makes, smell the grave mold on it . . . "

"Get to the point!" Reed snapped.

"Okay. She's down there, *it's* down there. It's coming after her, and she can't get away . . . so why didn't it get her!"

Reed choked, blowing Armagnac. "For fuck's sake, Arlen, it didn't get her because it doesn't exist!"

"But she thinks it does, or you wouldn't be here. And by the rules of the logic of hallucinations we just agreed on, it should have gotten her and didn't. That's sloppy, Reed, and Myra'd no more have a sloppy hallucination than a dirty bathroom."

He's right, Reed thought blearily. Myra, who was orderly to the point of compulsive, would not have a sloppy hallucination. It should have gotten her and did not.

Why?

He stared into the fire, then down at the immense, priceless Persian rug, the dark red of which looked black in the firelight.

Myra, Myra, he thought. My, honey, why didn't it get you? And what would it have meant if it had?

Breakdown; the total personality disintegration he'd seen a few times during his residency at Yale New Haven and only once in his practice. In the kitchen on Bowman, in Riverside, in the person of Belle Lambert. He could not begin to imagine what it would be like to live inside that hulk. He did know it was the last thing on earth he wanted to happen to him, and that included being eaten by a shark.

They could not let that happen to Myra. Could not let *it* come back, because next time . . .

He pulled his thoughts back to the question at hand. *Why didn't it get her?*

"She said Bob called her from the kitchen and it . . . disengaged . . . at the sound of his voice. Her word. *Disengaged,*" he told Arlen.

"She thinks Bob's the charm?" Arlen liked Bob, they all did. Bob had never been jealous of them or tried to get Myra away from them, the way Bill had Angie. But it was hard to imagine Bob Ludens as a charm against anything.

"No, Arlen. She thinks we are."

"The charm?"

"Yes."

"You and me?"

This could be the opening Reed had been waiting for. He said, "No, all of us."

"You've lost me."

"Myra wants us eight to perform a rite from that book you gave her, and bust the ghost."

"What?"

"You heard me. And I was so flummoxed by what she'd told me I agreed I'd get us to do it. I *promised* I would."

"That's nuts!" Arlen exploded.

"Is it?"

"You think maybe it's not?"

"I don't know what to think." Reed sipped the Armagnac, which slid down like silk. "I never saw the book, don't even know what a rite entails."

"Well I did see it, and it entails burning cat brain and dragon blood

... and that's the *sane* part. The simple, harmless fun part. If that's all there was to it, I'd say, hey, give it a shot and no harm done. But words go with it, words you have to say. Grand, terrible . . . awesome words. Shit, Reed, I only saw them for a second, but I can still see them. . . . " Arlen closed his eyes and recited in a booze-thickened voice, " 'By the dreadful day of judgment, and the sea of glass, by the beast with four eyes before and behind the throne . . . by the mighty wisdom of God, the holy angels, and the power of tetragamatron . . . ' " He stopped and opened his eyes. "You get the drift. It's the kind of stuff you can't say without laughing your ass off, unless you fall for it. She'll fall—already has or she wouldn't want us to do it. It'll only drive her deeper into—"

"No!"

"Into this pit our poor My's stepped over the edge of—"

"No!" Reed cried.

"What the fuck do you mean, *no!*"

Reed took another deep swallow, although his upper lip was already numb. A sure sign he was getting trashed. He could always stay here, as he and Don had a thousand times in their youth, as Arlen had at their houses. He wondered if Arl's old room was still intact, with the school pennants on the walls . . . and beaver shots from *Screw* in the desk drawer. How they had looked at them, as if expecting the camera to shift to a more revealing angle if they stared hard enough. No more need for that anymore; they were grown men, knew all about the real thing, a plethora of the real thing in Arlen's case. Arlen Pinchot, self-described pussy hound. Youngish, good-looking, monstrously rich man-about-town . . . several towns, including New York City. Handsome bachelor with hard dick and gigantic bank balance. Or was it hard bank balance and gigantic dick? Reed giggled.

"Something funny?"

"No." Reed made himself stop laughing. "Not funny at all."

"You were saying?" Arlen asked sourly.

He'd been saying . . . *no*, that saying those words would not drive Myra deeper. Now he must explain. Oddly enough the explanation was at hand, and no matter how mad it might sound . . . it made sense. Sense and sanity did not always tally, he thought. As in the case he was about to put to his oldest and dearest friend, Arlen Pinchot. *To you, Arlen,* he thought, and raised the glass a fraction in a toast that would embarrass them both if he voiced it.

To Arlen.

Arlen was going to do this with him, because it was for Myra. No question; they would all do anything for each other. But he wanted Arlen to understand as well as go along, so he'd be a real comrade in this project Reed had taken on. He just had to find words. He belched silently, then coughed and grinned, and finally told Arlen that they were dealing here with the saddest of all human experiences besides death. Helplessness. Terminal helplessness in Myra's case, culminating in the absurd spectacle of one of the richest women in the state—ergo one of the most powerful— rendered impotent by a basement and a barking dog. "She tried to get control," he explained. "She called the dog warden—a big step for My—but the dog kept barking. She remodeled the basement, but everyone, including her, still hates it down there. So she tells herself the answer must be beyond contractors and dog wardens; with Lambie's connivance, she consults a Ouija board, and then Bernie Samms, who tells her the basement's haunted by the ghost of an unjustly hanged woman. And her psyche, which I believe is a lot more savvy than Myra herself, sees a chance to grab some control at last. . . . "

"Control of what?" Arlen choked.

"The ghost!"

"Shit on a stick!"

Reed laughed. "Shit on a stick?"

"Go on," Arlen snapped.

"Where was I?"

"Control of the ghost."

"Ah, yes. Control. The thing we all want and can't get, and probably shouldn't have anyway. Control. In this case, of a ghost, and this is how I think it works. Myra asks us to perform a rite to bust a ghost, we do it, and the ghost that isn't there never shows up again. *Presto, chango,* Myra can tell herself, with the help of that indomitable psyche of hers, that she's gotten *that* much control over her life. Doesn't that make a little sense?"

"No."

"I was afraid it didn't." Reed slumped in the chair and took another swig of Armagnac. "We gotta do it anyway, Arl. She needs help."

"Of course. Help, not black magic. You find her the best shrink in the county and we'll make sure—"

"Noooooo . . . " Reed actually wailed, and Arlen stared at him.

"That's the one thing we can't do to her," Reed mumbled.

"What's so terrible about it?"

"What's terrible is that we're the only people she knows, including her husband, son, bankers, accountants, salespeople, and the fucking Avon lady, who treat her like a grown-up. For us to send her to a shrink, to as good as tell her she's hysterical and *we* know what's best for her, is radical rejection. As good as abandoning her to whatever she thinks is in that basement. And next time, Arlen, maybe logic *will* prevail, and it *will* get her. I can't begin to tell you how horrible that would be." He thought of Belle Lambert's dead eyes in the death mask of her face, fixed on the far wall of the filthy kitchen. "We can't let it. We've got to respect her. . . . "

"How?"

"Accept that *she* knows what's best for her and do what she's asked us to. In other words, the rite."

Arlen closed his eyes again and recited softly, " 'To be effective, the sacrifice and summoning, the calling up and casting out must be done at the site of the infection.' " He opened his eyes. "The basement, Reed."

The basement.

Suddenly Reed saw it as it had been; he saw the sweating, ancient stone walls, the packed, ugly dirt floor, and tiny windows too high in the wall to let in light or air; he smelled the dirt, mold, and that hot rot that wafted at you on breaths of icy air, and he thought, *She's not crazy . . . something's down there.*

"Can that," he mumbled.

"What?"

"I said can it. It's just a basement."

Arlen gave him an evil grin, the old mischievous grin Reed always loved because it was so utterly defiant, and hated because it usually spelled trouble.

"Who said it was anything else," Arlen said.

"Nobody."

Silence while they worked on their drinks, then Reed said, "Arl. It's for Myra."

"I know."

"We gotta do it."

"I know. You're the pro. You say it's what she needs, we do it. But how're you gonna convince the others without throwing Myra to them to pity? She'll hate that."

"She will. But I think we can manage."

After another Armagnac they didn't need, they came up with a scenario they thought would convince everyone without demolishing Myra's dignity. Arlen would warm them up, with Reed the pro, to whom they were more likely to listen anyway because he did work he got paid for, as the main attraction.

It could work, could get Myra what Reed believed she needed and keep the promise he'd made to her. An all-around desirable outcome, and he was feeling pretty good until he stood and had to grab the arms of the chair to keep his balance.

"Whoa ... buddy ..." Arlen exclaimed, but wasn't any steadier when he stood.

Sleet covered Reed's Porsche, which was the exact twin of Arlen's. They'd bought them on the same day, from the same dealer, had picked them up together and raced each other up 684 from Mount Kisco to Brewster, pushing ninety. Typical, Reed had thought; 180 was top on the dial, but he and Arlen thought they were pushing the envelope at 90. Arlen had won by a hair, because Reed kept thinking he heard sirens wailing behind him.

Arlen brought out a squeegee and brush on a stick to clean off the Porsche. He had on his robe and house slippers and was soaked through in a minute, which they thought was hilarious.

They got the windows cleared; Reed climbed in, started the motor, and waved as he pulled away. The car skidded at once and he grabbed the wheel hard, trying to concentrate on his driving through a haze of sleet and Armagnac. As he made the slight curve in the driveway that would hide the house from view, he looked back and saw Arlen still outside, in a shaft of light from the house that looked phosphorescent through the sleet.

He turned back and tended to his driving. The cold cleared his head a little, but conditions were abysmal, with visibility pushing zero. Everything was coated with ice; glittering tree trunks, branches, and the foot of road he could see shot out of the dark when the headlights hit them.

He lived a mile from Arlen; the drive took ten minutes.

An inch a minute, he thought. The final turn into his driveway was a long, slow sickening slide that missed the stone pillars guarding the entrance by what looked like half a millimeter.

The Porsche slid into the driveway; the taillights winked through the sleet, then disappeared.

"Now that's a car," said Rog Russell.

Dick Lambert wiped the windshield with his hand and peered through the hole in the condensation.

"Know what he drives to Riverside?" he said bitterly. "Know what he parks in front of our house?"

Dick twisted in the seat to look at the two in back: Bart Loamers and Ted Dukovsky.

"A fuckin' Honda." Dick bit the words. "A fuckin' 'eighty-eight Honda with a dented fender."

So what, Bart thought. Who gave a rat's ass what the doctor drove to Riverside.

"Wait'll you see the house," Dick said heavily.

Bart didn't want to see the house. But Dick put his old, well-tuned Trans Am in gear, made the turn, and crept up the driveway without lights. He hit the defrost, full fan, and the windows cleared, but visibility wasn't much better. Sleet pelted the car, the pavement underneath felt like jam, and the wheels gripped, then slid, then gripped. Bart was getting carsick.

He looked out; well-grown hemlocks, bowed down with ice, gave way to an acre or so of front lawn covered in white.

Then the lights of the house came through the sleet, and even from here, a hundred or so feet away, in the gray half-light reflecting on the ice particles, they could see the place was enormous.

Bart knew this was the point.

"So it's big," he said. "So he's rich. I think we knew that, fucko. This is Fallsbridge, not Calcutta."

Dick came to a slithering stop, twisted around again, and glared at Bart. Bart knew it was a glare, although he couldn't see Dick's eyes in this light.

"So he's rich, and when he takes the old bitch away, we'll be broke."

Dick had told them earlier about Lerner taking the old lady, over more beer than they should have had, and that now sat in a sour pond in Bart's gut.

"Can he do it?" Rog asked. "Can he really just drag her out of there?"

This time they all looked at Bart. If they'd been Mafia, he'd be their *consigliere*, he thought. The brains. He'd gotten into Oban Community, was applying for scholarships to four-year schools, and his adviser said he had a chance. His fantasy—his prime jerk-off, he called it—was to go to law school.

"Yeah," he said uneasily, "I think he needs another shrink for the court, but if he gets one, and the court goes along, they'll send the bailiffs for her."

"That like cops?" Ted asked. Ted Dukovsky was big and handsome with blue eyes, a wave of golden hair that fell across his forehead, and the IQ of a brilliant German shepherd.

"Yeah, Ted," Bart said without a trace of condescension. "That's like the cops. But not exactly."

"Jeez," Rog said softly, looking at Dick. "You'll have to get another job. . . . "

"I gotta get shit," Dick snapped. " 'Cause he ain't taking her."

"How'll you stop him?" Ted again.

Bart's uneasiness deepened. He knew the answer, but didn't want to hear it. Suddenly had an almost superstitious dread of hearing the words spoken in the overheated car that smelled of wet wool and sneakers.

He *was* going to be sick. He cracked his window a little and took a gulp of cold, wet air. Sleet blew in, tickled his nostrils.

"Close it the fuck up," Dick said. Bart took another deep gulp, then closed it. If he was the *consigliere,* Dick Lambert was the don.

Dick said, "He ain't gonna take her, because we're gonna let him know if he does, he'll really be in for it. . . . "

"In for what?" Ted asked.

In for a penny, in for a pound, Bart thought. He stared out the window, watching the fog re-form on it. His heart had started to flutter; sweat came out on his palms.

Dick said, "In for more of what we're gonna give him the first time to scare his Jew ass from here to Hartford."

"What's that?" Ted asked. He really didn't know.

"We're gonna beat the shit outta him," Dick said softly.

He was in profile to them, and Bart saw that slow grin spread across this side of his face. Bart knew Dick's eyes would look like wet granite if he could see them, and his heart started to thud.

"Yeah?" Ted said excitedly. "Beat shit . . . "

"Right outta him," Rog said happily. He was pretty drunk. "Beat shit . . . "

"You're forgetting a small detail." Bart's voice sounded shrill.

"Such as?" Dick asked.

"The cops."

Dick chuckled; the sound raised the hair on Bart's arms. He couldn't go along with this; this was finally the one thing he could not go along with. He was sorry about Dick's old lady, but she sat day after day in her own mess and should be put away. And Dick would be better off with a better job than jockeying gas at the 202 Amoco and ripping off the Coke machine. He might even find out that he was good at something.

"Uh-uh," Dick said. "I figured on the cops. The cops won't do him any good because he won't know who did it."

"Then he won't know who to be scared of," Bart pointed out.

"Oh, he'll *know.* But not really, because we'll cover our faces."

Bart let out a raucous guffaw. "Who are those masked men!"

"Not funny," Dick snapped.

"No. Because if he hears a voice, sees the car, finds one of our hairs on him . . . they'll grab us. They'll grab us anyway, because if he knows it's you . . . *they'll* know it's us. He's rich and a shrink—they won't stop for coffee on their way. They'll bust us for assault; that's three to five with no Big Macs and all the one-eyed salami we can eat!"

Rog and Ted giggled; Bart pressed his advantage. "Even if we never get to trial, we lose our jobs. . . . " His chance at UConn would go bye-bye. "Our folks'll go nuts. . . . " He stopped himself. They were pushing twenty; *folks* sounded babyish. But it was too late.

Dick gave him the *look* he must have gotten off an early Eastwood tape.

"He'll know it's me, they'll know it's us. But no one'll be able to prove shit, even to book us. He won't hear a voice, 'cause we'll keep our holes shut; we won't leave hairs around 'cause we'll have our heads covered; he won't see the car 'cause I'll get a junker without plates from Old Man Trimble's. And he won't see us, 'cause we'll wear ski masks. . . . "

"*Rubber* masks," Ted chortled, clenching and unclenching his hands between his knees. "Saw this flick where they hijack a bus wearing rubber masks of Nixon, Reagan, and Donald Duck!"

CHAPTER 4

Lambie and Myra stood in front of the shut basement door. The storm had ended in the wee hours; melting sleet gurgled through the downspouts and sun made slanting shapes on the kitchen floor.

"Why hide it at all?" Lambie wearily asked. "And why down there?"

"Because I didn't know how I'd explain it if Bob found it, and I picked the basement because . . . because I was sick of being scared of it."

Her head drooped. "Then only made it worse," she murmured.

"How?"

"Reed'll explain," Myra said.

Reed had called this morning to ask for a session five days early, "to discuss something important."

"What?" Lambie had asked, reasonably enough, she had thought. "All will be revealed," he had answered, followed by a brittle-sounding laugh. Myra had called a minute later to ask Lambie to come early, to "help her with something."

Getting the book out of the basement.

"Shit . . . " Lambie said quietly. She didn't want to go down there, even in broad daylight with Myra riding shotgun. But she'd do it, because she was absolutely not going to be intimidated by a goddamn basement.

She twisted the doorknob and tugged. The door stuck, and she felt a burst of hope that it would stay that way. But it squeaked open on the second, rather halfhearted tug, and light from the kitchen spilled out on the upper landing.

"I'll be right back," she said.

"Oh, no . . ." Myra cried. "You're not going down there, I am."

"Then what'm I doing?"

"I want you to stand guard, in case . . ."

"In case of what?" Lambie asked impatiently.

"Reed'll tell you. It'll make more sense coming from him."

As most things did for some reason, Lambie thought.

Myra started down the stairs; Lambie hung back a moment, then followed. Halfway down, two steps below the second landing, Lambie saw the book in its wrapper lying on the floor, and that inexplicable basement chill started its light-footed dance across her neck and down her spine.

Myra reached bottom, bent quickly and grabbed the book, then straightened up to face Lambie on the second-to-last step. The air was warm, dry, and silent, except for the faint susurrus of the blowers in the ceiling.

"Lamb?" Myra said in a strangled voice.

"What?" Lambie croaked.

"Move . . . I can't get past you."

Lambie gave a wild chuckle, then whirled around, and they raced back up the stairs to the sunlit kitchen.

Myra slammed the door, pantomimed nailing it shut, and they sagged against it, giggling.

The book was still in its wrapper on the sideboard when they finished lunch. Myra prepared to clear the table and bring out coffee and the strawberry meringue she'd bought at Baker's Table this morning, then realized her hands were shaking. Everyone would notice; she'd probably break a dish or two. She clasped her hands in her lap and let Arlen and Angie, who always offered, clear the table.

They came back with the coffeepot and the meringue. Lambie went back to get dessert plates. Don poured the last of the wine, just enough to give everyone a final taste.

Irene cut the meringue and passed it around.

The coffee and wine were drunk, the meringue eaten, and more dishes cleared; Myra wanted to scream.

Finally everyone was seated, the small talk died, and they looked at Reed to find out why they were here five days early. Arlen took the book off the sideboard and put it on the table in front of him. But *Reed* was supposed to do the talking, not Arlen. They must've consulted and decided this way was best.

Arlen put his hand on the book, like a Bible he was about to swear on, and started talking. Looking at him was an impossibility, and Myra turned to face out the bow window. The storm had beaten down the meadow grass, but the daffodil heads still bobbed bravely. The hives had been refurbished by Bob last weekend and were ready, but it would be weeks before the meadow bloomed, more weeks before they'd have honey, and they'd already opened the last jar.

Arlen told them about Joan Folger's reaction to the basement and went from that to the Ouija board. Don made a strangled sound but didn't say anything.

Don would be hardest to convince. He liked to say his feet were so firmly planted on terra firma you couldn't see his ankles. Meant to be funny, of course, but Myra thought it was a little sad. Irene would go along with Don, naturally, and Helen was another practical soul, who once admitted she'd given up Easter at First Cong because she found herself wanting to yell *Gimme a break* when they got to the Resurrection. But they were all practical, put their faith in what they could see and touch, in bridge scores and bottom lines on their trust accounts.

On Arlen went to the visit to his house and then to last night in the basement, exactly as Myra had described it to Reed. Finally, he told them about the book and how they could use it. Then he stopped talking.

Absolute silence around the table.

Myra swiveled back and looked at them, now wanting them to look back and see that she was sane and serious. But they stared at the tabletop or into space; Helen was enthralled with the dregs in her wine glass.

Arlen unwrapped the book. The tearing paper sounded cataclysmic in the silence. The book looked comically ordinary after its introduction, just a plain, clothbound book, not even that thick.

He put it on the table, and Don reached for it, opened it, riffled a few pages, then laughed.

"It's not funny," Myra cried.

Don looked at her. Her face was broiling by now; that rush of blood, like surf in a seashell, had started in her ears. Don put his hand over hers, which was clenched on the table. His felt warm and dry, hers like a chunk of ice.

"I know it's not funny," he said gently. She wanted to yell that she was not a wounded bird. He could argue with her, yell at her . . . just not humor her. "But I don't know how else to react," he went on. "It *is* creepy down there, My. I know that firsthand. But it's been dank, damp, and empty except for dead mice and millipedes for two hundred years. . . . "

Three hundred, Myra thought.

"Of course it's creepy," he said.

"Not anymore. It's warm, dry, and pretty, and everyone's still terrified of it. Joan was terrified, Don. Joan Folger was terrified!"

Don took his hand away from hers. "That doesn't mean we need an exorcism," he said firmly, and shut the book as if that were the last word.

She tried again to meet their eyes; no one would look at her. Angie was blushing almost as much as she must be by now. Lambie was chewing her bottom lip. Reed stared up at the brass chandelier over the table. The silence went on and on. Nervously, Helen reached for her knitting bag and pulled out the gigantic sweater she was making for her son Lenny, who'd finally stopped growing at about Reed's height. The click of her needles was the only sound in the room.

It was over; Goody Redman had won. Myra would call a real estate agent in the morning and confront Bob tonight. That was going to be pretty miserable, but he'd have to go along if he wanted to keep living with her. She was rich, did not need his permission to move. . . .

Then Reed laughed.

It was such an unexpected sound that everyone gaped at him. He was still looking up, his eyes crinkled, as he laughed; his mouth was open slightly. He had one of those good, deep, infectious laughs that made you laugh even when you didn't know the joke, and everyone smiled uncertainly. He shook his head, looked around at them. "Jesus, you'd think we were talking about knocking over Citibank or having an orgy. It's just a silly, harmless rite from a silly, harmless book."

"If it's so silly, why do it?" Don asked.

Reed said, "Because it might be fun, for one thing." They stared at him. "God. You look like you just heard a word in Venusian. *Fun*. You know . . . something you didn't plan on doing, but did anyway. Something besides playing bridge and golf, having little suppers at the club, and going in town to see shows no one wants to see. FUN!"

No reaction, and he said impatiently, "Look, it'd be like a game . . . getting what we need could turn into a treasure hunt. . . . "

"A treasure hunt for cat brain and bat blood!" Don cried.

"Pardon me?"

Don opened the book and showed him a page with a see-there look on his face. Myra remembered that look from the schoolyard when Reed, who'd been the biggest kid in school, protected Arlen and Don from Johnny Dukovsky, the bully from Riverside. Reed had been so big he'd never actually had to hit anyone. Myra had always wondered if he could.

Reed took the book from Don. It was the first time he'd actually seen it; he might decide it was lunacy after all. But he looked at it a moment, then said, "There're lots of less nuts alternatives, Don. Saffron, mace . . . cinnamon. Sounds like a bake-off."

"More like a jerk-off," Don said. Everyone laughed, the atmosphere lightened, and Myra started to hope.

"I can get opium and benzoin at the hospital pharmacy," Reed was saying. "Don't know about the vervain. . . . "

Helen looked over his arm at the book. "Bet those places in New York Lenny knows about have some of this stuff."

"What places?" Lambie asked.

"Outlets for this kind of thing," Helen said.

"Lenny into black magic?" Angie asked dryly.

"Of course not. He found the places when he did a paper on alternative medicine for anthropology."

"What the fuck're you talking about?" Don exploded.

Helen looked up from her knitting. "Where to get what we need to do it," she said mildly.

"You *want* to do it?" he cried.

She stopped knitting. "I don't know if *want's* the right word, Don, but I know Myra wants us to do it . . . and she'd do it for us if the shoe were on the other foot. I also know there's something down there that's got nothing to do with mold and dead mice. . . . and we'd be stupid not to admit it."

This time the silence around the table was breathless. Don started to say something, but a look from Irene shut him up, and Myra knew it was going to be all right.

There was a lot to do and get. Too much, they decided, for one or two people. They made lists, paired themselves up, and each pair took a list.

A few of the substances, such as galbanum and storax, even Reed had never heard of. And some, such as the powdered horn of a goat that's had intercourse with a woman, they decided, with much hilarity, to do without.

It was after five when they left Myra's with their "assignments." She waved from the door, but the dog was going full blast and she ducked back inside.

It had turned warm; sun hit the daffodil heads and gleamed on the road. The gurgle of the full stream foaming through a culvert under the road and windfalls on the lawn were the only signs of last night's storm.

Arlen's Porsche stopped at the end of the drive, then took off with a deep roar. The others straggled to their cars, except Angie, who passed her Range Rover and climbed into Reed's Porsche.

"What's up?" he yelled over the dog.

"Someone should strangle that mutt," she yelled back.

"Is that what you want to talk about?"

She turned away. From this angle, the swollen eye and spreading bruise were hidden, and she looked utterly lovely, one of the most beautiful women he'd ever seen. Yet he had never even thought of hitting on her

. . . or on Myra, who'd once been even lovelier. Or on Helen, or Lambie, who was an arrow of a woman on the order of Lauren Bacall, for whom he'd always had the hots. Irene had been coupled with Don since high school and out of the picture, but he could have tried with the others, and never did. Any more than Arlen or Don had (with anyone but Irene); nor had the women ever come on to them. It must have seemed too much like incest.

Angie turned. The wide splotch of discoloration on her face came into view, blasting her loveliness. Hatred for Bill Withers suddenly made him breathless.

Some day, he thought, savagely . . . some day.

But that was horseshit. If they hadn't done anything about Bill Withers by now, they never would. Couldn't . . . any more than they could watch that old horror flick . . . or turn to look if they'd heard *it* tinkle up behind them on the tile floor.

"Reed?"

"Yeah, Angie?" He yelled over the dog. Something else they couldn't do anything about.

The dog shut up suddenly. Angie spoke normally. "Reed, we're setting her up for a fall."

"Why?"

"Because we're going to go through all this crap, get her hopes up, and she's still going to have the basement from *Night of the Living Dead.*" That old horror flick that had shriveled his balls a generation ago.

Angie remembered it too; they probably all did. They should rent it, force themselves to watch it. An hour in the basement would seem positively jolly afterward.

"Maybe she won't," he said.

"You think we're going to bust the ghost?"

"There is no ghost, Angie. So whatever's wrong down there, is wrong up here. . . . " He tapped his head. "That being the case, just spending time down there could take the curse off."

"Time . . . down there. . . . " She sounded horrified.

He said gently, "Nothing'll get us, sweetheart."

"What if you're wrong?"

"You mean if something *does* get us?"

"Of course not," she snapped, then blushed. "I guess that's exactly what I meant. God, I can't believe how absurd that sounds."

"Like most fears when you put them into words."

Angie grinned. "You're the only person I've ever known who could say something like that without sounding like a pompous asshole." She stopped smiling. "You really think this'll be the best thing for her?"

"No. Myra does."

Angie was silent a moment; then she nodded, gave Reed a quick kiss, and climbed out of the car. The dog started yapping again, and she hurried to her Range Rover, climbed in, and slammed the door to shut out the noise.

"I got the names and addresses of those places from Lenny," Helen told Arlen on the phone.

"Fire away." Arlen was ready with pen and pad.

"First is Aphrodisia, on Bleecker, west of Sixth in the Village. Second is a place called Job's Resources. What a great name."

"Great."

"That's on Seventy-second. Number two-forty west, just east of West End."

They hung up, and he called Angie, who'd agreed to go with him. They'd take her Range Rover, which was ugly and much less likely than the Porsche to be vampired.

Aphrodisia was clean, well lit, and well organized, but it had only two of the items on the list: hyssop and asefetida.

Accent on fetid, Angie thought, because it stank. The cashier wrinkled her nose as she put it in a separate Ziploc before adding it to the small shopping bag with the hyssop.

She said, "People cook with that, you know. Can't imagine what it *tastes* like!"

They drove north under the abandoned West Side Highway with the old docks on one side, abandoned buildings on the other. Clumps of people whom Arlen said were the homeless clustered around stanchions along the road. Angie was shocked to see young women and even a few children among them.

It was warm in the city, two hours south of Fallsbridge, but the buildings on West End Avenue shaded the street so it looked like November instead of early May. Seventy-second Street was sunny, though, and lined with prosperous-looking shops.

"There." Arlen pointed up at a second-floor window that had JOB'S RE-SOURCES in gilt on the glass.

They entered a small, stone-floored vestibule with a bank of polished-brass mailboxes, and Arlen pushed the bell marked JOB'S. A buzzer went off, Arlen opened the door, and they climbed steep, narrow marble stairs with an iron railing to a small hall with doors that looked like metal coated with brown enamel. One read BOOKS OF THE ZODIAC, the other was to JOB'S, a long, narrowish room, with gray plush carpeting and the window on the street at the far end. A shining wood counter ran along one side, with a wall of apothecary drawers with shiny brass pulls and label slots behind it.

The room was hushed and smelled of lemon oil, reminding Angie of the vestry at First Congregational.

The door clicked closed behind them, a bell tinkled faintly, and a short, slight man of about sixty came through a door in the wall of drawers.

He had thick, gray hair springing from a widow's peak, a gray, curly beard, and the bluest eyes Angie had ever seen. Crayola blue, she thought.

He eyed them warily; Arlen stepped up to the counter. "A friend of ours told us we might be able to get certain . . . items . . . here."

"What friend?" the man asked. His wariness must come from keeping shop in New York, Angie thought, which was probably a hair more dangerous than driving at Daytona without brakes.

"Lenny Dumott," Arlen answered, and the man's face relaxed into a smile.

"Sure. Lenny. Nice kid, Lenny. You from his town too? I forget the name."

He had a faint accent.

"Fallsbridge, Connecticut," Arlen said.

"Yeah. Fallsbridge." He stuck his hand across the counter. "I'm Job Landau."

"Arlen Pinchot. And this is Angela Withers."

The blue eyes fixed on her, and he stopped smiling. He peered into her eyes behind the dark glasses and his face clouded with concern, *"Nu?* Husband give you the shiner?"

She wanted to tilt her head and say, coolly, *I don't see how that's any concern of yours.* Exactly as her mother would have done.

But Job Landau's expression and intonation were so concerned, so intensely kind, a lump filled Angie's throat, and she couldn't say anything but a strangled "Yes."

He came around the counter. "Sit," he said. "Those stairs're murder. Never mind they're steep as Mauna Loa, but the marble's murder on your feet. Sit . . . sit. I'll make you tea." He took her arm and led her to a round, dark wood table in front of the window with round-backed leather conference chairs on casters around it. He settled her in a chair, then let down a Mylar shade to keep the sun off her face, and for an instant she felt more cared for than she thought she ever had in her life.

He turned to Arlen. "You too, Mr. Pinchot? It's excellent tea. Winey Keemum I order special. Tea'll perk you up for the long drive home."

Arlen hesitated. Angie gave him a surreptitious nod, and he said, "Sure, tea sounds great."

He sat next to Angie.

"How about those items?" Landau asked. "I can get them together while the water's boiling."

Arlen slid the list out of his breast pocket and handed it to Landau, who put on a pair of half glasses. The hyssop and asefetida were crossed off and he said, "I see you have been to Aphrodisia."

"Yes."

"They're okay if you're into cooking." His eyes ran down the list. "But you ain't into cooking, are you?"

"No."

Landau looked at Angie. "D'ja know ambergris is whale vomit."

"No, I didn't," she said faintly.

"They used to use it as a fixative in perfume. Hundred years ago, women would dab whale vomit behind their ears." He looked back at the list. "I got pretty much all you need."

"Like powdered lapis lazuli," Arlen muttered, "storax and peacock feathers, hellebore root, and the brain of a fox?"

Landau laughed. "No fox brain, but you don't need it for what you're planning to do."

"And what's that?" Angie challenged.

Landau looked over the glasses at her and said, "Summon a demon."

"As a matter of fact, we are going to get rid of something," Arlen said.

Steam rose from the tea which Landau had served with fresh butter cookies, thin slices of lemon, and a squeeze bottle of honey. The honey was not nearly as good as Bob's, but the tea was superb.

"A ghost." Arlen was having trouble keeping a straight face. "We're going to get rid of a ghost."

"Cast it out," Landau said.

"That's the intention." Arlen grinned helplessly.

"You think it's funny, Mr. Pinchot?"

"I don't think it's anything."

"Ah . . . you don't believe in the ghost."

"Of course not."

Landau stirred his tea, then carefully put his spoon in the saucer next to the cup. "This seems like a lot of bother and expense—powdered lapis lazuli don't come cheap—to get rid of a ghost you don't believe in."

"It's a favor for a friend."

"Like a jar of Sanka for a housebound old lady?"

"Sort of."

"I see." Landau looked into his space, his eyes like washed sapphires in the Mylar-filtered sunlight. "The spirit must be very troublesome. . . ." He spoke absently, half to himself, leaving the feeling that the existence of the "spirit," troublesome or otherwise, was an established fact. Angie felt the hair on her arms and neck stir.

"I told you it's not anything," Arlen said jumpily, and Landau focused on him and smiled. "So you did, Mr. Pinchot, so you did."

* * *

The Fabric Barn on old Route 7 was vast, with a thirty-foot, steel-beamed ceiling and acres of tables covered with bolts of cloth. Lambie and Myra approached a high front counter, behind which a gigantic woman stared morosely at a computer screen.

"Excuse me. . . . " Lambie said. No reaction from the woman. Lambie raised her voice, "Excuse me. . . . "

The woman looked up.

"We're looking for satin," Lambie said.

"Silk or synthetic?" asked the woman.

"Silk."

"Silk'll run you seventy a yard or more." Her eyes scanned them, her expression said that was obviously beyond their means, and she went back to the terminal. "Synthetic's in aisle eleven."

Lambie and Myra looked at each other; Myra stepped up to the counter.

"Excuse me." Her voice took on a cold command Lambie had never heard in it before. The woman looked up. "We want silk satin," Myra said. "And we will pay what it costs. If you have it, tell us where . . . if you don't, say so, and stop wasting our time."

Myra was wearing an old L.L. Bean top, slacks that were shiny in the seat, run-over loafers, and that abysmal green jacket she'd ordered from somewhere.

The woman's chins trembled. "I don't have to take that . . . "

"You do if you want to sell silk satin at seventy a yard," Myra said. "If *you* don't maybe whoever owns this place does."

She was threatening her! Lambie couldn't have been more shocked if Myra had pulled a gun.

The woman's uncooked-looking face sagged. "I'm sorry," she whined, "but we lost a shipment from Taiwan and I've been trying to track it through fifty states."

Myra didn't say anything. The woman pulled over an old-fashioned mike on a stand. "Janie"—her plummy fat-lady voice boomed through the store—"Janie Spinks, front."

Janie was about sixteen, with hair streaked orange and five earrings per ear. But she knew the store, and she led them, forced-march pace, to a table in back covered with a sheet of thick plastic. "Here they are," she said, and whipped off the cover.

The colors of the silk seemed to pulsate under the harsh overhead light, and the women inhaled sharply.

"Yeah," Janie said with pride. "Real silk satin, and velvet, real silk moiré, and crepe de chine. Set you back a bundle."

Myra reached for a bolt of satin in a scarlet that made every other red Lambie had ever seen look faded or garish.

"Your hands clean?" Janie cried.

Myra looked at her hands and nodded.

"Okay. But Jesus, lady, don't sweat on it."

They unwrapped it in Helen's workroom at the back of her house, a mile from Lambie's, Arlen's, and Reed's. Don and Irene lived another mile north, on fifteen hundred acres of a baby Berkshire foothill. Myra's Redman Farm was in the other direction, close to the New York line.

Windows took up all of one wall of Helen's room; sun streamed through them, turning the red satin to a fall of garnet.

"Oh, God . . . it's wonderful," Helen said, reverently fingering the cloth. "And so heavy. It'll hang beautifully."

She looked up at them. "Must've cost a fortune."

They glanced at each other. It had cost almost eight hundred dollars, four hundred apiece.

"Uh . . . I know you said four yards," Myra said. "But we got all they had left, in case . . . " She trailed off, blushing fiercely.

Helen smiled. "In case I screw it up."

Myra looked down, loath to admit even the possibility.

"Good thing you did," Helen said. "I went to Notions, and the Sewing Room in Danbury, for patterns, but a bathrobe was as close as Vogue or Buttrick could come. So . . . I designed one myself." She unrolled a sheet of tracing paper with a Flair pen drawing on it. Lambie looked at it and suddenly felt disoriented to the point of dizziness because it looked exactly like what it was supposed to be; the robe of a sorcerer.

They were really going to do it.

One of them would don the robe in the drawing, brought to life in scarlet satin; they'd step into the magic circle diagrammed in the book, burn a bunch of weird substances in a brass brazier, and chant words people had been trying to control the universe with for a thousand years.

"How'd you know how it should look?" she asked shakily, and Helen grinned. "From Mickey Mouse in *Fantasia.*"

CHAPTER 5

At the same time, twelve miles closer to Hartford, in downtown Oban, Renny (for Renwick) Jarvis closed Belle Lambert's file and looked across his desk at Reed.

"Tapes?"

"Nothing to tape," Reed said, trying not to sound defensive.

"For how long?"

Reed looked down at his hands, folded schoolgirl fashion in his lap. "Four months. I kept hoping I could make it better, Ren. I never had this in my practice before."

Renny looked past him. "Don't suppose you would in a town like Fallsbridge."

Renny made it sound like the Emerald City, and maybe it was to him, Reed thought. He lived and practiced in Oban, a blue-collar town that had been down on its luck ever since Reed could remember. The recession years hadn't helped, and the main street was potholed, lined with empty storefronts that had yellowing FOR LEASE signs in the windows. Only the bars seemed to prosper.

But Renny Jarvis was hardly stuck here. He had been first in their class at Yale, could write his own ticket at any hospital clinic or research facility in the country. But this was his hometown, and he'd come back, he'd told Reed, because here was where he was needed.

"Nothing makes people crazier than being broke, idle, terrified, and about to be foreclosed on," he had said. "And these're my neighbors, Reed. People I grew up with."

Renny opened his daybook. "How's next Thursday, any time after ten?"

"A long time for her to wait."

Renny looked up from the lined page. "You can get someone else, Reed. My feelings won't be hurt."

There was Jennifer Macomber, who was as good as Reed . . . but not as good as Renny. And this was one time it had to be the best, because Reed didn't know precisely what was wrong with Belle Lambert, or where she should go.

To Limekiln, if she was catatonic, where she'd be drugged, shocked . . . treated. She might even come home again some day. People did. But there was another alternative, the bottom of the well in psychiatric diagnosis. Belle could be hebephrenic, and that meant Housatonic Valley, a warehouse almost no one came back from.

It was a crucial and subtle final diagnosis, and Reed could screw it up. Probably would. But not Renny.

"You saw the notes, Ren," he said. "I don't know where to send her . . . you will."

"What faith you have in me." Renny looked back at his daybook. "Okay, Thursday week, eleven," he said unhappily.

"Will it be that bad?"

Renny looked up. "We're taking her out of her home, away from her family against their will. How do you think it'll be?"

"I'm sorry," Reed said in a choked voice.

"Christ, don't do that," Renny snapped. "Don't apologize for expecting me to do my job. If I wanted it soft I'd've gone into . . . dermatology."

"Lupus," Reed said lugubriously, "melanoma . . . "

They grinned at each other, Renny closed his book, and Reed promised he'd buy the lunch afterward.

"At the Fallsbridge Club," Renny said. "Always wanted to see it."

Reed left with Belle's file under his arm after the secretary made a copy for Renny, and half an hour later stopped at the water fountain in the main corridor of Fallsbridge General.

Nervousness over what he had to do had left a tinny taste in his mouth, and he took deep draughts of icy, metallic-tasting water to drive it away.

It was almost four on Saturday afternoon; the pharmacy would close soon. He had been putting it off, but now must get the order in or the stuff would never be here by Wednesday.

He went down the hall to the closed door and looked through the glass inset. This would be hard enough one-on-one; impossible with an audience, maybe of another physician wondering what the hell storax was and why Reed Lerner wanted it.

The room was empty. He pushed open the door, setting off a buzzer, and crossed carpet the same no-color as in Renny's clinic, wondering what they called it on color charts.

Neutral, he thought, suppressing a giggle.

Joe Levine came out of the back and up to the counter.

Good, it was Joe. They were friends of a sort, had occasional lunches in the staff cafeteria together, joked about being the only two Jews in fifty miles.

Not such a joke, actually.

"Hey, Doc, how's it hanging?" Joe said brightly.

"Accent on hanging," Reed answered.

"Got problems?"

"Got a whole list of 'em." Reed took out the folded list of his "assigned substances" and put it down on the counter, resisting the impulse to slap it down like the ace of trump.

Joe looked at it; his thick, dark eyebrows drew together. "Jesus, Reed, what'm I supposed to do with this shit?"

"Get it for me."

Joe looked up at him. "You gonna poison the reservoir?"

It was a pretty good line, and Reed managed a strained-sounding hee-hee. He should've concocted a story on his way here from Renny's. A plausible lie Joe could live with. But Reed was a shitty liar, had been in-stilled with a hatred of lies by a white-haired Brahmin named L. Thomas

Lodge, his favorite Yale prof. "Always tell the truth," the old man had told them. "You won't be wrong any more often than if you lie, nor crueller in the end . . . and at least you will not be a liar."

But the truth was impossible in this situation; he didn't even think he could find words to describe it. He said, "Look, Joe, I need this crap, and I can't tell you why. So do me a favor—a mitzvah—and get it for me, no questions asked."

Joe gaped at him. "Mitzvah! You call opium and vervain *mitzvahs?*"

"I don't call them anything."

"Do you even know what vervain is?"

Reed shook his head.

"It's verbena, Reed. The stuff old ladies make sachets out of, and nineteenth-century practitioners used as an expectorant. You find it in herb shops or some New Age tea. . . . What the fuck could you possibly want—" Joe caught himself. "Right, right . . . you can't tell me. But I'm supposed to get it anyway. Including the opium."

"Including that."

Silence stretched on for what felt like a long time. The wall clock clicked to four, closing time for Joe. He could go home now, take his wife out to dinner, to the movies . . . see friends . . . things people did on a pleasant spring Saturday night.

Reed waited, aware of the beat of his heart.

Finally Joe said, "Okay, Reed. A mitzvah . . . "

The relief was draining; he hadn't realized it meant this much to him.

"Thank you." He grabbed Joe's hand and wrung it, making him grimace. He apologized for hurting him, let him go, apologized again, then thanked him some more. He told him he'd buy him lunch to thank him, and went to the door, where he thanked him again. Finally he got out of there, wondering, as he went down the main corridor to the water fountain to quell his raging, nerve-induced thirst, how he'd ever had the gall to become a psychiatrist.

As Joe Levine opened his dusty copy of the directory of suppliers of botanicals and "oddments," Don and Irene Forbes entered Trilby, the most expensive shop in Fallsbridge. It was carpeted in plush rose beige, with glass shelves and counters displaying Lenox, Royal Crown Derby, Royal Copenhagen, Wedgewood. It had place settings of Christophle silver, linen from Porthault, silk and leather from Hermès, and the best of the best pieces of folk art.

The door opened again and Janet Wilbur came in behind them and went to a rack of hand-dipped candles from Nantucket. Jason King, the shop owner, went to Janet, although the Forbeses were first.

Jason had owned this store since it was Flowers, a headshop that sold bong pipes, T-shirts with FUCK THE SYSTEM on them, and incense that smelled like moldy hay mixed with hairspray. Business went to hell with Reagan and the era of the yuppie, but instead of going belly up, Jason borrowed from the bank, remodeled, and renamed the store Trilby, Gifts for the Discriminating. He wound up making more than he ever had, even as a low-level purveyor of grass and hash (never coke).

Good taste explained some of his success, but it was mostly the result of knowing what his customers liked and what they could afford, so he never embarrassed them by suggesting something they could not.

He knew the Forbeses liked anything with birds or whales on it and could afford anything in the store . . . plus the store, the block of Main Street it sat on, and a couple of blocks of downtown Stamford thrown in. And Janet Wilbur, whose husband was a victim of the latest IBM "downsizing," could afford the candles. Yet he went to her because he also knew she'd have to get her kids from day care, do grocery shopping, and start dinner, while the Forbeses had nothing to worry about except getting home for cocktail hour, and were too old-line rich and good-natured to give a shit who came first.

Janet bought her candles, left with rushed thanks, and he turned to Don and Irene, who were looking at a blanket chest with a loon painted on it.

"That's supposed to have been done by an Adirondack hermit, around the turn of the century," Jason said, "but you never know with folk art."

"Mmmmmm . . . " Don fingered his collar and coughed, then plunged one hand into a safari jacket that looked as if it had come from a downscale Yukon outfitter thirty years ago.

He's nervous, Jason thought, and felt his interest quicken.

Finally Don cleared his throat harshly. *"Ugh* . . . we need a brazier."

"Ah."

"And a sword. Ornamental, you know. Like a saber . . . you know."

Jason kept his face blank. "I see."

"And a hazel rod," Don finished.

"Having a magic show?" Jason was joking, but Don leaped on it. "That's it . . . a magic show. How'd you guess?"

He's lying, Jason thought, wondering what they really needed the odd assortment of things for. Some new sex game, he thought, and got a mental flash of Irene playing dominatrix with the sword and hazel rod; the role of the brazier was beyond him. He coughed to keep from laughing and said staidly,

"A hazel rod."

"That's right."

"I can order the sword. It'll be ornamental and probably cost a fortune, but it's available. Ditto the brazier, which believe it or not I have in the basement from the days when we sold incense. But the hazel rod . . . " He trailed off, dipping into his considerable store of sixties lore. "Hazel . . . " The Forbeses looked eager, and younger than he'd ever seen them look, even when they *were* younger. A pretty glow had come to Irene's long face, and Don looked almost like the handsome youth he'd been when Trilby had been Flowers.

They were good customers, paid cash, never returned anything or tried to stiff him. He liked them, would help them if he could.

"You could cut a switch in the woods," he said.

"We want a finished piece . . . and it's supposed to be a rod, not a switch."

Jason nodded, repeated slowly, "Hazel . . . " then brightened. "They used hazel rods for divining."

"For what?"

"Divining water. The diviner would walk the land, and where he said the rod dipped you dug your well. Load of you-know-what, of course. But some folks set great store by it. Used to be a diviner right here in town . . . in Riverside. Name of . . . name of . . . "

They waited again, and he emptied his mind, looking down at the deep-piled rose-beige wool carpeting that had cost one twenty a yard five years ago. God knew what it went for these days.

"Loomis," he said triumphantly after a moment. "Charlie Loomis."

"What a memory!" Don cried, and they laughed, clapped each other on the shoulder, while Irene beamed from next to the Royal Crown Derby demitasse set.

"Yeah." Jason stopped smiling. "Only he was old when I knew about him years ago. He'll be ancient if he's still alive."

They looked crestfallen. Quickly, Jason said, "But, hey, it's possible. Look in the phone book while I get your brazier. It's downstairs, with stock I stored when we remodeled."

Irene was beaming again when he came up from the basement with the brazier, still wrapped in the pink tissue paper in which it had come from India twenty-five years ago.

"He's alive," she cried. "His wife said he'll see us."

Ida Loomis let Don and Irene into the tiny, talcumy-smelling foyer of a tiny house on Bowman in Riverside. She was in her mid-eighties at least, Irene thought, and so thin she looked as if she'd rattle when she moved.

"Charlie's ninety-seven," she told them, "and still got all his marbles. Only he's a little deaf, so you gotta speak up. He's waiting in the kitchen— warmest room in the house."

She led them down a short, narrow, carpeted hall, past small immaculate rooms, to an overheated kitchen at the back of the house. The cabinets were polished cedar, with a clean, shining, green linoleum floor so old it had buckled in waves. The old man sat in a wheelchair, facing a small color TV on the counter. Mrs. Loomis snapped the set off and said loudly, "Chuck, those folks that called about the rod're here."

The old man turned a denuded head on a wattled neck and looked at them. His eyebrows and lashes were invisible, his face a mass of sagging wrinkles like crushed wet paper . . . and about the same color, Irene thought. But then he smiled, his dark eyes in clear whites lit up, and she realized he'd once been a handsome man and did indeed have all his marbles.

"Got well trouble up yonder?" he asked. His voice was gravelly but strong.

"No, sir." Don spoke deferentially. "We . . . uh . . . need the rod for a magic show."

"A what?"

Don raised his voice. "Magic show . . . "

"What kind'a shit's that," the old man asked.

"A magic show . . . for the kids . . . " Don said lamely. "We'll pay for the rod, of course."

"Eh?"

"They say they'll pay for the rod," the old lady yelled.

"How much?" Loomis yelled back.

The old people looked at Don, Don looked at Irene.

How much?

The question hung in the air. How much could they give this thread-bare, immaculate, clearly proud old couple without getting their dander up.

How much.

"Will two hundred be enough?" Irene asked haltingly, and the old man cackled, "By my ass, lady, I'd love to get you in an all-night poker game. Two hundred! Rod's worth shit without the dowser . . . that's what we were called . . . dowsers. Gimme six bucks for it, and my time. No . . . make it seven on reflection, case that twerp Rowland comes after us for the sales tax."

He turned to his wife. "Mind, sweetie pie?"

She hurried out, the starched skirt of her housedress rustling, and returned with a stack of long, thin boxes faced in blue paper.

"That one," said the old man, pointing to the second from the top.

She handed it to him, and he opened it with a flourish to reveal a long forked rod of pale wood sanded so smooth it caught the light like metal.

"It's beautiful," Irene said softly.

"Damn tootin'. And it was a beloved tool, lady. So treat it with respect."

Across the street, Dick Lambert pulled up at the curb. He looked at his watch, then in the rearview mirror at the two in back.

"Ready?"

Ted Dukovsky nodded.

"Ass-face?" Dick's slate-colored eyes found Bart Loamers's. Bart said "Yeah" and looked out at the Rutherfords' two-family across the street from the Lamberts'. Ready meant they had their masks. Holding it made Bart's hands sweat, and he kept it draped over his knee. Ted kept running his through his fingers as if he liked the powdery feel of smooth, soft rubber. In front, Rog's and Dick's masks were hidden.

Dick killed the motor, then looked across at the front of his house, and said,

"Shit!" They all looked. In place of the Honda Dick said Lerner always drove "down here" was the silver Porsche.

"He never brings it down here," Dick said. "Why today? Why fuckin' today . . ."

"That tears it," Bart said. Relief left him needing to urinate. "We'll never catch him in that."

Dick caught his eyes in the mirror again. "We only have to catch him if he runs. Why would he do that?"

"Because we're chasing him," Bart said in his best how-can-you-be-such-an-asshole voice. But it was a sham.

Dick was right; Lerner wouldn't run because he wouldn't know he was being chased. He wouldn't recognize the junker Dick got from Trimble's last night: an '84 Chevelle that ran pretty well and had a solid floor.

The plan was simple, like all of Dick's plans. That alone gave it a shot at success.

Lerner would leave the house, where he was presumably winding up his last visit before the second shrink came to sign on to the committal.

He'd get into his car and pull away; they'd let a couple of car lengths open up, then follow. There was only one route he could take: that was Bowman, which bypassed the town center, to River. Then right on River, where the road narrowed and ran along a strip of marsh and reeds that smelled like tidal mud on hot days. No one but birders ever went there, and damn few of them, since it was muddy and buggy three seasons of the year, and frozen the fourth.

There, they'd pull out to pass; Lerner was a gentleman and would fall back to let them, even though he could easily leave them in the dust (or mud) even in the Honda. They'd pull around him, ride alongside for a moment (traffic was nil along that stretch), then force him over into the reeds. There was no guardrail, almost no shoulder, so the mud would grip the wheels. In a way he'd be worse off in the Porsche, since the Honda had front-wheel drive and a better chance of dragging itself out of the mud (which must be like quicksand after the storm). They'd pile out of the junker, plow through the mud in their knee boots, drag the doctor out of his car, and "beat the shit out of him."

Dick Lambert's version of telegraphy, with a message Dick was sure would be clear as clean glass. *Leave the old lady alone, or next time . . .*

Next time what? Bart thought helplessly as he watched the front of the Lamberts' front door.

Next time they'd kill him.

But there'd be no next time, Bart insisted to himself, because Dick's simple plans had a way of working out. The junker was the best junker ever, and Dick had filched it without mishap. Rog had gotten the masks from the leftover '94 Halloween merchandise at Drucker's Variety, where he filled in: a Dracula, a Frankenstein, and two generic goblins. Bart got one of the goblins.

Dick had even thought to have a crowbar under the seat to bust the car windows in case they couldn't reach Lerner before he got the doors locked. Shame to do that to the Porsche, Bart thought. Shame to do it to *Lerner.* But he *would* get the message; this would start and end this afternoon, with no serious injury.

The door to the Lambert house opened slowly, like the horror-movie door behind which will be the MONSTER. Reed Lerner in this case, looking singularly nonmonstrous, and Larry Lambert, Dick's old man. As they stood on the stoop, Bart realized what a big man Reed Lerner was. He'd seen him around town all his life, but never thought of him as being especially large. Maybe because he was well proportioned, with legs not too long or waist too short, shoulders too big or small. Everything seemed to fit, making him appear average size. But Larry was almost six feet, and Lerner towered over him.

Maybe Lerner'd show *them* a thing or two, which would almost be

worth getting kicked around for. But there were four of them, Dick had the
crowbar, and his knife was probably stuck in his belt. At least Bart hoped it
was the knife, not Dick's old man's .32.

Lerner and Lambert said a few words to each other. The light coming
from the foyer cast a glow behind Lerner, giving him an ethereal look at
this distance.

Then Lerner held out his hand, probably in the spirit of *I know what this
is doing to your family, Larry, and I'm sorry . . . but it'll be for the best . . .* or some
such bullshit. Larry looked at the hand: Bart thought he would refuse it.
But at the last moment, he shook, then went inside.

The door shut, the backlight was doused, and Lerner was just a normal-
looking man again . . . except for his size.

He headed down the cement path with weeds that seemed to grow
through the cracks at all seasons. Bart realized he was holding his breath,
praying for something, anything, to intervene.

Then it did.

The door to the Loomises' next door opened; a couple Bart recognized
as the Forbeses, who gassed up their Wagoneer at Trimble's, came out.
More rich folk from Upper Fallsbridge.

"Reed . . . " called the male Forbes. Lerner turned around, and Bart
thought, *Reprieve.* He was going to wet his pants if he didn't take a leak
soon.

They looked at each other across the strip of ragged grass that separated
the small houses.

"What're you doing here?" Don asked.

"Got a patient." Reed nodded at a house about the same size as the
Loomises', but in a terrible state of neglect, Irene saw, with roof shingles
that were actually mossy, giving the roof an algaic cast, as if it were at the
bottom of a pond.

"And you?" Reed asked. Don held up the long, narrow blue box.

"Ah, success," Reed said.

Irene thought Reed looked terrible. His face was gray, there were dark
rings under his eyes. He came down here to help people the state, town,

and country wanted no part of, and they were draining him.

He probably missed the kids, too, was the kind of father who hugged his sons unselfconsciously even though they were college age.

He and Riva must be lonely in the huge, empty house, as Irene and Don were in theirs. Only *they* didn't have kids coming home for summer break.

She had her usual miserable vision of the years to come, with her and Don, old, infirm, and alone, with old, infirm servants and stacks of Audubon field guides. . . .

And the gang of eight, who'd never abandon each other, she thought.

She slipped her hand through Reed's arm. "Come home with us."

"What?"

"Right now. Come home, have a drink and dinner with us. I'll call Riva and browbeat her into walking over. It's a gorgeous evening, it'll do her good. I'll defrost the quail we had sent from D'Artagnan. I'm sure Cook's laid in some asparagus . . . we'll have a feast."

"And play bridge," Reed said tonelessly.

"Absolutely not. We'll get drunk and watch our latest tape of the rarely sighted yellow-bellied pussy-sucker. . . . "

"The what?"

"You heard me," she said primly, and the men exploded in laughter. Reed hugged her with one arm and nodded that he'd go.

They were moving; Bart's heart gave a whump like an oil-furnace back puff.

Dick hunched way over, and Bart knew he was reaching for the ignition wires to start this wreck. "Easy does it," Dick was saying softly. "Easy does it. No peeling, no squealing, guys. We just wait our turn, then pull away nice and easy. Much better things ahead than peeling rubber one more time, right boys?" He sounded like the mate, Starbuck, in the *Moby Dick* movie. *Pull, lads, pull, nice and easy, pull my lads,* as they bore down on the unsuspecting whale.

It's a whale, the same Starbuck had said, *no more, no less. A monstrous great whale, but just a whale, and killing whales is our business. . . .*

Or words to that effect.

But poor Starbuck had been wrong, it was not just a whale, and Bart suddenly knew this was not just your everyday old assault on a sunny afternoon.

He knew they should not go after Reed Lerner, M.D., any more than those ill-fated denizens of the *Pequod* should have gone after the white whale.

A cold, smooth sickening sense of dread settled over Bart Loamers like a gigantic cape of kelp, and a few drops of urine leaked into his drawers.

Hey, guys, he wanted to whisper. *We've had our fun. Anticipation is greater than realization, and all that. We've had our anticipation . . . let it go. . . .*

But this isn't for fun, Dick would say, his cruel gray eyes settling on Bart, *this is for survival.* And Bart would say, with the hair on his body waving like seaweed, and the utter confidence of the surely damned, *But this is the surest way not to survive, Dickie.*

"What the fuck're you mumbling about," Dick hissed from the front seat.

"Something about being damned," Ted said happily.

"Wait," Rog whispered to Dick urgently before Dick could say any more. "This tub fires like a fuckin' jet, they'll look over, see us. . . . "

"Yeah, yeah," Dick whispered back. "Tell me when he pulls away."

"I don't have to tell you nothin'," Rog said. "That fucker's a Porsche, you know it when you hear it."

"Maybe, maybe . . . we ought'a just kind'a . . . " Bart said from the seat, sounding massively weak.

"Maybe we kind'a ought'a shut your fuckin' hole," Dick hissed.

"Don't jive him like that. . . . " Ted raised his voice a little. He always stood up for Bart. He was as strong as he was good-looking; a clop from him would put Dick in dreamland for a second or two anyway.

Dick hissed, "Sorry . . . Fart Breath . . . " and the Porsche started with the fine, deep-throated roar of four hundred horses in sync. Bart kept whispering, but knew he was speaking too softly to be understood and wasn't too coherent at this point anyway, what with piss leaking into his shorts from his absolute terror of what they were about to do to Lerner, and what he somehow knew that would bring down on their heads.

Then another motor started up, gears grinding a little, and Rog said,

"Oh shit . . . " They all straightened up (from the hunch they'd assumed to keep from being seen from the street). The Porsche had moved away from the curb and was heading down Bowman at a fairly stately pace, only right behind it, barely a car length away, was the Forbeses' Grand Wagoneer. That wasn't all; the Wagoneer could turn off on Ridge, Prospect, or even King before they got to the appointed spot, still leaving Lerner alone and vulnerable. But Bart saw one person in the Wagoneer, and two in the front of the Porsche, and the Porsche driver was a woman. Wherever they were going, they were going together, and Lerner was giving Mrs. Forbes the treat of driving a 911.

That really did tear it; they all knew it.

"Okay, okay, okay, fuck . . . " Dick mumbled. "But that's for now . . . there's later . . . lots of later . . . there's the lot at the hospital, staff parking's over on the dark side . . . or that lousy lot at the clinic. Shit, you can't find a silver dollar at dusk it's so fuckin' dark. . . . "

But Bart wasn't listening. He'd thrown open the junker's rear door, ripped down his zipper, and shoved himself halfway out of the car to urinate gushingly in the gutter.

On Tuesday, Joe Levine called Reed on the scratchy, interhospital line, and asked, "Where's my lunch?"

"You got the stuff?"

"Got it. And bring your checkbook, buddy. All that old-New-Age bullshit don't come cheap."

"Bet the opium cost more than the galbanum," Reed said.

"Bet you're right. Cafeteria . . . twenty minutes."

"You're on."

"I'll have the stuff in a plain brown shopping bag." Joe was having fun with this. "And I'm getting the most expensive dish on the steam table."

"That will be brown meat product in brown gravy substitute for four-fifty."

"Don't I know it," Joe said mournfully.

CHAPTER 6

By one on Wednesday, lunch was over, and the eight of them were a little drunk. They always had wine with lunch, but today they'd started an hour early, polished off four bottles, then made their way to the basement door, where they had stood single file.

"Like campers at the crapper," Angie had said with a giggle.

Myra had opened the door, led the way down, and the others had followed with the "supplies." They had rushed through the preparations, as eager as ever to get out of the basement, Myra thought. They had pushed the furniture back, with Reed doing the heavy work that had involved single-handedly moving the rock maple coffee table it had taken three men to carry down.

Then they had lined up as they once had to play Red Rover, bent in unison, and started rolling up the rug. A feeling of camaraderie had run down the line of them as they worked, and they'd looked up, grinning at each other.

With the rug out of the way, Arlen brought out a big wooden compass the likes of which Myra had not seen since grammar school and drew a chalk circle, whereupon, Helen, who had the steadiest hand and had painted signs for school, painted it in red kiddy tempera guaranteed to wash off, even after a year. As she printed strange words from the book that they didn't understand, but were afraid to leave out—BALLATAR, HALLYA, SOLUZEN, others just as odd—Myra remembered Helen's other signs from thirty-five years ago:

HALLOWEEN PARTY, MIDDLE SCHOOL GYM. COSTUME AND JACK O'LANTERN CONTEST ... APPLE DUNKING, REFRESHMENTS. And, CHRISTMAS PAGEANT, DEC. 21, BRING ONE WRAPPED PRESENT FOR THE NEEDY ... SANTA WILL BE HERE!

Helen straightened up, holding the red-dipped brush, looking down at her handiwork. "God, why's it got to be red?"

" 'Cause that's the color Billy had the biggest jar of," Angie said.

"It looks so ... " Helen trailed off, and Don said, "Bloody."

Maybe it did seem a little hemorrhagic, Myra thought, but she suspected that was how it should look and felt her heart lighten as they went back upstairs. Then it got tense, because after lunch—vegetable pâté and duck salad, all homemade—and the last of the fourth bottle of wine, Reed looked at her and said,

"My ... it's your house."

Her basement, her ghost ... her problem. She knew exactly where that was leading, and her heart sailed into her throat. "I can't," she whispered.

No one spoke. The red satin robe hanging on the door looked ghostly under the plastic cleaner's bag.

Lambie put her hand over Myra's. "My, you're the one who believes ... "

"I thought you all believed ... at least a little." She looked around at them.

"But you're the one it showed itself to," Reed said gently. "I think you've got the best shot at ... " He halted; everyone leaned forward a fraction to hear what he'd come up with. He grinned, looking a little the worse for the wine, and said, "Getting its attention."

He was right. It had appeared to her, it *was* her ghost. Besides, being sorcerer probably wasn't any more nerve-wracking than playing the virgin in the elementary school Christmas pageant year after year. She'd never understood why they thought Mary must be blond.

"Okay ... my house, my ghost," she mumbled. She drank the last of the wine in her glass, then looked at the robe.

"Do I have to take everything off?"

"Well, some," Helen said, "or it won't hang right."

"But not my underwear . . ."

"Of course not," Helen said. A ribald crack from Arlen that Myra was too nervous to take in.

She pushed back her chair.

"The book says you have to wash," Reed told her.

"Why?"

"God knows."

"How thoroughly?" she asked. *Are we talking about hands and face, or shower, shampoo, and douche?* She smothered what would certainly have come out as a drunken guffaw.

"Your hands," he said, looking at the book.

"Anything else?"

"Not that we're going to do." He was still examining the book.

"What're we *not* going to do, for instance?" That was Don.

Reed grinned. "We are not, for instance, going to cut off the head of a virgin white cock and burn it." He looked up with a winey glow in his eyes. "At least, I take it we're not."

Everyone giggled briefly and self-consciously, then fell silent. Myra stood and reached up on tiptoe to take the robe off the door, looping the skirt over her arm so it wouldn't drag on the floor.

The bathroom in the guest wing downstairs was cavernous and chilly. Myra opened the window to let in some warm air from outside, but the floor tile and porcelain sink were freezing. She undressed to her underwear, washed, and dried carefully so she wouldn't get water marks on the satin. Then she slid on the robe. It was cold at first; her skin pimpled as the slick cloth slid around her.

She secured it with hooks and eyes Helen had sewn on, and tied the sash. Her waist looked slimmer than usual. It could be the cut of the robe, or she might have lost weight. She avoided scales and couldn't be sure.

She pulled her comb through her hair, brushed off the shoulders of the robe to get rid of any stray hairs, then looked at herself in the mirror.

In contrast to the scarlet, her skin looked almost pale, and she hadn't seen her hair look that . . . golden . . . in years. For the first time since she could remember, a semblance of the old, pretty Myra Fox looked back at her.

Not just pretty . . . beautiful.

"Gosh," she whispered, a little startled by the reflection in the mirror.

She picked up the robe skirt, went to the door, and opened it, then let the skirt fall around her with the gentle hiss of heavy satin.

Smoke filled the basement; the smell was not bad so much as strange, redolent of herbs and spices you'd never normally put together: cardamom and dill, basil and cinnamon. The smoke was thick, the basement was warm, Myra's hands were sweating. She had to hold the hazel rod and book in one hand, the sword in the other. "I can't hold all this *and* read," she said. Her breath made the smoke billow.

"Hand me the book," Arlen said. "I'll read, you can repeat after me."

She went to the edge of the circle. "Don't step on the line," Reed cried, as if it really mattered.

" 'Step on a crack, break your mother's back,' " Angie singsonged.

The smoke thickened; it could set off the fire alarm or choke someone who was allergic to some of the junk in the brazier. What a ridiculous mess this was turning into, Myra thought.

"I'm opening a window," Reed said. "Didn't see anything in the book about us having to smother."

He cranked one of the awning windows open, and a breeze blew in, tearing the smoke to shreds and bringing a welcome gust of fresh air.

"Ready?" Arlen asked.

She nodded, feeling dizzy from the wine and fumes.

Helen's eyes were watering; Angie suppressed a cough; Don's face was pink and sweating, and Myra saw him give his crotch a surreptitious scratch.

Some exorcists, she thought.

Arlen leafed through the book.

The sword was getting heavy, her arm started to ache, and she was sweating. Sweat would stain the robe, but it could be dry-cleaned in the unlikely event it was ever to be worn again.

Her arm started to ache. "You said you were ready, Arlen. . . . "

"I know . . . I know . . . lost the place."

Lambie smothered a yawn; Helen pulled at a leg of her sagging panty-hose. God, why didn't Helen buy decent pantyhose, Myra thought with annoyance. She could certainly afford it.

Then Myra remembered *her* twenty-two-dollar top and 100 percent polyester elastic-band slacks waiting for her in the bathroom upstairs.

"Got it," Arlen said, holding the book at arm's length. He needed bifocals, Dr. Faye had said; Arlen told the gang he'd told Dr. Faye to stuff it. "Ever hear of a stud wearing bifocals?" he'd asked.

"Okay, My. First we consecrate the instruments. Look at the sword, then the rod and brazier, and repeat after me. 'I conjure thee form of instrument, by the virtue of heaven, and all the stars which rule . . . ' "

She repeated the words.

He went on: " 'By virtue of the four elements, by that of all stones, all plants, all animals whatsoever, by the virtue of hailstorms and winds, to receive such virtue herein. . . . ' "

The words were grander than she'd expected; the others seemed to be listening.

" ' . . . that we may obtain by thee the perfect issue of all our desires . . . ' "

She recited after Arlen and thought, "The perfect issue of all our desires." How utterly marvelous! Nothing from Quaker meeting had ever been marvelous. Or much of anything, come to that. The "service" (if you could call it that) had been conducted in silence, unless someone was moved to speak.

Yet she remembered it lovingly, as an hour out of time every week when you had to be alone with yourself in silence and "wait upon the Lord." She especially remembered the moment, made almost awesome by its "plainness," when the hour was over, and you turned to each other, took hands, and said, "Good morning, friend."

Arlen intoned, " 'Which also we seek to perform without evil . . . ' "

She repeated it and thought, *Absolutely without evil; all I want is a normal basement.*

" 'Without evil, without deception . . . ' " Arlen's voice had gotten deeper, as hers had. She felt the words rumble in her throat. The others were staring at her, and for once she didn't mind being looked at, the . . . cynosure of all eyes.

Cynosure was one of those words she must look up someday.

" ' . . . by God, the Creator of the sun and angels . . . Amen. . . . ' "

"Amen?" It was over too soon, she thought. Then Arlen said, "Now the incantation itself, Myra."

The others drew closer, Arlen turned a page of the book, Myra grasped the sword more firmly and raised it higher. Her arm had stopped aching; she was no longer sweating.

Then Arlen's voice rang out. " 'By the dreadful day of Judgment, by the sea of glass which is before the face of divine majesty . . . ' "

Sea of glass, what a gorgeous image. She repeated it and he read, " 'By the four beasts before the throne having eyes before and behind, by the holy angels and the mighty wisdom of God . . . ' "

The atmosphere in the basement had done an elemental shift. The silence was deep; Angie swayed to the words; Helen had closed her eyes. So had Don, of all people, and his head was bowed as it would be in church.

More words came through the light smoke left in the air, across the red circle . . . and Myra repeated them. At first she cajoled and summoned the spirit, by the *this* and the *that,* show yourself! Come to me, speak to me; do it pleasantly, clearly, and without deceit.

Then the content changed, as if the spirit *had* shown up (although nothing at all happened) and it was time to cast it . . . her . . . out. But that was still more cajoling than demanding, and Myra thought the approach extremely savvy. More flies with honey than vinegar, and all that. *Honey!* The word stuck in her mind, unlike the other words. *Honey-honey* swam thickly through her mind; she must be very high on the wine and smoke. Had no idea how much time had passed. Twenty, maybe thirty minutes; maybe more. *HONEY.*

She repeated, " 'Because thou hast answered my demands, I hereby license thee to depart, without doing injury to man or beast. . . . ' "

In spite of the terrible injury done to you, Goody Redman, Myra thought, *for which I am deeply, truly, painfully sorry.*

HONEY.

" 'Go, I say . . . ' " she repeated after Arlen. " 'I conjure thee to withdraw in peace, and may the peace of God ever continue between thee and me. Amen. . . . ' "

A perfect ending, Myra thought . . . and the vent fan came on.

Not the ceiling blower triggered by humidity in the air, but the vent fan on the washroom light switch.

Only the light was off, the washroom a black oblong across the basement. Its door creaked in the draft, then started to shut; it gathered speed and slammed, making the awning window Reed had opened gape wider. Air pressure dropped, smoke was sucked out, the exotic scent went with it, to be replaced by a rushing gust of the old basement stench. Then it all stopped; fan, wind, and smell, and there wasn't a sound.

Arlen croaked, "The fan."

"It's on the light switch," Myra said faintly.

Helen said, "You said 'amen.' "

"Yes."

"Then it's over."

"Over . . . " Arlen slammed the book shut and edged toward the stairs. Myra put down the sword and rod and stepped over the rim of the circle, careful not to step on it. But her foot caught in the satin, and she stumbled. Reed grabbed her arm. "Pick up the skirt and let's . . . " His voice rose. "Get the fuck outta here!"

"What a bunch of Weeeeennnnnnieeeessssss," Don wailed, laughing, shooing Irene ahead of him to the stairs, and Angie wailed, "Nathan's Famous . . . " And they ran, stumbling, mock-moaning and giggling wildly. Reed kept hold of Myra's arm and half helped, half dragged her up the stairs to the kitchen. Lambie was the last one out, because she'd actually had the guts to stop and crank the window shut.

*   *   *

"A short ignited the fan," Don said. "Call an electrician."

"And the smell?" Myra insisted, looking around the table at them. "You smelled it."

Helen raised her hand as if they were back in second grade and she had to go to the bathroom. "I think I know. The window wells are stone. Stone soaks up smells, and when that gust of air blew in . . . "

"It brought the smell with it," Angie finished for her.

"Eau de slime," Lambie said, and everyone but Myra laughed.

"Then it's gone," she said.

No one answered.

"Well, is it gone?" she demanded. They looked at her, then at each other, then didn't seem to know where to look.

"You don't believe in it, do you?" she said softly. "You never did."

"What difference does it make?" Don asked. "We still exorcised the shit outta it."

"Then why did we run away just now?" she asked, and again, no one answered.

Myra hung the robe back on the padded hanger and sniffed at it. The folds still harbored the smell of smoke, but no sweat, and the underarms were unstained. She brought it back to the breakfast room, to Helen, who was taking it home with her; she would loan it to Christy Perkins's daughter for a costume party.

"If no one minds," she said.

No one did.

Next week they'd spend their first hour cleaning up downstairs; most of the hundreds of dollars' worth of exotica would be thrown out, but Myra and Lambie would split up the culinary spices, and Reed would return the opium to the pharmacy.

"The pharmacist'll be relieved I didn't smoke it all," he said.

Don and Irene wanted the hazel rod. "It's the smoothest wood I've ever felt." Irene smiled. "And we *could* have well trouble one day."

Angie said she liked the brazier, and Arlen wanted the sword. Something for everyone; souvenirs of the afternoon.

* * *

They left. The dog waited until the last motor faded, then started yapping again.

Myra went back inside, shut the door, then crossed the kitchen to the basement door. She hesitated, then opened it and stepped out on the landing. The fan was quiet; no lights were on, not even a glow was left from the ashes in the brazier. Everything was dark and silent; she leaned over the railing, and whispered, "Are you there?" She braced herself for the fan to whir or a breath of that stench to blow up the stairs at her.

Nothing happened.

She told herself that was because the rite had worked, and *she* was gone. But she was still mightily relieved to get back into the kitchen, and shut and bolt the basement door.

CHAPTER 7

The dog was still barking. Bob put his fork down next to the plate of half-eaten food.

"Goddamn it..." It was the first time he'd mentioned the dog since the night Myra had gotten trapped in the basement.

"I'll call the dog warden in the morning," she said.

He looked at her.

"I mean it, Bob. I'll call first thing, give 'em hell."

He put his hand over her fist clenched on the table. "My, My, you've never given anyone hell in your life."

"Well, there's a first time for everything... and this will be the first time for that." She had put on a red satin robe, stood inside a magic circle, and cajoled and commanded a denizen of the netherworld (maybe). She was not going to be intimidated by Pastori the obnoxious, or a Jack Russell terrier the size of her foot.

"In fact, I'll do it now," she said suddenly and stood up.

"No one's there at this hour."

"I don't mean the dog warden, I mean Pastori. I'm going over there right now...."

She was not the least bit afraid of Antonin Pastori, or his dog, his wife, or his kids if he had any. For once, she didn't seem to be afraid of anything, and it was a wonderful feeling. But she'd had wonderful feelings before that turned out to be delusions, she reminded herself.

"No, My," Bob said. "It's too late."

"No, it's not. The news isn't even over. I'll just talk to him, one neighbor to another. My God, Bob, you can't even eat your dinner."

"My . . ."

She kissed his cheek. "I'll be right back."

She rushed through the kitchen, and out the back door before he could argue anymore.

It was warm out; she didn't need a jacket this time. Spring had come in one day, it seemed, and the meadow was in full bloom and needed cutting. The leaves on the trees were unfurled and the air smelled of fresh grass and apple blossoms from the abandoned orchard at the edge of the old farm.

Halfway down the path to the road, she heard a high, sighing hum that rose and fell like surf. It was coming from the hives. The bees must be swarming or whatever they did. Before long, workers would leave the hive to collect pollen and they'd have honey again.

The hum got louder.

It must be very loud for her to hear it this far away and over the yapping dog.

When they got the honey, she'd call Barb Potter and offer her a jar. If Barb didn't want to see her (as she probably wouldn't), Myra would wrap it in bubble wrap and send it to her.

She suddenly felt expansive, almost joyful, the way she used to at this time of the year when school was almost over for the summer.

She reached the road and looked both ways; she didn't see any cars or hear any motor noise, and she hurried across the narrow road to the foot of the Pastoris' driveway.

She could see the house more clearly now than on that bone-chilling night last month.

It was about a quarter the size of her house, and very well kept, with trimmed evergreens around the foundation and impatiens bedding next to the stoop.

She rang the bell; the dog went nuts and she wondered, as she had before, if anyone would hear her. Only this time, she wasn't sweating bullets; her blood pressure was not heading for the stratosphere.

She raised her hand to knock, and the door opened.

She'd forgotten how unwholesome-looking Antonin Pastori was, as if he'd eaten, drunk, and smoked too much for fifty years.

His yellow-whited eyes glared at her. "You again!"

"Yes, Mr. Pastori, I'm sorry to bother you, but I thought we might have a chat."

"A chat!" His voice growled with malice. "A chat! I said all I got to say to you last time, lady."

He made "lady" sound like an epithet.

"I know, but I thought . . . well . . . last time I said all the wrong things and I thought I'd try to make amends."

A spark of interest in his muddy eyes. "What kind of amends?" She got the feeling he expected her to offer him money.

He must know she was rich. He'd have heard in town, *You live on Redman, across from the Ludens? Her old man was Starret Fox, left millions.*

Half to her brother George, half to her, and the eighties had doubled, maybe trebled it; she had not kept track. She'd open the weekly statement from New York, glance at the bottom line, then give it to Bob to deal with. She remembered the figure sixty or sixty-five from the last one. So she must have sixty or so million dollars. A lot of money; a humbling, shameful amount of money, and she *was* ashamed.

She said humbly, "Amends by trying to establish a neighborly relationship so we can solve our problem. . . ."

"*Our* problem? *I* got no problem."

"But we're neighbors, we're supposed to consider each other. . . ."

"You just don't get it, do you?" The dog shut up, suddenly, and Pastori growled in the silence. "You just don't get it, you fat, dumb, rich bitch. . . ."

The words hit Myra like icy slaps; she couldn't believe she'd heard right and found herself bending closer with her head tilted as if she didn't want to miss a syllable.

"You just can't get it," he raged. "It's my dog and my land. And maybe I

only got two lousy acres, not three hundred and fifty like some people...."
He sprayed her with saliva. "But it's MINE. And I'll leave my dog out all
fuckin' day and all fuckin' night if I want to. You got that? All fuckin' night!
So you can take your 'neighborly chat' and your snooty ways and stick 'em
up your snooty ass!"

Shock kept her in the listening pose for a few beats.

She was not furious or even angry. She wasn't anything except surprised at being called snooty.

She started to say she wasn't snooty and never had been. She didn't
think about her money; she hadn't made it, never paid any attention to it.
It was just zeros after commas, nothing to do with her. And, it had certainly
never made her feel snooty or anything but guilty.

She opened her mouth to say that and try to salvage something from
the dreadful way this had turned out one more time, but words she'd never
thought or imagined saying to him or anyone else came out of her mouth.
"I think you're going to be very sorry, Mr. Pastori."

It wasn't what he expected either, and his eyes widened in surprise,
then narrowed, and she thought if that look had substance it would blister
her skin.

"We'll see who's going to be sorry," he shouted, and slammed the door
in her face.

She waited a moment, still more surprised by her "you're going to be
sorry" remark than she was angry. After a moment, she turned, noticing
how full of buds their impatiens were. Hers were ratty by comparison. She
wished she could ask Mrs. Pastori what her secret was.

That was obviously out of the question.

Myra made her way back down the path to the road.

She looked again, then crossed to her own land. She went up the stone
path to the back door and felt something underfoot. She moved her foot
and in the fading light saw a dead bee. It must have been crawling around
on the stoop, and she'd stepped on the poor thing.

"Sorry," she murmured, and brushed the small corpse off the stoop into
the grass with her foot.

* * *

Pastori left the dog out even later out of spite, Myra thought, and it was still barking at eight-thirty. Bob and Myra were in the den watching TV.

"Thought you and Pastori parted friends," Bob said.

She'd told Bob they had, because if he knew the truth, he'd have trucked his six foot some inches (he was almost as tall as Reed) and two hundred and twenty pounds across the road and wiped the floor with Antonin Pastori. She was pretty sure that was exactly what the little man was waiting for, so he could call the cops . . . then his lawyer.

"He must've forgotten, or maybe the poor little dog whined to stay out because it's so nice out. It'll stop soon." She spoke confidently, then changed the subject, saying, "I heard the bees."

"What?"

"The bees, found a dead one on the stoop."

"Impossible, it's much too early."

"But I saw—"

"Not before June, it's just not possible."

When Bob was sure, he was very, very sure, she thought. She wasn't going searching through the grass for the dead bee to show him.

Across the road, Ruth Pastori said, "Please, let the damn dog in, Tony. I can't hear the movie."

"It stays out until I say so. No one tells me when to let my dog in. Specially not those snot-assed fuckers across the street."

"Road."

"What?"

"They call it a road."

"They call it a road," he mimicked.

"Nothing wrong with calling it a road," Ruth said, staring at the TV screen. It was a Jeff Bridges–Glenn Close movie she'd missed in the theaters and had looked forward all day to seeing. Now she couldn't hear a word because of the damn dog. Nice damn dog, she thought. Dora the dog, cute and affectionate, if you treated it like a dog and not a weapon against people you hated.

She punched up the volume on the TV remote, but it didn't help much.

Poor Dora must be very hungry by now, but Tony wouldn't give in. He hated the Ludenses, even though he'd only talked to Mrs. Ludens the two times she'd come here about the dog. Ruth had seen her around town many times and thought she was a meek, pink, plump little woman she couldn't imagine *disliking*, much less *hating*. But Tony could hate anyone. He was Brooklyn Calabrese (who'd inherited the good hardware business in Oban) and could find insults to his manhood anywhere.

Yiiiipppppp, yiiiipppppp.

It was eight-thirty; the dog sounded famished. Tony compressed his lips in a line and stared at the TV, although he couldn't hear any better than Ruth could.

He must *want* another confrontation with the Ludenses, but Ruth did not. The Ludenses were rich, from old-line Fallsbridge families. The dog warden would be on their side, as would everyone else, except for the few Italians in town. Ruth wanted no part of a feud. She loved this town, wanted to stay here; still got a thrill out of giving her address at stores or on phone orders: "Number Ten Old Redman Road . . . " then a pause to drive the point home, "Fallsbridge, Connecticut."

Yiiiipppppppp . . . Dora had to lose her voice soon (if that ever happened to dogs) or collapse.

The *yiiiipppppp* suddenly changed to a *kiiiiyyyyyyyiiiiiyyyy* that was as close to a scream as Ruth had ever heard from a dog. She and Tony looked at each other; she rayed off the TV.

Kiiiiiiiyyyyyyyiiiiiiyyyyyyyyy, the little dog screamed.

"What the fuck." Tony got up on his short, bow legs. "She's doin' something to the dog."

"Don't be ridiculous, Tone. She wouldn't hurt a fly."

"Fuck that . . . " He grabbed the poker from the fireplace tools and ran out of the room. Ruth followed him.

Kiiiiyyyyyyyiyyyy . . . The dog screamed in agony. It was a horrible sound, and Ruth grabbed her husband's arm. "Don't go out there, Tone. . . . "

"You crazy? They're hurting my dog!" He wrenched his arm away and ran across the kitchen to the back door. Ruth went after him, then stopped halfway and listened. There was another sound under the dog's wailing screams, a high, keening hum that rose, peaked, and fell, and was even worse in a way than Dora's shrieks.

"Don't go out there," Ruth cried at her husband. "Don't!"

He ripped open the back door, the hum got louder, then sank back when he slammed the door. She ran to the window and saw him go down the back steps, with the poker raised like a club. She didn't see Dora, but it was almost dark; the outside lights were not on.

She hit the light switch next to the door, then back to the window, but even with the lights on, she couldn't see much, except what looked like clouds of black specks in the air, motes of some kind or flies.

There were lots of flies this time of year, only these were bigger than mayflies, and their buzz was harsher, higher, more threatening. Like bees, but it was too early for bees, except for the gigantic, lethargic carpenter bees Tony waged yearly war on.

Abruptly, the dog stopped screaming. Maybe just seeing Tony, and knowing it was going to be finally let in, and fed. . . .

Tony gave a short, shocked-sounding shout as if he'd been . . . stung. Then came another shout, then a wail as anguished as Dora's. It turned to a screech that scaled up, took on the sound of tearing metal; she ran to the door, but was afraid to open the screen in case it *was* bees out there.

"Tony . . . " she screamed. "Tone . . . "

He kept shrieking, and she knew he had not heard her. Some of the black dots headed for the screen, attracted by the light. They butted it; a couple fell and crawled on the stoop. They *were* bees. Beyond the light, she saw the cloud of them thin into a line. A beeline, she thought stupidly, and it headed right at her. She leaped back and slammed the inner door as the bees hit the screen. They batted madly against it; then she heard something plop . . . *inside the kitchen* . . . and whirled around. Two bees crawled on the cooktop. As she watched in horror so stark she was beyond screaming, two more plopped out of the hood fan onto the stainless steel.

Myra opened her eyes to the buzzing of bees Bob said couldn't be there. She'd been dozing in front of the TV. She looked at Bob, who was intent on the game, and probably couldn't hear the *bzzzzz* over the crowd yelling.

"Bob."

"Mmmmmm."

He didn't look at her.

Bob, did you hear that? she wanted to ask. But what if he *didn't* hear it, what if the hum was in her mind, and she'd imagined the dead bee, the way everyone seemed to think she imagined everything lately, especially that flutter of movement and the sly scrape-tinkle in the basement last Thursday.

The buzz got louder, and she thought he stiffened as if it had gotten through his concentration. She started to say her stupid, *Bob, did you hear that?* But the noise faded and disappeared, except for a faint residual hum that could come from a failing TV tube.

The dog stopped yapping; the hum stopped; the silence was welcome. Then the TV crowd roared and the dog cried; the crowd noise sank but the dog's cry went from the usual squeal of a dog being trod on to a banshee shriek of animal agony. Myra jerked straight up in the chair; Bob's head snapped around to face her. "What the hell was that?"

"The dog."

"Sounds like they're skinning it. . . . " He got up, went to the window, and opened it. The shrieks, backed by that hum, got much louder, and he shut the window and looked back at her. The shrieks went on until Myra felt them in her teeth.

"Holy shit," Bob whispered. "What're they doing to it?"

The shrieks stopped; Bob took a deep breath, to say something, and the shrieks started again, only in a different timbre this time, and Myra knew it was a human being making those impossible screams of agony. A man.

"I'm calling the cops," Bob yelled.

They rushed out the side door, down the path to the road. It was still warm out, but Myra was shivering; she should have put on her jacket this time. Bob took her hand when they got to the verge of their lawn with their house behind them . . . and the screams stopped.

They looked at each other. In the light from the house, Bob's eyes and cheeks looked sunken.

"Maybe we should wait," he said.

"No . . . they must need help."

He nodded, and, clutching each other's hands, they crossed the road to the Pastoris' land. Halfway up the driveway, Myra felt another of those lumps underfoot. She stopped, dragging Bob to stop with her, and rocked back her foot.

Another dead bee.

Her heart started to slam in her chest; heat rose into her face.

"Don't let it," she whispered. "Oh, please . . . don't let it . . . "

Bob let go of her hand. "What're you mumbling about?"

"Bee . . . "

"I told you . . . "

She pointed down at the tiny corpse on the asphalt driveway. Bob shone the beam of the flashlight he'd brought (Bob thought of things that never occurred to her) and saw the bee. Then raised the beam and they saw the blacktop dotted with fuzzy little bodies.

"What the fuck," Bob whispered.

I told you, Myra wanted to say, but restrained herself.

They went up the drive together, trying not to step on the corpses, but they got thicker as they got closer to the house until their feet crunched with every step.

"Walk on the grass," Bob said sickly. They moved from pavement to grass; Myra still felt myriad little lumps under her shoes, but the grass cushioned the crunching. They got to the front door; the stoop was carpeted with bees. Most were dead, but a few live ones crawled over the bodies of their fellow bees.

Bob leaned across them and rang the bell. Ridiculous, but they didn't know what else to do. No one came, and Myra started around the house. "Wait for the cops," Bob cried.

"They'll need help. . . . " She kept going, trying not to think of the soles of her shoes squishing the bees, which got thicker as she approached the side of the house. There was a freshly painted white fence (Pastori was the kind who was always fixing and painting) with a gate to the yard. The fence was not very high, but the dog, which she'd never seen, was supposed to be small.

She unlatched the gate and went through it, treading on a thick layer of dead and dying bees. Some could come to life enough to sting her, but she knew they would not for some reason, and she kept going.

Bob caught up with her, and they crossed the yard; a path of white stone was black with bees. The lights were on back here, and she saw two lumps, one large, one small, on the grass behind the house.

From behind her, Bob trained the flashlight on the larger lump. It was Pastori; she knew him from the plaid shirt and green twill work pants he'd had on before, not from his face, from which all features had been erased. Which was now a swollen mass of welts with black centers, like gigantic blackheads. The most fulminating acne eruption in history . . . one for the books. She choked down a crazed laugh and was suddenly reeling with nausea. A few live bees crawled across the lumps and the excoriations that had been Antonin Pastori's face. One crept out of the ear hole in swollen flesh, a few more out of the matter-filled crater that had been his right eye.

The light disturbed them; they took off. "Duck," Bob screamed, and she went down on one knee in the grass, feeling dead bees burst under her weight, and the bees flew harmlessly over their heads in the direction of the meadow. At the same time, blue and red strobes flashed on the Pastori lawn and trees, and tires crushed more bee corpses as the first police car arrived.

CHAPTER 8

Myra made tea automatically, barely aware of what she was doing. The pot was still steeping and Bob sat at the table staring into space when the first cop came in the back door. He introduced himself as Sergeant Nolan Lemon and put a printed card on the table. He wore plain clothes, was very tall, with a long, square-jawed face, and kindly, close-set dark eyes.

She tried to pour tea for him, but her hand shook so the top of the pot rattled. He took the pot from her and poured for the three of them.

"What about Mrs. Pastori?" she asked. "She must've been home. . . . "

"She was badly stung," he said quietly. "About fifty or so bees got in the kitchen. They must've come through vents and down the chimney. But they say she'll be okay. I know they were your neighbors. . . . "

"Not really. I mean, they only bought the house last year. I didn't even know her first name."

"I see."

He sipped the tea, looking at her over the rim of the cup. "Tea's nice, but we could probably use a shot of brandy, Mrs. Ludens. Would you have some?"

"Of course. . . . " She started to stand, but her legs wouldn't hold her. She flopped back in the chair. "I'm sorry." Bob started to haul himself to his feet, but Lemon said quickly, "I'll get it. Just tell me where."

"In the pantry, first cabinet on your right. First shelf . . . I think."

He came back with the fairly decent brandy Myra used for sauces, poured generous dollops into their cups.

Myra took a sip; the brandy blew up her nose and made her eyes water.

Bob sipped and coughed, but some life came back to his eyes.

Lemon took a deep gulp of steaming tea that must have burned his mouth, but he gave no sign. "Don't know why, but brandy always helps," he said.

The back door opened again and a uniformed man who was much younger than Lemon came into the kitchen. His smooth, boyish face was about the same shade of pale green as the background of the kitchen wallpaper, and there was a splotch on his uniform blouse that looked like vomit.

He said, "Sergeant, HQ called in. They're sending the full team."

"Good. Why'n't you go on home, Lou; we got plenty of men there."

The kid nodded and ducked out the door, and Lemon looked back at the Ludenses.

"Why don't we start at the beginning; you called nine one one . . . "

"It's too early," Bob said. His voice sounded far away, as if it were coming through a large empty box in his chest. "It's way too early. There shouldn't have been any bees. . . . "

"I understand," Lemon said. "And we've asked the state police to try to round up an entomologist. . . . "

"I'll kill them," Bob said tonelessly. "First thing tomorrow, before the sun comes up, I'm going out there and burn the hive."

"I wouldn't do that until the entomologist has a look, Mr. Ludens. See, we might have a bigger problem here than we realize. Regular bees just don't act that way, do they?"

Bob shook his head, shook his whole body with it, and jarred the table. "NO . . . no . . . oh, my God . . . . no . . . "

"So, we're a little afraid that maybe we've got some kind of invasion. You've heard about the African killer bees coming from South America? They've been reported in Texas and a few other states, and we're thinking

... we're afraid they might have made it north ahead of schedule."

No, Myra thought. The dead bees she saw were just their regular, docile bees that droned, spread pollen, and made honey. They'd only stung Bob a couple of times in all the years he'd been keeping them. Something had happened to them; something had driven them berserk, made them murderous. But then why had they attacked the Pastoris and their dog and left her and Bob alone?

"Mrs. Ludens?" Lemon said, in the voice you use to recapture someone's attention, and Myra realized she'd been staring at the basement door.

Lemon took a tiny cassette recorder out of his pocket and put it on the table. It looked like a toy.

"Hope you don't mind," he said. "It's a lot easier than taking notes."

"Of course we don't mind," Bob said, then looked at Myra.

"We don't mind," she echoed, wishing for the millionth time he'd ask her first, just once.

Lemon turned on the recorder. Little spools turned, and the phone rang. Myra rose; her legs held her up this time. Lemon said,

"I wouldn't answer, Mrs. Ludens. It's probably the press, and talking to them on the phone's an invitation to every dink stringer on the East Coast to call. I'd let it ring if I were you."

It went nerve-rackingly on and on; the little tape unwound, recording rings.

Finally Lemon got up, took the receiver off the hook, then depressed the key to disconnect and put the receiver on the counter. It buzzed to let them know it was off the hook; a raucous, computer voice came on, then stopped, and it was quiet. Lemon rewound the tape, Myra drank the last of her brandy-laced tea. Her eyes felt heavy; she had to suppress a yawn.

"You first, Mrs. Ludens," Lemon said.

She looked at the recorder. "Just speak normally," he said. "It'll pick up your voice. Start at the beginning...."

The beginning was about six-forty when she'd gone over there about the dog. She didn't want to tell Lemon about it, but Mrs. Pastori probably would when she recovered.

Haltingly, leaving out Pastori's profanity, Myra described her after-dinner visit to the house across the road.

Bob interrupted, "You said . . . "

"I know. But I was afraid there'd be a fight if I told you what really happened."

"Fuckin' A there'd be a fight," Bob grumbled, but Pastori had died horribly only an hour ago; Bob couldn't get up much animus.

"How did you leave it with Mr. Pastori?" Lemon asked.

Hatefully, Myra thought. Aloud she said, "That he'd do what he wanted, and I'd live with it. Or deal with it somehow."

"Such as how?"

"I don't know. Call the dog warden, I guess."

"They're notoriously ineffective in situations like this," Lemon said.

"I know."

"Oh?"

She wanted to call the words back, but it was too late.

"How did you know?"

"From before," she mumbled.

Lemon waited with his head cocked.

"From April," Myra said. "I think it was April. I called the dog warden."

"And?"

"He was notoriously ineffective." She smiled shakily.

"And?" Lemon persisted.

She swallowed with an audible click, and Bob said, "I made her go over there, Sergeant. She didn't want to. I . . . insisted."

"And was the first meeting with Mr. Pastori any more amicable than the second?"

Myra didn't answer, and Lemon said easily, "Don't suppose you drugged those bees. . . . " He smiled, meaning to lighten the atmosphere that had gotten terrible heavy.

But Myra cried, "Oh, God . . . no. No . . . how could we . . . "

"Take it easy, Mrs. Ludens. It's all right."

But it's not all right, she wanted to shriek, the man's dead . . . his face . . .

The massively swollen, featureless glut of masses Antonin Pastori's face had turned into appeared to her, and her head swam. She was going to faint and couldn't wait.

She grabbed the table edge, waiting for the dizziness to become profound enough to black everything out, so she could slide bonelessly, ignominiously under the table.

Nothing happened, except the dizziness receded and the young trooper stuck his head in the door.

"Thought you'd gone home," Lemon said.

"Started to, then saw the Channel Six van turn in. Thought I'd better warn you."

"Shit!" Lemon went to the door, and looked out toward the road. "Shit." The trooper left again; Lemon turned back into the kitchen and shut the door.

"Walsh and his minicam are out on the road."

Rob Walsh, the local roving reporter for Channel 6. Bob watched him; Myra was usually in the kitchen preparing dinner when he was on.

She and Bob went to the side windows above a counter. Lights bathed the road and front lawn. Closeness to the road was one disadvantage of living in a converted farmhouse, Myra thought. The other seven had big, gated estates in Upper Fallsbridge, and Walsh and his minicam would have to trespass an eighth of a mile before they even got within sight of their houses. But here, they could film from the public road.

The side of the van opened; a tall man climbed down and joined the others on the road shoulder.

"They'll head for the crime scene first," Lemon said, "but it's cordoned off by now, so they'll come over here."

It happened as he said. The lights crossed the road, figures were silhouetted in their glare. Troopers in campaign hats clumped around Walsh and his crew, and there was some angry-looking gesticulating. This was the face-off between press and troopers, Myra thought, knowing the troopers would win. Then the clump of black forms broke up; lights moved back to the road.

At the same time, a dark-colored van, with its roof rack of lights dark, pulled down the driveway, around the newspeople, and turned onto Redman. Myra saw a seal on its side.

"Coroner," Lemon said. He backed away from the window and turned to them.

"I'd talk to the TV people, get it over with if I were you. It's a terrible occurrence, but it *is* an accident, the bees're the only mileage they'll get out of it. If they *are* Africanized, they'll play up the earlier-than-expected migration. In any case, I can't see them caring enough about the people across the street to harass you. Unless they discover bad blood between the two households. I don't have to tell you what those assholes'll make outta that...."

The front doorbell rang.

Rob Walsh had a thin face, orange-ish with makeup. His hair was brown and styled in waves that dipped over his high forehead.

He was a couple of inches shorter than Bob, but still tall. He smiled, showing predictably perfect teeth.

"Mr. and Mrs . . . " He hesitated.

"Ludens," Bob said. "I know who you are."

Walsh held out his hand; Bob shook it and Myra saw the excitement of the moment . . . of lights hitting him and the front of his house, and of the camera trained on him . . . in his eyes.

She slunk back in the shadows and stealthily slid the door partway shut to hide herself.

"Reed . . . Reed, quick. Bob's on TV. . . . "

Reed came out of the bathroom, toweling his hair, and stood to the side so he wouldn't block Riva's view.

On screen, Rob Walsh was holding the mike for Bob, and Bob was saying, "I don't know, except that it's much too early for them. . . . "

"Early for what?" Reed asked.

"Bees," Riva said.

"Bees?"

"Wait . . . listen."

But there wasn't much more. Walsh said, "But they *were* here, early or not. . . . " and Bob nodded slowly, looking exhausted and lost. Walsh thanked him, then turned to the camera. "There you have it, folks. A freak occurrence that shouldn't have happened but did. And left a man and his dog dead, and his wife critically injured. So what kind of bees were they? Has the Africanized strain made it north years before expected? Are the killer bees among us even now, supplanting and contaminating the gentle European strain in our gardens and flower beds?"

"What man's dead?" Reed asked tensely.

"I don't know . . . I didn't hear the whole piece."

Reed went to the phone to call Myra and got a busy signal. He hit redial a few times with the same result, then hung up.

"I better go there," he said.

"I'll come too?" Riva made it a question.

But a man was dead, the death bizarre enough to bring out the press and get Bob Ludens on the late news looking old, sick, and confused about his bees.

Reed didn't want Riva anywhere near the place.

Myra let Reed in the kitchen door. Bob was at the kitchen table with a man Reed had never seen before. They both stood.

"Sergeant Lemon," said the stranger, stretching out his hand, "State Police Troop B. You're Dr. Reed Lerner."

"How'd you know?" Reed asked, shaking his hand.

Lemon smiled, making his face look a little less drawn. "Wife took me to a lecture you gave on tranquilizers and bed-wetting. Back when my boy was . . . bed-wetting."

"Did the talk help?"

"We took him off the trank since you said he'd probably get over it on his own. And he did. Then I read later that some kids had maybe OD'd on the drugs and died."

"Oh." Reed tensed, knowing what was coming.

Lemon said huskily, "I suppose you could, without too much stretching, be said to have saved my son's life."

Reed thought, *But there's the one I didn't save, Sarge. Her name's Belle, and about twelve hours from now I could be consigning her to what you could call, without exaggeration, the snake pit.*

"Thank you," Lemon said, quietly.

You're welcome would be like taking credit for something he didn't deserve, and Reed changed the subject. "I didn't hear all of what happened here...."

Myra came to the table with a cup and saucer. "Have some tea first. We've been lacing it with brandy."

She giggled, and he realized Myra was pickled. He grinned at her. "Sure, My... tea."

She poured tea that was black from steeping and added a horse-sized dollop of brandy. He sipped. The tea was muddy; the brandy tasted like cough medicine without the syrup.

He took another brave sip and sat back.

Lemon turned off the same brand of cassette recorder Reed used, slipped it in his pocket, and stood up. "It's not a tale I care to hear again," he said. "I'll be across the road if you think of anything else you want to tell me. Nice meeting you, Doctor." He left, the pocket of his jacket sagging slightly from the weight of the recorder.

Bob wiped his hand shakily across his eyes. "I'm going upstairs, Reed. Everything's okay... I mean, as okay as it can be... under the circumstances...." He drank the rest of the brandy-tea in his cup and left the kitchen, his feet shuffling, as if they were too heavy to raise.

That left Reed and Myra alone at the table.

"Under what circumstances, Myra?"

She looked across the kitchen at the basement door with the smoked-looking wood slats and black iron hardware. "You'll think I'm drunk."

He grinned. "A little tiddly, maybe."

"Tiddly. Haven't heard *tiddly* since my mother died." She dragged her eyes away from the door and looked at Reed.

"Our bees killed Pastori and his dog, Reed. Some of them got into the house and almost killed his wife. But they say she'll be okay. I saw the dog and the man in the backyard, afterwards. The dog looked like a big oven roast. The man... didn't look like anything I've ever seen or imagined ... or ... "

"Myra!"

She glared at him. "Don't *Myra* me, Reed. Don't soothe me, humor me, or try to figure out what's best for me. *Listen* to me. Imagine I'm CEO of GE, and *listen* to me."

"Listen to you say what, Myra?"

"That I'm terrified of what I think *really* happened tonight," she said, then told him.

Seven miles away on the outskirts of Oban, Barbara Potter had also seen Robert Ludens on the late news.

She rayed off the TV and sat with her feet up on a hassock, staring at the blank screen.

The report had been live; the Ludenses must still be awake, and it was only ten-thirty. Not ridiculously late to call, even in the exurbs.

She looked in her phone book, dialed, and got a busy signal. She tried again a few times, then gave up. She was only calling to offer poor, pink Myra Ludens a few words of sympathy and support anyway.

Sympathy is the word between shit and syphilis in the dictionary, her ex used to say.

A real cutie, he'd been.

She tried one last time, then put the phone back in its wall cradle and looked across the kitchen at the cabinet where the jar of honey had been. Honey . . . bees . . . death . . . and that basement.

She'd finished the honey weeks ago; just as well, because if there'd been any left now, she'd have thrown it away.

CHAPTER 9

Renny Jarvis barely looked at Larry Lambert's dreadful little room, giving Reed the impression he'd seen others like it.

"I'm signing the committal with Dr. Lerner," Renny told Larry. "Do you understand what that means, Mr. Lambert?"

Larry gave a short nod that brought a lock of dark, oily-looking hair down on his forehead.

"Once the judge issues the order, it will happen fast," Renny said. "This afternoon . . ."

"What if I don't let them in?" Larry asked slyly, looking up without raising his head.

"Then they'll break the door down, and you'll have to pay for a new one."

Larry looked down again.

"There'll be two orderlies and a bailiff. The bailiff is an officer of the court, Mr. Lambert. Interfering with him is a crime. He will be armed. Do you understand?"

Larry gave another nod and muttered something.

"What?" Reed asked, bending closer to him. Larry's eyes shifted from Renny to him. "Will I ever see her again?"

"Of course. They have visiting hours like any other hospital."

"Where'll she be?"

The big question. Reed looked at Renny, who stared at the wall over the blank TV.

They'd been here over an hour, while Renny had gone over her. Pinched her skin, looked at her nails, encrusted with dirt that made Reed queasy, but didn't seem to faze Renny. He had looked into her eyes, prying up the lids, opened her mouth, and sniffed at her breath. The examination seemed to go on for a slice of eternity; then it ended, and Reed and Renny had gone down the narrow hall to Larry's room.

Now Reed would hear the results of the poking, prodding, and smelling, and Renny's reading of the tests and Reed's notes: the final diagnosis, and he had to force himself to exhale.

Renny said, "Housatonic Valley, Mr. Lambert."

The Warehouse.

"It's an excellent facility," Renny went on. "About forty minutes from here. I'll leave the number, they'll give you directions to get there, and let you know when you can see her. Probably not for the first day or two, though. To give her a chance to get settled."

Renny's voice was extremely gentle, and just before they left the room he put his hand on Larry's shoulder. "She really will be better off, Mr. Lambert. So will you in the long run."

Larry looked at his hands, clasped between his thighs, and didn't say anything. The men said good-bye to him and left the room.

As they passed the kitchen, Reed turned to go in, to say something to her, touch her. He wasn't sure what. But Renny grasped his arm firmly. "What's the point, Reed?"

There was none, and they passed the kitchen and left the house.

The exterior of the county court in Oban was typical postcard New England: a frame building, with imposing wood doors and many-paned, double-hung white-framed windows.

Also typically, Reed thought, it was filthy inside: the carpet was worn, pilled, and stuck with leaves that must have been tracked in last fall.

Judge Wild's office was on the second floor; the steps were granite that looked like they had not been washed or polished in a decade; the dirty ivory enamel on the radiators was peeling.

Wild's desk was dirty brown wood of some kind, the window behind it grimy. The chair the judge sat in was black leather that had faded to brown, with beige streaks where the leather had cracked.

The judge had a doughy face, with dark-lashed blue eyes and ancient acne scars. His head bent over the papers Reed had presented to him, showing a ragged part in his gray-brown hair; dandruff speckled the shoulders of his musty-looking blue jacket.

He raised his head and looked at Renny. "Housatonic Valley?"

"I'm afraid so."

The sharp blue eyes went to Reed. "You look about to shit in your pants, boy." Wild was only about ten years older than Reed, and Reed resented the *boy*, but he spoke equably. "That's about how I feel."

The judge smiled; the room lit up as if a Kleig light had gone on, and the ugly man became handsome. He said, "That's how you should feel, Doctor. Only don't beat yourself up too much. It's not your fault the lady's bonkers."

"I should've been able to do something. . . . " The words that had haunted Reed for weeks, that he'd been unable to say to Renny, his colleague and friend, or even to Riva, Arlen, or any of the others. But four minutes in this office, and out they'd come. Something decent about Hector Wild, Reed thought, decent with a capital D.

"You *are* doing something," Wild said quietly. "You are sending her someplace where she's got a chance of getting help." He looked from Reed to Renny. "The family knew they had the right to representation, and a full court hearing."

Renny looked at Reed, who said truthfully, "I told the son some time ago. Either he didn't believe me or wasn't interested . . . or . . . wasn't sure what I was talking about."

"But he was informed?"

Reed nodded, and Hector Wild signed the order committing Belle Lambert to Housatonic Valley.

* * *

The maître d' showed Reed and Renny to a table overlooking the golf course. It was another sunny day; people in brightly colored shirts and pastel trousers or skirts walked across grass as smooth and green as felt. Carts made into tiny toys by distance rolled across flats and gentle rises.

They were in the grill room of the Fallsbridge Country Club. The walls were paneled; the tables were heavy octagons of lacquered wood, with round-backed armchairs on casters.

Renny Jarvis looked out through the wall of glass, then around the room, carpeted in green a few shades darker than the perfect lawn beyond the terrace.

"The Fallsbridge Country Club," he said with mock reverence. "Always wanted to see it."

"Mmmmmmmm. Wait till you taste the food."

"Good? Bad? Indifferent?"

"Slightly less foul than the crap in the staff cafeteria." Reed meant at Fallsbridge General, and Renny winced.

"Except for the hooch," Reed said. "They've got a fabulous cellar, and it's the only place north of New York that serves Delamain cognac."

Reed closed his menu. "I advise the club sandwich, or maybe a minute steak if you're feeling lucky. On no account have crab anything."

"Oh?"

"Everyone gets sick on it."

"Not to be obvious, but maybe they should stop serving it."

Reed pulled his mouth down and lowered his voice an octave. "What, my dear . . . and not have crabs?"

They laughed a little; a waiter in black pants, white shirt, and red bow tie came to the table. Renny ordered a Bloody Mary, Reed the Delamain, and both ordered club sandwiches.

The men were quiet. Reed let guilt and sorrow for Belle Lambert sweep him for a moment; then he took a deep sip of the Delamain, which was so smooth it was almost sweet. "When'll she be there?" he asked.

"I take it you mean Mrs. Lambert."

Reed did not think he'd ever heard her called Mrs. Lambert.

"You take it right," he said.

"This afternoon sometime. I'll give you the same advice I gave her son. Let them get her settled."

Silence again, while they sipped their drinks. The sandwiches came; Reed took the toothpicks out of his, but didn't eat.

Renny devoured one quarter of his in two bites and wiped mayonnaise from the corners of his mouth with the club's big damask napkin. If only the food were as good as the linen, Reed thought.

Renny took a deep sip of the Bloody Mary, ate a handful of potato chips, and picked up the next quarter of the sandwich. Suddenly Reed asked, "Could you be wrong about her, Ren?"

Renny Jarvis put the quarter back on his plate as if the question ruined his appetite. "I can be wrong about anything, Reed. But I wouldn't put money on it this time."

"What'll happen to her?"

"Probably exactly what you think."

That meant *nothing*, now and for the rest of her life. Nothing.

Reed made himself take a bite of the sandwich, but the mayonnaise had the consistency of machine oil, the turkey of cotton. He put the sandwich down and took another swig of Delamain. "I've got one more problem, Ren."

"Great. That's just great."

Reed grinned. "Not like today."

"Mucho gratitudinous, buddy."

"Today wasn't as bad as I thought it'd be," Reed said truthfully.

"I have indeed seen worse. What's the other problem?"

"Something that happened to a woman I've known a long time." The waiter poured more Delamain, Renny finished his Bloody Mary, and Reed launched into the tale of Myra and her basement, the hallucination, and the rite they'd performed to bust the ghost that wasn't there. Renny listened with total, rapt, nonjudgmental attention, and Reed found himself thinking you could say anything to this man, that he'd have listened with the same faintly sympathetic dispassion to Jeffrey Dahmer.

Reed finished, feeling drained, and thought a lot of time must have passed, but it was still lunch hour and the grill room was full of men and women eating between golf and tennis games. Reed never played either. He had joined the club because the other seven belonged, and it was a good place for them all to meet with their spouses. Not many restaurants could seat sixteen with no advance notice. And they were used to the food. Reed had actually gotten to like a dish they called cauliflower gribiche.

"What do you think?" he asked after a moment of silence.

Renny stared through the wall of glass at the tenth green. "I think I need more information about this friend of yours to think anything."

"Like what?"

"Like . . . were there any symptoms or anything leading up to this . . . some triggering event?"

"Not that I know of, and I would know."

"Any indication of metabolic brain dysfunction."

"None."

The waiter cleared the table; they both ordered coffee, and Renny switched to Delamain. He took a deep swallow when it came, and put the glass carefully on the cocktail napkin. "Keee-rist, that's good."

"The hallucination was the only 'symptom,'" Reed said. "And along with what I guess you'd call profound shyness. But she's had that all her life."

Renny's look sharpened. "You've known her . . ."

"Since kindergarten."

"Friends? lovers?"

"Friends, for God's sake. Best friends. It happens."

"Sure. But that means you're the last shrink on the planet who should be trying to diagnose—"

"I'm the only shrink on the planet she'll talk to, Renny. So help me."

"If I can," Renny said after a moment. "Okay, no metabolic problem . . . no thyroid . . ."

"She's a little overweight, but has been for years."

"Schizo—"

"Definitely not."

"She taking any drugs?"

"She is a labile hypertensive on hydrochlorothiazide and aspirin."

"How much aspirin?"

Reed shook his head. "I thought of that. It's baby aspirin, once a day."

"And she's never had anything like this happen to her?"

"Never."

Renny sipped coffee and Delamain alternately, then held up the cognac glass. "What's this ambrosia run a bottle?"

"Hundred, maybe . . . "

"Shee-it . . . "

More silence. It was two; the grill room was emptying out. More figures appeared on the golf course.

At last, Renny said, "It could be an idiosyncratic response to panic. Does she leave the house?"

"Yes. She's not hysterical or phobic. In fact, in spite of the timorousness I mentioned, she's very, very bright, and I've always thought she was pretty . . . solid. That's why I went along with the rite. I thought . . . I thought . . . I don't know what I thought."

Renny smiled. "You thought she had a self-limited problem that'd be solved when you busted the ghost."

"Yes."

"And now you're wondering if that didn't make it worse."

"Exactly. And I—"

Renny held up his hand, and Reed shut up. They'd always had a good relationship, with Renny as the mentor. He was smarter than Reed, a better shrink. Not that Reed was bad; he knew he was not. But Renwick Jarvis was a virtuoso, Itzhak Perelman to Reed's first violin, and Reed waited on his opinion.

Renny said, "Okay, Reed. You humored her and shouldn't have. You let your affection for her get the better of your good sense. . . . "

"I didn't mean—"

"Of course not, you meant to make her better, and you thought that meant doing what she wanted you to. Like an indulgent parent. Dumb, sure. But we've all done it. Done is done, though, and I'd just let it go for now. Not mention it; try to get her off the subject when she does. Sometimes behavior is the best medicine. . . . 'Use can almost change the stamp of nature' and all that shit."

"But now there's more," Reed said, and told Renny about the death of Antonin Pastori and his dog last night. It was a hideous story, and Renny shivered and motioned the waiter to bring more brandy. He was quiet for a moment after Reed finished, then asked, "What's that list of horrors got to do with the ghost in the basement?"

"She says *it* did it."

"Did what?"

"Something to the bees to turn them into killers. She said the rite didn't get rid of *it* . . . it brought it out, gave it focus. A purpose."

"What kind of purpose."

Reed shrugged. "To avenge Myra, I guess."

Long, long silence this time. The grill room was almost empty; the waiter had presented the bill for Reed to sign and was now leaning against the bar waiting for them to leave so he could set up for dinner.

Then Renny said the last thing Reed expected him to, and on later reflection, he decided Renny must have been drunk.

"I'd say it was crap on a cracker, Reed. But what *did* happen to those bees?"

"Okay, heave!" said Harry Sherms. The other orderly, Tom Nesbitt, grabbed Belle Lambert's big, soft arms as gently as possible and heaved when Harry told him to. They got her forward in the chair; the smell of excrement rose in a wave, and they looked at each other. Harry grinned weakly. "What'd I tell you? These are so bad they're funny."

He was referring to ICs in general: involuntary committals.

Another heave got her to the edge of the chair, ready to fall to the floor but balanced so she wouldn't. Harry held her while Tom got on his rubber gloves and plastic apron; then Tom held her while Harry did the same. The bailiff, Jessica Shannon, stood to the side, with her fingers tucked into her belt, from which hung her radio, a club, a flashlight, and a nine-millimeter snapped in its holster.

The man of the house—the son, Lawrence Lambert—stood next to the sink, watching teary-eyed. Jessica gave him a glance, then turned her attention to the men heaving the mound of flesh off the chair and, hopefully, onto the collapsed stretcher on the floor.

Jessica hoped she wouldn't have to help as she'd had to on other occasions and been pissed, defecated, and thrown up on.

They seemed to have it in hand now. The mound teetered on the edge of the chair; they eased her a millimeter at a time toward the waiting expanse of plasticized canvas; Jessica and Larry Lambert watched breathlessly as the two men, each weighing over two hundred pounds, maneuvered the silent, limp woman weighing even more into a controlled flop.

They did it, she landed right, and a moment later, Harry Sherms was working the hydraulic mechanism. The stretcher rose on its insectile legs; they started wheeling her toward the kitchen door, and Jessica stood aside to let them through. As the stretcher-gurney rolled past her, the woman's eyes met hers, and into them came a look of such rage and malice, Jessica felt her innards cringe. Then the gurney was past Jessica and in the foyer heading for the door.

Jessica raced after it for another look, but the woman's face was slack again, mouth loose, eyes blank and unseeing.

"Sergeant Lemon?" Reed said from the doorway.

"Sure . . . sure . . . come in."

Reed entered an office smaller than Judge Wild's, with a gray metal desk and gray file. A window let in a bar of sun that hit Reed in the eyes, and he raised his hand to shade his face.

"Sorry." Lemon pulled down a crumbling, yellowish shade, and the office dimmed. Reed came up to the desk.

"We met last night. . . . "

"I remember." Lemon gestured at a metal chair padded in gray plastic, and Reed sat. On the desk was one of those plastic cubes displaying photos of a girl and boy in their early teens, and a round-faced woman with thick, dark wavy hair, blue eyes, and a couple of extra chins.

"That the boy did the bed-wetting?" Reed asked.

"Yup. Girl never had the problem."

"Girls usually don't. That was our first clue that enuresis might be physiological."

"Ah . . . " A pause, then Lemon asked, "What can I do for you, Doc?"

"Do you know any more about what happened last night?"

"Some. But you'll have to give me a reason to tell you."

"Pardon?"

"A reason . . . you know . . . " Lemon was sending him some kind of message.

But he'd had three brandies at lunch, the day was in its 3:00 P.M. doldrums, and his mind wouldn't work.

Patiently, Lemon said, "A reason. Like you're the Ludenses' physician and information will help them deal with the shock. A reason that justifies giving information to a civilian."

"Oh."

Lemon smiled. "Gotta cover my ass with the brass."

"Oh."

"So what do you need to know to help your . . . patients."

"What the entomologist said."

"He said they were plain old honeybees." Lemon consulted a sheet of paper lying on his desk. "*Apis mellifera*, the bees that pollinate my squash vines, and yours if you grow any."

"Not the killer bees . . . "

"No. The bug man, name of Monro, said killer bees are a variety of African bees that contaminate the gentler European strain. Sounds kind'a racist, don't it. Anyway, these were just plain honky bees."

"Then what happened to them?"

"That's the question."

"And why didn't they sting the Ludenses?"

Why did they kill Pastori and the dog and not sting me or Bob? Myra had asked.

"That's one I *can* answer," Lemon said. "At least Monro can. He said the bees' stings are barbed and stick into whatever they've stung, then pull out, taking the bees' abdominal parts with them. Naturally, the bees that stung the man and dog died." Lemon ran his fingers through his light brown hair, which had thinned in a deep widow's peak. "Nature is truly repulsive, isn't it?"

That sure was, Reed thought, imagining the bee's horror (assuming a bee could feel horror) when it realized it had left the bottom half of itself in whatever it had stung.

What nature had done to Belle Lambert was almost as repulsive.

"Leave her alone a day or two," Renny had told him. "Let them get her settled." He assured Reed most of the staff at Housatonic was good. Oh, they had their quota of living dead, like any state facility. The ones who'd gotten pushed off welfare and weren't literate enough for the DMV, and/or were too inert to flip burgers at McDonald's. The bottom feeders, Bob Kelner at Yale had dubbed them. Renny would never refer to people that way; Reed hoped he wouldn't either.

"Doc?" Lemon said.

"Yes, Sergeant, nature can be repulsive. What about the other bees?"

"What other bees?"

"The ones that didn't sting Pastori or the dog and were still alive when the Ludenses crossed the road. Mrs. Ludens said there were hundreds of them."

"Maybe thousands," Lemon said. "The bug man said it turned chilly last night. Chilly enough to make the bees logy after they'd been out for a while. He also said that whatever triggered the frenzy . . . some bee hormone rush, maybe . . . would have dissipated by the time the Ludenses got there."

Bee hormone rush?

That sounded as ludicrous as anything he had ever heard, but that didn't mean it wasn't true. At least it was an answer to Myra's *Why did they kill Pastori and the dog and not sting me or Bob?* If he could get out *bee hormone rush* with a straight face.

CHAPTER 10

Reed saw plumes of black smoke across the Ludenses' meadow. He climbed out of the car and shaded his eyes with his hand. The hives were burning, sending two rigid-looking columns of black smoke into the cloudless sky.

Bob must be incinerating his bees: the queen, workers, drones, and the eggs and larvae they tended. Reed felt a sudden, stupid, pang of grief for the poor dumb beings, victims of biochemistry gone awry; *bee hormone rush.*

He trudged up the path to the back door, rang, and Myra let him in. She confirmed the bees were gone.

"He poisoned them first with some kind of spray," she said, "then poured gas on the hives and lit it up." Her eyes were teary. "He feels awful, Reed, but he didn't know what else to do . . . and he had to do something."

Reed sat down at the table to tell her what he'd just learned from Lemon and maybe ease her mind a little about what happened last night.

Then she said, "Can I fix you a cup of tea?" And he came as close as he ever had to losing his temper with her. "For Christ's sake, Myra, I do not want tea or cookies or a nice glass of lemonade."

He was instantly contrite, expected that searing look of hurt in her eyes that some women got when you turned on them. But as usual, Myra Fox Ludens surprised him. "Okay, no tea," she said evenly and returned to the table, where her cup was steaming.

"I'm sorry, My."

"Don't be." She smiled. "I've been offering people tea like a character on *Masterpiece Theater*. Offered it to the Pastoris' son and daughter this morning, and they didn't want any either."

"What *did* they want?"

"Only to find out what had happened to their folks. They didn't know anything about . . . you know . . . the trouble between me and their father."

"I see. . . . " he said, and his beeper went off. He went to the wall phone and dialed his service, which answered before the first ring stopped.

"Doctor Lerner—thank heaven. A Mrs. Withers called, sounding very upset. I could barely make out what she said."

He slammed the phone down and turned to Myra.

"Angie called. Barely able to talk, the service said."

They both knew what that probably meant, and Myra grabbed her purse. "I'll go with you." He started to tell her no, then realized he wanted her with him. Angie would want to see her, plus Myra would stand with him if he had to face Bill Withers.

Angie's house sat on a rise about three acres from the road. It had a gate and gate house, which had been built in the days when Angie's family, the Brookses, had balls and a gatekeeper to check invitations.

Now there was a handsome bell pull that set off chimes up at the house . . . and a very sophisticated alarm system that was silent. But the gates were open, and Reed drove through and up the long driveway.

He stopped at the front door; Myra jumped out and ran up the stairs without waiting for him.

She rang; Reed came up behind her.

"We should've called the police," she said. "We could now . . . with your car phone."

"Let's see what's happened first."

She rang again. No one answered.

"Bet the new housekeeper's left already," Myra said. Angie had a hard time keeping help because of Bill.

Myra rang again, then turned the knob. "Reed, it's unlocked."

She opened it, and he eased past her into the interior of the house.

The foyer ceiling rose three stories, with the fabled crystal chandelier a Brooks patriarch had carted from Europe around the turn of the century.

The house was big, with many surfaces of hard material—tile, marble, polished stone—and their footsteps echoed along the floor and off the walls.

"Angie . . . " Reed called. There was no answer.

Then Myra called, her higher voice shattering the house's stillness, and a sound that was half sob, half moan echoed back. They looked at each other, then rushed down the long hall, past shut sets of double doors to the room Angie's mother, Lydia Brooks, had called the morning room.

As they neared the rear of the house and the courtyard with the carriage house, now the garage, they heard heavy rhythmic thwacks, followed by the crack of wood.

Bill Withers was working off his rage, or winding down from the exertion of beating his wife, by chopping wood.

The morning room door was open; Angie was lying on Mrs. Brooks's prize Aubusson with her bare legs bent up and the phone on the floor next to her. She must have pulled it off the table by the cord.

"Wait," Myra hissed at Reed and ran into the room.

Reed stood at the door while Myra straightened Angie's legs and pulled her skirt down to cover her; then he came into the room.

Angie's eyes rolled up and looked at him. All the veins in the whites appeared broken, making her tears look bloody. There was a gash on her cheek where it must have hit the brass andiron when she fell, since it also had blood on it. Worst of all, one of Angie's eyes looked sunken and off kilter as if Withers had broken the eye socket . . . and that could be lethal.

Reed forgot the rest and grabbed the phone. He ripped the receiver off the cradle, and yelled at Myra, "Don't touch her, My."

On her knees, Myra slid back a few feet; Angie's pallor was deepening. "Get a blanket," Reed shouted at Myra. Angie could be concussed and going into shock or the broken eye socket (if that's what it was) could be the external sign of a fractured skull. This time the prick—the lousy, rotten son of a bitch prick still driving his ax up and down in the courtyard—this time he could have killed her.

Reed punched 911; a woman answered "Emergency . . . please state—"

"This is Dr. Reed Lerner. I want an ambulance and paramedics to Ninety-two Belden Road, Upper Fallsbridge. I want them prepared to stabilize a possible skull fracture. Victim is going into shock and I'm going to hang up. You have the address?"

"Yes, sir," the woman said smartly. At least English was her primary language, Reed thought. He'd once called 911 in his New Haven days and gotten a man fluent only in Hindi.

He put the phone down and ran back down the echoing hall, out the front door to the Porsche. Stupid, unthinking, and half hung over from the brandy at lunch, he'd left his bag in the car. He pushed down the rubber-tipped brass door stop to keep the huge door from swinging shut and raced to the car for the bag.

Whack went the ax as he returned to the back of the house; *crack* went the log Withers split.

Myra had come back with blankets and was gently folding them over Angie, one after the other. Reed ripped open the bag and took out his pre-filled syringe of epinephrine. He'd never used it in all his years of practice, but would never think of leaving the house without it.

He held the syringe and looked carefully at Angie. Her skin was moist and grayish . . . like Belle Lambert's. The marble mantel clock bonged four. Belle was at the gates of the asylum by now . . . or inside them . . . her time in the outside world over. From now on her view of the sky would be laced by mesh inside the heavy-paned windows of Housatonic Valley.

Angie's skin was cool, dropping toward cold. Her pulse was thready; her eyes looked at him, at Myra, at the ceiling. Roving too much, but still seeing, he thought, because when she looked at Myra, she smiled, and Myra smiled back and took her hand.

"Your hand's cold," Myra said, chafing it in both of hers.

Angie moved her lips, which looked dry and cracked, as if she hadn't had water in a week. "Cold hands, warm heart," she said in a ghastly whisper.

Reed doubted she could have a skull fracture and respond like that. But her skin was too cold. There was blood caked in her lovely red-gold hair; more blood ran down her forehead. "Better safe than sorry," he mumbled. He pushed up the sleeve of her oxford-cloth blouse, pinched the flesh of her upper arm hard, and drove in the needle.

"Ooooowwww . . . " she cried, but not very loudly.

Thwack-crack came through the window open to the courtyard. *Thwack-crack*. Then in the distance, he heard a siren, and he and Myra looked at each other, then back at Angie. Her eyes were a little wild, her lashes were stuck together with tears . . . and Reed saw more blood oozing from a smaller cut on her temple.

Thwack-crack. Bill Withers split another log.

"You didn't call the police!" Angie croaked.

The epinephrine was doing its job; her color was better and her skin was losing that cavelike cold.

"No police," he said.

"Good . . . "

Her eyes closed; the off-kilter eye looked even more sunken. She could be dying, and Reed wouldn't know what to do. He had an M.D. from Yale, a Ph.D. in psychology from Johns Hopkins, and all he could do was shoot epinephrine into her. Maybe that was all anyone could do.

Maybe this was, as his mother would have said, in the hands of God.

Myra was on her knees next to Angie, holding her hand. Myra's nails were unpolished and cut (or bitten) almost to the quick. Her skin looked rough as a scrubwoman's, but her hair, which fell in a thick curtain as she bent over Angie, was the color of some extravagantly sweet heirloom corn—Kandy Korn, they'd call it, or Golden Queen. She rocked a little as if lulling a baby.

"I don't think so," said the paramedic as he applied a pressure bandage with exquisite skill. "Looks like edematous flesh, not deflected bone. . . . "

Referring to Angie's eye socket. "I think she's just gonna have the mother of all shiners."

Again, Reed thought.

The paramedic, who was big, red-faced, and blond, gave her a shot, and she lay deathly still as he and a much smaller man got her onto the stretcher-gurney, the same sort of device that must have been used to move Belle Lambert.

It was almost four; in an hour or so, Belle would have her first meal in her new home. Something soft, fed to her with a plastic spoon, Reed thought with an inner shiver.

As they raced Angie out into the hall, the big blond who'd given her the shot raised his head. "What's that noise?"

"Someone chopping wood," Reed said.

"Helluva time for it."

"Helluva time," Reed agreed.

Helluva time, Reed thought. Beat up your wife, maybe crack her skull—maybe kill her—then go out back and chop wood. He must confront Withers, must somehow get up the balls to face the son of a bitch. But first they had to find Billy in the big rambling house and tell him where his mother was.

He'd be home from school by now, probably with Peg, the nanny.

Myra went upstairs to look for them; Reed searched downstairs. The sitting rooms and dining room were empty. So was the guest washroom. Back here the *thwack-crack* of wood splitting was very loud. It was a mad thing for Withers to do, and Reed wondered as he had many times at the psychic quirk behind it.

He went through the butler's pantry to the large, echoing, mostly stainless-steel kitchen and found a skinny woman huddled at the kitchen table.

The new housekeeper Myra had mentioned.

She jumped up when she saw Reed and backed away until she was pressed against the counter.

"It's okay . . . everything's okay," he said stupidly. *Thwack-crack* went Withers's ax in the background.

"Nothing you can do here," Reed told her. "Why don't you take the rest of the day off."

She jerked her head like a marionette on a string and repeated, "Day off."

"Someone will call you later about when to come back," he said. "Unless you live here?"

Some of them still had live-in servants. But not the Lerners. Riva came from a family of Upper West Side, Eastern European socialists, and after they were married and living in the big house, she'd told Reed that live-in help was as alien to her as suttee. After his father died and his mother moved to Palm Beach, Riva let the live-ins go with generous severance or pensions, and they'd made do with dailies. It was much easier now that the boys were away at school.

The woman told him she went home nights, to Oban.

He left her pulling on a colorless raincoat and made his way back through the pantry to the back stairs. The woman must have gone out a side door, and he heard her car start up and pull away, then nothing but the *thwack-crack* of the axe.

There didn't seem to be anyone else on the first floor, and he climbed the stairs to a long narrow hall with a strip of carpet, and doors lining it. He opened one and saw an unfurnished, moderate-sized room with a small, neat bathroom.

This section of Brooks House, which he'd never been in before, must have been the servants' wing in the old days.

He went down the hall toward the front of the house, along a gallery with a rail overlooking the entry hall and that incredible chandelier, and heard voices across the way.

Myra and another woman he supposed was the nanny, but not Billy.

The kid was there though, sitting on the bed, back to the wall and knees drawn up with his chin resting on them while the women packed a small suitcase for him.

He leaped off the bed in a tangle of scrawny arms and legs when he saw Reed, raced across the room, and threw himself at him. Reed was a huge man and withstood the onslaught. He picked the boy up, and Billy wrapped his legs around Reed's middle and buried his face in Reed's neck, sobbing. Reed hugged him until the boy wriggled to be let down, then Reed set him on his feet and stood back.

Billy Withers was a long, scrawny eight-year-old with knobby knees and elbows, ears like pitcher handles, and a thatch of thick, straight, straw-colored hair. He'd have been a homely kid, except for huge, thick-lashed eyes, the exact blue-green of his mother's. His disposition was as lovely as his eyes, with just enough deviltry to keep him from being a nerdy little pain in the ass.

Pain in the ass was a good place to start what was bound to be a miserable conversation, Reed thought. He crouched down, eye level with the kid, and said, "How's this for a humongous pain in the ass."

"Humongous," the kid wiped the tears off his face.

"I think she'll be all right," Reed said, referring to Angie, and the boy nodded and looked immensely relieved.

They couldn't leave him here with just Nanny Peg between him and the madman chopping wood in the rear court. "Want to come home with me or go to Aunt Helen's?" Reed asked. A man had been stung to death across the road from Myra's and the cops, and/or the press would be back. Don and Irene had never cared much for kids, and Joan Folger was at Lambie's. Almost as bad as leaving Billy here.

Reed missed his boys, hoped the kid would pick his house. Riva would also love having him. But Billy worshipped Helen's son Lenny.

"Lenny home?" Billy asked.

Reed nodded. "Spring break."

"Will Aunt Rivie be sad if I go to Lenny's?"

"Yup. But she'll get over it if you and Lenny come for dinner."

"Can Peg come?"

Reed looked up at her folding little-boy Jockey shorts across the room. She nodded approval at the arrangement, and he said, "Sure she can."

"Aunt Helen's please," said the kid, then shot a fast, round-eyed look of hate and fear at the window through which still came the sound of splitting wood. "Does *he* know?"

Reed took a deep breath and said, "I'm going to tell him."

Reed found the phone downstairs to call Helen, then heard the mantel clock in the morning room bong half past. They'd had time to evaluate Angie by now, and he called Fallsbridge General instead.

"Your wife does not have a fractured skull," Reed told Bill Withers.

Withers had stacked the split wood neatly; unsplit logs waited against the wall of the carriage house. He must have wood delivered by the cord for his post–wife-beating exertions, Reed thought.

Withers swung the ax down, rested the head on the ground, and draped one arm across the end of the handle. He was bare-chested, his yellow chest hair shimmered in the sun, and his skin was slick from the sweat of his exertions.

He was probably the best-looking man Reed had ever seen, with the kind of perfect, aquiline blondness that would have looked stupendous in an SS uniform.

"A fractured skull?" Withers asked.

"That's right, Bill. She doesn't have one."

Withers laughed; Reed felt his hands bunch into fists.

"Didn't know that was a possibility," Withers said. "It's like hearing your kid walked away from the wreck, when you thought he was safe in bed. . . ."

Withers's eyes were red-rimmed, his skin, slick and greenish. He was on the verge of a hangover, a doozy, Reed hoped. With pounding head, the taste of tidal mud in his mouth, and loose, jittery, griping bowels.

"Surely you must have noticed she hit her head when you knocked her down." Reed's throat was tight, talking hurt.

"Now that you mention . . . it . . . " Withers's gorgeous gray eyes glittered with malice.

"Reed . . . " Myra stood in the open French doors from the morning room.

"We're ready." She stepped out on the terrace.

Withers picked up the ax and balanced a new log carefully on his splitting stump. "Hey there, My. Long time no see and all that shit. . . . " He raised the ax, hit the log dead center. It split in a shower of splinters and Reed jumped a foot.

"Now, now," Withers mocked, and Reed felt himself flush.

"Billy's ready." Myra looked from Reed to Withers.

"Ready for what?" Withers said easily.

"To go to Helen's. Peg's going with us. Then, I imagine we'll stop at the hospital."

"Hospital!" Withers finally sounded jarred. It must have just gotten through that he'd put his wife in the hospital, and her friends were taking his son away.

"That's right," Myra said, with amazing equanimity. "We'll call when we know how she is."

"He said . . . she's okay."

"No." Myra's eyes narrowed. "He said she didn't have a fractured skull. That's hardly the same thing." Withers and Myra stared at each other; Withers looked away first.

"So you called the paramedics . . . "

"Of course."

"And the cops . . . "

"We didn't; the paramedics said they should, and may have by now."

Withers's eyes fixed on Myra again, not a nice look. "You better hope not," he said softly. "Because if the cops or you . . . or anyone . . . tries to interfere . . . " He raised the ax again, blade dazzling in the sun, and brought it down whistling. Reed flinched, but Myra didn't move. The new Clint Eastwood, he thought, smothering a crazy snicker.

The ax hit the stump and lodged in it; Withers yanked it free and grinned at Myra, drawing his perfectly formed lips back from his perfect teeth. "You take my meaning, My?"

He meant he'd kill Angie, or Myra if she were handy, or any of them he could get his hands on.

"Perfectly," Myra said without a quaver. "But it's a position I'd rethink if I were you. If there's still time."

It was an extraordinary thing for her to say. They all knew it.

Withers tried to hold on to his macho cool, but the words rocked him visibly, in spite of their oddness.

Reed took Myra's arm. "C'mon, killer, time to go...."

Reed wanted to ask her what she'd meant, and why she'd added the "If there's still time." But Billy begged to ride in the Porsche, leaving Peg and Myra to the Range Rover, and he didn't get a chance.

CHAPTER 11

"She's still a little rocky on her pins," the resident told Myra. "I'm going to admit her for the night."

"But I thought . . . "

"It's just a precaution." The resident's name tag read Jonathan Shaw, M.D.

"He's right," Reed said. "Better to be sure."

"I've got a CAT scan scheduled for six, Mrs. Ludens. If it's okay, we'll let her go first thing in the morning. Believe me, we don't keep anyone ten minutes longer than we have to."

He and Reed left, presumably to see to the admission of Angie, who was still in the emergency room, and Myra found herself alone in a lounge with some vending machines and a TV playing without sound. The news was on, and she tried to turn up the volume to see if there was more about Pastori's death. But the controls on the console were disconnected, and the remote was missing.

She went to the vending machine and saw a Milky Way, her favorite. But she didn't have change, and the change maker had an Out of Order sign taped to it.

She'd had Dave in this hospital; her mother had died here five days after a massive coronary. (Her father had been killed in his Chevy Caprice—a good plain Quaker car—on I-84 many years ago.) Myra still volunteered here once a week, manning the register in the gift shop with Lambie and Angie; Reed was on staff here.

It was *their* hospital; their families had left it millions through the years. But the change machine was caput, and someone had ripped off the TV remote.

At loose ends, she wandered into the main lobby, then thought of Mrs. Pastori, who must be here recovering from the stings.

She might be glad for a visitor, and might also know something, have seen something that would squash the monstrous notion that had formed in Myra's mind, that had nothing to do with the bee hormones Reed had mumbled about a few minutes ago.

She went to the information desk and asked for Mrs. Pastori's room number. The woman behind the desk was Dorothy Higgins, whom Myra knew from volunteering here and at other nearby hospitals.

"First name?" Dorothy asked.

"I don't know. We're not friends. I live across the road from her and thought there might be something I could do . . . about the house or some-thing. You know."

"Nice of you." Dorothy beamed at her, and Myra blushed at the lie she'd told.

"Well, Pastori's hardly a common name." Dorothy said, "We'll find her."

She typed in the name on a console, then looked at the computer screen. "She's in three twenty, Myra. Third floor this wing. Her name's Ruth."

Myra left a message for Reed so he could find her and went to the elevators. Dorothy called after her,

"Be sure to stop at the nursing station before you go into the room."

At the third-floor nursing station, she was issued a pink card with a 3 on it, indicating there were already two visitors in 320.

She thanked the woman behind the desk, who had on what looked like blue cotton fatigues, and went down the hall to the room.

Last night she'd told Pastori he'd be sorry . . . today she'd told Bill to rethink that position. If there was still time. Time for what? And why had she spoken those half-threatening words when she had no idea the men were in danger?

That dreadful notion slid back into her mind. She pushed it away as best she could and went on down the chilly, tiled hall to 320.

Half of Ruth Pastori's face was bandaged; the exposed half was red and swollen and dotted with scabs where they must have removed stingers. Myra wondered how bad the other, covered portion was.

The Pastori children were there. The son, a nice-looking man about Dave's age, offered her the chair he'd been sitting in. She started to decline, then realized that the muscles in her legs were jumping from strain and would probably cramp if she didn't take her weight off them. She thanked him and sank gratefully into the molded plastic chair.

Ruth Pastori's visible eye was closed.

"She's napping," Myra whispered, ready to rise again and leave. But the son said, "She was awake a second ago. I know she won't want to miss your visit."

He leaned over to say something to his mother, but before he could, the lid that was swollen and crusted opened. Ruth Pastori's bloodshot brown eye rolled past her son and fixed on Myra. Myra, not knowing what sort of expression she should have on her face, felt her mouth stretch in what she knew was a totally inane smile.

Ruth Pastori's eye widened and stared fixedly at Myra.

Myra shifted in the molded plastic chair; the young man saw the intentness of his mother's look. "Ma . . ." he said uncertainly.

Then Ruth Pastori opened one side of her mouth (the other side appeared to be bandaged shut) and shrieked, "Nooo . . ."

Myra and the girl jumped to their feet.

"Noooooo . . ." the bandaged woman screamed. "Get away . . . get her away . . ."

The young people looked at Myra in horror. She reared back, sending the chair crashing to the floor.

"Nooooo . . ." Ruth Pastori screamed, thrashing in the bed so the IV stand threatened to fall. The son backed away from his shrieking mother; a nurse wearing the same sort of blue slack outfit as the woman at the desk raced into the room.

"Mrs. Pastori . . ."

"Noooo . . ." Ruth Pastori screamed, her eye bulging, the exposed portion of her face going from red to purple. "Nooooo . . ."

The daughter grabbed Myra's hand, which was shaking so violently the girl had to capture it.

"We better go," she said, pulling Myra toward the door. Ruth Pastori's eye followed her. "Get away," she screamed. "Get away . . ."

Myra pulled her hand away from the young woman's and dashed out into the hall. She ran to the counter and leaned against it, head down, gasping for breath.

The woman Myra didn't even know had looked at her and screamed in terror; nothing like that had ever, ever happened to her before. She slumped against the counter; the woman in blue behind it watched her curiously.

"Mrs. Ludens . . ." Myra turned her head. It was the Pastori daughter, a pretty girl about twenty-five.

"I'm so sorry," the girl said.

"Oh . . . I never meant . . . I never thought. What happened? Why did she scream when she saw me?"

"Come, let's sit down," the girl said.

She led Myra to yet another lounge with a TV, one that had its remote. Stupid, stupid, stupid to even notice such things, Myra thought. But she couldn't help herself. She sat on a hard black plastic couch; the young woman sat on a chair at a right angle to it.

"She told us you'd come to the house last night," the young woman said.

"What's your name again? I've forgotten. . . . " Myra spoke in a shaking voice. She had stood up to Bill Withers and his ax without fear. But Ruth Pastori's screams had engendered such horror, she was still shaking.

"Roseanne," the young woman said. "Roseanne Silvio. As I was saying, mother told us about last night. . . . "

"It was about the dog," Myra said, half moaning. Tears ran down her cheeks; she dragged her purse into her lap and pulled tissues out of the pack she always carried. "The dog kept . . . barking."

"The dog *yapped,*" said the girl, "and it was awful. My father wouldn't listen to reason about it. We all hated the racket; we didn't come over as often as we used to because of it."

"Oh . . . " Myra wiped tears off her cheeks, and a cold, chilly sweat off her upper lip.

"Mrs. Ludens . . . "

"Oh, dear . . . I don't know what happened. Your dad and I . . . I'm so sorry. But we had . . . words, I'm afraid. . . . "

And I told him he'd be sorry. Then walked away, as calm and collected as you please. Just like today, with Bill. Rethink that position if there's still time, I told him.

Time for what? She balled up the Kleenex in her hand.

"We had words," she repeated. "Very rude ones, I'm afraid. On both our parts."

"You didn't tell us when we saw you this morning."

"I was ashamed. I mean . . . we'd had these . . . words . . . then he was dead, and I felt horrible. I *did* tell the police about the . . . quarrel."

She wanted to amend the word, tell the girl *quarrel* was too strong. But that was garbage, the quarrel had been an all-out fight. Everything but the two of them punching each other.

You'll be sorry, she'd said.

Schoolyard words. *You'll be sorry, nah-nah, nah-nah.* And he had been very, very sorry.

And now . . . *Rethink that position, Bill Withers. Do it fast.*

"Mrs. Ludens . . . "

"I'm just so . . . at sea, I don't know what happened, Roseanne. Neither did the police, even after they'd investigated . . . except . . . "

Myra gathered herself, said a silent *Thanks, Reed,* then told the girl what Lemon had told Reed, who'd told her.

"Bee hormone rush?" The girl made it a question.

"That's right," Myra said weakly, "bee hormone rush . . . "

They looked at each other and burst out laughing at the same time. They laughed for a moment; then one of the women in blue fatigues came to the door and glared at them.

The girl said, "I can't believe I did that. My dad's been dead less than a day...."

Myra looked at the wall clock over the lounge door. Twenty-two hours, she thought.

The girl stood up.

"I'm so sorry," Myra said. "But it wasn't me ... I mean I didn't have anything..."

"To do with it?" The girl looked into Myra's eyes with an expression of humor and kindliness. "Of course, you didn't, Mrs. Ludens. And I'll make sure Mother understands that, as soon as she's up to understanding anything. Of course you didn't. I mean, my God, Mrs. Ludens, how could you?"

"Bee hormone rush?" Angie asked.

"That's what the entomologist said," Myra told her.

Angie was sitting up in the hospital bed; there were stitches on her forehead and cheek and a compress bandage over her eye, probably to keep down the swelling. Some paler-than-blood-red stuff—Betadine, Myra thought—stained the split in Angie's bottom lip. Her visible eye was bloodshot, her face very pale, with dead white lines around her mouth. She still looked a thousand percent better than she had two hours ago.

"Bee hormone rush ..." Angie giggled, then grabbed her side. "It only hurts when I laugh...."

Next to her was a bouquet of exquisite, but short-lived, spring flowers, and across the room, a huge basket of fruit, candy, and jars of preserves covered in yellow cellophane, like an Easter basket. Only Easter had been over for weeks.

"The basket's from Don and Irene, the flowers are from Arlen. He brought them both himself and stayed to eat with me. Yellow ooze and brown goosh...." Angie said. "I suppose it's a good sign they fed me at all, no matter how lousy it was."

"It couldn't be *that* bad," Myra said. People complained about the food here as if other hospitals ordered out from "21".

"It was horrible." Angie started to cry. Myra got out of the chair and sat on the bed next to her, holding her hand. "Angie . . . honey, it can't be good for your eye to cry. . . . "

"But I called *Reed* to come to the house," Angie sobbed. "I never thought he'd be with you. I never meant you to see that. . . . "

"I know . . . I know . . . "

"I'd've spared you, My. You know that."

"Yes."

Angie looked past Myra, tears pooling in her visible eye. They were quiet a moment, then Angie said, "Helen called. Billy's eaten half a four-pound roast and Lenny the other half."

Myra nodded distractedly.

"And Lambie's coming by later," Angie went on. "With Evan."

"Nice."

Myra slid off the bed and went over to the basket, then back to the chair. It was time to say what she had to, but it was not easy. She sat foursquare, hands in her lap, purse on the floor, trying to look sedate, to counter the outlandish words she was about to utter.

"My?" Angie said softly.

Myra looked at her. "Angie . . . I think something's going to happen to Bill."

She enunciated each word so Angie could not mistake them. Angie stared out of the good eye and Myra's heart raced. *She's going to scream at me to get out of her sight, like Ruth Pastori,* she thought. But Angie said in a low voice, "What're you talking about, Myra?"

Myra rose again and paced to the fruit basket.

"Myra!" Angie said sharply.

Myra turned around. Angie's lip had split open again; blood oozed through the Betadine. Myra yanked a tissue out of the box on the bed table and put it gently against the spot. Angie took over and held it with her long, pale fingers. She used to get manicures, Myra remembered suddenly, but these days her nails were dull, with cuticles almost as ragged as Myra's.

Gingerly, Angie took the tissue away from her lips. She licked the spot and grimaced at the taste of the Betadine. Myra had used gallons when Dave was little and couldn't make it down the stone walk without falling over something. The *klutz,* Bob called him, a word he'd gotten from Reed.

"Is it still bleeding?" Angie asked.

Myra shook her head.

"I don't want to get it on the linen," Angie said. "They won't change the sheets again. . . . "

"Oh, for God's sake, Angela. Your mother donated two lounges and a maternity wing to this hospital . . . they'll give you a clean pillowcase."

"What about Bill?" Angie asked.

Myra did not answer.

"Myra, you can't just drop a bomb like that, then clam up."

Myra sat back on the edge of the bed.

"You already think I'm nuts, don't you?" she asked quietly.

"You mean because of the . . . uh . . . basement."

Myra nodded.

"I did, My. I guess I still do a little, but only a little because of two things. One because was when Arlen and I went to New York, we met this old guy named Landau, who was very nice . . . very . . . how can I say it . . . *together*. And not really that old. Just that he had very white hair, you know. . . . " Myra nodded. "But with this smooth, fair skin," Angie went on, "and the most amazing blue eyes I've ever seen. Like washed sapphires."

"Angie."

"Sorry, you know I get carried away. Anyway. He was the kind of man you'd ask directions of in a strange town or to protect you if someone was chasing you. A good sort of man, My. If you had an accident that wasn't your fault, you'd want him for a witness."

Myra smiled. "Believe it or not, I get the point, Angie."

"But you *don't*," Angie said with sudden ferocity. "You don't get it at all . . . because *he* believed in the ghost! Called it troublesome . . . or no . . . asked if it were. As if there could be a ghost that was troublesome or anything else. He *believed* in it, and that shook me to my core because I believed in him. Arlen did too, I think, though he'd never say so."

"And the second thing?"

"What?"

"The second thing that keeps you from thinking I should be committed?" Myra asked.

"Being down there with the smoke and smells, and that fan coming on blowing that breath out of hell. . . . " Angie stopped, her good eye on Myra. The focus must be off from having the other one covered, loss of depth perception or something, Myra thought. Then Angie said, "There *was* something down there with us . . . wasn't there?"

Myra went back to the huge basket. The fruit and candies looked trapped behind the cellophane; she felt sorry for them. She could feel sorry for anything or anyone, even Bill Withers.

She reached in her purse, took her penknife out of the zipper compartment.

"Myra . . . answer me. . . . "

She opened the smallest blade, nicked the taut cellophane, and it split all the way down.

"Myra!"

"That's right, Angie. Something's down there . . . and I think whatever it is killed the man across the road and his dog." She reached for a pear.

"What are you talking about!" Angie exploded. "Bees killed him. It was on the news . . . you said so too, *bee hormone rush*. Bob's bees went crazy and stung . . . " But Angie was no fool, she knew what Myra was implying, and after a minute of pushing out words, she stopped, then went on slowly. "You think whatever *it* is did something to the bees."

Myra nodded. She polished the fat rosy pear with a tissue and handed it to Angie.

Angie took it, her eye fixed on Myra.

"Okay, say I believe you. For the sake of argument. What do murderous bees and the whatchamacallit in the basement have to do with Bill?"

Myra sat back down and described the confrontation with Pastori last night.

"Nasty bastard," Angie said, bit into the pear, and winced. Myra hadn't eaten hospital food since she'd had Dave, almost thirty years ago, but the food *was* lousy by all accounts. Poor Angie must be hungry. Myra would bring her something from the cafeteria before she left: custard or rice pudding.

"Very nasty," she said. "But I knew he would be. I don't even know why I went over there, except that hope springs eternal, I guess. Anyway, he didn't say anything I didn't expect him to, except about my being snooty.

That caught me off guard. I'm a lot of things . . . mousy, silly . . . compulsive, I guess . . . with the conviction of my eccentricities, as Dave says. But I've never been snooty."

"No, My," Angie said gently. "You've never been snooty."

"So *that* surprised me a little. But it's what *I* said back that really shocked me, Angie. I opened my mouth to say something conciliatory, I'm sure. Just to make things a tad less murderous between us. Hoping, I guess, that maybe we could try to be at least civil someday . . . and I said, 'I think you're going to be very sorry.' "

Angie stared at her.

"Don't you see, I sounded as if I knew what was going to happen," Myra said.

"But you didn't. . . . "

"Of course not. How could I?"

"No way." Angie grinned tightly. "Bee hormone rush sounds pretty unpredictable. I still don't see what that's got to do—"

"Angie, I said the same thing to Bill this afternoon."

"You told Bill he was going to be sorry?"

"I didn't use those words. He was chopping wood . . . and he said no one better interfere with his family, then raised the ax to scare us . . . and I said, 'It's a position I'd rethink if I were you. If there's still time.' Different words, same meaning. It was a threat!"

"What did you mean by *if there's still time?*"

"I don't know. I didn't even know I was going to say it."

Angie stared at her with her one uncovered eye, then reached for the phone. Myra settled back in the chair; Angie got an outside line and dialed. Myra heard the muffled ringing; then Angie said, "Bill? I'm glad you're home . . . no . . . no . . . it's okay. They did a CAT scan, it's normal. . . . " A faint, forced chuckle. "I've got a brain." She listened, then said, "I know, I know. But they put packing on it, so maybe it won't discolor."

Angie was calmly discussing her injuries with the man who'd given them to her, and for the first time, Myra felt a touch of that disgust with her that Lambie said she'd felt for years.

"Then it's good I caught you," Angie was saying. "They gave me something, and I'm half asleep as it is. No . . . tomorrow sometime. I'll let you

know. . . . Oh, he's fine. Having a ball with Lenny, eating like a horse."
Another chuckle.

How could she? Myra thought.

Then Bill must have said he loved her, or missed her, or was desolate
about what he'd done, because Angie flushed, and stammered, "Yes . . . no
. . . me too. . . . " Then she hung up.

"He's okay, Myra."

"So I gathered."

"You don't really think. . . . "

"I don't think anything, Angie. I just told you what happened."

"Okay, okay . . . don't get annoyed."

They were silent a moment; then Angie said, "My? I do hate him sometimes. Most of the time, and I suppose I want to get rid of him."

"Suppose?"

"Suppose. Things happen between men and women. You know that.
Things that you can't explain to anyone. I *do* want to get rid of him . . . but
sometimes he's the old Bill. The man I fell in love with. And . . . oh, God,
he's still beautiful, and he's still Billy's father . . . and Myra . . . I don't want
him hurt. . . . " Angie laced her fingers nervously across her middle. "Will
you talk to him. Warn him to be careful."

Watch out for bees, Myra would tell him.

"I mean if you can without getting his back up. It's gotten super easy to
get Bill's back up. . . . " Angie was saying.

Myra remembered his reaction to her *That's a position I'd rethink if I were
you.* She'd sounded like a lawyer trying to settle out of court; yet the
strange, oblique, stilted warning . . . if warning it had been . . . had scared
him. She thought he'd listen to her if she could figure out what to say.

"Pop . . . " Dick Lambert shrieked from the door of the empty kitchen.
"Pop . . . "

It was getting dark; he turned on the light and saw someone had been
cleaning in here; the dishes were washed, the table clear . . . and her chair
was gone. Probably too rank to even try to salvage.

"Popppp . . . "

He raced down the narrow hall to the open door of her room, and there was the old man at her dresser. The drawers were open, with some of the clothes already packed in boxes; the mattress in a roll on the bare springs.

Larry Lambert grinned doggily at his son. "They did it, Bub. Lerner and another guy came about eleven, carried on a little, then left. And a few hours later, here comes a lady bailiff rigged up like Robocop. And two men in white coats. . . . " He cackled shrilly. "They really had on white coats, Bub. Strapped Ma to this hydraulic business and hauled her off. They had papers all signed, sealed, and blue-backed."

"Oh, God . . . " Dick moaned.

"Got them in my room. Wanna see them?"

Dick sagged against the door frame, head hanging.

"What's the matter," asked his father with a touch of irony. "You gonna miss her so much?"

Dick looked up at his father without raising his head, so his eyes gleamed from under his brows. Larry took a step backward.

"It was supposed to be Monday," Dick said softly. "He wasn't supposed to come for her until Monday."

"Yeah . . . well, guess they didn't feel the need to check their schedule with you. They came, saw her, got what they needed from the judge, and had the whole thing rolling lickety-split. Makes sense, I guess. Once you're going to do something like that, no sense crapping around, letting everyone tense up, if you know what I—"

"Fuck," Dick screeched and charged his father. Larry tried to get away, but the room was cell-sized, and he backed into the wall. Dick grabbed a fistful of shirt front and hefted him up until his toes just scraped the floor.

"You limp old prick . . . you total hunk of shit . . . " Dick screamed and spat, and Larry blinked against the splats of saliva. He turned red, then a sick dusky color as his son's fist dug into his windpipe, and he gagged. Dick let him go. He toppled, grabbed the ajar drawer to save himself, and it slid out and upended. A cloud of soft, diaphanous, pastel-colored cloth puffed out, filling the air. They stared in amazement as the cloud separated into scarves and slips, panties, bras, and hose, and pale-colored nighties—and settled around them, soft as mist.

"Undies," Larry said in a hushed tone. "Her undies . . . "

Dick stared at the lovely things, unable to imagine his grandmother owning, much less wearing them; yet she must have, because they were not new, but had been carefully laundered and ironed and put away in this secret drawer, in this tiny filthy room.

He felt a jarring stab of grief for the woman who'd folded these lovely things and put them away years ago. His eyes burned, tears threatened for the first time since he could remember, and he thought,

Nana, oh, Nana, I'm so sorry. . . .

Larry picked up a pale blue slip with ribbon straps and held it to the light. "My God," he said reverently. "My God . . . can't believe she ever wore . . . "

Dick slammed out of the room and raced down the hall to the kitchen. He yanked open the refrigerator, took out a can of Rolling Rock, popped the top, and took a deep swig, then sank back against the sink.

Lerner had done this, had taken her and the nine hundred a month that meant nothing to him, and everything to Dick. Had done it on the sneak, beating Dick cold by the simple expedient of showing up four days before he was supposed to.

There had to be a way to make Lerner backtrack, to bring her back and the money with her. Only Dick already knew he was jerking off and that was not going to happen. She was gone, the money was gone.

He'd get by without it somehow; get a better job, or an extra job, or spend what he made now more carefully. He could live with that; he could sure live without two hundred pounds' worth of old lady filling her pants at the kitchen table. He could *not* live with Lerner beating him and gloating over it. Laughing about it to the rich shits of Upper Fallsbridge for whom Dick pumped gas every day, day after day.

That was unbearable.

Lerner must be made to pay for what he'd done.

"Bub?" Larry stood in the doorway, still holding the light blue slip. "Called out to that place they took her to. Lady told me we can see her tomorrow. Said there're grounds around the place, like a park, and families have picnics there on nice days. Maybe we could get some KFC and take her out on the grass—"

This was too absurd to even try to deal with. Dick took his beer and pushed past the old man into the hallway, heading for his room to wait for Ted's call, as he'd been waiting all week.

The others would balk at going after Lerner now that the old lady was gone . . . if they knew she was gone. The plan was laid on, ready to roll. All Dick had to do was let it happen.

They strapped Belle Lambert to the potty chair and left her alone with Bailiff Jessica Shannon in the big, chilly, third-floor reception room.

Jessica sank down on a black vinyl couch, like the couch in every other waiting room she'd ever been in.

She was waiting for Aaron Mendel, M.D. (whom she'd never met), for the final, formal signing over: the committal that would shift Belle Lambert from one arm of the state to another.

From cop to shrink.

Then Jessica could go home after ten hours' duty, most of it on her feet.

She looked at the hulk of Belle Lambert, whose head tilted forward, chins resting on her puff pouter chest.

Jessica had never seen anyone look more zonked, and she risked closing her burning eyes. A moment later, her head canted back against the cool plastic cushion . . . she heard dream surf . . . that changed to a peculiar squishing sound. It got louder, came closer . . . and her eyes snapped open.

Belle was coming at her, rolling the chair by its wheels, rubber rims squishing on the tile floor. Her head still tilted, chins multiple, but out of eyes that had been vacuous as air an instant ago blazed hate, mayhem . . . the will to murder.

She was going to attack.

The front of the chair would smash into Jessica's shins, pinning her to the couch while fat, grubby thumbs went for her neck . . . or eyes.

Jessica leaped to her feet, sidled along the front of the couch, then backed up and hit the wall! Smartly, the woman who was not supposed to be competent to change her clothes changed direction and kept coming. Jessica was trapped between a jog in the wall and the couch, with Belle only feet away, gaining speed. Jessica unsnapped her holster. Somehow she'd have to justify using the Glock, definitely deadly force, on the poor loony in a wheelchair. But as a nameless police chief from some prairie state had observed on the tube, "I'd rather be tried for their murder than have them be tried for mine."

She gripped the butt to draw. *Freeze or I'll shoot,* she'd say, and Belle Lambert would have no more idea than a lizard what she was talking about.

"Bailiff!"

A voice floated into the room from the doorway. Belle Lambert halted as if she'd run into a wall, and a short, dark man with a lot of thick, dark, curly hair came into the room.

Belle's eyes were blank again, and Jessica let go of her gun.

"But that could not have happened," Aaron Mendel gently told Jessica a few minutes later. "Simply could not." He'd been a quarter of a second too late to see Belle in action.

"You think I'm lying?"

"Of course not. But these patients give everyone the whim-whams and I think you were spooked."

These patients? How many hulks emptied of reason and refilled with murder resided in this building, Jessica wondered, and shivered.

"Like that," Mendel said, without a hint of *see—there* in his tone, or she'd have decked him. Could do a good job of it, since he was a good few inches shorter and maybe twenty pounds lighter than she was.

She liked small men, though, was sorry they were having this argument because she thought he was kind of cute, with his smooth, pale skin, large soft, dark eyes fringed with thick lashes. He had that sort of pippin' chicken look that brought out all her protectiveness—her macho side, she thought ruefully. And he was not wearing a wedding ring.

"Look at her." He nodded at Belle. Her head still had that broken-neck tilt to it; a strand of drool connected her chin to her shoulder, and her eyes were blanker than blank. Jessica had seen more expressive marbles. She could barely remember how they'd looked with that storm of malicious vitality blazing out of them. But it *had* happened; she wasn't going to pretend it hadn't.

"That wasn't how she looked a minute ago," she said stubbornly.

"Maybe, or maybe it's just time for you to give up this duty. No one stays on it for long."

He meant well, but with special duty came special pay. Her kid's SAT scores were stratospheric and he could go to Harvard, Yale, Dartmouth on scholarship if Mommy could come up with about ten thou a year living expenses. She had to keep hauling loonies around, or doing any other special shit with special pay they'd let her.

Mendel must've realized some of this and said, "I'm sorry. I guess no one would do this if they didn't have to."

"You must."

He was an M.D., could presumably write his own ticket.

"Used to." He looked sadly at Belle. "Back before I ran up against my own limitations—" He stopped suddenly, flushed, then said,

"Look, no reason why we can't do the signing-over in comfort. Want a cup of coffee?"

He meant downstairs in the huge, high-ceilinged, hard-tiled cafeteria. Hardly a date, yet she knew that's what it would be, and she flushed too.

"What about her?" She nodded at Belle.

"I'll get someone to look in, but she's not going anywhere. Belle Lambert's not in there anymore."

Maybe she's *not*, Jessica thought as they passed her on their way out, *but someone is.*

It was dusk when Bill Withers hung up from Angie.

The huge house was silent, and he went from the kitchen, where he'd taken the call, through the butler's pantry to the back stairs. He'd go up, take a shower, then go out for something to eat.

A cheeseburger at Rusty's, the gin mill in his old neighborhood in Riverside. Rusty's smelled of a septic tank in the back and stale beer in front, but it was a place where he could have food and a couple of drinks without everyone eyeing him as they would at the Inn in Upper Fallsbridge.

That? That's William Withers, Angela Brooks's husband, and a total bum by all accounts. Isn't that a boilermaker he's drinking with the pâté maison?

He reached the stairs, glanced out the window, and saw the ax resting against the wall of the carriage house. Burns, the sometime chauffeur and general factotum, would be here by 7:00 A.M., long before Bill got up; he'd see the ax, *tsk,* and feel abused at having to put it away.

Bill didn't blame him. His own father had ground into him, *Take care of your tools, and they'll take care of you.*

His father had died when Bill was still in high school. He remembered going into the workshop afterward, seeing the tools racked, hung from hooks or squeeze holders. The metal hasps, heads, drill bits, blades, saws, wrenches, shone; the shed smelled of oil his father had used to keep the metal rust-free and the wooden handles from drying out and splitting.

He looked out at the ax lying on the ground.

Take care of your tools . . .

He left the house by the back door and went out to the courtyard to the ax. He picked it up, then noticed an unsplit log on the stump. The last log, he realized. Split it and he'd have finished the cord.

He balanced it on end and grasped the ax handle in one hand. He was good with tools, had the gift, his father had said. His father had owned a repair service for tractors, mowers, weeders, brush hogs, motor rakes, and the like. No cars. Bill would have liked to work on cars. Having his own garage had been his dream, killed when he met Angela Lodge Day Brooks of Upper Fallsbridge.

Not because of Angie, never Angie. It was the old lady, the Dowager Brooks, Bitch Brooks. Dead five-plus years now, but he could still hear her cracked, raucous upper-class voice. The Muffy Set voice that shrieked whatever it had to say, sure the whole world must be enthralled. The spoiled set, on the order of putrid chicken, he thought. He had truly hated Lydia Brooks. *Of course Angela's husband cannot possibly run a* garage. She'd made it sound like a crack house. End of discussion as far as she was concerned. He had wanted Angie more than he'd ever wanted, or believed it was possible to want, anything; for sure more than he had wanted a garage on Route 25. So he had taken a job at the ad agency the Brookses owned a big piece of, and they lived miserably ever after.

But he did take care of his tools.

He raised the ax, feeling the satisfying pull in his muscles as he brought it down. It lightened suddenly, something flew past his head, and the head-less handle hit the log, jarring his arm to the shoulder.

The ax head had flown off and must have sailed into the bushes behind him. He dropped the handle and waded into the bushes, then crouched down, feeling among the twigs, branches, old leaves, and soft earth with his bare hand. It was getting dark; if he couldn't find it by feel, he'd have to get the flashlight out of the carriage house. Then his fingers contacted metal; he got a grip on the head, straightened up, and brought it out of the bushes to the courtyard. He put it back on the handle, tamped it down hard to settle it, then raised it again. This time it came off at once, slid down his back, and clattered on the stone-floored court.

He tried to refit it, then saw that the tip of the handle that should anchor it had dried out and split; it was beyond repair.

He sighed and dropped the whole business on the flat top of the stump. He was lucky it had whizzed past his head, not hit him. It would have broken something if it had; at least given him a shiner equal to Angie's.

Angie . . .

Not her fault about her lousy mother. He should have told Lydia Brooks to stuff it, and taken Angie away. They wouldn't be rich, but they'd have the kid and each other. Could still have if he could just cool it on the hooch.

No boilermakers tonight, after all, he vowed. Just beer with the cheeseburger.

He felt something on his wrist, looked down and saw a black dot in the faint light. He sort of knew what it was, and his insides slithered; he rushed to the carriage house, flicked on the spot, and looked at it in the light. A tick was battening on him, engorging as he watched. It was shiny and disgusting, but was not one of the tiny, Lyme-disease deer ticks, thank God. He grabbed it to tear it off his arm, then remembered it would leave its sucker in his skin to infect. Gasoline would make it let go, but the smell would stay on his skin no matter how he scrubbed it. Heat would also work, and he pulled out his disposable butane lighter and twisted his arm to hold the tick to the flame without burning himself. It wasn't easy; some of the hair on his arm sizzled, but the tick finally shifted. It was getting bigger as he watched; he held the flame closer, not caring about a little scorch or blister. Not caring about anything but getting it off of him. Finally it let go and fell with a faint click to the pavement. Bill stomped on it, dropped the lighter back in his pocket, and heard the phone ring.

He ran up the back stairs, opened the door to the delivery alcove, and raced across the kitchen to the wall phone, praying it was Angie.

He grabbed the phone, and Myra said, "Bill?"

A moment of silence; then he said hoarsely, "Yeah, My. It's me. My . . . I'm sorry."

On the other end, Myra had braced herself, not knowing what kind of reception she'd get from him, hating to be yelled at on the phone.

But it was the old Bill, suddenly: contrite and sweet. The gorgeous young man who'd danced with all of them tirelessly while the other men clutched around the bar, talking stocks, or soccer, or whatever men talked about. Bill wasn't such a great dancer, but he was so enthusiastic, so eager to please, you didn't mind getting sort of pulled around the floor, and occasionally trod on.

The old Bill, the one they didn't see very much anymore. Maybe because they didn't see Bill much at all anymore. He'd always been a heavy drinker, but it used to make him funny, not violent. He'd twirl an imaginary Victorian mustache and chortle, "Gad, you're a beauty, woman."

"Or would be if I lost forty pounds," Myra would say, and he'd answer, "Well, maybe only thirty." Then they'd laugh . . . too much. Bill ate, drank, laughed too much. Was too handsome, too ebullient and ingratiating, had turned too mean too quickly.

Excessive Bill was now apologizing over the phone, had already said he was sorry about fifteen times. Even apologizing too much, Myra thought, at the same time remembering how much she had liked him.

"Will you forgive me?" he bleated.

"I . . ."

"Get Angie to, too, My. She's okay, isn't she? I mean, she's really okay."

"Oh, Bill. She had to have a CAT scan, and they've got this compress on her eye that has to stay there for a couple of days to make sure there is no permanent damage. And she had about thirty stitches on her forehead and down her cheek. Of course she's not okay. How can you even ask that?"

He was silent.

"Bill."

"Yeah, My," he said heavily. "Why'd you call?"

"I need to come over, if I can. Get some stuff for Angie. The clothes she had on are unwearable."

"I'll bring—"

"No," Myra said quickly. "She isn't ready to see you yet, Bill. You understand. She'll be home tomorrow."

He didn't say anything.

"Besides, I have to talk to you about something." Wrong tone, she thought. She sounded like a school principal.

"Like what?" he asked warily.

"I'll tell you when I get there. . . . "

"I was going out for dinner."

"I'll be there in about ten minutes, and this won't take long."

That could be a lie; she had no idea how long it would take or what she'd say when she got there. The threat was vague; she'd have to put him on guard without making him think *she* was threatening him.

"Then you can go out and eat," she said.

And maybe leave town, she thought. The ad agency he worked at was over the state line in Millerton; he could stay in a motel there for a few days or at one of those cutesy bed and breakfasts where the proprietress would probably fall in love with him.

But he was not home when she got there.

The alarm was unarmed, the door unlocked.

"Bill . . . " she called. Her voice echoed back from the marble floor.

She went down to the kitchen, called again, then again from the foot of the back stairs. No answer.

She looked outside.

It was dark; she pressed the switch next to the door and the outside spots came on, lighting up the stump and the ax he'd been using lying next to it.

She turned the spots out and went upstairs, making her way down the long halls and gallery to the master suite in the south wing of the house.

The quilted coverlet was smooth, pillows on the bed plumped. Everything in order thanks to the new housekeeper . . . or Peg, or one of the dailies they all used these days.

She slid open mirrored closet doors and saw Bill's clothes. Then in the next closet, Angie's. There weren't many, mostly outfits she recognized, including a plaid suit she could swear Angie had back in high school. And there to the side was her white chiffon coming-out ball gown from 1967. Myra was sure it was the same dress. Lambie had worn marquisette; she didn't remember what Helen or Irene's dresses were made of.

The closet smelled of Angie's White Linen cologne.

Tomorrow was supposed to be sunny and warm again. It was suddenly spring, a brief, treacherous season that could swing back to winter, as it had with the sleet storm last week, or on into the dead, enervating wet heat of Connecticut summer.

But they said tomorrow would be clear, in the sixties. Myra took out a light wool skirt, a pullover knit jersey top that matched, and found underwear, half slip and stockings, a green cardigan, and a pair of low-heeled brown shoes.

She packed it all in the tote she'd brought, then took some toiletries from the master bath. She stood still, staring blindly at herself in Angie's mirror, over the shell-shaped marble sink, trying to think of what she'd forgotten.

Nothing came to her, and she zipped the bag and left the master suite. She went to the rail of the gallery overlooking the huge, marble-floored foyer, dominated by that incredible chandelier she secretly thought was hideous, and called again, "Bill . . ."

He could be outside in back, or maybe down in the basement that Angie's grandfather had made into a game room, including a bowling alley no one had used for years. The pin setter probably didn't even work anymore, she thought, but they'd had fun with it when they were kids.

"Billlll . . ." she called again, in case he was in the washroom. The crapper, Angie called it; she'd always had a rough mouth.

No answer. Myra hoisted the tote bag and went down the grand front stairs. The girls had used them to appear to their dates on prom night, sweeping down the curving last flight to the marble-floored foyer under the giant crystal chandelier.

Myra had had a husband and baby by then and hadn't gotten to go. She remembered being more relieved than anything; still would be, she thought.

She got to the main floor and went through the house to the courtyard in case he'd driven in while she was upstairs. But it was empty except for the ax on the ground, and this time the sight of it troubled her. Bill was a brute, a creep, an abuser. But she remembered him as also orderly, the way she was. Orderly to the point of compulsive, she thought, remembering the perfectly squared-off state of his closet she'd just gotten a peek of. With summer clothes waiting under plastic, shoes on their rack on the floor, ties on a holder.

And there was the woodpile in regimental alignment, stacked to a fare-thee-well against the carriage house wall.

The broken ax on the ground was almost shocking in its incongruity, and she thought, *Bill would never leave it like that.*

But he had, so something must have happened. Such as the hospital calling to say Angie had taken a turn and he'd better get there.

She whirled around and went back to the big, stainless-steel institutional-looking kitchen. A kitchen the lady of the house was only supposed to enter to give orders to the cook. She went to the phone on the wall next to the ovens and dialed Fallsbridge General with her heart hammering in her neck.

A woman answered, put Myra on hold, and a moment later, another woman said, "Fourth-floor desk."

Myra asked about Mrs. Withers in 418.

"You can dial direct, you know," the woman told her.

"Yes. But I'm afraid I might wake her up. I just want to know how she is."

"Hang on," the woman said kindly.

Myra waited, staring at the front of the six-burner Fox restaurant stove, which must have been installed in the old days when the Brookses gave balls.

"She *is* asleep," the woman said, unexpectedly loudly, making Myra jump. "Good you didn't dial direct."

"And she's okay?"

"Fine. She's being discharged in the morning."

"Is Mr. Withers there?" she asked, already knowing he was not. Bill wasn't the type to hang out while his wife slept, would never be one of those worried-looking men you saw in hospital snack bars or cafeterias.

The woman came back to say he was not there, and Myra hung up. Angie was okay; Bill was out on the town, as much town as there was to be out on, Myra thought. He'd left the ax . . . because he'd just left it—end of story.

It felt wrong, but so did half the things in life, she thought. She went back through the alcove to the back door. She had locked the front door, but left the back unlocked, and stepped out into the courtyard.

It was a mild evening with soft light still in the western sky, a sort of grayish-pink glow, impossible to describe or probably reproduce from any palette.

She stopped next to the ax and looked across the slope of the land to the woods that made thin, black, clawlike lines against the sky. Soon they'd leaf out all the way, changing the shape of everything. Nothing was ever the same up here, unlike cities, which were static all seasons, except for potholes and the dirty clumps of snow you'd see on TV.

She crossed the court to the path around the house and heard something thump in the carriage house.

A can of paint or a tool could have been knocked over by a small animal, but that wasn't how it sounded, and Myra stared at the doors.

They had once been made of thick vertical wood slats with long, black iron hinges and had been hell to open. Mr. Brooks got sick of the inconvenience and had overhead doors installed. Four doors for three cars: Angie's Range Rover, Bill's Corvette, and the big Caddy they didn't use very often. The fourth stall must be empty, or maybe had a riding mower or other equipment in it.

She stared at the doors, her heart hammering, the faint susurrus of her blood pressure in her ears. Whatever it was thudded again, as she sort of expected it to.

She bent and grabbed the heavy metal garage-door handle, heaved up, and the door rose smoothly, revealing Bill's red Corvette and the interior of the carriage house, with shelves for cans of paint, weed killer, plant fertilizer, and tools on pegboard. The riding mower hunched in the last stall, casting an outsize, misshapen shadow, inside of which a figure writhed.

Myra froze in the doorway, staring at it.

It twisted and rose, assumed the shape and size of a man, although it was covered with beaded skin like a lizard.

Myra opened her mouth, tried to make a sound, but only a faint gasp came out. The figure flung out arms; some of the beads flew off and landed on the walls and floor with little clicks. She looked down helplessly and saw engorged ticks.

She tried to scream and couldn't; tried to move, but was rooted to the spot. Inside the round of beads that was the head, pale-colored eyes rolled in agony, and the figure writhed harder, sending out gas fumes. It was doused in gas . . . a red metal gas can rolled on the floor.

Ticks were crawling toward her; she stepped back; her heels popped crisp bodies, as they had the bees.

She strained again to make some sound, and couldn't, then saw a tick on her shoe, making its laborious way up toward her ankle, and she finally screamed. At the same time, the writhing figure across the carriage house struck a flame with one of those disposable butane lighters all smokers carried these days . . . including Bill Withers.

"Billlllll! . . . " Myra shrieked and got back a screeching gurgle of mortal agony. It brought the flame toward the gas-soaked ticks that should have dropped off, but were shifting like an undulating swell of motor oil.

"Nooooo! . . . " Myra screamed. She leaped forward, hitting the car fender, crunching more ticks underfoot, and Bill touched the flame to what must have been his chin. His head went up in a whoosh, flames dripped off him, found dribbles of gas, and crept across the floor, incinerating ticks. More of them sloughed off his burning body, but they were burning too and scuttled in little dots of flame across the carriage house floor.

She screamed and shrieked and tried to get to him, but the heat was fierce. Lines of fire raced across the floor at her. She backed out the door and saw the garden hose coiled around its holder, fixed to the side of the

building. It was attached to a spigot at one end, nozzle at the other. She
wrenched the valve on, grabbed the nozzle, and raced back to the door.
She aimed at the figure now covered in a scrim of flame and opened the
nozzle. Water gushed out, the hose whipped in her hands, and a muffled
concussion shook the courtyard. The Corvette tank had ignited, flames
filled the carriage house, and she dropped the hose and ran. The nozzle hit
the paving and water shot out wildly, drenching her. Behind streamers of
water from the spewing, rampant hose, Bill Withers's blackened, burning
figure staggered toward the light, hit the side of the flaming Corvette, and
fell to the ground.

CHAPTER 12

"Yes?" the woman called down.

"I've got to see Mr. Landau. . . . " Myra called back, hauling herself up the stairs by the iron railing. Her legs were shaky; she was sweating over the itchy coating left by the last bout of sweating. Her face must be green, with its usual splotches of red.

The girl for Technicolor, she thought.

She topped the stairs and faced the woman in the doorway of Books of the Zodiac, the bell Myra had rung when Job's Resources didn't answer.

"Job's not here," the woman said. She was about fifty and fat, with massive hips and breasts like couch cushions. She had on a print tent dress that came almost to her surprisingly trim ankles above tiny feet, and her face was small-featured. Almost pretty, Myra thought, with warm, dark eyes and thick, dark brows.

"I'm sorry, honey," the woman said. "Today's his day off."

"Oh . . ."

"It's his Sabbath," the woman explained.

"Oh . . . " He must be Seventh Day Adventist, or was it Jehovah's Witnesses who had Saturday Sabbaths, or Orthodox Jews . . . or all of them.

She could have come yesterday, should have. But she'd been too hung over from the drug Reed had given her Thursday night and on Friday even to contemplate driving to New York. The hangover had been gone by noon, but by then it was too late to make the trip. Besides, it had never occurred to her that a store open to the public would be closed on Saturday, most people's shopping day.

"Come back tomorrow," the woman said. "He'll be here ten sharp."

"Nooooo . . . " Myra wailed, and heard Bill Withers's blood-curdling gurgle from under the slowly undulating cloak of ticks covering him.

She swayed; the woman cried, "Oh . . . dear . . . "

And the next thing she knew, she was being helped into a large, sunny room that smelled faintly of shellac. The woman guided her to a low table, with low, conference room–type chairs around it, and eased her into one.

"You look like shit, honey," the woman said gently.

Not a patch on Bill Withers, Myra thought, and this time saw the beady ticks fly through the air as he flung out his hand with the lighter in it.

She was going to faint.

"Let me get you some soda," said the woman. "You need the sugar."

Myra nodded dumbly; the woman left her alone in the big, sunny room.

Bill had the lighter in his hand and flicked it: *Flick your Bic,* and *burn, baby, burn.* She was stuck in the seventies. The lighter must have been in his pants pocket; had he reached through the tick barrier to get into the pocket? Was the pocket also filled with ticks?

The floor shook as the woman trod back to her, carrying a striped, frosted glass. "Ginger ale, honey." She handed the glass to Myra. It was cold, damp, slippery; Myra got a death grip on it and brought it carefully to her lips.

Bill had gotten the lighter out of his pocket, flicked it, and applied the flame to his gas-soaked head.

Go soak your head, they'd yelled in grade school. Horrendously mild now, but a bad thing to say in those days. Go soak your head, Bill Withers, and that's exactly what he'd done. Then set it on fire.

Such pictures, thoughts, fragments of thoughts had chased her down 684 to the Hutch, to the Cross County and Henry Hudson. Two and a half hours of driving her usual fifty-three miles per hour, while everyone, including about seven hundred eighteen-wheelers, flew past her at ninety.

She was sick to death of it, couldn't stand another minute of what was going on in her mind, and she drank half the ginger ale in a gulp. It was regular, not diet, and the sugar hit her like a mainline jolt. She ignored the inner wrench of icy liquid hitting bottom and drank again. For the first time since she'd come out of the drug-induced sleep Reed had put her into Thursday night, the vision of Bill lost focus.

"Could I have some more?" she asked.

The woman brought out a moisture-beaded can of Canada Dry and poured the rest into the glass. Myra drank, suppressed a viciously acid belch that forced fumes up her nose, and actually stopped seeing the mask of ticks over Bill's head catch fire.

She slumped in the chair.

"Better?" the woman asked.

"You have no idea."

"I guess whatever it was was pretty bad?" The woman was inviting Myra to confide in her.

"I can't talk about it. It's not a secret, I just can't get the words out."

"I understand." The woman sat down across from Myra and held her hand out.

"Zelda Fineman," she said. "The Zelda's for real—my mother was a total jerk."

"Myra Ludens . . . " Myra had never liked her first name, but had to admit it was better than Zelda.

"About Mr. Landau . . . "

"Yes."

"I've got to find him, Zelda."

"Something to do with why you needed ginger ale and looked like death in clown paint a minute ago?"

Myra nodded.

"In other words, an emergency," Zelda said.

Another nod from Myra.

"You know what Job sells?"

Another nod.

"Excuse me, Myra. But it's really hard to see how dried toad and mandrake root figure in an emergency."

"It's him I need, not what he sells."

"With you there." Zelda nodded sagely. "Rather have Job Landau on my side when the sky falls than anyone on earth. . . . "

He believed in it, I believed in him, Angie had said.

"But please understand, I can't cock up his day off without knowing why," Zelda said.

And I can't tell you without sounding like a maniac, Myra thought. Even if she could get the words out.

They'd reached an impasse, but a good-willed one. She knew Zelda would help her if she could. Myra sipped the ginger ale, thought for a second, then said, "What if you call him, tell him I need to see him. He doesn't know me, but he knows two of my friends. Arlen Pinchot and Angie Withers. We're from the same town."

"What town?"

"Fallsbridge, Connecticut."

Zelda smiled. "Sounds like a picture postcard with a steepled church, village green, and more antique shops than people."

Not an unfair description, but Myra didn't like it, and it must have shown on her face.

"No offense meant, honey." Zelda patted her arm.

None taken, Myra thought, *as long as you get me to Job Landau.*

"Go on, honey."

"Well, that's it, really. My friends have already told him the . . . uh . . . situation . . . and he'll either agree to see me or not. If not, you've just wasted a couple of minutes of his phone time . . . no harm done. . . . "

Zelda stood up. "Like a doctor's answering service," she said lightly. "Job'll get a kick outta that."

She moved to an old-fashioned black rotary-dial phone on the counter with slabs of fat swaying with her dress, and picked up the receiver. "Tell me those names again?"

Myra repeated them, then leaned back into a shaft of sunlight. The room was lined with shelves of every size and description of book. More books were arranged on the table in front of her with a hand-lettered sign, SELECTIONS OF THE MONTH, and fanned-out copies of a magazine call *Fate*.

* * *

Seventy-sixth between West End and a park along the river was pretty and unexpectedly residential-looking, with trees planted in squares hacked out of the cement surrounded by short iron fences, probably to keep dogs off, Myra thought.

The address Zelda had given her was a neat brownstone, with one bell.

She rang it; a moment later the door was opened by a thin, gray-haired woman wearing an elegant gray slack outfit.

"I'm Myra Ludens," Myra said quickly. The woman smiled, causing nests of wrinkles to appear around her eyes. "Zelda described you perfectly." *Plump, pink, and sweaty,* Myra thought.

"Please come in. I'm Harriet Landau, Mrs. Job Landau."

She led Myra down a short hall to dark wood double doors that slid open to a long, narrow room with heavy, European-looking furniture.

The room faced north and was full of shadows. It appeared empty until a form in the shadows stood up, and there was the man Myra felt as if she'd come a million miles to see.

Job Landau was a little taller than she was and very slender; his eyes were the intense blue Angie had described, his beard and hair silvery as the spun-glass angel's hair they used to drape on Christmas trees. He was wearing a light blue shirt and the type of cardigan with pockets Myra thought of as a "janitor sweater."

In front of him, on a heavy, carved-legged coffee table with a glass protector top was a large silver tray with a tea set of the most magnificent china she'd ever seen.

He smiled at her and held out his hand. "How do you do. I'm Job Landau." They shook hands; Harriet Landau slid the doors shut, leaving them alone.

The tea was good, the honey so-so. The buttery cookies he handed to her on a plate were delicious. It was almost noon; she'd only had coffee this morning.

"How is Mrs. Withers?" he asked.

"He . . . I'm sorry to tell you . . . he beat her up again."

"Oh . . . " Landau looked away, and Myra thought he truly cared.

"But she'll *be* okay," she said quickly. "And it's not going to happen again."

"Except it usually does in such cases."

"Not this time, Mr. Landau. Her husband's dead."

The blue, blue eyes, bluer even than hers, fixed on her. "What happened to him?"

She saw Bill's tick-covered hand rise to his tick-covered head; the lighter flared, illuminating glossy, blood-engorged bodies. He touched the flame to his chin, his head burst into flames . . .

Myra gripped the arms of the chair hard enough to hurt. The vision lost focus; she was able to see Landau again.

"He burned to death," she said tonelessly. But it was really ticks that killed him, as bees had killed Pastori. Pastori on his back with his massive, stinger-embedded face turned to the moon: another vision she'd never shake.

"Oh God . . . " she moaned.

"Tell me about it, Mrs. Ludens. Myra, right? Can I call you Myra?"

She nodded.

"So, Myra, tell me about it. That's what you came to do, isn't it?"

Another nod from her.

"So . . . I'm listening. . . . "

At first she spoke haltingly, then warmed to her story until it flowed out. She told him things she hadn't meant to, going back as far as the session with the Ouija board and the visit to Bernie Samms. She even described performing the embarrassing rite in the scarlet satin robe. Then came the deaths in all their horrific detail, though she got the feeling he was not particularly horrified, as if he'd heard or seen worse in his life. She didn't want to know what that might be. She ended her recitation with sirens screaming onto the Brooks estate, probably for the first time ever. And cops and firemen stumbling through the pall of smoke from smoldering automobile components and flesh, trying to figure out what had happened. Lemon tried to get her to tell him, but she was beyond coherence by then. It was

Reed who saved her, who had shown up in the middle of everything and made some sort of excuse, undoubtedly medical, then spirited her home to her own blessed kitchen, where Bob was waiting. He seemed to know what had happened; Reed must've used the car phone to call ahead, but Myra could not remember him doing so. Then Reed had given her one of those little powder-blue pills and waited to make sure she swallowed it.

The end, she wanted to announce for Landau's benefit, but just stopped talking.

Silence for what felt like a long time, then Landau fixed on the one aspect of it she could hardly bear to think about. "Sounds like you knew what was going to happen, Myra. Did you?"

"God, no."

"But what you said to the men who died, sounded—forgive me—but it *sounded* prescient."

"Only I didn't even know I was going to say it, don't you understand? How could I have known when I didn't even know what I was going to say . . . ?"

"So when you warned Mr. Withers, then went back . . . "

"I knew it was a warning. I don't deny that. And I went back to reinforce the warning. Even though I didn't know what it was a warning against."

"But you were too late."

Bill's tick-covered hand touched the tip of the flame to the tip of his tick-covered chin, and flames whooshed up his face with the snap crackle of a winter fire started with fat-wood kindling.

"Too late . . . " she gasped.

Silence again. She shifted in the chair, sweat ran down her ribs, she rubbed her upper arm against the side.

"It's a horrible story," Landau said quietly.

"It's not a story."

"A horrible chain of events. But I don't know how I can help. . . . "

"Don't say that. Please. You must help. You're my only hope. . . . "

"Of what?" He tilted his head.

"Keeping it from happening again."

He frowned; his eyebrows were thick and sooty gray. Darker than his beard.

"Do you think it *will* happen again?"

"No. I don't know."

"Have you issued any more . . . uh . . . inadvertent warnings."

"No!"

He took another sip of tea; Myra took another cookie and gulped tea to keep from choking on the crumbs.

"Tell me more about these warnings," Landau said, setting the wonderful china cup in the saucer.

"What do you want to know?"

"Do you think they were coincidences, or did you somehow sense what was going to happen?"

"Maybe deep down I did sense . . . but I think . . . " She hesitated, trying to find words. "I think . . . it might have been just my sense of . . . fair play at work."

"Fair play?" He seemed disconcerted for the first time.

"They had something coming to them, especially Bill. He'd been using Angie for a punching bag for years and getting away with it. . . . And Pastori . . . "

"You think they *deserved* . . . " Now Landau *did* look horrified.

"No, no," she said quickly. "Not that. Of course not. But maybe in both cases I sort of figured deep down that it was time for the worm to turn, for something bad to happen to them if they didn't mend their ways. Maybe that's what I meant when I told Mr. Pastori he'd be sorry, and Bill that he should rethink his position."

"*Is* that what you meant?" He leaned toward her.

"I don't know. I'm not what you'd call an aware person, Mr. Landau. To put it mildly. I often don't know what I mean by what I say, and in this case I didn't even know what I was going to say."

"I see." He raised the teacup again, and she noticed a monogram in the middle of the saucer with a curlicued *L* as the primary letter. For Landau?

How did you get Limoges, Haviland, or Sèvres to monogram their china for you?

He saw where she was looking and put the cup back in the saucer. "My family china," he said. "From the old country."

"You must've had your heart in your mouth when they shipped it here."

"I didn't know it was happening."

"Pardon?"

"The china and I became . . . separated. I happened to see it in the window of an antique store on Madison Avenue years later, thousands of miles away." He smiled at the cup and saucer. "Like a fairy story, *nu?*"

"You bought them," she said, her mind sliding into a totally different track from the china.

"Mmmmmm. They were very expensive, as you can imagine, and I couldn't afford them at the time. Had just started my little business. But the store owner was very kind; he put them on what you call layaway, and after a year or so, they were mine. . . . "

He took one of the cookies, bit into it with short teeth too perfect-looking to be his own. But Myra's thoughts about his teeth were surface; her mind stayed on that other track, gaining speed. He'd been separated from his family china thousands of miles away, years ago. Very expensive china, from the old country. He was a Jew from his name and closing his shop on Saturday, and some other indefinable thing about him. Unlike Reed, who could be anything from anywhere. Job Landau was a European Jew about sixty, who'd been relatively unmoved by her description of two appalling deaths . . . *because he'd seen worse.* As she suddenly knew he had. Much worse. Old film clips of bodies being bulldozed, rolling over and over like broken dolls, came to her. That turned into the famous picture of the little boy of five or six, dressed like John-John Kennedy at his daddy's funeral: little coat, little hat, arms raised, hands behind his head as a grinning beast in a Nazi uniform held a gun on him.

Job Landau had been *there.*

She gasped.

"Mrs. Ludens?"

"You were *there.*" Her voice was hushed with awe.

"Where?"

"Those camps. That's why you lost your china . . . you were *there.*"

Landau's eyes narrowed to blue glass slits; Myra's were wide, her face broiled; that hateful rush like surf in a seashell started in her ears.

"What amazing insight you have, Mrs. Ludens," Landau said. *What big ears you have, said Red Riding Hood to the wolf,* Myra thought.

"I don't know anyone else who'd have put that together from my comments about some dishes. Amazing . . . " Landau was speaking very slowly, his eyes drilling into hers, as if trying to see something through her head.

She hunched back in the chair, wishing she could get farther away from him. Angie trusted him; Myra supposed she did too, but to do what?

He kept staring, and she started to squirm. Then he said, "Of course you're right. A matter of being born at the wrong time, in the wrong place. Poland in 1930. Though I honestly remember very little. Now . . . " His focus shifted. "Where were we?"

"I'm sorry, I didn't mean . . . "

"Let's get back to the matter at hand, Mrs. Ludens."

"But I *am* sorry . . . I don't mean about *that*, I mean about reminding you. Of course I'm sorry about that too, very sorry. . . . "

She stopped herself, and knotted and unknotted her fingers.

"You're sorry about a lot of things, aren't you?" Landau asked gently.

She smiled; the roaring in her ears lessened. "I'm sorry about just about everything, Mr. Landau, just about all the time."

He nodded as if he understood (although he looked like the type who never had to be sorry about anything). Then he said, "There's a great deal I don't understand about what you've told me. And that I suspect you can't explain to me or anyone else. Maybe there is no explanation. But one question stands out. You seem to credit the rite in the basement for initiating what happened. Yet I got the impression you've lived in the house in relative peace for many years."

"Yes . . . "

"So what happened to make you perform the rite to rid yourself of this . . . bête noir . . . after so long."

"I had the basement remodeled."

"**W**ait a few days, let them get her settled," Renny had said. It was good advice, and Reed had tried to take it. Had gotten through Friday without leaping into the car and driving ninety miles an hour to Housatonic Valley. But he knew he could not get through today, because the vision of Belle not only haunted him, it became more vivid every hour.

Last night, he'd taken Xanax, the same anxiolytic he'd given Myra. He'd fallen asleep easily, then woke with a start at predawn (hour of the wolf, according to legend), with his jaw clamped so hard it cramped and his eyes staring at the far wall of his bedroom, on which was projected the image of Belle Lambert strapped to her metal-framed hospital bed, with huge, fulminating abcesses pulsing all over her.

He couldn't go back to sleep after that, knew he'd probably have to take enough Xanax to OD to sleep tonight unless he saw for himself that she was okay.

He had no idea how he'd get rid of the image of Bill Withers in the carriage house.

"Don't come here," Lemon had said. "You don't have to see this."

But he was a physician, had seen worse, he'd told Lemon, remembering some choice scenes from the ER at Yale-New Haven of a Saturday evening. But he'd been wrong; he had never seen anything remotely like the smoking, charred, black lump that Bill Withers, best-looking man in town, had turned into. And to make it worse, a little icing on the cake of horror, some of the ticks had survived the fire and were creeping across the carriage house floor like beady dots.

He'd have to stay high on crack a year to get rid of that one.

He turned into the parking lot of Housatonic Valley, a huge red brick holdover from early in the century that looked like it belonged in the Rust Belt.

All the spaces within a block of the building were taken except those marked Handicapped. He circled and saw an old woman, with an empty-looking shopping bag flapping in the breeze, climb painfully into an old Volvo. She started it in a puff of smoke and pulled out. He whipped the Porsche into the space, beating out a Ciera hidden on the other side of the Volvo.

Reed expected the finger or some other sign of rage from the driver, but the man behind the Ciera's wheel gave a defeated shrug and drove on.

Reed crossed the lot, climbed wide, shallow stone steps worn swaybacked in the middle, and entered Housatonic Valley State Psychiatric Hospital.

The Warehouse.

The lobby was cool and cavernous, with a stone floor that had a thirties-looking sunburst design in the middle. Some stone was missing, giving it a toothless, off-kilter look, which was entirely appropriate, Reed thought. Housatonic Valley was the nadir, the pit. *Number nine,* some smart-ass at Yale had called it, referring to the final circle of Dante's Inferno.

It was the place you never wanted to send anyone, for your sake as much as theirs, because it signified unconditional defeat for both of you.

He crossed the stone to a half-round desk with a beaky-faced woman behind it.

"Help you?"

"I'm looking for Aaron Mendel," he said. "My name's Lerner. I'm Belle Lambert's physician."

It was a lot of information to hit her with in one breath, but she nodded, touched keys on a computer console, and looked at the screen.

"Dr. Mendel's in the building, Dr. Lerner. I'll page him."

She'd gotten it all; he wondered if the rest of the staff was that competent.

He waited across from a large, gray-painted blank wall, the size, color, uncompromising emptiness of which were disturbing. Maybe he'd make a donation earmarked, *Flower prints for the big, blank lobby wall.* . . .

"Dr. Lerner . . ."

Mendel was short, dark-haired, and sallow, with soft brown eyes and a slack handshake. "She's on Three," he said. "But I wanted to talk to you before we go up there."

Reed's heart lurched. "Nothing's happened to her . . . ?"

"Something happened *around* her that I wanted to discuss with you. Let's get a cup of coffee."

They sat at a clean orange Formica table in a spotless cafeteria, drinking coffee that was not just potable, but downright good, and Mendel told him Bailiff Shannon's account of yesterday evening. Reed shook his head. "Never happened."

"The bailiff's a pretty solid lady."

"It still didn't happen."

"You're saying it's impossible?" Mendel asked gently.

"Nothing's impossible. But it's about as unlikely as . . . " He couldn't think of a for-instance.

Mendel grinned. "As a cadaver chasing her around a dissection gurney was the example I came up with."

"Yeah."

They rode up to Three, and stepped out on a shining ceramic tile floor that was cleaner than the floors of most of the restaurants Reed ate in. This part of the country, in spite of its quaint, cute, sometimes beautiful exteriors, was squalid within, with dirty floors, dirty bathrooms, crescendos of dirt in gorgeous, eighteenth-century town halls, grimy tile on ice-cream parlor walls. The floor of the best bakery in rich, stunning, butter-wouldn't-melt-in-its-mouth Fallsbridge was a disgrace; he'd seen a roach on the wall of the local gourmet emporium where you could spend two bucks on a single, out-of-season peach.

But the madhouse was spotless.

Mendel hung back. "Reed . . . "

Reed kept going. "Aaron, I'm going to wet my pants if I don't see her soon."

"It's just . . . I spent last night with Jessica Shannon, the bailiff."

Reed stopped, not knowing what to say. Mendel rushed on.

"The point is, Jessica's not hysterical or easily spooked or looking to dramatize herself. I wish you'd keep in mind when you see Mrs. Lambert that she might have undergone some . . . " He couldn't find a word.

"Metamorphosis?"

"Too strong. But something."

"Sure." They moved on, reached the ward and entered, and Reed finally saw Belle.

She was in a proper wheelchair at the end of a clean, all-white bed. They'd washed her hair, which was much redder than he'd realized, with few strands of gray for a woman her age, and her skin had a glow with the grime gone, but her eyes were glassy as ever and stared a fraction of an inch to the right of his. Her head had the same broken-necked tilt to it and her mouth was slack. But they had put her in a clean blue gown, with a white lap robe and blue slipper-socks, and someone had tied a blue ribbon in her auburn hair.

A blob of something yellow—egg, he thought—smeared the corner of her mouth. He took out his handkerchief, gently wiped it away, and she snapped at him like a riled dog.

He jerked his hand back and stared at her.

"What happened?" Mendel asked.

"I don't know."

It must have been one of those involuntary movements common in vegetative states, a meaningless twitch, but it sent adrenaline pumping through him.

"Reed?" Mendel said tentatively.

"She should see a neurologist."

"Of course. It's laid on for next week, but you did tests. . . ."

"The whole alphabet soup: EEG, MRI, CT, EMG, SEP."

"So?" Mendel asked.

So. Maybe it was nothing, and the lady bailiff was a whole lot jumpier than Mendel thought, but Reed couldn't chance it. If Belle went from stuporous to manic, she could hurt someone, most likely herself.

Hating himself, he asked, "You got padded restraints?"

In the upscale Fallsbridge psych ward, where the alkies and dopeheads and odd psychotics were rich, the restraints were fleece-lined.

"We do," Mendel said.

"I mean fleece-lined, not those miserable nylon—"

"I said they're padded," Mendel said in a what-do-you-take-me-for tone.

"I guess you better use them."

"What happened just now?"

"Nothing probably." The spasm of a dead frog, he thought.

"What about night restraints?" Mendel asked.

Night restraints would be terrifying if she came to in the dark. He'd also read that night-restrained patients had a higher incidence of aspiration pneumonia and death. He said, "No, let's give the lady a break and leave them off at night."

Dick Lambert saw the silver Porsche heading for the parking lot exit, and he slammed on the brakes, throwing his father against the dashboard.

"What!" Larry Lambert cried.

Dick jammed the car into reverse, squealed around the end of the lane, and headed the wrong way, straight at a VW with a white, startled blob of a face behind the windshield. He missed the VW by centimeters and careened into the next lane, trying to find his way through the maze of the lot to the exit road he had seen the Porsche on.

But he was in still another lane, still going the wrong way, and this lane was blocked by a gigantic eighties DeVille with a codger behind the wheel.

"Move it, you old shit," Dick screamed out the window and laid on the horn. But the noise only unnerved the old man, and he looked blankly out at Dick with faded blue eyes. "Fuck," Dick screamed, reversed again, and this time he wound up going the right way around on what looked like the exit road.

But the Porsche was gone.

"What was all that about?" his father asked in a quavering voice.

"None of your fuckin' business. . . . "

More or less the answer Larry Lambert expected, and he wondered for the millionth time where all his boy's anger came from. And whose Porsche that was and what Dick would have done if he had caught him.

They headed back and he returned to dreading the half hour he was about to spend looking into his mother's dead eyes, chafing her limp hand, trying to be a dutiful son.

CHAPTER 13

"Barb . . ."

"Myra?"

Myra's face was cooking; beads of sweat dotted her forehead and her hair was damp. She wanted to hug Barb, but she had been sweating for hours in traffic up the Saw Mill, 684, and the connector to Fallsbridge. She was sure she smelled by now and held out her hand to shake. Barbara grabbed it and pulled her gently through the door into the tiny foyer of her condo.

"To the kitchen," Barb cried gaily. "I'll finally return the favor and make *you* a cup of tea!"

They went down a short, narrow hall, past a living room with beige carpet and furniture and a mirrored wall that gave an illusion of space. Sliders to a small patio with stone planters let in wide bars of sunlight.

The kitchen was sunny, with a gray tile floor, stainless steel surfaces and polished granite counters. Only the oak pedestal table was old, with the deep sheen of years of waxing. Myra would have bet it was probably Barbara's most prized piece of furniture.

Through an open door she saw a small room with shelves of large-for-

mat books, paper spines of what looked like catalogs, and a drafting table.
Barbara's workroom.

Barb poured the tea into bright blue mugs from a bright blue pot and pushed a pot of honey toward Myra.

"It's supermarket honey, My. Nothing like Bob's. Maybe when you make up the next batch, you'll think of me."

"There won't be a next batch," Myra said. "Bob gassed the bees and burned the hives yesterday."

"Why?" Barb cried.

"You heard about the man killed across the road."

"I caught the tail end of the story on the late news. I tried to call, My. Truly. But the line was always busy."

"The cop who came told us the press would be calling and took the phone off the hook."

"Oh, Myra, it must've been dreadful."

"Dreadful. Then Bob killed the bees that were left. I guess he thought it was the right thing to do . . . to atone, or something. But it wasn't their fault . . . they're just bees, how could they know?"

They sipped the tea in silence a moment; then Barb said, "My, you're not here to talk about bees. I'm glad to see you and all, but it's not like you to just show up out of the blue." Looking like she'd been chased across three states by demons, Barbara thought.

Myra looked at her. "Barb . . . what happened in the basement?"

"Something must've happened," Landau said. "Until you remodeled, it was quiet, right?"

"Awful . . . but yes, quiet."

"Then something stirs after thirty years. . . . "

"Three hundred," Myra muttered.

"Whatever." Landau waved his hand, doing away with two hundred and seventy years in a blink. Talk about taking the long view, Myra thought.

"So, something must've activated it," Landau insisted. "Something made it go from passive to murderous. What, Mrs. Ludens?"

"I don't know."

"Who would?"

"The designer?" Myra made it a question.

"Happened?" Barbara asked, way too casually. "What makes you think anything happened?"

Myra's heart speeded up.

"I just know it did," she said.

Barb sat stiffly on her side of the table, then suddenly deflated. "You found out about the bones, didn't you?"

Myra had to remind herself to breathe.

"Bones?"

"Will told you, or Dale. It was Dale Hale, wasn't it? The chickenshit tile man with the rhyming name. He told you. . . . "

"What bones?" Myra's voice rose. She couldn't remember the last time she'd yelled at anyone.

"Bones!" Barb jumped up and raced to the sink. She emptied her cup, then opened a cabinet overhead. "Want a drink? I've got Scotch, bourbon . . . vodka." She took down a bottle of vodka. "Not a bad brand." She pretended to study the bottle. "Not as reminiscent of paint thinner as some of the cheaper ones."

"For God's sake, what bones?" Myra cried.

"Dale found them and called us down to look at them."

"Why didn't you tell me?"

"Because then you'd've told someone, and they'd've told someone, and pretty soon it would've reached the ears of some archaeological big brother . . . and they'd've shut us down. Will's got five kids. I've got one . . . but he's at Amherst. We couldn't afford to be archaeologically correct. . . . "

"What kind of bones?" Myra demanded, though she already knew. *"They wouldn't want to pollute their churchyard with her remains," Bernie Samms had said, "so her husband buried her on the farm . . . your place."*

In the dirt-floored basement.

"What kind of bones?" Myra fought to control her voice.

"Oh, for Christ's sake, Myra. Human bones . . . a woman's bones. We wouldn't be going through this for rat bones. They were small . . . people back then were short, but Will said she was full-grown; he seemed to know what he was talking about and you could just sort of tell it was a woman by the delicacy. They were pretty much intact, and very dirty, except in a couple of places where the digging had scraped away the mold and stuff, and there they were sort of ivory." Barbara gave a wretched-looking grin. "The color Pratt calls Hepplewhite on their paint chart." She looked away. "I'm sorry, My. You make light of things when you're ashamed of them."

"What did you do with . . . her?"

"Buried them deeper."

"Oh . . . no . . ." Myra groaned.

"What's so terrible, for God's sake? *She* didn't care. We didn't show her any less respect than whoever dumped her there in the first place."

"She was not dumped. She was buried; her husband buried her after she was hung as a witch, and they wouldn't let her into the churchyard. . . ."

Barb turned a terrible greenish color; Myra was afraid she was going to pitch forward across the table. Barb was still holding the bottle of vodka. Shakily, she poured some into her teacup. "Shit, My, we didn't mean anything but to keep on working. We reburied her, a little more deeply, a little more securely, if anything, and as close to where Dale unearthed her as we could."

Myra stared down at the flat surface of dark tea in her blue cup.

"Myra?"

Myra looked up at her without seeing her. Barb had never seen Myra look like that before: cold and distant, so far removed she could have been looking down on her from a great height. Barbara found the look disconcerting, a little frightening.

"Myra . . ."

Myra blushed and looked like herself again.

"Yes, Barb."

"What're you going to do?"

"Rebury her, I guess. In the churchyard, with the right prayers and so on this time."

"You'll have to break up that floor."

"I know."

"All that beautiful tile work . . . and dust everywhere."

"I know. I hate to do it. If you had just—" Myra stopped herself, then smiled. "God, I hate people who do that. Like Cokie Roberts on ABC. If you'd just done it right the first time . . . nah-nah, nah-nah. I'm sorry. But I can't just leave her there. Under . . . " Myra swallowed, her throat worked. "Under the house."

"Are you sure it's the hanged woman?"

"Yes." Myra closed her eyes, which burned from so many hours of driving in the sun, fighting glare on the road.

Barb asked, "When did this witch hanging and do-it-yourself, at-home burial take place?"

"June sixteen ninety-five. No one knows the exact date."

Not even Bernie Samms, Myra thought.

"I see." Barb raised the vodka-filled teacup, then put it back down. "I never drink before dinner; I must feel like shit to even try. Look, I'll do what I can to help. I'll talk to Dale and supervise so it won't be any worse than it has to be. You realize that tile's set in cement. They'll have to jack-hammer."

"Yes."

"It'll be an abysmal mess for a few days."

"I know."

"There's another consideration too, Myra. If the archaeological Nazis do hear about it, they could agitate to take over your basement."

Myra smiled grimly. "They're welcome to it."

She stood; Barbara stood with her, and held out her hand. "No hard feelings?"

"No hard feelings," Myra said. That wasn't strictly true yet, but Myra knew it would be soon, given her nature, and she shook Barbara's hand.

"I really am sorry," Barbara said, and Myra answered, "Not as sorry—" then snapped her mouth shut before the rest could come out, and her eyes widened to the bulging point.

"Myra . . . "

"Barbara, oh God . . . Barb . . . "

"What is it?" Myra had gone from pink, to red, to white, with splotches of high color on her cheeks and between her eyebrows.

"Myra . . . sit down," Barbara said solicitously.

"You've got to get out of here."

"What're you talking about?"

Wildly, Myra looked around the kitchen, then through the door to the workroom. "Just take a few things."

"Myra, what is it?"

"I don't think you have to go far. Just out of town; maybe across the state line to be sure."

"What state line?"

Myra took the question literally. "Massachusetts, New York, whatever's closest."

"Damn it, Myra. What are you talking about?"

Myra sat back down. She must stay here and keep calm until she somehow got Barbara safely away.

"Myra!"

"You won't believe me, but you must do what I tell you anyway, Barb. You must get away."

"From what?"

"That's what you won't believe." Myra looked at the pretty terra cotta wall clock. It was almost five; still hours for Barb to get on the road before dark. But light was no guarantee. It had been dusk when the ticks got Bill.

"Myra . . ." Barb sounded a little scared, probably at being alone in her kitchen with what she thought was a wacko.

"Sit down." Myra spoke as calmly as she could. Barbara sat. "Just now, you said you were sorry." Myra spoke as calmly as she could manage.

"And I am, truly—"

"You said you were sorry, and I almost said, *Not as sorry as you're going to be.*"

Barbara grinned. "Well, maybe that's a little Hollywood Mafia, My, and not at all your style, but—"

"No," Myra said sharply. "Don't make light of it, Barb. Don't even think of making light of it. The last two people I spoke to like that are dead. . . ."

Job Landau rose from the camel-backed sofa next to the fireplace when Reed and Arlen entered the club lobby.

They had been in the middle of their weekly squash game when the message came that Landau was downstairs, asking to see Arlen. They had rushed through showers and dressing and arrived in the lobby with wet hair and damp patches sticking their shirts to their backs.

Landau looked neat and compact, in a good blue blazer, gray slacks that had kept their crease on this unexpectedly hot day, and an oxford cloth shirt with a rep tie. He was dressed like a clubman, Reed thought, but could never be mistaken for one. Maybe because of the length of his silvery beard or the intense blue of his eyes. People with eyes like that don't belong to country clubs.

Arlen introduced them. They shook hands, then Landau turned to Arlen. "A friend of yours came to see me this morning. Myra Ludens." Arlen and Reed exchanged glances, and Landau went on, "I think I should talk to you about her visit. . . . " He looked at Reed, then back at Arlen. "Alone."

He meant to exclude Reed. Which was fine with Reed, but Arlen said, "Doctor Lerner has known Mrs. Ludens as long as I have, sir. Is as concerned with her well-being. You can tell him anything you'd tell me." Reed expected protest from the other man, but he nodded, then looked out the sliders at the close-cropped lawn stretching to the ring of trees. "Maybe we could find someplace else to talk?"

It was warm and sunny, tee-offs must be running hours behind, and the lobby was full of golfers wearing this year's in-color of lime green, and talking at the top of their voices. "Perhaps outside," Landau said with a trace of longing. To a man from the city, the landscape beyond the glass must look like paradise, Reed thought.

"Better not, sir," Arlen said solicitously. "It's May, flies're out . . . we'd be eaten alive. The folks you see out there are slathered in buggo."

"Ah . . . " Landau gave a last look at the green expanse and turned away.

"The grill's right over there." Arlen nodded at the quilted vinyl double doors. "It'll be quiet this time of day."

The grill was where Reed and Renny Jarvis had eaten lunch after they'd committed Belle Lambert.

Ted Dukovsky rode the mower off the grass onto the tarmac and saw the Porsche. He braked, put the mower in idle, and sat there with it chuffing softly while he stared at the back of the gorgeous little car.

Silver Porsche, Dick had said, and there it was. Ted had seen it for himself twice now and would know it without Dick. Silver Porsche, Connecticut tags. Another one just like it usually showed up at the same time . . . and there it was, just a couple of rows away. One of them had to be the silver Porsche with Connecticut tags Dickie was looking for. Couldn't be *three* such cars even in the parking lot of the Fallsbridge Country Club.

He put the mower back in gear, rode it to the shed, and a minute later entered the guard house. Pops Boyle was having his supper of bologna on whole wheat, with a tomato, hard-boiled egg, and salt in a twist of wax paper. He was reading a tattered three-day-old *USA Today.*

"Hey, Pops," said Ted, "that news is as old as you are. Ha, ha."

Pops looked up at him. "That's when it gets really good, Sonny." He took a giant bite of sandwich and, chewing slowly, went back to the paper, leaving Ted totally confused.

Maybe he meant that news needed aging, like deer meat and whiskey, but Ted couldn't be sure. Probably Pops was just having fun with him. A lot of people did, because he couldn't get what they said. Bart was the only one who never teased him, who always took all the time needed to explain things to Ted. Sometimes, Ted would pretend to catch on when he didn't just to let Bart off the hook.

Bart was the smartest person he knew, Dick Lambert the meanest.

At the thought of Dick, Ted's shoulders slumped. Dick wanted Ted to call him when he saw the silver Porsche in the club lot, since Doc Lerner was a member here. Nice enough guy, the little Ted had to do with him, and he didn't know what all the fuss was about. But Dick had made him promise to call the second the Porsche showed up, and there it was . . . second rank from the clubhouse, third slot in.

At least it had been half a minute ago. He'd better get on the horn to Dick before it moved.

"Can I use the phone?" he asked Pops.

"Gonna call your lady friend in Honoruru?"

Ted didn't know how to answer and just stared in his bland, good-natured way. Pops snorted and snapped the paper. "Okay, okay . . . you know where it is."

Inside on the desk, Ted thought. And he went through the door to the empty inner office to call.

The grill waiter was spotty and about eighteen. He was wearing a dirty shirt and a sullen expression that didn't change when he saw Reed and Arlen. He ambled to their table at an insultingly slow pace and Reed knew the kid knew they would take whatever snot he dished out, leave a tip anyway, and not complain to the brass. In other words, they were what Reed's Dad would have dubbed, with total contempt, *putzes*.

Then Landau turned to survey the room, the kid saw his face, and stuttered to a stop. When he moved again, his back was straight, his bearing almost military. He hurried to the table and snapped open his pad, looking at Landau. "Sir?"

"You got espresso?" Landau asked.

"Yessir."

"Good. I'll have it."

The kid took orders for Steamboat Ale from Reed and Arlen, then went on his way.

"Myra must have had something pretty crucial to say to bring you all the way here," Arlen said, to get things started.

"Depends on how you take it," Landau said evenly. "I'm sure I don't have to tell you what it was about."

"The ghost in the basement . . . " Arlen grinned.

"That's right. And I thought what you seem to be thinking. That I was dealing with a woman in midlife crisis, or whatever phrase is fashionable just now, and all I had to do was listen with all my attention and sympathy. That's what I thought she needed: attention, and sympathy . . . and a kindly but dispassionate ear. A Dutch uncle to hear all, judge nothing." He turned the fork over and over on the table. "A nonpriestly confessor . . . " His mouth twisted. "I'm not usually such an asshole."

But that was the tack Reed would have taken. Nothing asshole about it that Reed could see.

The kid arrived with the ale and espresso and served them with a flourish, then asked Landau if he could get him something from the Happy

Hour buffet, which consisted of limp fried shrimp, fish paste on crackers, and incendiary chicken wings that produced instant murderous heartburn.

Not the chicken wings, Reed started to warn. But Landau said, "Can't, Sonny, gotta watch my figure, but thanks anyway."

Sonny.

Reed tried to imagine the reaction had he called this kid, or any kid including his own, *sonny*. But Landau did it, and the kid beamed at him and backed away as if from the presence of royalty.

Landau raised the tiny cup, sipped, and said, "Execrable," giving it the French pronunciation. He put the cup down. "As I was saying, I thought she needed sympathy, being premenopausal and overweight. Though pretty, gentlemen, in case you haven't noticed. Very, very pretty."

"We were always her buddies," Arlen said. "Never saw the attraction. Knew it was there, of course . . . heard ad nauseam what half the boys in high school would do to Myra Fox if she'd let them."

"Indeed. I thought that must've been part of it," Landau said. "Her looks, I mean. Many people expect more of beauty than it can ever give them, then become disappointed, sometimes bitter. So I figured that's what had happened to her, that she thought the power her beauty conferred was gone because she'd put on weight, lived to be forty . . . whatever. So she'd made up a ghost in the basement, an entity that had supernatural power, but was still amenable to her control, and when she and the rest of you performed the rite and exorcised the ghost, she'd get back some of the power."

Reed realized he'd started nodding in rhythm to Landau's words; Landau noticed and stopped dead. He waited until he had full attention from both of them, then said, "I was wrong."

"Why?" Reed cried. "That's what I'd've said was exactly—"

"And you'd have been wrong."

"Why?" Reed cried again, and Landau looked at him as if he'd lost his mind. "Because two men are dead, Dr. Lerner."

Silence from Reed and Arlen.

Landau said, "They are dead, aren't they? She didn't make it up?"

"They're dead," Arlen croaked.

"And they died as she described? One stung to death, the other in an *auto-da-fé* to keep from being sucked dry by ticks."

They nodded.

"That didn't happen because Myra Ludens put on a few pounds, gentlemen . . . or maybe you think it did."

"Of course not," Reed said. Landau looked intently at him. "Then what do you think *did* happen."

No response from them.

"Maybe the deaths were the result of coincidental freaks of nature?" Landau suggested.

As in bee hormone rush . . . or tick hormone rush, Reed thought. He saw the charred lump that had been Bill Withers, smelled it . . . and his gorge rose. Quickly, he raised his water glass and drank. The ice cubes clicked against his teeth; the water was pure, almost blue, sweet and fresh. The best thing they served here. It helped, and he put the glass down.

"Well?" Landau looked from one to the other.

"That sounds even less likely than the ghost in the basement," Arlen said morosely.

"I thought so too . . . and unwillingly came up with an alternative."

"What?" Arlen leaned on the table, rocking it and spilling a few drops of espresso into Landau's saucer. "You won't be so eager when you hear what it is," Landau said, and Arlen laughed. "What could be worse than a ghost in the basement?"

"No ghost in the basement."

"Ah, please, sir, no riddles," Arlen begged. "If you know, tell us."

"I don't *know*. How could anyone *know* such things? But an idea came to me after she left. Not long after, mind you. I had suggested to her that something must've happened to trigger the . . . uh . . . activity. She told me about remodeling the basement, and we agreed something might have happened during it. I had no particular faith in that, but she jumped at it as a possible explanation and was on her way to talk to the designer when she left me. It was something she *could* do, and I swear, she was in better shape when she left than when she'd arrived. For my part, I planned to go on with my day off, stupidly congratulating myself for my sensible handling of a touchy situation.

"Then something she said came back to me. Not in a burst, mind you,

but slowly, insinuating itself into my consciousness, and when it did . . .
when I let myself remember her words . . . I swear my flesh crept and every
hair on my body stood up like wire. I still shudder at it; it's what made me
make this trip to see you."

"*What* made you make this trip?" Arlen asked impatiently.

"She told me she warned those men. The warnings were oblique—she
only knew them as warnings after the fact. Didn't even know what words
she was going to say until she'd said them. But they *were* warnings, and
initially I put them down to a bout of prescience, or just that sense of doom
many people get before a disaster. I was ready to forget again, but then I
also remembered her saying that the men deserved to be punished—that
something bad should have happened to them and did. She said that, gentlemen, and in my arrogance of being so sure I knew what was happening,
and what she needed, I let it go right past me."

"Let *what* go right past you?"

"That she thought the men who died should be punished."

Reed said, "They were shits, Mr. Landau. We *all* thought they should
be punished."

"But you didn't warn them they were going to be. She did. My mind
forced me to remember that, then I put the rest together. A few minutes
later I was in my car on my way here."

"Put what rest together!" Arlen wailed, causing Chuck Worth at the
next table to look up from his first martini of the evening.

Landau looked from Arlen to Reed and back. "It's in her house, *she* saw
it move, heard it. The men who died were her enemies. . . . " He paused;
they said nothing. He went on. "This has not occurred to you . . . ?"

"*What* has not occurred to us," Arlen demanded. But something was oc-
curring to Reed, something so noxious he'd have done anything to get rid
of it, but it sank in, developed to the point where he half knew what he was
going to hear when Landau said, "That the ghost isn't in Myra Ludens's
basement, but in her mind. She *is* the ghost."

Myra set Barb's monogrammed overnight case on the floor on the passenger side of the BMW. Barb's packed two-suiter was in the trunk with a

shopping bag of designs and catalogs so Barb could work while she was
gone.

Myra went around the front of the car to the driver's side. Barb grinned
tremulously at her, then tried to fit the key into the ignition. Her hand
shook wildly; the key hit the steering column and fell out of her hand to
the floor. She bent to retrieve it.

"Watch your head," Myra cried.

Barb straightened up carefully, tried again, and failed.

"I'll do it," Myra said.

"Shit, no. If I'm too shaky to start the car, I'm too shaky to drive it."

Good point. But shaky or not, Barb had to get out of here.

"I'll drive you there if you can't yourself," Myra said. Barb was going
to Springfield, where she said she had a roommate from Smith who'd put
her up.

It would be Smith, Myra thought. Irene, Lambie, and Angie had gone to
Radcliffe; Helen, to the Rhode Island School of Design. While Myra
learned to cook, clean, and change diapers. She needn't have, of course.
Could have hired all the help required, but she came from a long line of
Quaker elders and eldresses, to whom it was wrong to pay people to do
your dirty work.

Not that all the great schooling had done the rest of them much good.
Helen meant to be a great artist and wound up a great knitter and seam-
stress. The others' dreams had also not come to much, except Reed's.
He'd wanted to be a doctor and was. But it was hard to see how he got
much joy out of it when he had to do things like committing Belle Lambert.

Myra remembered Belle as young with mounds of curly red hair and
glowing skin. She'd worn dresses a tad too tight then, maybe a little trashy-
looking, and it had been rumored that the men she took to her bungalow
paid her. But that was talk, Myra thought. She'd just been young and full of
life; a party animal, they'd call her these days.

How terrible for her to end up at Housatonic Valley.

Volunteering sometimes took Myra there, trips she dreaded because it
was a gruesome place. The patients you were allowed to see didn't seem to
know you were there, and the ones you weren't were supposed to be dan-

gerous. Belle probably wouldn't know Myra from the bedpost if Myra visited her, but might sense her presence deep down. Just because you couldn't respond to things didn't necessarily mean you weren't aware of them. . . .

"Myra . . ."

She focused on Barb, holding the car key in her hand. She was still pale with fear over what Myra had told her, which was how Myra wanted her to be so she'd get away and stay away. Starting now, since it was almost the time of day it had been when Myra opened the carriage house door.

She shivered.

"My?"

"Goose on my grave," she said. Or ghost, but she was not going to utter that word.

"My, you really will—"

"I really will see the reverend tonight or tomorrow. As soon as possible. Next week, week after at the latest, she'll be in hallowed ground, you'll come home. . . ."

And I'll sleep my first drug-free sleep in a long time, she thought.

"You're sure?"

Myra smiled; there'd be no First Congregational in Fallsbridge without contributions from Don, Irene, Helen, Angie, and Arlen. Reverend Bodgett would perform last rites for a chimpanzee if they told him to.

"I'm sure," Myra said.

"Okay. Meantime, I'll call Dale Hale, the tile man, remind him how much work he gets from me, and tell him he'd better do a perfect job if he wants any more."

"Thank you . . ."

"Don't thank me," Barb said a little sharply. "If it weren't for me—" She stopped with a gasp and put her hand to her mouth. "That's not true. I didn't have anything to do with what happened to those people. . . ."

"Of course you didn't." Myra sounded surer than she felt. "Of course you didn't. . . ."

Then she noticed that a crooked shadow from the locust tree branches had crawled across the hood of the BMW. It was getting late. "Try again," she said.

Barb raised the key in a still-shaky hand, but managed to get it into the ignition this time. She turned it, the motor fired smoothly, and she cried, "Yes!" Sounding thrilled at performing the simple task of starting her car.

She blew Myra a kiss and put the car in gear.

"Call me Wednesday," Myra told her. "I'll know something by then."

Barb put the car in gear and rolled away down the drive to the entrance to Hillgate and the main road. She stopped and signaled a right turn. So she was avoiding the highway and taking 7, a smallish road that ran North through pretty, pokey, New England towns to the Canadian border. It was slow, but much nicer than 84 or 91, where you had to play unwilling tag with trucks and felt like a slug if you didn't do eighty.

The BMW made the turn and disappeared around a curve, and Myra sagged with relief.

It was over; Barb was safe, or would be when she crossed the town line, Myra thought. It was a Fallsbridge spirit: born and raised in Fallsbridge, falsely accused, and hanged here. . . .

Here, Myra thought suddenly. *Right here,* on the rise she stood upon, below which the town was a sprawl of white frame cubes bisected by the village green, now a park, with the river twisting through it like glitter-ribbon in the setting sun.

Right here, from the old oak DaSilva developers had cut down when they built Hillgate Condominiums. There had been protests, but Planning and Zoning had gone along with the DaSilvas. Paid off, no doubt. The Landmark Commission of five blue-haired ladies had tried to save the oak, to no avail. They had asked the DaSilvas to at least put up a plaque to mark where the oak had been, but that didn't work either. No developer was going to erect a tablet reading: *Here stood a magnificent oak tree that had been old enough, big enough, grand enough in 1695 to support the weight of a grown woman, and we hacked it down to make a few extra bucks.*

"What're you saying?" Arlen choked.

"I'm not exactly saying anything," Landau said gently. "It's just an idea that came to me . . . that I thought I should tell you about. Warn you about. And now I've done it." He looked past Arlen at the sliders, through which the light was starting to fade, and pushed back his chair.

"You can't do that," Arlen cried.

"Pardon?"

"You can't drop a bombshell like 'Myra is the ghost,' then walk out."

"I've said all I can, Mr. Pinchot. My night vision isn't what it used to be and I'd like to get on the road . . . to get home before dark."

He was already too late, Reed thought.

Landau stood; the waiter rushed over. "Sir?"

"Time to go, sonny. Thanks for everything." He gave the kid a million-watt smile, then spoke to Arlen. "Walk out to the car with me; we can talk a little more. . . . "

He walked away with Arlen right behind him, leaving Reed to sign the check and add the kid's tip. He gave him a whopper, but the kid gave him a snotty look and went back to his post against the wall.

They were gone when Reed reached the lobby, which was almost empty; the last golfers must be teeing off by now.

He hurried out of the building, saw them in the lot, next to a snappy blue Dodge that looked new, and reached them as Landau was saying, "I know how mad this sounds . . . and maybe is. And maybe I shouldn't have said it, but once it occurred to me, I couldn't leave you in ignorance of the possibility. . . . "

"What possibility?" Arlen raged.

"That one of your nearest and dearest friends . . . someone close to you emotionally and physically . . . has a power you'd never expect her to."

"Power!" Arlen was close to screaming. Landau shook his head. "I'm sorry. This must seem terrible to you . . . both of you. . . . " The blue-blue eyes fixed on Reed; then Landau nodded to him as if they had an understanding, and he looked back at Arlen. "If you notice, your doctor friend here's been very quiet. I suspect he's got a notion of what I'm talking about. . . . "

Only a notion, but Reed did have it.

"Talk to him," Landau said. "Things like this . . . things that push the limits of what you think are possible . . . of what you bank on being true . . . are probably easier to hear about from a friend than from a stranger you have no reason to trust. . . . " He tucked a business card he had in his hand into Arlen's shirt pocket, then, moving quickly for a man his age, got into the car and started it. He rolled the window halfway down. "You know where to reach me if you need me," he said, then rolled the window back up, probably to shut out any more of Arlen's protestations, and drove away.

The car paused at the club gatehouse with the setting sun winking blindingly on the trunk. Then it turned west toward New York and disappeared, leaving Arlen and Reed standing stiffly in the parking lot.

The pavement had soaked up the sun and was soft and hot underfoot. Reed knew he was in for a session with Arlen, and moved off the asphalt to the cooler lawn. Flies came up from the grass in a cloud. Arlen went after him, grabbed his arm, and whirled him around.

"What the fuck was he talking about . . . what power?"

Reed tried to find a way to answer.

"He said you knew." Arlen made it an accusation. "Knew what?"

Reed looked off at the ring of trees around the golf course. They'd leafed out just since the sleet storm last week. The night Myra had seen *it*, heard *it* rattle up behind her. She'd come up with the quintessential ghost story cliché of rattling bones, but hallucinations didn't have to be imaginative. Neither did reality.

Only Job Landau had suggested an extremely imaginative version of reality. Excruciatingly imaginative.

"What power?" Arlen was yelling. "What was that old fucker talking about?"

Reed saw the Simmonses in the parking lot, wearing his-and-hers lime-green golf outfits. They watched worriedly, probably thinking he and Arlen were having a fight.

Reed gave a phony smile and a Richard Nixon wave. Arlen looked around and saw them, and instead of making things worse, as he could have (and often did), he stalked away across the grass. Reed hesitated; the Simmonses seemed to decide it was none of their business and climbed into their S-class Mercedes. They backed out of the space; Reed went after Arlen.

"Arl . . . please, Arl . . . " Arlen stopped and turned around. Flies made a cloud around his head.

"Talk to me, Reed. Tell me what that old fuck meant by suggesting ... even suggesting that Myra was responsible for two deaths."

"Not knowingly."

"How could it be unknowingly?" Arlen cried.

Reed mumbled, "PK ..."

"PK?" Arlen's voice scaled up an octave. "What the fuck is PK?"

Phenylketonuria, Reed thought: a malignant metabolic flaw that left kids retarded and crippled if you didn't catch it in time. Landau's PK was almost as bad.

Reed said, forcing the word out, feeling his face catch fire, "Psychokinesis."

It was probably the hardest single word he'd ever spoken in his life.

"What?" Arlen yelled.

"You heard me."

"You mean like what they put in monster movies and low-grade horror novels ... like Uri Geller bending spoons ... and old Russians turning on lights without touching them ... ?"

"Arlen ..."

"Don't Arlen me! That old fucker's just cast Myra in a grade-Z horror flick, and you seem to be going along with it."

"Of course I'm not. But in his defense, there've been cases—"

"Cases!" Arlen's voice hit falsetto. "What fucking cases!"

"You've heard about them ... everybody has. Stones that rained down on a roof, dishes flying around, trees uprooted with no wind and no one near them. You've seen it in movies, on TV. It makes headlines in supermarket rags. ... " Reed paced a few feet to get away from the flies, then stopped; they caught right up to him. "One case involved Jung himself. A table in his house split in two for no reason, with no one near it; made a believer out of the old fart."

"Tables and dishes, sticks and stones're *objects.* Bees and ticks are not objects!" Arlen cried, in a crazed tone. Fortunately they were alone on the lawn by now; the flies must have driven the golfers inside. Clouds of flies whizzed around Arlen's head; one dive-bombed Reed and hit him in the eye.

"Jesus, let's get out of here."

They rushed off the grass back to the tarmac, leaving most of the flies behind and stopped next to a green Seville that looked solid enough to knock down the clubhouse. Next to that was an old Lincoln Town Car that could demolish the Seville.

Arlen leaned against the Seville's bumper and looked up at Reed. Reed was older by four months, better educated . . . slightly richer. He'd always been the one to whom Arlen turned for advice he generally ignored. But Reed knew he would not ignore whatever Reed said now. Reed sank back against the Lincoln, facing Arlen across the few feet between the cars.

"I don't know what to say." He spoke softly.

"Say the truth, Reed."

"I don't know the truth."

"You mean you think it's possible?"

"No!" The word burst out of his mouth. The instant it did, he knew he did not for a nano-instant believe Myra had willed bees and ticks to kill. "No," he affirmed, raising his voice. "No matter what Landau said."

"Landau's a hard man to discount," Arlen said. They appeared to be reversing roles.

"Discount him anyway, Arl. Myra didn't do it, PK or no PK, and there are no ghosts." He sounded utterly certain. *Was* utterly certain he told himself. Arlen scuffed the side of his shoe against the soft tarmac like a bashful kid. "Then what happened to Bill and Pastori, Reed? What the fuck happened to them?"

"I don't know. But as they say Sherlock Holmes said, when you eliminate the impossible, whatever's left, no matter how improbable, must be the answer. It was not Myra or a ghost. So what does that leave us with?"

After a second, Arlen said, "Coincidental freaks of nature."

"Exactly."

"Jesus." Arlen brushed flies out of his hair. "That sounds almost as off-the-wall as the ghost. . . . "

"But not quite."

Arlen stood away from the Seville fender. "Then that's got to be it. Of course it does. It can't be Myra . . . she gets sick every time someone kills an ant. And there are no ghosts, for God's sake, no matter what my

old man's degenerate books say. It was just a freaky set of natural occur-
rences. . . . "

" . . . that can never be repeated," Reed finished for him. "At least it
would be in the quark and black hole category of odds if it was."

Arlen nodded eagerly, almost smiling. "Coincidental freaks of nature."
He held out his hand; they shook on it, then gave each other an enthusiastic high five that left their palms stinging.

"Coincidental freaks of nature!" Arlen crowed with relief. "CFN!"

"We'll toast that tonight."

"Tonight?"

"Dinner . . . tonight, you and the lady from Yale Riva wants you to
meet?"

From one of Riva's classes.

Now that the boys were at school, she'd gone back to finish the Ph.D. in
psych she'd been working on when she met Reed twenty-three years ago.

"I forgot," Arlen said grimly.

"Don't sound like that. The lady's not an ax murderer. . . . "

"You sure?"

They were joking, getting their equilibrium back in spite of Landau the
Cassandra. Reed dearly hoped he never laid eyes on Job Landau again.

"What time?" Arlen was asking.

"Seven-thirty, so you better get moving." It was almost six-thirty.

"I'll bring the Dom, get the evening started with a bang. But I should
warn you, if the lady does not resemble Quasimodo I fully intend getting
into her knickers."

"We expect no less," Reed said solemnly.

"Coincidental freaks of nature!" Arlen cried, raising a hand in a salute.

"Coincidental freaks of nature," Reed repeated, and thought, *bee hormone rush*. Maybe the entomologist had come up with something just as
ludicrous to explain the ticks by now.

Arlen climbed into his Porsche; Reed had left his bag behind in the
locker room and went back to get it.

*   *   *

Arlen drove out the club gate to the road to town.

He'd showered after leaving the squash court, but still had to shave and change, and he got a move on. It was a glorious evening; he'd walk to Reed's carrying the champagne. Two bottles, he decided in a burst of generosity. Two bottles in a shopping bag from Caldors if he could find one in the bag collection in the pantry.

He hummed to himself, then broke into song (Amazing grace, how sweet the sound, to save a wretch) and glanced in the rearview mirror.

A hunk of seventies junk behind him was snorting out puffs of blue smoke, and he put on a little speed to get away from the fumes. The heap fell back, leaving about four car lengths between them.

They turned into River Road, started the slow, circuitous climb out of the flatlands to Upper Fallsbridge, and the heap that didn't look like it could maintain forty without falling apart started to gain on the Porsche.

The front right tire of Barb Potter's BMW blew. The car veered, she fought the wheel with all her might, and managed to muscle the car off the road onto the shoulder, where it ground for a few feet, spitting gravel, and finally came to a listing stop without hitting anything.

She sagged in the seat a second, then got out and went around front to inspect the damage.

Her $350, top-of-the-line Pirelli tire, which had come with the car last year, was demolished. Not just blown, but exploded as if a bomb had gone off inside it. The car sat on the rim in a leering tilt.

This was on Forrest, a mile and a half from Fallsbridge Center, almost to the Oban town line. It was the section of land where the riverbank disappeared, and water spread, creating a marsh of skunk cabbage, toads, snakes, and mosquitoes. Devil's Marsh it was called on survey maps, probably because it was green and dank and gave up a miasma of rotting vegetation and mud, except in the dead of winter, when the surface froze in a gray slick, with thin streams of muddy water running under the ice. Dogs and cats had been known to break through the ice and drown, or get caught in the mud in spring and starve to death before anyone found them.

Not a nice place.

Water rats had been seen out here; Sally Dukovsky, who worked for the upholsterers in Oban, said she'd seen them run across the road at dusk, "big as Portuguese breads." Meaning either the four-inch-long rolls . . . or the full-size Chaves Bakery round loaves, ten inches in diameter.

Big rats, Barbara thought. Her innards slithered.

She stared into the darkening, damp woods, smelled mud . . . and that musty rodent scent. The smell could be her imagination, but one thing was *not*. Bees had killed Antonin Pastori; ticks had killed William Withers. Insects gone mad, and there was no reason to think the same thing couldn't happen to the rats in Devil's Marsh.

Barbara looked desperately around. The road was deserted; ahead was the sign: LEAVING FALLSBRIDGE. SETTLED 1680.

Barbara looked up the road toward the sign and heard something rustle in the underbrush. She backed up to the car fender, staring into swampy woods where the sun never shone.

She couldn't see anything; the rustling stopped; she started to exhale in relief, then heard a faint but definite squeak. Mice squeaked . . . so did rats. Water rats as big as Portuguese breads. They'd normally avoid people, as did most creatures . . . but bees didn't sting for no reason either, and ticks didn't swarm like bees. Barbara gave a low moan and rolled her body around to face the passenger-side door. The tire was flat, she was not going to fix it, or call the Amoco on her car phone and wait for them . . . or even the cops . . . to show up. She was on a road she'd been on a thousand times, in a town where she'd lived since college and thought of as home, and she knew she was being insane, but she also knew she was not, and true madness meant staying here one second longer.

She ripped open the passenger door, terrified of the time it would take to go around the car where her back would be to the woods, and threw herself into the car. She slammed the door, grabbed the steering wheel, and hoisted herself over the gearbox into the driver's seat, then reached for the key. Her hand jittered but the key was already in the ignition; she just had to turn it. The car had never failed to start, even mornings after last winter's dead, icy nights that broke all records. But she knew that it could conk out this time. That this time all bets were off, and if she searched back along the road or looked at the blown tire, she would *not* find a nail, glass shard, or pointed stone.

With her heart slamming in her throat, she turned the key. The motor caught and roared as she raced it. She jammed the gear into first, let up the clutch . . . and the front left tire blew.

She kept pressing her foot until the car moved squishily forward. She kept going; behind her the squeak she thought she'd heard was repeated, got louder; other squeaks joined it. She kept her foot on the accelerator, pushing the car on its flat front tires toward the LEAVING FALLSBRIDGE sign. She looked in the rearview mirror; the road, shaded by trees, was almost dark, and she couldn't see anything. She pushed the pedal a little harder, and the left rear tire blew. She didn't hit the brake but kept her foot on the gas, as the crippled car humped reluctantly forward on its rims. Her eyes darted to the rearview mirror every few seconds. The road looked empty; she was behaving like a maniac, destroying a thousand bucks' worth of tires, and probably the wheel rims (God knew how much they would cost), for nothing. But she kept going . . . and the last tire blew. The car collapsed; she felt as if she were a few inches above the pavement; the rims slashed through the rubber, ground against the pavement, and the shredded rubber flapped. But she kept going, and a quarter of a mile over the Falls-bridge town line, well into Oban territory, she took one hand off the wheel to punch 911 on the car phone.

They'd be furious at her calling for something as nonlethal as flat tires, even four of them . . . but she didn't care.

CHAPTER 14

Reverend Bodgett poured and drank, poured and drank again, then held the bottle up invitingly.

"Uh . . . no thank you," Myra said.

He poured and drank once more, then set the bottle down, but eyed it longingly.

She took pity on him. "My, but these glasses are tiny. Maybe I will have another." She drank off the sherry, smothering a shudder. It was that too-sweet, nine-fifty-a-half-gallon variety you got at the Liquor Warehouse on Route 7.

She held out her glass; he poured for her and for himself, emptied his glass, and poured one more time. That made four or five for him; Myra had lost track.

Color came to his chalky cheeks; his eyes brightened. He settled back in his chair, nursing the sherry.

"I don't have to tell you how . . . strange . . . even outlandish your request is, Mrs. Ludens." But he was treating her very carefully, given who her friends were. Without their money, Reverend Bodgett could be stuck in Oban, Hartford, Bridgeport . . . Detroit.

"I know how strange it sounds, Reverend. But you can check with Mr. Samms about the authenticity of the bones. . . . "

"If you find them."

"If we don't there'll be nothing to bury and nothing to worry about."

"Quite so." He sipped.

"Mrs. Potter, the designer, must have gotten in touch with Mr. Hale, the tile man, by now. I'll make an appointment with him, then check that it's convenient for you. So you can be there . . . for the . . . uh . . . " She couldn't think of the word.

"Exhumation?"

"Yes."

"That makes eminent sense," he said, leaving Myra thinking she'd never heard anything sillier.

"However," he said gravely, "even if the bones *are* there, and Mr. Samms *does* attest to their authenticity . . . I still have a problem."

"What problem? She must have been Puritan. They became Congregationalists, didn't they?"

"Some. Later . . . "

"Well, can't we just assume she would have if she'd lived long enough?"

"That's not the problem."

"What is? She *was* falsely accused, hanged, and not buried. . . . " Myra insisted.

"We don't know that."

"We know she was hanged, unless Mr. Samms lied."

"Bernie'd never do that. She *was* hanged. . . . "

"And not buried in the churchyard. I don't think he'd lie about that either."

"No . . . "

"Then what's wrong? Certainly she was falsely accused. Unless . . . unless, Reverend Bodgett, unless you think she was a witch?"

A moment of silence, then he said morosely, "I see what you mean."

He still looked very unhappy, maybe because of the sherry. It was the kind that would give you a hangover before it got you really drunk.

Gently, she asked, "What *is* wrong, Reverend?"

"Nothing, I guess. It's just such a . . . strange situation. But I guess I said that before."

"Yes, sir. You did." He still looked sad, though, and her heart went out to him with his cheap sherry and threadbare little vicarage. When they were done, and Goody Redman was properly buried and prayed over, Myra would get him a case of the good Sandeman amontillado she kept at home.

She stood; he rose with her and saw her to the study door. The drapes in the room were drawn and she didn't realize until she went out into the windowed foyer that it was almost dark, and Bob had no idea where she was.

She spied a black, rotary-dial phone like Zelda's on a rickety-looking table in the hall.

"Can I use the phone?"

"Of course."

Bob answered in the middle of the first ring, sounding a little wild. "Where the hell have you been?"

She turned away and lowered her voice, not wanting the reverend to hear her harmless little lie.

"Danbury Fair Mall, Bob. It's been so long since I was there, I just lost track of the time. And Bob, they had this wonderful art show from the local schools. . . . " That had been last month, but he'd never know. "And the kids' stuff was really wonderful. So free and full of color," she babbled.

Silence from him.

"Did you eat?" she asked, knowing the answer. He couldn't scramble an egg on his own.

"No. I was waiting for you." A beat, then, "So's Sergeant Lemon."

"What?"

"Sergeant Lemon. He's been waiting since seven."

Myra closed her eyes.

"You okay?" Bodgett hissed.

She covered the phone mouthpiece. "Fine, fine." Then uncovered it and told Bob she'd be right home.

But she couldn't call Dale Hale, the tile man, with Sergeant Lemon hanging over her, listening.

"Can I make one more call?" she asked.

"Of course."

"It's to the tile man I'd told you about."

Bodgett made a be-my-guest gesture. She looked in the white pages for Bridgeton, Millbridge, Fallsbridge. Towns named when the Fox River was so wide and swift you needed bridges to cross it. Most of the water had been leached off by development and you could now jump across it in some places. Slowed current was causing silt-up; environmentalists worried about its effect on the Housatonic, into which it fed.

She expected to get a tape at Dale Hale's number, but he answered. "Yes, Mrs. Ludens. Barb called and told me all about it. . . . "

Barb called; Barb was all right!

"I'm sorry for what we did," Hale was saying. "We didn't mean no harm."

"Where did Mrs. Potter call from?"

"Millerton, just over the state line. Had the damnedest thing happen to her. . . . "

"What?" Myra's heart gave a whump.

"Had all her four tires blow at the same time. Can you feature that? New, top-of-the-line tires on a new eighty-thousand-dollar buggy. I'd be fit to be tied."

"Me too," Myra said weakly. "Wh-when can you . . . ?"

"The sooner the quicker as they say. Barb said you'd want to do it on banker's hours so the hubby don't know."

"Yes, yes . . . " How wise of Barb. Myra hadn't even thought about Bob knowing.

"Trouble is, I'm tied up until Wednesday morning."

He sounded worried about the delay, and Myra wanted to laugh, because it had been three hundred years; a few more days wouldn't matter.

She covered the mouthpiece again and asked Bodgett if Wednesday morning was all right with him. He said it was, and she made the date with Dale Hale.

Lemon rose from the kitchen table when he saw Myra.

She said, "Please don't get up. . . . " He sat back down. Bob stared at her without moving. She saw teacups on the table and plates with crumbs on them.

"We had tea and cookies," Bob said, "then tea and brandy and cookies. . . . " His cheeks were flushed; he gave her a crooked smile.

She unwound the silk scarf she'd had on all day, under which her neck felt sweaty and itchy, and put it with her purse on the counter. Then she shrugged out of the standard, two-button blue blazer every woman in fifty states must have at least one of, she thought.

"Just let me hang this up." She was buying time, trying to calm the flutters in her middle before she faced Lemon.

She went down the hall to the front closet and hung the jacket on a padded hanger. The horrid blue-green jacket was still there, shoved to the side. Would probably be there when she died.

She tensed suddenly, waiting to hear the dog yap, she realized, *then* saw its pitiful little body swollen to bursting and shut her eyes, but that only made it more vivid; to be followed in flashes by the litany of visions: Pastori's balloon-shaped, black-dotted face turned to the moon, Bill's tick-covered hand raising the flaming lighter to his chin. . . .

She slumped against the wall, waiting for the pictures to fade. It took a while, but they did, and at eight by the chimes of the mantel clock, she straightened up and headed down the hall to the kitchen, where Sergeant Lemon waited.

At eight fifteen, Reed drained his flute of champagne and got to his feet. "I'm going to call."

"You did tell Arl seven thirty?"

It was the eightieth time Riva had asked that question, and he didn't bother to answer. Arlen's blind date, Temma Myer, was also waiting. She was tall, with knobby knuckles and elbows and a long, bony face. But she also had thick auburn hair (sort of like Belle's), warm brown eyes, and was one of those ugly-beautiful women that Arlen would probably find intriguing.

She was getting morose by now, feeling stood up. But Arlen would never stand anyone up on purpose. He might be ten, fifteen minutes late at the most without calling. Never forty.

Something had happened.

Reed went to the sitting room phone and looked back at Riva. Her face was drawn, with the strained look around the eyes she'd had the night Bob called to say something had happened to Myra.

Reed picked up the phone and dialed Pinchot House, as he'd been doing since he was old enough to use the phone.

George answered.

"No, he's supposed to be with you. 'Dinner Reed,' right on the calendar. But without the time."

Reed told him the time, and George said, "He knew that?"

"Yes."

Silence; then George echoed Reed's thoughts. "He'd be ten minutes late . . . maybe twenty, not forty-five. Something's happened. . . ."

The minute hand on the mantel clock hit eighteen after; George spoke with uncharacteristic informality. "Okay, Reed. We can crap around and call around, wait and worry, but I think we should cut to the chase and call the cops."

Cops.

Something cold and heavy broke loose in Reed's middle, made a long, fast descent and hit bottom.

"Cops," he croaked.

"You heard me."

"Do you want to call or should I?"

"Both of us."

Reed nodded at the phone. Two would be more credible to the cops, would be taken more seriously. On the grounds there was something to take seriously: that Arlen would not turn up after a foray to a favorite singles bar in Hartford or the one in the East Fifties where he had picked up top-level female executives. "You ain't lived 'til you get head from a CEO," he'd told Reed.

Reed hung up and faced the women. "That was George. Arlen's house-man," he explained to Temma. "He thinks we should call the cops."

Lemon asked Myra his questions, got no answers that satisfied him, but he persisted. "I'm sorry, but you see my dilemma, Mrs. Ludens. There was bad blood between you and Pastori . . . about a dog, I know. And I know how superficial that sounds. But a few years ago a man in Oban, who shall remain nameless, blew away his next-door neighbor with his Vietnam M16 because of the neighbor's barking dog. You'd be amazed how much bad blood can be generated by a barking dog . . . or a biting dog . . . or a dog that takes a crap on the neighbor's lawn, or back or front porch.

"People don't like having their space violated. Even their air space, as in the case of the noise the dog made. So I don't for a second discount how bad this bad blood might've been. . . . "

Myra listened in silence. He went on, "Even worse blood between you and Mr. Withers, and that's not superficial. Mrs. Withers . . . " He looked at his notepad. "Angela Withers is a good friend of yours, if I'm not mistaken."

"You're not," Myra said softly.

"She's part of a group of you who are, by common knowledge, all very close friends."

"Yes."

"It's also common knowledge that Withers kicked the—uh . . . was abusive to his wife. So you see what I'm hung with here. Two men who could be called your enemies die horribly, and you were *there* both times. Almost to the minute. . . . "

"Sergeant—"

"I know. I know what you're going to say. These were disturbances of nature, acts of God no one could control. I know that. I approached the entomologist they'd sent from Storrs to ask him if there was any way these . . . events . . . could have been . . . uh . . . generated. Without, of course, at all implying that you might've had anything to do with them."

He took out his handkerchief and mopped the glow that had come to his face from the brandy, or from remembering his interview with the en-tomologist, Myra thought.

"What'd he say?" she asked.

Lemon smiled grimly. "Nothing. But his demeanor let me know that if I ever suggested human intervention in these deaths again, he'd look into having me certified." He mopped his face again. Myra would have liked to do the same; it was very warm in the kitchen and sweat made itchy trails down her ribs.

She said, "I understand."

"You must also understand that these deaths are not merely coincidental; they are wildly, freakishly, grotesquely concurrent, and I have to ask if you have any idea . . . any idea at all how—"

That was when his beeper went off.

He quieted it and nodded at the wall phone. "May I?"

"Of course."

He put the beeper to the phone mouthpiece, then the receiver to his ear. "Lemon."

He listened, inhaled sharply, shot a look at Myra, then looked away, something else must have happened. Maybe to Barbara! But Dale Hale had just spoken to her in New York State, and she was fine. Besides, they wouldn't beep a Connecticut state cop about an incident in New York.

She was being paranoid; they'd had a pileup on 84 or 91. Or a holdup in Oban or Torrington. Nothing to do with her.

He'd turned his back to her, was hunched around the phone, mumbling into it so she couldn't hear because it wasn't her business.

But when he hung up and faced her, and she saw his pallor and the dark depressions around his eyes, she knew it *was* her business. Her mouth dried up; that surf-in-a-seashell roar rose in her ears.

"What?" she croaked.

"Mr. Pinchot . . . Arlen Pinchot. You know him?"

"Yes."

"He's one of your little group, yes? Same bridge club as Angela Withers and so on. . . ."

"Yes."

"He's been hurt, Mrs. Ludens."

"He's dead. . . ."

"No. Just badly hurt. He's at Fallsbridge General."

Reed stood at the side of the bed in the Intensive Care Unit. Arlen's face was swollen; a bandage covered his head. They'd operated to relieve pressure against his skull, and maybe had succeeded.

His eyes were closed; he puffed into the ventilator while letters and numbers flashed on the screen. He was breathing some on his own: a good sign. Surely that was a good sign.

"Reed . . ."

He turned. Ralph Malone, head of neurology here and of neurosurgery at Yale-New Haven—a world-class sawbones—stood in the doorway of the cubicle.

"We'd better talk," Malone said. Reed nodded and looked back at Arlen.

Arlen had been the first human being in his life who'd assumed the dimension of a separate person: the first one Reed had seen the morning his mother had his nanny take him to preschool to be with other kids.

"Arlen." He realized he'd spoken aloud.

"Reed . . ." Malone was waiting. Arlen Pinchot was not his only patient, although he was probably the richest.

Reed wanted to touch Arlen, but there didn't seem to be any safe place to do it. He backed up a step, then turned, dragging his eyes away from Arlen's face, and followed Malone out into the corridor.

On their way to the conference room, they came to the glass-walled lounge where Myra, Helen, Don, Irene, Angie (still fighting shock about Bill), and Lambie waited for news.

Their faces looked like sick white blobs under the fluorescent light. Angie's eye was still bandaged, the black stitches ghastly against her pale skin.

Reed and Malone passed the lounge and entered the conference room, which was kept overheated. They must think people needed extra warmth to handle the news they got in this room.

It was beautifully furnished, with a polished teak table, and roll-up, upholstered chairs; not like the vinyl couches and molded plastic chairs in the lounge. Boxes of tissues were spotted around on tables.

Malone sat down across from Reed and folded his hands on the table. He looked awful.

"Should I get the others?" Reed whispered. He sounded like a rummy with laryngitis.

"No. You'll understand what I say to you, be able to convey it to them better than I could...."

"Convey what to them?"

Malone blinked, keeping his eyes closed a second longer than normal, then said, "He's flat-line, Reed."

It took Reed a minute to make sense of the word.

Flat line . . . the line was flat. The line on the EEG, Malone meant. That black line that was supposed to have those staccato ups and downs, those precious blips and glitches of cerebral activity, was flat.

Arlen was brain-dead . . . Arlen had ceased to exist.

"I did it," Arlen had yelled thirty years ago. "I did it, shit-breath!"

Arlen had meant he'd gotten laid, fucked, screwed at least. Had dipped his wick, hauled his ashes, become a man. An event Reed knew was probably still years in the future for *him*.

"Who?" He had tried to keep his envy out of his voice.

"Helen Sturgis." The old man's secretary's daughter.

"Taking advantage of the help," Reed had said sourly.

"Yeah." Arlen had looked dreamy.

Silence; then Reed had asked softly, "Arl? What was it like?"

A serious question, and Arlen had done his best to answer it seriously. "Not like I expected, fucko. My pants were around my ankles, the change in my pockets clanked, and I got more bug bites on my butt than she's got zits on her face."

Reed had grinned; the grin carried over from the past to the present in a spastic grimace that twisted his face.

* * *

"Are you sure?" That was Don, asking one of the stupid questions Malone had avoided by getting Reed to tell them.

"Positive." Reed spoke without inflection.

"But he's alive?" Helen asked that, and Reed looked at her without actually getting her into focus.

"Yes."

"But how can he breathe if he's brain-dead?" Don had a gotcha-there-pal tone, but his face was gray; the dark circles he'd had under his eyes since he was a kid—the result of a variety of allergies—had turned black. They'd all aged years in the past few hours. Even Myra had lost her plump prettiness to become almost ascetic-looking.

"Certain functions . . . " Reed said, then had to clear his throat. "Certain functions are controlled by areas of the brain that have nothing to do with cognition or personality, and continue after activity in the rest of the brain ceases." He took refuge in pedantry.

"For how long?" Lambie asked. It seemed to take him half an hour to turn to her and get her into focus.

"Sometimes indefinitely. But in Arlen's case, they had to put him . . . "

Him was the wrong word, Reed thought wretchedly; there was no gender to the hulk hooked up to the ventilator. Arlen was gone.

" . . . on a respirator," Reed went on. "Malone says he'll stop breathing without it."

No one spoke.

"Another indication of the extent of the damage." Reed dropped the words into the silence.

"Then he'll die if we unhook him. . . . " That was Lambie again.

"Yes."

"He'll suffocate," Don whispered, and started to cry. Tears spouted out of his eyes, his face twisted and turned red, and he sounded like he was choking.

The women sat stony-faced. Then Myra went to him and put her hand on his back; Irene took him in her arms. Reed sat still, not thinking about

Don crying and the women keeping it all in when it should be the other way around. He was hearing Arlen's fourteen-year-old voice shout, "I did it, shit-breath . . . I did it . . . " And himself, bitterly asking, "Did what?" Although he had known that Arl had gotten laid, fucked, screwed; Arlen had dipped his wick. . . .

The voices in his head stopped. Don was still crying; Lambie was knotting and unknotting her fingers—wringing her hands, Reed thought. Helen had called home to tell her husband, Max, what had happened and ask him to look in on little Billy, and to tell him his mother would be late, but was okay.

Reed hadn't seen the kid since Bill died.

But that was only yesterday. Or no, it was almost two A.M., making it the day before yesterday.

He bowed his head. Lambie had said, *He'll die if we unhook him.* He had to explain that that decision must be made by Arlen's sister, Betty.

"Don't you want to see him?" Betty asked Reed.

She meant for a last look before they disconnected everything.

But that was not Arlen down there, he had to keep telling himself. They were not killing Arlen . . . Arlen was gone.

Reed shook his head; Betty left the conference room, where she'd signed the papers at the table. They'd been whisked away by Harold King, the hospital's chief administrator. He'd gotten out of bed in the wee hours to do this . . . so Arlen would not suffer (which he was not doing anyway, since *that* was not Arlen) . . . and the Pinchots, Lerners, Folgers, and Forbeses would be accommodated. Not to mention the Ludenses, Dumotts, and Angie Brooks Withers, whose mother had donated the maternity wing.

The door hissed closed after Betty, leaving Reed alone in the softly lit, overheated conference room with its plush carpet and solid teak furniture. He knew there was a bar behind the dark wood cabinet, and, wonder of wonders, his staff key opened it. There were Scotch, bourbon, vodka, and gin. No white wine or Campari, he noted with satisfaction.

He grabbed the gin bottle: Gilbey's. Surely Fallsbridge General could do better, but why? No one worried about insults to their palate by the time they got around to drinking gin in the ICU conference room.

He unscrewed the bottle, tilted it, and took a long, vaporous swig. He waited for it to singe its way down his gullet, then took another, and one more for good measure. He recapped the bottle and was back at the table, staring at nothing, when Betty returned. Her pretty face was blasted-looking, as if a high dose flash of ultraviolet had exfoliated the top layer of her skin.

"They took it all away," she sobbed, "except one line into the back of his hand. . . . "

"Fentanyl," Reed said absently.

"What is that?"

"Synthetic morphine . . . mother's little helper."

"What for?" she cried.

"To make sure he's comfortable." Reed dredged up a tone of sympathy from somewhere, but it was not easy. "To ease him on his way." Gin fumes blew up his nose, making his eyes water.

"You make it sound like they're killing him," she sobbed.

"Then I make it sound wrong, Bets. He's already dead, at least the part of him that was Arlen. Nothing left but impersonal function. . . . " Like Belle. "And that will now ease itself, with the help of the fentanyl, into a slow gentle stop."

Unlike Belle, who could grind on for another twenty years.

The table rocked a little as Betty sat down across from him and leaned on it.

"Reed?"

He looked up into her swollen, bloodshot eyes, which looked as if all the veins had broken in the whites.

"What, Bets?" he asked as gently as he could.

"What happened to him?"

Car accident, he almost said; the beloved Porsche killed him. But all at once that wouldn't wash, and he realized for the first time that he didn't *know* what had happened to Arlen. He had supposedly run the Porsche off River Road and met his doom. But that stretch was marshy flatland and reeds, with nothing to "run into" except the river itself. And then all that would happen was that you'd sit hubcap-deep in the mud until they towed you out.

So what *had* happened?

He went back to the beginning. Arlen had lost control of the Porsche. Easy to imagine, given the car's proclivities and his (and Reed's) tentative style of driving. Arlen lost control, the Porsche zoomed through the marsh and hit *something:* an old piling hidden by the reeds, say. But then what? Don went to the site before he came to the hospital, in a very Don-like fit of having to see what happened. He reported the driver-side door was sprung, window smashed. That was all. No crumpled front fender or hood, and Don would have noticed and said so.

But something had hit Arlen on the head hard enough to cause massive cerebral swelling and brain death. Maybe the windshield. But it would have left a bruise, welt, red mark. There was nothing but the diseased-looking swelling in his eye sockets from cerebral edema.

"Reed . . . "

He'd been staring fixedly at Betty without seeing her. He brought her into focus. "I don't know what happened, Bets, but I'll find out."

He had taken Betty down to the lot, where her driver helped her into a Caddy as big as a bungalow in Riverside. Reed gave the driver a supply of Xanax for her. Same stuff he'd been pushing on Myra and swallowing himself.

After they were out of sight, he pulled out of the lot and drove to Ralph Malone's house.

It was almost 4:00 A.M.; nights were short this time of year, and the sky was already pale. Malone was not going to be happy to see him, but if he'd wanted to sleep nights he should have become a golf pro.

Malone lived in South Millbridge, almost but not quite across the line of Upper Fallsbridge. He was a top neurosurgeon who didn't lift a scalpel for under twenty thousand. Yet Fallsbridge, where the eight of them (seven now, and that was going to take getting used to) lived, was beyond his reach. Land went for two hundred thousand an acre, and estates of the type the eight of them owned started at around two million.

Malone lived on a stretch of nice lots of about five acres, in a sprawling Colonial, set back from the road in a neat patch of ornamental shrubs and flower beds.

All the windows were dark. A key panel next to the front door, part of an old-fashioned alarm system, showed a small, baleful dot of red light.

Reed took a breath and rang the bell. It pealed through the house and died away like a truncated change-bell rhapsody. Nothing happened; the family must be in their third NREM (nonrapid eye movement) cycle of the night. Too bad. Too fucking bad, Reed thought, and rang again.

This time a square of light appeared on the walk behind him. He looked up, saw light in a second-story window. He turned back to the door as heavy, exasperated-sounding footsteps pounded down the stairs and across a floor to the door.

"Who is it?" Malone sounded annoyed and shaky.

These towns were supposed to be safe, but it was late, the spring moon was full: the season of madness, crime . . . and paranoia.

"It's me," Reed called softly through the door.

The red panel light changed to yellow, a deadbolt shot back, the door opened, and there was Malone in ragged pajama bottoms and a T-shirt that said DORK, with an arrow pointing down.

"You'll never make the cover of GQ in that getup," Reed said. Malone managed a short, angry-looking smile that didn't reach his sleep-puffed eyes. He must have started to say something appropriately nasty, given the hour, then remembered who the man in the coma was and what he meant to Reed, and his expression softened. He opened the door all the way and let Reed into the foyer.

The floor was white marble tile that was freezing even through Reed's shoes; must be like blue ice through the thin soles of Malone's slippers.

The ceiling soared; a hideous black iron chandelier that was probably supposed to look Shaker hung from a misshapen black rod.

"Reed?"

"What happened to him, Ralph? I'm sorry . . . and yes, I know what time it is, but I gotta know what happened to him."

"But you do know. Cerebral trauma, cerebral edema. . . . "

"But how, Ralph? I gotta know how."

"The cops didn't tell you?"

"No."

"Jesus . . . shit . . . Jesus . . . "

He walked across the icy floor and flicked a wall switch. Strategically placed lamps came on in a step-down room that was beautifully proportioned but hideously furnished in the tradition of that chandelier: someone's idea of Shaker mixed with Bauhaus. The work of the decorator from hell, Reed thought. Or maybe it was the lady of the house's taste. He must not say anything, which was kind of funny since he couldn't believe he'd even noticed the furniture.

"Sit down," Malone said, and parked himself on a white leather excrescence that looked too small for two people, too big for one.

Reed sat gingerly on the edge of a pale sectional that wrapped itself around a pale wood "Shaker" coffee table the Shakers would never have conceived.

"I'm sitting," he said. "What didn't the cops tell me?"

"I guess they're still not sure . . . "

"About what?" Reed kept his voice calm, but feelings he couldn't identify started to slip out of control.

"I couldn't tell. I mean it's impossible to be sure, and I was moving fast, Reed, not caring about the *how* of what I was dealing with. You know."

Reed nodded.

"There was still a chance, one in a million, but a chance, so I only paid attention to what was right in my light beam."

"Yes."

"But I think . . . no, I know the blow was to the side of the head."

"Blow . . . " The word fell out of Reed's mouth like the toad out of the fairy-tale maiden's mouth.

"Blow," Malone echoed.

"From debris from the car . . . "

"Probably not . . . "

"Ralph . . . what are you saying."

"Shit . . . *they* should'a talked to you, not me. I'm not an M.E., for Christ's sake. I can't be sure . . . but I think . . . it looked like . . . I believe . . . but wouldn't bet on it, of course . . . but I think someone hit him."

Reed stared at him, frozen to the slick surface of the sectional couch. Then a click sounded in the room's chilly but stale air, then another. It took a second for the sound to get through the haze of *someone hit him* in Reed's mind. Then he turned toward the sound and saw a call light on a phone blinking on and off.

No ring, just the light.

Clever, Reed thought. Really *clever* . . . he'd get one like it. Only people rarely called him in the middle of the night.

Malone heaved himself to his feet and went to the phone, while Reed dragged his eyes away from the mesmeric flash of the light and tried to find someplace to look. It was as hard as it had been earlier to find space on his oldest, best friend's body to touch. Arlen's face had been distorted from the tube in his mouth; even so, his cheek had been clear. Reed should have kissed it.

A huge, boiling, roiling, gasping sob clutched his whole body. It took all his strength to stifle it, but he did, and it came out a sick choking gasp that could have been a suppressed cough . . . or a belch. Then came an equally horrific snigger, and it took as much power to choke that down. He heard Malone's voice, but was too engrossed with controlling his hysterics to make out the words.

He heard a harder click, different in tone from the light. Malone had hung up. Reed clenched his jaw and swallowed, almost swallowing his own tongue with the gigantic glob of spit that suddenly filled his mouth. A method of suicide, swallowing your own tongue. He'd learned that from the novel *Silence of the Lambs*, not from one of the ten thousand psych classes he'd taken.

He looked up at Ralph. His eyes itched; the lids felt sticky. A tear he couldn't stop broke free of the lid and made an interminable, burning trail down his cheek.

Ralph Malone stared back at him, with eyes that looked almost as haunted as his own must.

"He's dead," Reed said softly.

Malone nodded. Then, without a word, he went to a cabinet next to the ghastly white marble fireplace, with a painting two steps up from big-eyed kids on black velvet hanging over it, and came back with a bottle of clear liquor.

Beefeater.

More like it, Reed thought. He said, "Just had a quarter of a bottle of the rotgut at the hospital."

"So you'll have another quarter of a bottle. Then go home and take something else."

"Xanax."

"If that's your pleasure."

"Been dishing it out like Eskimo Pies in July. Turning into a real pusher. But it's a bad idea to take with booze. . . . " His voice started to crack.

Arl was dead. And all the crap he'd been telling himself about how he had *been* dead for hours, how that was not Arlen in the ICU cubicle with more wires and tubes coming out of him than a robot getting tuned up, was . . . crap. Only *now* was Arlen dead, for the first time ever.

"On the contrary," Malone said. "Once you're home, I think taking Xanax with booze is a fine idea. And who're you gonna listen to, your neighborhood neurosurgeon or some mail-order pharmacologist venal enough to take money from a drug company?"

Reed took a long, deep swig from the bottle Ralph handed him, then another, and did indeed get down a quarter of the bottle before he staggered out of the house to the Porsche, waiting faithfully in the driveway, looking like a casting in frozen mercury in the gray dawn light.

It *had* been a blow to the head, Lemon told him the next morning. Indications were "just indications, so far, but good ones," that the Porsche had been forced off the road on River Road midway between Bowman and Forrest sometime in the evening yesterday.

The longest day, Reed thought, in the last phase of his gin-Xanax hangover. Second only to D Day. But that was garbage thinking. There was no war; Arlen hadn't been out to save the world or do much of anything except keep himself in books and bridge and get laid regularly.

He had planned to have a wife and kids someday. "But I'm too rich to sweat it," he'd told Reed. "When the time comes, it will happen."

Should've sweated it, shit-breath buddy, Reed thought, feeling his throat tighten. *Should've sweated it.*

"We found lots of crushed reeds," Lemon was saying, "but no tire tracks. Of another car, I mean. So what we figure happened, and Dr. Lerner, please ... this is abject speculation. What we figure happened is someone went after the Porsche, forced it off the road. Not too hard to do with a car as responsive as that, and a driver who ... " Lemon paused delicately, and Reed said, "A driver who should have stuck with a Town Car."

"Probably. Anyway, they forced him off the road into the marsh and the Porsche got stuck in the mud. He should've just jumped out, forgotten the car, which I'm sure is insured, and gotten out of there. But he got mad, maybe, decided he wasn't giving up his car, and he locked the door. *Sounds cool* ... "

It didn't sound cool. It didn't sound anything, but Reed kept quiet.

"Only it was not. In fact it was dumb." Lemon stood behind his desk and turned to the window, back to Reed. "Dumb ... because whoever wanted that car *really* wanted it, and they had a crowbar or a tool like it. They smashed the window, unlocked the door and dragged Mr. Pinchot out.... "

He was still facing the window; Reed had to strain to hear. "What?"

Lemon turned around. "They dragged him out of the car ... then must've all gotten bogged down in the mud."

"All?"

"At least two, more from the look of the reeds around the car."

Reed took a deep breath and another of those swallows that seemed necessary to get rid of floods of spit, then said, "He was murdered."

Lemon didn't bother to answer.

"It was murder ... " Reed pressed.

Still no confirmation, or expression of horror or regret, from Lemon.

Reed gave up. "What happened then?" he asked.

"When?"

"After they *all* dragged him out of the car."

"Then we get into more heavy conjecture. What we call in the trade a handjob.... "

Lemon smiled; Reed smiled back before he could stop himself. And it was at that moment he knew he would get over Arlen's death. Not by next Saturday, when he'd avoid the club and try to block thoughts of calling Arlen about having dinner or lunch . . . or to hear of his singles bar exploits of Friday night, best night of the week to get laid, he'd said. But Reed knew the Saturday would come, next month or next year, when he wouldn't have to take Xanax washed down with gin to get rid of Malone's voice saying, *Flat-line*, with that instant reply of Arlen at fourteen, crowing, *I did it, shit-breath.* . . .

"And the heavy conjecture posits?" Reed asked Lemon.

"That they all staggered around in the mud in a scene that was probably hilarious to watch . . . and would've stayed hilarious, except one of the motherfuckers hit Mr. Pinchot, probably twenty million times harder than he meant to."

"With . . . ?"

"Probably the same thing they broke the window with. Metal, from the shape and width of the wound in the snaps. . . . "

"Snaps?"

"Police photographs, Doctor."

"Oh."

"The M.E. tells us more, of course. But not much more, because they had to operate before he could get a look, and I gather that meant peeling the scalp forward. . . . "

Reed's gorge sailed into the back of his throat and he looked around wildly for something to throw up in. Lemon had seen it all before, and with a look compounded of sympathy and wary disgust, he kicked forward the metal wastebasket. "Unless you can make it to the can down the hall," he said. Reed hung over the wastebasket without answering. It was already lined with a white plastic garbage bag; he must not be the first person to lose his lunch in it. But he didn't after all; a minute passed, he sat up straight, pulled out his handkerchief with weak, shaking hands, and wiped his face, which felt cold, damp, and gray, about like a mushroom, he thought.

Unfortunate image; the nausea returned. But nothing came up this time either, and he sank back, shaken and probably even paler.

"Thought doctors didn't get sick over stuff like that," Lemon said—harsh words but spoken kindly.

"I'm a shrink, not a surgeon."

"And you knew the deceased."

"He was my best friend."

"I'm sorry. I didn't know. I'm really sorry." There was a long period of respectful silence from Lemon, then he said, "Okay, so because of the . . . uh . . . surgery . . . we might not know exactly what did it. We do think it was just the one blow, probably delivered without that much punch from what little we could see. But it was in the exact right spot to put out his lights. Rotten luck."

"Who . . . " Reed got the word out in a burst of breath that made him sound like a startled owl; the hysterics that almost got the better of him at Malone's last night bubbled up again.

"That's the kicker, Doc. We got no clue and probably aren't going to have. I could carry on about how we'll do our duty and get the fuckers. Probably string along you and Mrs. Pinchot-Raines and anyone else who cared until you stop caring *so* much. But I'm not going to do that, Dr. Lerner. I'm going to play it straight with you and hope you appreciate the honesty enough to forgive us someday."

"You mean you won't get them."

"I'll be shocked to shit if we do."

"Oh, God . . . " Reed slumped in the chair; his chin sank to his chest. Lemon leaned across the desk. "We'll try," he said earnestly. "We'll try but the . . . site . . . is a mess. I mean mess. The Oban cops were called first and showed up first and made it a worse mess. . . . "

"Called by whom?"

"No way to tell. Whoever it was used the 'all other calls' number instead of nine one one. My instinct tells me kids tried to grab the car, and that's all they meant to do. Then it got out of hand. Maybe Mr. Pinchot went for them, maybe he threatened them, maybe he tried to run and one of them panicked. Lots of maybes, but I *do* think it was kids. Pros don't carjack, and I don't think the kids're local."

"You mean not from Fallsbridge."

"Or Millbridge or Bridgeton, where kids have their own Porsches. Those communities are too rich."

"Except for Riverside," Reed said. Something tugged at his conscious-ness that he tried to catch, but it slid away and dissolved, leaving him twisting in frustration in the wood slat-back chair. It was like not finishing a sneeze.

Lemon was saying, "Yeah, except for Riverside. But the population of Riverside's comparatively big and straggles over the border into Oban. About half the people in it are between eighteen and twenty-two. So that doesn't pin it down much. Of course, we might get lucky and find the weapon in a trash can on Main Street, or in the dump or river. But we probably won't, and short of something like that . . . " He shrugged, then looked hard at Reed. "There is one thing you could do."

"What?"

"You're not poor folks, from what I understand."

"We're not."

"That's what I heard."

For a wild second, Reed wondered if Lemon was about to solicit a bribe to find the killer . . . killers.

Then Lemon said, "Could you get together to put up a reward?"

"For what, how much?"

"For 'any information,' just like you see on TV. Someone might've seen something, and the money will overcome their natural not giving a shit about what happens to anyone but themselves."

Lemon rocked back in his chair, causing it to squeal softly, a plaintive sound. "Amount's up to you. Just don't make it too munificent or we'll have 'em crawling out of the walls claiming to have seen everyone from Hillary Clinton to Elvis clobber your buddy."

"You're not from around here," Reed said suddenly.

"How'd you know?"

"That's not the kind of thing a local cop—even a local state cop—would say."

"Why is that?"

"Because we're too nicey-nice to talk that way about each other. Too committed to looking like characters in a Tide commercial."

Lemon laughed and held his hand out across the desk. "Nolan Birch Lemon, Lieutenant, Boston PD, retired. Took my pension and took a job out here because I wasn't ready for full-time golf and afternoon TV."

They shook and Reed settled back in his chair, glad that Lemon was not from Oban, Washington, Bridgeton; that there was more to his expertise than answering false alarms on the estates of Dustin Hoffman and Meryl Streep. It gave him hope that Lemon was being too modest and might catch the killer after all.

CHAPTER 15

"And friends and family of the victim have offered a reward, ladies and gentlemen," intoned Rob Walsh on the local news. He
was the creep who'd made Bob Ludens look like a self-serving, camera-
hungry swine the night Pastori was killed, the Night of the Bees, Reed
thought.

"A reward large enough to impact almost any life, tempt almost any
person." Walsh paused to build suspense, and was so good at it, Reed
tensed to hear the amount, although it was his money put in escrow by
him a few hours ago.

"Two hundred thousand dollars!" Walsh trumpeted, then stared into
the camera. "That is two hundred *thousand* dollars, ladies and gentlemen.
So if you saw anything out on River Road in Fallsbridge on the night of
June second, if you happened to be passing that way at dusk . . . if you
know anyone who was, here's your chance to perform a civic service *and*
get rich." He looked past the camera at the viewer with a one-venal-cynic-
to-another grin that Reed found sickening, and he rayed off the set.

"Lord," Riva said. "What a . . . a . . ."

"Schmuck?" Reed said helpfully, and she laughed.

Reed tried to laugh with her but only made a pathetic, strangled sound.

This afternoon, he'd accompanied Betty to Keane's to pick the casket. She chose a gigantic thing of what looked like carved bronze costing a fortune. Arlen would not have approved, but Arlen was dead, and that was the casket Betty wanted. Reed had kept his mouth shut.

The funeral would be Wednesday, with a "viewing" tomorrow. Like a wake, if Congregationalists had wakes.

"Can I see the rest of the news?" Riva asked gently.

"Sorry." He rayed the set back on. Walsh was over; it was the turn of the Democrats and Republicans to tear at each other as elections loomed, with attacks so gratuitously vicious, Reed couldn't imagine voting for any of them. His eyes burned, from watching them, then closed. He heard an audience roar and Pat Sajak's voice. The news must have ended, and Riva put on *Wheel of Fortune*, one of her few guilty pleasures . . . then chimes broke through his doze. He thought a contestant had blown it on TV, but the game show had a buzzer, not chimes.

He opened his eyes and saw Riva staring at the door from the sitting room to the ill-lit, shadow-filled foyer, and the chimes rang again.

Ding-ding, ding-ding.

A less melodic front door bell than Ralph Malone's. Deliveries to the Lerner house came to the rear, and the other seven let themselves in the side door, which was left unlocked until bedtime. Reed couldn't imagine who'd come to the front door this late.

Ding-ding, ding-ding.

Persistent bastard must have seen the Porsche under the porte-cochère and the lit downstairs windows.

Ding-ding, ding-ding.

"Guess he's not gonna give up." Reed hoisted himself to his feet.

"I'm going with you," Riva said. He looked at her; she looked back pallid and wide-eyed, with cords standing out in her neck.

Riva was scared because the doorbell had rung.

Day before yesterday, she'd have left him in the chair, crossed the foyer, and simply opened the door. Then Arlen got clubbed to death on River Road, in the town he'd been born and raised in and the safety they had always taken for granted was exposed as an illusion.

Together Reed and Riva went out into the almost dark foyer; he paused to turn on the porch lights and the massive, many-armed brass chandelier that sent shafts of light from a hundred candle-shaped bulbs across the floor and walls of the foyer.

Ding-ding, ding-ding.

He approached the door, remembering the wretched father in Kipling's "Monkey's Paw" opening the door to the fulfillment of his second wish . . . his son's mangled body.

Reed shuddered; Riva murmered, "Honey . . . "

"Goose on my grave," he said and shot the dead bolt on the door. He remembered the squeaking hinge on the old radio show he and Arlen and Don had listened to tapes of when they were kids.

Welcome to the inner sanctum, he thought.

Unless it was a swarm of bees, a sea of ticks waiting on the other side of the door. Or something even worse.

His heart beat in his throat as he reached for the carved oval brass door-knob that had been too big to grab one-handed when he was a kid.

He turned it, the door swung in . . . and there was a kid he knew from around town.

Bartholomew Loamers.

The anticlimax of finding on his doorstep, after that gigantic buildup, a postadolescent who used to be a cashier at Fallsbridge Market brought a helpless grin to his face.

"Something funny?" the kid asked coldly with a hint of a snarl in his voice.

Only that I cast you as swarms of bees or ticks, Reed thought, *or one of the zombies from that old cult classic you and every other kid from sixty-whatever to now must've seen. Things have gotten bad, kid, but you gotta admit, nothing on the evening news rivals the dead roving the countryside to devour the living.*

He stopped grinning. "Bartholomew?"

"Bart."

"Bart. No, nothing is funny. I just wasn't expecting guests."

"Can I come in?"

Reed looked past him at an eighties Escort in the driveway with some-one in it.

"Who's with you?"

"Ted Dukovsky."

A groundsman at the club, a sweet, dumb boy with bland white-lashed eyes like Myra's. Although hers were mild, not bland. In fact, they sparkled with vitality and intelligence. It was a little known fact that Myra was, in fact, brilliant, had scored off the chart on the Wechsler they gave the kids in high school. Higher than Reed (he had found out much later) or any of them. So of course, she was the one who had never gotten to college.

"Ted'll wait in the car," Bart said.

"Ah, and what'll you be doing while he waits?"

"Talking to you."

"About?"

The kid looked down at his feet in an attractive display of shyness. He had acne scars à la Richard Burton, thick, shining hair, and was wearing some brand of supersneaker that probably went for $150. He should be too old by now to care about such symbols of manhood, Reed thought, then remembered that he and Arlen had bought ninety-thousand-dollar high-performance cars they could barely handle, for roads unsafe over forty.

"What do you want to talk to me about?" Reed asked gently.

The kid looked up with dark miserable eyes and said, "Arlen Pinchot."

Reed thought of the reward.

Too much'll bring 'em outta the woodwork, Lemon had said.

"Lot of money," Reed murmured.

"Huh?"

"I said it's a lotta money."

The kid looked honestly at sea. "What's a lot of money?"

Riva stepped into the light, and the kid bobbed his head to her. "Miz Lerner."

"Why, Bart, I haven't seen you for some time. Mr. Robbins said you'd started at Oban Community."

"Yes. And working at Trimble's now, ma'am. They pay more than Robbins." He looked back at Reed. "What's a lot of money?"

He did not know or was an Oscar-class actor.

"Never mind." Reed opened the door all the way and Bart entered the foyer, his eyes rising at once to the gigantic brass chandelier, then darting around to cream plaster walls hung with oil paintings and the forty-foot expanse of marble floor under his sneakers.

"Jesus," he breathed.

"This way."

The kid's sneaker soles squeaked on the marble as they crossed the foyer. As they entered the sitting room, Reed watched the kid take in the furniture, books, state-of-the-art TV, and the forty years' worth of knick-knacks Reed's mother had collected with good taste and unlimited funds.

It was a lovely room; Reed had forgotten how lovely until he saw it through the eyes of this kid from Riverside.

Riverside.

Dick Lambert was from Riverside; the kid might know him . . . and Belle. He wondered if Bart Loamers had any idea where Belle Lambert was this second, at eight fifteen on a Monday night. Probably in the day room of the nuthouse with the other psychoplegics, watching TV, Reed thought. With the picture reflected in her empty eyes, her head in that broken-doll tilt with a glistening strand of drool worming its way down her chin.

"Sit, sit," Reed said quickly, and the kid sat on the down couch, looking startled at how deeply he sank into the cushions.

"Would you like a drink . . . a beer?" Reed asked. The kid shook his head. Riva said, "Maybe something else . . . " She was thinking of the chocolate milk and cookies their youngest, Mort, would want at this time of night. Bart Loamers shook his head, staring at his hands clenched in front of him. He was in agony, Reed realized suddenly; he'd been too taken up with his own angst to notice.

The kid looked up at Riva in misery, "Mrs. Lerner . . . I . . . uh . . . " He couldn't get it out, and Riva, who had the real talent in the family when it came to emotional crises, said, "Would you like to talk to my husband alone?"

The kid nodded, and she smiled. "Let me know if you change your mind about wanting anything." He nodded again and she left the room, shutting the door noiselessly.

Reed went to the cabinet and took out his Delamain. He held up the bottle invitingly. "Sure? It's really primo stuff."

"No. No thank you."

Reed poured himself a generous tot, then came back and sat down across from the kid with the coffee table between them. He sipped the Armagnac, waiting.

After a moment, Bart blurted out, "I want to be your patient."

"Oh?"

Loamers reached into his shirt pocket, drew out a folded check, and handed it to Reed. Reed unfolded it and saw it was made out to him for one hundred and twenty-five dollars.

"I got the amount from whoever answers your office phone," Bart said. "I figured an hour'd be enough to start."

"Start what?"

"My being your patient. I mean formally your patient."

Reed started to object, then saw the kid's agony was now mixed with desperation, and he refolded the check and stuck it in his shirt pocket. "Okay, Bart. You're my patient. Now what . . . "

He waited for what seemed a long time, then Bart Loamers gave a drawn-out, quavering sigh, and said, "We did it, Dr. Lerner."

He meant killed Arlen.

Reed knew this without thinking about it and was floored to find he was not shocked, or even surprised, that he'd subliminally known this was what he was going to hear the moment he'd seen the kid at the door.

We killed Arlen. This young man . . . and whoever else comprised the *we.*

Reed let it sink in and was further floored to find he was not enraged, at least on the surface, because if this kid had done it, it had been unmeant, with all the malice and intent of a lightning bolt.

Still, it was a horrendous revelation, and Reed found it had knocked the breath out of him. He took a long drink of Armagnac.

"You know what I mean. . . . " the kid whispered.

Reed nodded.

The kid said, "I said *we* because I was there. I didn't hit him."

Say something, Reed screamed in silence at himself. He had to say

something. They were talking about Arlen, whose death had plunged
Reed into a loneliness he had not known since the long-ago morning when
he had first seen Arlen Pinchot. It had been in the fifties, at Mrs. Walsh's
Nursery School in Fallsbridge Center. Long before the days of punk or
grunge, and they would have been wearing crisp little shirts and pants and
round-toed little-boy shoes that were miniatures of their fathers'.

Reed cleared his throat so hard it burned, and croaked,

"If you didn't, who did?"

"I can't tell you."

"I'm calling the police."

"I'm your patient, remember? Besides he was real careful. The car's a
cube of junk by now."

"What?"

"Like in *Goldfinger*. Remember they cubed a Lincoln with the corpse inside in *Goldfinger*, the James Bond movie."

"I remember."

"That's what happened to the car we used. Same night. One of us . . . uh
. . . knows how to run the crusher, see . . . and he ran it that night. . . . "

With moonlight beaming down on mounds of wrecks you just glimpsed
from Super Seven, the never-to-be-finished highway, Reed thought.

"And we wore gloves . . . and masks," Bart said. "Rubber masks, goblin
masks . . . " That last came out in a ghastly croak.

"Ah," was all Reed could manage.

"It's all marsh grass and mud out there except for a couple of blinds for
birdwatchers," Bart ground on. "They won't find anything to hang on us. If
you see what I mean."

"Someone might've seen," Reed said doggedly.

"Might've, but I don't think they did. And what'd they have to see anyway, except a heap that doesn't exist anymore, and four creeps in goblin
masks."

The masks, Reed thought. Lemon might find the masks. . . .

But Bart Loamers killed that hope. "Masks're in the car . . . in the cube
the car's turned into, and it's gone. They move 'em every few weeks.
Today a couple'a hundred were hauled away, are probably on a rail
flatbed heading for Texas."

"Texas?"

"I don't know that. I just always think of them being sent to Texas. Point is, even if you betray my confidentiality and tell the cops, they're not going to find anything to back it up unless I talk. Which I won't."

"Ah."

"But I had to tell you it wasn't me or Ted out there. Ted steps over cracks in the sidewalk to keep from treading on ants."

Reed swilled more Armagnac.

"Or Rog . . . " Bart mumbled.

So, it was not Bart, Ted, or Rog (whoever Rog was). Didn't take Aquinas to figure the next question.

"Then who was it, Bart?" Reed's voice sounded remarkably steady.

"I can't say the name, Doc. Literally can't. But you know. Or will if you think about it."

"But I don't."

"Yeah . . . you do."

"Don't tell me what I know. I have no idea who'd do that to Arlen Pinchot—or anyone else—for a *car*."

Bart's eyes widened in surprise. "Car? What's the car got to do with it?"

Reed stared at him.

"Why'd you think—" Bart stopped, then nodded. "I get it. Cops saw ninety thou worth of silver buggy and figured we were carjackers."

"Yes."

"That's shit, Doc. The car meant nothing, except . . . except it did in a way."

Reed finished the Armagnac, but didn't get up for more. Another drink would put him over some edge, on the other side of which was uncontrollable rage. Another drink of silky, delectable brandy, and all six four and two hundred pounds of him would shoot out of the chair and tear this kid's head off his neck.

He compelled himself to sit back and ask quietly, "If it wasn't the car, what did you kill him for?"

"We didn't know it was him."

It wasn't for the car, but the car was a factor, and whoever wielded the crowbar (or crowbarlike implement) had not known it was Arlen.

They had not wanted the car or Arlen. They had wanted . . . whoever was driving a silver Porsche like Arlen's, but not Arlen because they didn't *know* it was Arlen.

They had wanted Reed.

"Lambert," Reed said softly.

Nothing from the kid, but that was answer enough.

So Lambert had gone after Reed and gotten Arlen. . . .

"It was supposed to be me," Reed said.

The kid nodded.

"But it wasn't, and he still killed Arlen."

The boy looked down at the floor.

"Why?" Reed whispered.

The kid didn't answer.

"It was about seven, according to the cops. They're right, because it was six thirty when Arlen left me in the club parking lot. It wasn't dark; Lambert had to see it wasn't me. So why . . . "

The kid opened his mouth, nothing came out, and he shut it.

"Why?" Reed screeched and shot out of the chair. He grabbed the kid by the front of his shirt, hauled him to his feet, and drew back a fist that looked gigantic out of the corner of his eye. The size of a honeydew. It would split the kid's mouth open, break his nose. Blood would flood down his face and soak his shirt—clean shirt, Reed noticed unwillingly. Clean and ironed without the stiff laundry folds. His mother must've washed and ironed it for him . . . he was that young. His hair was shining, his face freshly shaved, and he smelled of aftershave. Something cheap he'd probably gotten at Rusk's Discount in Oban.

He went to a bottom-of-the-heap two-year college and had to work at Trimble's even to pay for that, yet he kept up his appearance, his . . . dignity, Reed thought, and a jolt of pity shot through him.

His fist stayed balled for a second, then he relaxed it and let the kid go. Bart flopped on the sofa, sweat popped out on his face and streamed down it. He wiped it with his sleeve and looked up at Reed.

"I thought you were gonna cream me."

"So did I."

"Why didn't you?"

Wearily, Reed sat back down in the wing chair, across from the kid. "I suddenly remembered creaming people is not my style. Okay, Bart. Tell me the rest. You got Arlen off River Road into the marsh . . . thinking he was me. I was your target."

"You know why?"

"Because I committed the old lady and ended Dick's ride on the entitlement trolley."

"Yeah."

"So, you thought it was my car. You must've forced it over. . . . "

"That part was easy. We had a heap we didn't give a shit about; he was driving a silver nine eleven without a mark on it."

"So you forced him off the road, then got the door open. . . . "

"Smashed it open, because it was locked. I mean smashed the window with a crowbar . . . "

Crowbar.

"Pinchot had time while Dick did it, Dr. Lerner. He could'a gotten out the other side, put some distance between him 'n' Dick. It was muddy, he couldn't move fast, but he could've gotten a few yards, anyway . . . but he just sat there with his arms up to protect his face from the flying glass. That's why we didn't know until we pulled him out of the car into the mud . . . then . . . we saw who it was. . . .

"Ah, Jesus," the kid moaned. "That should'a been it. Right car, wrong man, and that should'a been toot fini and would'a been. We all stood around like we'd been poleaxed as it sank in what we'd done. Then we all seemed to decide *screw this* at the same time, and we turned and started slogging back through the mud to the heap mumbling to ourselves . . . so relieved we could'a wet our pants. At least I was. We didn't want anyone to really get hurt, no one was supposed to get *killed,* and seeing Pinchot was the end of it, only then he did the dumbest thing he could'a. I don't blame him. I mean, bunch'a guys in rubber fright masks run you off the road, break your car window, drag you out in the mud . . . then drop everything and walk away. You'd wanna know why. Pinchot wanted to know why, and he grabbed the one nearest him—Dick—and started yelling what the fuck did he think he was doing and all that kind'a shit . . . and Dick turned on him, Doc. But not just on him. That second, I think Dick turned on the whole world. The old lady and her money were gone, he'd have to get another job or a better first one . . . or something. His life was in shambles, courtesy of you. He meant to give you back some of the grief he figured you'd given him. But he couldn't even do that, because he'd run the wrong fuckin' car off the road. Then suddenly here's this guy who's supposed to be someone else, screaming at him . . . and he's got a crowbar in his hand. . . ."

Bart stopped. He was shaking all over, his face ran with sweat, the underarms of his shirt were drenched.

"Oh, God, Doc, you know what happened. Dick swung the crowbar"— Bart swung his arm, pantomiming the scene—"and it connected. . . . " Bart's arm arced. "I heard it hit. . . . "

Crunch, Reed thought, and became instantly, violently sick. He took a deep, long breath; the nausea eased.

The kid moaned, "I saw it, can still see it . . . I'll see it forever. It took a year to happen, like the slow motion they use in flicks to show you something's important, and shit, fuck, and bleedin' Christ, this looked important, Doc. The most important-looking thing I ever saw . . . or ever will . . . "

The kid sobbed and buried his sweltering face in his hands. Reed stared dumbly at the top of his head, waiting.

The boy raised his head; his eyes were red and swimming, tears mixed with the sweat on his face. "I'll see it when I'm an old man," he said. "It'll probably be the last thing I see before I die."

Reed nodded, and the kid went on brokenly, "He just dropped straight down in the reeds. Pinchot I mean. Just dropped without a sound . . . "

"But he was in the car when he was found."

"We put him back."

"Why?"

"To make it look like that's where it happened. They must'a seen right through that shit."

"Then?"

The kid shook his head. "Then we got outta there. . . . I made 'em stop, and I called nine one one. In case there was a chance to save him. I mean, he was still breathing when we left him."

But flat-line, Reed thought, feeling that rage stir again. *He was flat-line, you little sack of shit.*

He took a breath so deep and slow it burned his lungs, and he collapsed back in the chair and mumbled,

"You should tell the cops."

The kid said quietly, "That'll just flush my life, and he'll still be dead."

"Then why'd you come here. Why tell me . . . why torture me . . . ?"

The kid stared at him as if he'd spoken in tongues.

"Was it to confess?" Reed urged. "To get it off your chest? To shift the burden from you to me?"

"Jesus Christ, get your head outta your ass, Doc. Dick meant to get you, and he got Pinchot. Made himself a killer in your name, and you're still walking around like the Teflon head-candler. Whaddaya figure Dick's gonna do when he stops being scared about getting caught and guilty about getting the wrong man?"

"Try again," Reed said dully.

"Bingo. So I came to warn you, so you can cover your ass."

CHAPTER 16

"Cover your ass . . ."

How, Reed thought, as Bart Loamers's Ford backed and filled and headed down the drive to the road.

It was a glorious night; the almost full moon spread a soft gray light on the pale green spring lawn.

"What'd he want?" Riva's voice startled him and he turned swiftly, banging his shoulder against the window frame.

To save my life. And I almost creamed him for his trouble. Aloud he said, "To talk."

"About?"

He turned to gaze again out the window. "Things that trouble nineteen-year-olds . . ."

"At this hour, at our house?" Riva wasn't fooled, and some deep, barely detectable quaver in her voice told him the visit had unnerved her.

You don't know the half of it, sweetheart, he thought. He'd do his best to see she didn't find out . . . while he *covered his ass.*

He didn't know how to even start.

He was rich and soft, not given to strenuous pursuits. He had never even joined the Boy Scouts or played anything except squash and occasional tennis with Arl or Don. How did he even start to cover his ass?

Get a gun.

There were two in the house, his father's idea. He didn't even know where they were . . . except probably in the main master suite that had been unused since his mother moved to Palm Beach.

Cover your ass . . .

"Reed?"

Her hair looked like silk in the moonlight coming through the window; her shadowed eyes were huge. He'd make love to her if this had been any other night.

She said, "I hope you can help him. He seems like a nice kid."

"Sure . . ." A prince. Except for this little glitch of having been an accessory, before and after the fact, to Arlen's murder. A real prince.

We pulled him out into the mud. The *we* was not lost on Reed.

Still, Bart Loamers had made the effort to save him, warned him to *cover his ass.*

Riva returned to the TV in the sitting room. Reed looked up the stairs toward the shadowed landing at the top. The gun (guns?) would be up there if they were in the house at all.

Noiselessly, in his soft-soled slippers, he mounted the stairs to the second floor of the gigantic house. Too big for just the two of them, since it was unlikely the boys would ever come back to live.

They should sell it, get something smaller but still special, like Myra's sprawling farmhouse.

But without the specter in the basement . . . that Job Landau said was in Myra's head. *Was* Myra. And that was as deranged as anything he'd ever heard. He forced it out of his mind and concentrated on what he had to do to *cover his ass.*

Find the guns.

He reached the second floor and made his way to the main corridor by pale light from the lamps and moonlight streaking in the window at the end of the hall. He passed the present master suite and rarely used guest rooms and came to his folks' suite, consisting of a bedroom, sitting room, dressing rooms, and two huge, all-white space-module bathrooms, with the sauna and Jacuzzi his father had adored in the one.

Though cleaned regularly, the rooms still had an air of disuse, like his office after the weekend.

He went to the middle of the sitting room, facing the tiled fireplace, then turned around in a deliberate circle, asking himself where he'd have kept the guns if he were the old man.

Out of reach of the kids, out of sight of his wife, who'd hated them. But they still had to be handy to take care of a thief in the night . . . the only reason for having them.

The bedroom, he decided.

He entered the room and was hit with the old, worn-down sadness at seeing the stripped bed, empty dresser tops, and his mother's vanity, without the jars and bottles, silk flowers, photos slid in the mirror frame.

"Okay, Pop," he whispered, "where'd you hide 'em?"

The closet or the bathroom, which had been the old man's sanctum sanctorum. Going in there seemed a breach of the old man's privacy, even seven years after his death. So he went first to the closet, a walk-in empty of clothes but still smelling faintly of the bready scent of his father, mixed with thin whiffs of masculine cologne and old, cold cigar smoke.

He liked being in here, found himself inhaling deeply as he advanced into the space with its built-in drawers, tie holders, shoe racks.

He found the guns in under a minute, hidden under the second shoe rack behind the strip of wood that made the bottom riser. They were in a felt-lined wooden box, with ammo for both.

One was a .38 of good weight and heft for Reed's hand. The second was a 9mm monster that would be impossible to hide, and Reed chose the .38.

He replaced the 9mm, left the closet, and shut the door, facing himself in the full-length mirror on it. Seeing himself holding a gun was shocking, beyond anything he'd ever imagined.

He stuffed the .38 into the back of his waistband.

Full face the gun was invisible; in profile it made a discreet lump he thought would be undetectable under a jacket.

He faced himself again, then crouched, pulled the gun, and growled, "Freeze."

He was awkward; his thumb had trouble finding the safety.

He put the gun back in his belt and tried again, and again, until he felt comfortable drawing and cocking it.

He straightened up, holding it more confidently than before.

Reed Simon Lerner, M.D., F.A.C.P., healer of the mind, member of the gang of eight (now seven) . . . and gunslinger.

"Cover *your* ass, Dicko," he hissed at the mirror.

The coffin was closed, with white, cloyingly sweet flowers covering the lid. Everyone knew funeral flowers stank; they were reviled in books and movies; people hated them, yet persisted in having them—a hangover from preembalming days, Reed thought.

Betty and her husband, Tony, who was tall and emaciated-looking, wearing a stovepipe-cut dark suit that made him look more emaciated, sat in the front row. Their sons, sixteen and nineteen, Arlen's nephews and heirs, sat next to their parents.

The seven were together in the second row, with their spouses in the third.

Don and Irene had identical-looking deep, dark lines under their eyes. Helen's face was gray and slick, and she looked on the verge of fainting. But she had looked that way for the past hour, and Reed stopped worrying about it. Lambie stared fixedly at the coffin, shifting quickly to peer around anyone who blocked her view. Myra sat between her and Reed, and he noticed a faint sound, like a single-horsepower motor in another room, coming from her. Myra was humming tunelessly and pointlessly under her breath. He must tell her to cool it on the Xanax tonight. At the same time, he would tell Don, who looked like he needed a little time in oblivion, to take some.

Helen probably needed a good dose of iron. Lambie seemed okay, except for that fixed stare at the coffin, and Angie's lips kept moving, even after condolers she'd been talking to were gone. She needed more than Xanax, Reed thought. Maybe Thorazine . . .

Angie and Billy were staying in Helen's guest wing, and Reed doubted they'd want to (or should) go back to Brooks House for a long time.

Reed shifted, trying to ease the pain in his back from the gun, but it slid into an even worse spot. He excused himself, sidled out of the row, and found the men's room off the hushed, carpeted mourners' room, which had big couches, boxes of Kleenex, and vials of smelling salts spotted around.

Break and sniff, he thought. Stay conscious, and in agony.

Whoever put smelling salts in this room was a sadist.

He went into the men's room, used the commode, and reshifted the gun to the other side of his back, where it immediately started fresh bruising. His lower back would be a mass of purple by tonight; he'd have to keep his pajamas on.

Arlen never wore pajamas, said sleeping in the nude ensured waking up with a hard-on.

Not this morning, Reed thought.

He pressed paper towels soaked in cold water to his eyes, then made his way back.

At noon, they "broke" for lunch, like actors at a rehearsal or a Senate investigating committee.

It was too far to the club and back, so they went to the Fallsbridge Coffee Shop on Main, then back for the afternoon shift.

Reed climbed out of Riva's big, blocky, comforting Volvo and, across Governor Street, saw the dark red Trans Am that was usually around when he visited Belle.

Dick Lambert's car.

He froze with one leg out of the car, and his hand slid around his waist under his jacket.

Riva had gotten out and was halfway to the side door before she realized he wasn't with her. She turned back, the Trans Am's tinted window slid smoothly down, and Dick Lambert looked out at Reed from a few yards away. Reed's hand grabbed the gun butt but didn't draw; Lambert stayed in the car, eyes on Reed. His still boyish cheeks bloomed as he smiled. His hand came up, Reed jerked the gun out of his belt, and Dick made a gun of his finger, aimed at Reed with one eye closed, and pulled the imaginary trigger. Then he laughed, jammed the car in gear, and peeled away from the curb, laying a trail of smoking rubber.

*   *   *

Reed's legs trembled, and he half staggered down the funeral parlor aisle to his place in the second row.

Coward, wimp, he screamed silently at himself; *weenie!* The kid pointed a *finger* at him, and he was pissing in his pants . . . all hulking six foot four of the craven, faint-hearted, white-livered *chicken* he was.

The shakes got worse. He had to stop in the aisle and hang on to the back of a chair. At least it was lunch hour; the room was almost empty. Someone put a hand on his shoulder. "Reed . . . " It was Myra, her arm stretched full out to reach his shoulder. Her lovely face looked woeful, with a crease of worry between her pale eyebrows. No one could look as worried as Myra, he thought, and heard Job Landau's voice out of nowhere: *Myra is the ghost.*

With those few words came an idea so horrible, such a betrayal of everything he believed and of this plump, sweet, pretty woman he honestly loved, that he could not believe he'd had it. Yet he had, and it sank in and put down roots so deep and so fast he couldn't remember what it had been like not to have it.

One instant he'd been innocently looking into Myra's worried blue eyes, the next he was consumed by this crazed notion he wasn't sure he'd ever get rid of.

He spent the rest of the afternoon trying to cleanse his mind, but *the idea* had become like the old saw of not thinking about an elephant. After the afternoon "viewing," he ate dinner, drank Delamain, watched TV with *the idea* entrenched. He went back on Xanax, washed down with gin, and finally fell asleep. The next morning, the day of Arlen's funeral, he woke with a raging hangover that he figured was part grief, part Xanax, plus gin mixed with Armagnac. *The idea* was there, but had faded considerably, and by the time he was able to keep down a thimbleful of cranberry juice and a slice of toast, it had lost its vitality.

He shaved carefully, only nicking himself once. He tended the cut with tissue and styptic until it stopped welling blood. Then he dressed in a suit as dark and funereal as Betty's husband's, with a shirt stiff as plastic, a tie the dark scarlet of arterial blood, and a shroud-white handkerchief spiking out of his breast pocket. He checked himself in the mirror and confronted a primly dressed fellow who looked eighty.

He eased the tissue off the nick on his chin, returned the gun to his waistband, and judged himself as ready as he was ever going to be. Then, with *the idea* sunk to the level of something he'd seen in *Tales from the Crypt* about thirty years ago, he went downstairs.

The idea would have stayed at that level, eventually becoming a nuts notion that had come to him in '95—assuming he ever even thought of it again—if Dick Lambert had not come to Arlen's funeral.

CHAPTER 17

Half an hour before the service was due to start, Lambert appeared in front of Betty, Tony, and the two nephews in the first row.

His hair was slicked with mousse; he had on a pink dress shirt, no tie, and a blue blazer, with loose-legged tan slacks. He looked past Betty's perky little black straw hat at Reed in the next row, waited for Reed to see him, then spoke to Betty and gave Reed a slow, sly, arrogant grin.

Reed sat frozen in his funeral finery, with the gun digging into his back.

Lambert finished whatever he was saying and moved up the row to the side aisle.

He had come to the funeral of the man he had murdered to mock Reed's grief, mock the grief of all of them. *The idea* came flooding back.

Reed looked over at Myra in the seat next to him, then faced front, aware of Lambert watching the back of his head.

It was insane. He shouldn't even begin to entertain it because it meant telling Myra things she didn't need or want to know. It was cruel, unfair . . . but he knew he was going to do it because he *could* do it.

He stood and looked down at Myra sitting between him and Lambie, who seemed as transfixed by the coffin today as she'd been yesterday.

Myra looked up at him.

Sun from a high window shone through her thick, silky, blond hair, turning it to a gilt halo around her face.

"Reed?"

"I've got to talk to you . . . in the mourners' room."

The others turned to see what was going on.

"About the catering." He spoke in a stage whisper.

If it was about food, you would naturally talk to Myra.

"Right now?" she whispered back. Fifteen minutes before Arlen's funeral was set to start?

"Now," Reed said. He was Arlen's best friend; asshole buddies, Don had called them, always feeling a tad left out. No one expected Reed to behave rationally today or for some time to come.

Myra followed him up the aisle; they passed Dick Lambert seated in a middle row. He gave Reed that same thin, vicious grin.

The mourners' parlor was hushed as before, the rose carpeting streaked with vacuum trails, the Kleenex and smelling salts ready, along with dishes of hard candy for those who needed a sugar rush, Reed thought.

Myra unwrapped a round green candy and popped it in her mouth.

She was much more alert today, must have knocked off the Xanax as he'd advised.

"The caterers are John Frawley and his sister," she told him, with the candy clicking against her teeth. "They did last New Year's Eve party at Helen's. . . ."

Where he, Arlen, and Don had gotten blasted and gone outside to clear their heads. They'd sat on the front steps of Helen's rambling brick Georgian on Last Road (literally the last road in Fallsbridge), gulping freezing air to sober up enough to drink some more. The stone had been icy; Don had jumped up, rubbing his posterior and shouting, "My hemorrhoids!" They'd roared as if *hemorrhoids* were the wittiest word ever spoken.

Arlen's eyes had shone with tears of laughter, making him look about twenty in the winter moonlight.

"I remember," Reed said hoarsely.

Myra rummaged in her purse. "I've got the menu. . . ." She pulled out a folded sheet of pale green paper, then stopped suddenly and looked up at him. He watched her usual vague, slightly foolish expression disappear as that stratospheric IQ of hers kicked in. He had looked it up as part of a psych project he'd been involved in in med school, suspecting that the mind behind those wide, sky-blue eyes was way beyond what people thought, and he had been superright. Myra Fox had scored in the 170s, with quantitative skills beyond what they called "any known rating scale."

She said, "You don't care about the food, Reed."

He could still say he did, that this meeting in the mourners' back parlor was about him wanting everything to be perfect for Arlen's last party, and Myra would not argue.

But there was that outside almost-but-not-quite-impossible chance that Job Landau had been on target with his *Myra is the ghost*. Reed waited a beat, then said, "Right, My. It's not about food . . . it's about Arl. What really happened to him."

"What really happened to him?" Don asked from the doorway.

Lambie and Irene squeezed into the opening with him; past Don's shoulder, Reed saw Helen's black hat and Angie's dark blond hair.

They'd followed him and Myra to the parlor.

He slumped in his chair. "Shit, guys . . . "

Don charged in and threw himself into a roomy leather chair facing Reed. "What did happen to him?"

"You can't know and not tell us." That was Lambie, as they came into the room, taking seats or leaning against the paneled wall.

Helen said, "He was our comrade, too, Reed. If *you* know, we should, too."

"Just give me a second." He looked up at each one of them, letting them take in his pink-rimmed, swollen eyes, pale skin with the shadow of his beard like smudged charcoal, and the nick on his chin. They would see how tortured he was, would not urge him to speak. But they *did* have a right to know.

Of course they'd been told it was murder, but he doubted any of them had actually thought the word, much less said it out loud. He thought, *Okay, fellahs, you asked for it.* And he launched into a narrative of Bart Loamers's visit the night before last. He watched them pale as they listened, and when he got to Arlen being dragged out of the car into the mud, a hiss came up from the six of them, like air escaping, and Don groaned, "Shits. Brutal fuckin' shits."

Reed went on to Arlen mortally wounded, left face down in the muck, then finished the tale and looked at the wall clock. Three of, time was almost up.

Naturally, Don asked who had done it, and Reed lied that he did not know.

"But you know who told you," Don accused.

"But I can't tell you."

"Why?" That was Helen. Reed looked at her. "Because he's my patient. I can't breach—"

Don exploded. "What the fuck're you talking about? You've *got* to tell."

"I can't. . . ."

Don leaped to his feet and stood over Reed with clenched fists. All they needed to put the icing on this horror of a day was for Reed and Don to have a fight.

Myra said, "Don, please. He'd tell if he could."

Bless Myra, good, dear, loyal, Myra, who always helped if she could, never hurt. *The idea* sank deeper into the realm of mad fiction.

The clock clicked to two; Angie stood. "We better go."

Her stitches were out, leaving red dots running down her temple and cheek. Mirror sunglasses hid the shiner, and she'd never have another, because Bill Withers was dead.

Rethink that position, Myra had told him.

"So what're we supposed to do?" Don mumbled.

"Pin our hopes on a witness coming forward for the reward. What else can we do?" Reed said.

"Tell the cops who told you," Don cried, then looked miserably at Reed through lashes stuck together with tears. "I guess you can't, or you would," he said, and David Keane, overseer of this and other funerals that ran five thousand or more, stuck his head in the door.

"Reverend Bodgett's ready, folks."

* * *

Someone else was in Dick Lambert's chair, and Reed felt a shock of relief that was staggering, until he saw him in the back, on the far aisle, with his legs stretched out. The other chair must have been too confining.

His eyes met Reed's and that slow, slimy grin spread itself across his face again.

Reed twisted around to face front; the .38 dug anew into his back.

Organ music to wait by came through speakers. Myra turned to him, wide-eyed. "He drinks," she whispered. "I mean the reverend. What if he's drunk."

"We'll get a few laughs," Reed said. They grinned quickly at each other and faced front. A moment later she turned again. "I was the only one you were going to tell, wasn't I?"

Organ music swelled before he had to answer. The door in the wall behind the dais opened and the Reverend Bodgett came out. He strode to the podium with his white robe billowing out behind him, opened the Bible on the podium with a slap, and exclaimed, "I am the Resurrection . . . "

A tenet Arlen had no truck with any more than he would have had with this folderol of organ music, flowers, and a ten-thousand-dollar casket.

Myra's shoulder pressed against Reed's; her breath was warm on the side of his face. "You were going to tell me who it was, weren't you?"

He didn't answer.

She whispered, "Tell me now if you want, Reed. I'll never repeat it."

She would not. Like the best Mafia bag man, Myra's word was gold.

He looked into her earnest blue eyes fringed with pale lashes. *The idea* had never seemed more ridiculous, but he suddenly knew that no matter how ridiculous, how frankly insane it was, Arlen would want him to give it a shot, and without hesitation he whispered, "Dick Lambert."

The Reverend spoke of Arlen's charity, decency, probity. Myra faced front, seemingly listening intently, but a second later she turned back to Reed.

"I know him from Trimble's," she hissed, meaning Lambert. "I saw him here, in back—"

"Cool it, My," Bob said from behind them; Lambie gave them the look you give whisperers at the opera, and they settled down to get through the rest of the service.

Reed figured it would all take about an hour, less with any luck. Then would come the stint at the graveside, then the reception, then . . . nothing.

Life without Arlen.

This was not the time to think about that, and he fixed his eyes on Bodgett's moist, pink face with capillaries making darker strands across his cheeks.

The Reverend finished his spiel, leaving Reed with the impression he'd genuinely liked Arlen, as most people did.

A moment of rustling as Don made his way to the podium. The room had gone from hot to stifling. It was much hotter out than predicted; Keane's had started up the central air-conditioning too late to counteract the heat of a couple of hundred bodies.

Don's voice was deep, strong, soporific; Reed took in about one word out of ten.

He looked over at Myra, who stared at Don as if hanging on his every word, but he doubted she heard any more than he did.

Myra, Myra. Myra the polite, good, gentle, and loyal. Myra, whom Job Landau had suggested was the engineer of two outlandish killings.

Reed might have heard greater absurdities, but none came to mind. And for that absurdity Reed had betrayed Bart Loamers, a lousy thing for him to do, one he would hate himself for when the ludicrousness of why he'd done it sank in.

Then the service ended, Dick Lambert literally bumped into Myra as she was leaving the funeral home, and it stopped being ludicrous.

It ended at three, when the heat of the day was at its height. Myra mopped her face with her hanky, damp patches stuck the silk of her dress to her back, her stockings felt glued to her legs.

People moved up the aisles to the shut doors. The heat shut down on everyone, the doors stayed shut with people jammed up against them, then opened suddenly, and blessedly cool air blew in. David Keane appeared, looking shame-faced. "Sorry, folks, some idiot locked them."

People streamed out into the lobby; Myra trudged up the aisle with Bob ahead of her. She paused to look back at the coffin covered with odoriferous flowers wilting in the heat and suddenly thought this was her real good-bye to Arlen, not the stage-managed graveside ceremony that came later.

Good-bye, Arl, she thought. *Good-bye, my dear friend . . .* and a body slammed into her side, sending her reeling. She went down hard on her knees, jarring her spine to her skull, but the thick, plush carpet cushioned the fall and she was sure she hadn't broken anything. Riva crouched next to her; Bob and Reed were rushing back to get to her.

"Myra!"

Riva grabbed her arm, Myra grabbed a chair seat, and they boosted her to her feet. "No harm done," Myra said to no one in particular. Then she turned to see who'd rammed into her and faced Dick Lambert.

"Sorry . . . sorry . . . " he was saying. "I tripped or something . . . Jesus! You okay? Jesus, I'm really sorry. . . . "

This was the killer, according to Reed. But he sounded so worried and sorry, looked so sincere. *Poor thing,* she thought in spite of herself, and started to say, *That's okay, no harm done,* or words to that effect, and out came, "You don't know what *sorry* means. . . . " A gasp, then, in the sudden silence around her, she added, "Yet . . . "

No one moved. Reed, Riva, and Dick Lambert looked like statues of themselves. Then the kid's long-lashed eyes narrowed; his full lips (which would probably be considered sensual when he was fully grown) turned down and he snarled, "What the fuck's that supposed to mean, lady?"

Antonin Pastori had also called her *lady.*

You'll be sorry, she had told Pastori, then advised Bill to *rethink that position.* And now . . . *you don't know the meaning of sorry.*

"Get away," she said softly, and the kid's eyes widened.

"I mean it," she hissed so Reed and Riva wouldn't hear. "Get out of town."

She sounded like the sheriff in a stock western. *Don't let the sun set on you . . .* etc. It was the wrong tone. She added, "I beg you."

He tilted his head as if listening to her, and she suddenly knew he was. She was scaring him; he really might pay attention if they sat down, just the two of them, and she warned him as graphically as she had Barb.

But Reed stepped between them and in a low, deadly voice said, "Get your ass outta here, Lambert." That ended the moment of rapport between her and Dick Lambert, if it had existed.

Lambert stepped back, grinned at Reed, and popped his middle finger at them. *Up yours,* he meant, and she felt herself blush, and heard that horrid roaring in her ears. But this was not about her or her blood pressure. It was about a boy of twenty (if that) who was in mortal danger.

Please, she mouthed at the kid, but he grinned evilly at her and swaggered up the aisle, joined a small clump of people, and exited the side door that opened to the churchyard.

CHAPTER 18

"Yo, shithead, this is 555-0068." Dick Lambert's taped voice came over the phone. "Leave a message at the beep, or don't leave a message...."

After three calls, Myra gave in and said to the tape, "Please call 555-8099. It's urgent...." Then came words she'd never used in her life: "A matter of life and death."

She did not leave her name. He might remember her voice from the funeral parlor, but he might not; she thought it more likely he'd return an anonymous call. Probably at two in the morning, just as she finally started to drift off.

It was already after midnight.

Bob had had too much champagne at Arlen's. She'd driven home, and he had staggered up the stairs and passed out in the middle of the bed. She had gotten his shoes off, loosened his collar, tie, and belt, then gotten his jacket off by rolling him from side to side.

After the warm day, a blanket of chilly fog seeped in the open window, and she had covered him with a light blanket, left him snoring on his back. She had undressed in the bathroom, showered, and, wearing her robe and nightie, gone downstairs to call Lambert, and had kept calling, until finally leaving this mortifying "life or death" message.

She hung up and her eyes went helplessly to the door to the basement.

"She must'a gone ten feet straight up," Dick Lambert said thickly.

They were in the Riverside Roadhouse, the town's only gin mill, the only place in a ten-mile radius where you could get a beer without a fifty-dollar plate of food.

Rog chuckled at the picture of rich-bitch Myra Ludens flying through the air, and Ted smiled vaguely. But Bart looked grim.

"What's'a matter, scab-face?" Dick asked.

"What were you doing there in the first place, fucko?"

Dick looked into his glass of flat beer.

Bart had expected snot and gotten unhappy silence.

"Fucko?" he asked almost gently.

"Just went, that's all."

In wordless sorrow, Bart suddenly thought. Maybe to honestly pay his respects, only to run afoul of the Ludens woman.

Her reaction was a mystery inside a puzzle over a riddle. *You don't know the meaning of sorry . . . yet,* clearly meaning he would in time.

It was a threat, and it came from Starret Fox's daughter, who was worth about a hundred million by all accounts. Bart believed it, because she looked just the opposite. Drove a three-year-old Buick and dressed like a Kmart cashier. He knew, because his mother *was* a Kmart cashier.

Myra Ludens, with clout up the kazoo if she chose to use it, had threatened Dick Lambert—a little like shooting a fawn with a bazooka. Something you'd never do unless you just like seeing flesh fragments fly.

So why?

Lerner might have told her about Pinchot, but then she'd probably tell the cops instead of threatening poor Dick in public.

Unless it was not about Pinchot, but then what was it about? Dick could tell him, only he never would as long as he had the other two around to play to.

*   *   *

Dick dropped Bart off second to last, then peeled down Ruxton, leaving Bart on his front porch. Fog from warm air hitting ground still cold from the long chilly spring hid the street, muffled the car noise.

Bart went inside the dark house and stopped to listen.

Not a sound, though he saw light under his mother's door. She'd probably fallen asleep over a book.

She would not hear him, but his little sister Kaye had the ears of a cat. He slipped off his shoes and padded through the house to the kitchen, turning on and off the lights he needed to get the keys to his mother's Escort. He slipped his shoes back on, and left the house, moving stealthily across the slats of the back porch. The fog had gotten thicker just in the last few minutes; the street lamps were dazzling smears that barely lit his way to the car in the driveway.

A few minutes later Bart parked in front of Dick's on Bowman, climbed out, and made his way around the side of the house to the back.

The fog was much thicker in the narrow space between the buildings; he waved it away from his face only to have it fold back around him like a pale, diaphanous curtain. He stayed close to the house, finding his way by feel to the rail of the porch. The back door was usually unlocked, on the sensible assumption that no one would be stupid enough to bother ripping off the Lamberts.

Bart went up the steps to the porch, avoiding the third step, which had squeaked ever since he could remember. Light streamed through the back window, but could not penetrate the dank-smelling fog. The whole state was mildewing, he thought, needed a good, clean prairie wind to blow the miasma away.

He felt for the knob, opened the door, and stepped into the kitchen, which was a little startling in its hard-edged light and its cleanliness. It was cleaner than he'd ever seen it, with no dirty dishes in the sink or bits of food rotting under milky water, and no smell of excrement.

A woman's scratchy voice came down the hall from Dick's room, and he went toward it.

The door was shut; tacked to it was the sign, CALCUTTA, 10,335 MILES, that they'd ripped off from Barrow's Tag Sale shop when they were about twelve and still into petty crime. Before they had gone big time and killed someone.

Before *Dick* had killed someone.

But Bart had been there and done nothing to stop it, was an accessory before, after, and during. He would get fingered for it or not and there was no point rehearsing that particular disaster before it happened.

He had things to do that could be done. For instance, to keep Dick from going after Lerner again, and, even more important, to get Dick to take heed of the enigmatic warning/threat delivered by Myra Ludens this afternoon.

The scratchy voice had stopped. He knocked on the door, rattling the sign.

"Fuck off," Dick snarled, probably thinking it was his old man.

Bart opened the door slowly, unsure of his reception, but Dick grinned when he saw him. "Hey, scab-face, what're you doing here?"

"Visiting," Bart said dryly. "Who's the broad I just heard?"

Dick gave a leering grin. "You ain't gonna believe it." He pushed the play button and a woman's voice crackled through the speaker. "Please call. It's a matter of life and death."

"She didn't leave her name, but I know her voice," Dick said. "It's *her.*"

Myra stood at the basement door, praying it could be dislodged by nothing short of dynamite. But a half-hearted tug opened it, letting out warm, dry, fresh air.

She stepped out on the landing, turned on lights, and looked down.

The rug was still rolled up, the "magic" circle exactly as they'd left it with the pentagram and strange words in red kiddy tempera.

She took a step, stopped, and said, "I mean no harm." Then went on down the stairs, expecting that prickling to start its run across her neck and up her arms, a little surprised that it didn't. She reached bottom and stepped down on the tile over *her* bones. Maybe *right* on them, and she leaped back up a couple of steps, smothering an impulse to say she was sorry.

She waited a beat, then said, "I know they shouldn't've moved you, *they* know it too. But they have families and needed the work. They are sorry, very sorry, and whatever harm they did will be undone, you have my word on it."

The poor moss-covered bones would be dug up again, this time to be carried out into the fresh air and sunshine for the first time in three hundred years. They'd make the short trip to First Congregational, and there, in a lovely shady spot, with wild yarrow and phlox blooming in the slightly overgrown grass, Goody Redman would be tucked away in the good earth at last.

Myra choked up, her voice sounding thick and teary when she spoke again. "They committed a transgression, I admit, but not such a serious one. Not like what Pastori and Bill did. But Pastori . . . and oh, God . . . even Bill. . . . " She had to stop for breath, then went on. "I know what happened to them. I mean I know it was done for my sake in a way. At least it seemed to fall in with what could've looked like what I wanted. But I didn't . . . I swear . . . I didn't. No one . . . no one could have deserved what happened to those men.

"That's what I've got to talk to you about, because I'm afraid . . . terrified . . . it's going to happen again. This time to a young man. Very young. . . . "

She was having a conversation with a pile of bones! She should be in the bed next to Belle Lambert's, the boy's grandmother. Reed used to talk about her, until he became afraid her committal was inevitable and he'd failed, then he stopped mentioning her.

"He doesn't deserve it, either." She spoke gently. "The boy, I mean. Dick Lambert. I don't believe he meant what happened to Arl. I believe it was the awfulest accident, and he's suffering for it, no matter how uncaring he acts. But even if it wasn't an accident . . . even if it was the most brutal, premeditated murder, with the special circumstances they use to sentence people to death . . . even then, Mrs. Redman, he wouldn't deserve what happened to the others."

She stopped herself, suddenly terrified that she'd given offense. After all, if her premise was correct, the woman she was addressing had been hanged for witchcraft in a time when such things were commonplace, when the Inquisition was still in full swing on the Continent, and people were strangled, impaled, burned alive—a time that would make this one, for all its drugs and murder, look like a stroll in the park.

Being stung to death, or burned to death to keep from being sucked dry by ticks might not seem so horrible to a woman from such a time. But it *was* horrible, no matter what Goody Redman had been through. Myra would not back down on that point.

After a moment to let her words about the horror of the other "executions" sink in, she went on to talk about the boy and his grandma, the little she knew. She described Fallsbridge today, and explained how hard it must be to be poor in a town full of rich people. The basement cooled down as it got later and colder outside; her skin pimpled, her legs started to ache. She used the stair rail to ease herself down to sit on the fourth step, with her feet in their woolly slippers on the second, and tucked the skirt of her robe around her legs. She kept talking until she was really freezing, had started to repeat herself, and was sure Goody Redman had gotten the point . . . if she was ever going to. Then Myra grabbed the stair rail and hauled herself to her feet. She looked down at the expanse of gray tile, hoping for and dreading some sign from the spirit she believed was here.

Nothing happened, and she started back up the stairs, aware of the basement at her back, anxious to get out; but halfway up, something else occurred to her, and she had to stop and turn back.

"Another thing," she said, trying not to lecture. "Reed said it was just the one boy. The others were there, but only Dick Lambert hit Arlen. I know that—now you do too. But will ticks, or bees, or mice, or snakes . . . or whatever . . . be able to make such distinctions? I mean, the wrong boy could be punished . . . and that would be terrible, ma'am. Worse than what was done to Arlen . . . as bad—forgive me—but as bad as what was done to you."

That said, she turned again and went the rest of the way up the stairs. At the door, some of the old panic returned. That Old Black Magic, she thought, with the tune running through her head. She was suddenly sure the door would stick and she'd hear the click-clack of toe bones, metatarsus, metacarpus, all the small and large bones . . . all hundred and whatever of them . . . coming at her across the tile.

But the door opened easily, and she stepped out into her kitchen and saw the red light shining steadily on the answering machine.

Dick Lambert had not called back.

Bart went back through the Lambert kitchen.

His car was out front, but going that way meant passing Larry's room. Larry might hear him and come out to talk, and a conversation with Larry Lambert was like a week in a dark closet.

The mist had gotten thicker. He retraced his steps around the house by feel, then struck out across the front yard blindly, heading for the Escort on faith, without any sensory evidence of its position.

He had tried to convince Dick to call Myra Ludens back, to hear her "life and death" message, but Dick had refused. Then Bart had gone on to the other goal of his visit and asked Dick about Doc Lerner. Nothing so crude as *Will you leave the poor shit alone now that you've killed the wrong man,* but he wasn't too subtle about it either.

He had braced himself, in case Dick adopted the cock-measuring stance he tipped over into so easily. But Dick Lambert had been uncharacteristically quiet, and it had struck Bart again that Dick was miserable about what he'd done, and it was that misery that had taken him to the funeral.

Then Dick had broken the silence with the words Bart longed to hear. "What's the fuckin' point, fucko? Let's leave Asshole Lerner alone."

Bart's knee rammed the car fender, bringing tears to his eyes, and he heard a faint but definite chirp with the undertone of a chatter. Like a squirrel or mouse.

He stared blindly into the fog.

Antonin Pastori being stung to death across the road from the Redman Farm had made all the local stations. They'd quashed the press on William Withers's death since no local was going to risk the Brooks heiress's wrath. But Bart had heard what had happened to him, and he now listened with all his might through the fog.

Senses need each other, he thought. His lost sight seemed to impair his hearing instead of sharpening it.

Then he heard it again. It was coming from the next block, where Bowman ended, the many marshes along the river began, and snakes, rats, toads, bats—every creepy crawly native to the northwestern Connecticut slice of southern New England—hung out.

Bees had gotten Pastori, ticks Withers, now something was chirping out there in the fog. A whole lot of somethings from the sound, and they were getting louder, which translated to closer. Close enough to give off a musty smell that warred with the moldy odor of the fog. He knew that smell; it came into the basement at home in the fall when *they'd* come in after the first cold snap, and he'd have to put out traps to get rid of them.

Rodent smell.

"Oh God . . . oh shit . . . " he moaned, his breath blowing a hole in the fog that closed right up again. His mind raced over what he knew and what he could figure: Pastori had lived across the road from Myra Ludens and William Withers had been married to Myra Ludens's buddy.

Two men in her sphere died horror-flick deaths, and this afternoon she'd told Dick he didn't know the meaning of *sorry*. Now a swarm of somethings was chirping out in the fog, and Bart knew he could twist and turn and try to make something everyday out of whatever it was, or he could act. Myra Ludens had given Dick the warning, if it *was* a warning, so they were after Dick if they were after anything.

Bart whirled around, sending the fog swirling around him, and headed back. Higher up the fog thinned enough for the faint outline of the roof to guide him. Almost there, he reached out blindly, felt the stone supports of the front steps, then veered left and used the stone foundation to feel his way between the Lambert and Loomis houses.

Lambert, Loomis, Lerner, Loamers, Ludens. Lots of *L*s in this affair, he thought, suppressing what was bound to be a totally nuts snigger.

The chirps were louder, more clearly in a bunch. They were getting closer, and there were more than a few. Much more. He even thought he heard their distant scuttle, the barely audible click of tiny claws on asphalt as they came out of the marsh.

He slid along the stone foundation to the back-porch rail, flowed up the stairs to the back door, praying it had not locked after him by some fluke.

It was open. He slammed it back against the wall, letting in a cloud of fog, then pounded across the kitchen and down the hall to Dick's room.

Dick sat cross-legged on the bed, with his nineteen-inch Sony (nothing but the best for ol' Dickie boy) playing softly.

"What the fuck . . . ?" he cried when he saw Bart, who was gray as the fog, with his hair curled into wild knots from moisture.

"C'mon . . . " Bart gasped.

"What the fuck?" Dick repeated, and the phone started to ring.

"Never mind that," Bart cried and grabbed Dick's arm. He was not as big as Dick, but had mad purpose on his side and pulled him easily off the bed. It was going to get harder when Dick collected his wits enough to resist.

"The phone," Dick said.

"Fuck it . . . c'mon . . . Jesus, Dick, something's coming out of the river marsh. A lot of them . . . c'mon!"

Dick pulled back; Bart had to let him go.

"What the fuck . . . ?" that was the third time and Bart didn't know what to do. He couldn't muscle Dick out of there, but didn't know how to explain any better than he had, except to blubber, "They're after you, Dicko. Like the bees after Pastori, ticks after Withers."

The phone stopped ringing. Dick muttered, "You're nuts."

"Yeah? Listen." Bart raised his finger like a teacher making a point, and they listened. The chirps weren't loud, but they were definite.

Dick looked at him with suddenly scared eyes. "What the fuck?"

"If you say that again, I'll smash your face in. Now let's get outta here."

"And go where?"

"My house."

"*They* won't go there?" Dick's narrow eyes had rounded; his face was the color of oatmeal.

"I don't know." Bart grabbed Dick's arm again and pulled him out into the hall. Dick didn't resist at first, then he dug in and they had to stop.

"The old man—I ain't goin' without the old man. . . . "

So, Dick Lambert had mourned his victim and cared about his old man. It was a night of revelations, and later (if there was a later) Bart would reflect on how little "best buddies" knew about each other.

"Okay, get him," he said. The chirps didn't sound any louder or closer.

Dick pounded on Larry's door.

"Pop . . . hey, Pop . . . "

No answer; the door stayed shut. Out here in the hall, the chirps—or one chirp from many throats—was very clear.

"Pop! Oh, shit . . . Jesus, Daaaadddddddyyyyyy. . . . " Dick wailed, and Larry Lambert came out of his room in his underwear.

"House on fire?" he asked, blinking in the light.

"No—we're going to Bart's."

"What'n tarnation for?"

"Listen," Dick said, and the old man raised his head, listened, then looked at his son. "We going to Bart's 'cause peepers're out?"

"Peepers . . . " Dick and Bart looked at each other.

"Frogs, boys. Frogs're out in the marsh fuckin' to make lil' frogs. And best a luck to 'em. But why's that cause to head for Bart's in the middle of the fuckin' night, answer me."

"Peepers," Bart groaned.

Larry looked at him, eyes bright. "Sheeyit, son, we used to hear 'em every spring. Pipes of Pan, they'd be called. They disappeared for a time—no one knew why. Now seems they're making a comeback. Heard it on TV. All the green types're shittin' in their pants 'cause frogs're back fuckin' and sounding off about it. Guess I'm sort'a glad to hear 'em again, too." He got a dreamy look. "Pipes of Pan's what you hear, boys, spring peepers. What the fuck d'ja think it was?" His look sharpened.

"We didn't know." Bart blushed furiously.

"Strikes me you two seen too many movies," the old man said and went back into his room. He shut the door, and springs squealed faintly as he climbed into bed.

Bart and Dick looked at each other.

"Peepers," Dick said softly.

Bart giggled; a second later Dick joined in, and they howled until the old man yelled at them to shut up, as he used to when they were kids and Bart stayed over.

Back before the old lady, who'd always been a little weird, hit bottom.

*   *   *

The phone rang again as they passed Dick's room on their way to the kitchen for a beer. Dick answered it.

"Yeah?" He listened while Bart leaned against the door frame. His legs were weak and he kept his hands jammed in his pockets to keep them from shaking.

Spring peepers.

He had heard spring peepers . . . not mice from hell, or rats, cats, snakes . . . or killer tomatoes.

Dick said into the phone, "Yes, ma'am . . . I hear you."

It must be the woman on the tape, Myra Ludens, reiterating her mad threat that had seemed real and murderous five minutes ago. It was now as ass-wipish as Bart's hearing spring peepers and deciding he was living through the middle half hour of that dear old giant-bug flick, *Them!*

"I'm fine . . . that's F-I-N-E," Dick told Myra Ludens. "And I plan to stay that way. So do yourself a favor, lady . . . get a life."

F-I-N-E . . . get a life.

Dick Lambert was fine. By this time after she'd issued the first two threats, Bill and Pastori were dead.

But the kid was fine.

She looked at the basement door. Maybe Goody Redman had heard her, maybe it was a delusion after all and the ticks and bees were instances of nature gone berserk.

The hall clock bonged one.

Dale Hale was coming at 9:00 A.M. to disinter the bones. Then Myra would attend another funeral, one that had been delayed three hundred years almost to the day. That would finally be the end of it, she thought, heading upstairs for what she was sure would be the best night's sleep she'd had in months.

At the same time, on the other side of Fallsbridge, Reed watched the fog fold softly against the windows of his bedroom.

He had to get up, fought doing so, still trying to fall asleep. But it was barely one, still hours before dawn. He'd never make it. He dragged himself out of bed and went to his bathroom across the sitting room from Riva's and urinated in a gushing stream he swore smelled of champagne.

He'd gotten blotto on Arlen's Dom, as Arlen would have wanted him to, but was now sober and unhungover, except for a pain behind his eyes that sharpened sickeningly when he bent over the basin to wash.

He straightened up fast, wet a cloth, and pressed it to his eyes. The warm, wet pressure helped, the headache sank a notch, and he went back to sit on the edge of the bed, watching the fog again.

It was now 1:05 on the first day of whatever . . . if anything . . . he had set in motion. He was scared, longed to talk to Landau. To hear the older man's steady voice with its trace of accent tell him that on reflection, his notion about Myra was insane, too mad for him to have even entertained, much less spoken.

Then Reed could sleep.

But it was too late to call Landau, who probably prized sleep as much as Reed's old man when he had reached that age.

There was another call Reed could make, and he stood up again, this time taking his house slippers. They tended to flap, would wake Riva, and he carried them. He put them on in the sitting room, then went out and down the hall to the phone on the refectory table against the wall. No phone book up here, his own address book was downstairs, and he called information and asked for the Lambert number in a hushed voice.

There were two at that address, a bored-sounding operator informed him. Lawrence and Richard.

The kid had his own phone.

He got the number for Richard, dialed, and held the phone plastered to his ear as it rang. It must be in the kid's room; he'd answer fast if he answered at all.

On the second ring, Reed got a click, and a sleepy sounding, "Yo . . . " in Dick Lambert's voice. He waited a moment to be sure it was not a tape. "Yo . . . " said the kid again, more alertly, and Reed hung up.

Dick Lambert was alive and well, and answering his phone in Riverside. Whatever Reed had hoped, dreaded, longed for had not happened.

CHAPTER 19

"I know it's a bad time to call. . . . " Myra said tentatively.

"Terrible." Reed was with Rosemary Page and they were at the point in the session when she always started to cry. He'd taken the call because Myra had told Miss Mohr it was important.

"You don't know how terrible," Myra said. "Wait till you hear what I want."

"Can't wait." He smiled reassuringly at Rosemary.

He was no brilliant diagnostician like Renny; he *was* a world-class reassurer and that could be pretty powerful medicine. Rosemary smiled back through her tears.

She was nice, and in pain. Pain without portfolio, because she had money, a gorgeous home, good kids, and a mostly loving husband she still found attractive. You don't know how lucky you are, people would tell her. Get it together, straighten up and fly right, they'd say, along with the other standard, cruel absurdities folks came up with. Even those who should know better.

Rosemary's pain might be baseless . . . it was also real and agonizing. As Belle's had been before she went bye-bye to get away from it.

Myra was saying, "I will make it short, Reed. But it's going to sound pretty bizarre."

"So what else is new," he muttered, making Myra laugh.

He had Rosemary's intense attention.

"I'm inviting you to Goody Redman's interment today," Myra said. "Noon or thereabouts, at First Cong churchyard. . . ."

"To what . . . ?"

"You heard me, Reed." Excitement bubbled in Myra's voice. "The bones were there—"

"Bones . . . "

"Bones. *Her* bones . . . Goody's bones. Listen Reed, Landau said something must've happened to make it—her—come to life after so long. So I went to see Barb." She told him about the bones while he sat in silence, aware of Rosemary listening. She edged her chair closer; he edged his away and swiveled half back to her.

"We found them," Myra crowed. "I mean he found them, and now he's being very, very careful—"

"Who's being careful?" Reed forced himself not to shout.

"Dale Hale, the tile man," Myra answered. Rosemary inched forward.

"Oh, Reed . . . they're really there. I saw them, a portion of them, anyway. Dale's uncovering the rest now. It's painstaking, but it's almost done. And Reverend Bodgett's here. He'll perform the service—"

"Service . . . "

"At the graveside. The grave should be dug by now, and Reverend Bodgett arranged for a white pine box, such as they'd've had in those days. And Bernie Samms'll be there. . . ."

This was truly nuts. On the far side of nuts and still running. But that was consistent with everything else that had happened the last few days. Since Antonin Pastori's death by bees. Or even before. Since Myra had the basement remodeled and decided it was haunted, and Bernie Samms gave the haunt a name. Elizabeth Redman, aka Goody. What had brought the idea of Goody Redman to life after all these years? Why did Myra suddenly decide her basement was haunted?

Because she'd spent thirty thousand remodeling it, and it was still hellish, and she couldn't take that. But why was it still hellish?

A soft mew from Rosemary, and he turned his head. She was getting impatient with him, and he could hardly blame her, since he'd used up about five of her minutes on a personal call.

But he could not let the question alone: Why did the basement stay hellish enough to make Myra invent a ghost?

Because as Don had said, it had been empty except for dead mice and millipedes . . . and a corpse quietly putrefying . . . for centuries. An atmosphere you could not expect to dissipate immediately in spite of new paneling, floor, and ceiling tiles. And in not changing, the basement became another testament to Myra's helplessness. So she'd made up a ghost that flickered in the recessed lighting, and tinkled on the new quarry tile. . . .

Unless there was something to Landau's *Myra is the ghost*.

Mad, mad, mad . . .

"Whattaya need me for?" he asked Myra, trying not to sound exasperated. But Rosemary picked up the undertone and grinned hugely, being at that stage when she was jealous of his contacts.

"To bear witness," Myra said quietly. "The way we did for Arlen. Some people should be there, Reed. It's been three hundred years . . . it'd be terrible if no one came after so long. I'm asking Lambie, Helen, Don—everyone. They'll probably be annoyed with me too." So she'd also heard it in his voice. Myra rarely missed anything. "But maybe they'll come," she finished.

"They'll come. We'll all come because you asked us to," he said gently, and Rosemary pushed her chair back and turned away to punish him for the affection she'd heard him direct at whoever was on the phone.

The Reverend was resplendent in his white shift, or whatever they called it. His eyes were bloodshot, bright pink bloomed across his nose and cheeks, and he had trouble keeping his half-glasses on his nose.

Reverend Bodgett had kept himself sober yesterday out of respect for Arlen, Reed thought, and fear of Arlen's friends. But Goody Redman's friends had been in the ground for centuries . . . if you could call people who'd hanged you friends.

Some of their descendants might be here, though, such as Lambie or

Helen. Not Myra, because her people had been Quakers, who'd have had no part in the execution.

The Reverend was winding down: *ashes to ashes,* etc., and *in the certain hope of the resurrection.* Nothing like that in Judaism that Reed knew of: no resurrection, no promise of paradise. What dour people we are, he thought, and Lambie nudged his arm. He came out of his reverie and saw she was handing him the trowel with a scoop of dirt for him to scatter. This had not happened at Arlen's grave; the Reverend must have been admonished by Betty to keep it streamlined.

Reed took the trowel, a chased silver thing with a smooth wood handle stained almost black, probably from the sweat of countless hands gripping it to spill earth on loved ones' graves.

He held it a moment, suddenly struck by the solemnity of this moment. In the pit before him, in a plain, smooth pine box that had been beautifully sanded and finished, were the bones of a woman who'd been accused, tormented, tried, convicted, and hanged for a crime that did not even exist.

Witchcraft.

He sprinkled the dirt slowly, moved his lips in a silent *God rest your soul, Elizabeth Redman.* The dirt hit the lid with a hollow, lonely sound. No flowers to cushion the top as there'd been on Arlen's casket. But there were flowers around the grave, waiting to rest on it once it had been filled in. And he'd bet his entire fortune that Myra had arranged for a headstone in slate or limestone, in keeping with the other stones in the old churchyard.

They stuck up crookedly around them, some dark stone, some lighter, all with carvings of willows, vases, or angels, and one he couldn't understand anyone wanting on a grave . . . a chiseled skull. A sort of defeated-looking symbol of the inner knowledge that resurrection was an empty dream, and death ruled all.

He shivered in the hot sun, dug the trowel into the pile of soft earth, and passed it to Bernie Samms, who stood next to him looking grave and unkempt, with his hair frazzled and old stains on his jacket.

Samms passed on sprinkling dirt; then came Myra, and she did it with her lips moving silently, as Reed's had done. Probably saying the same words with a Quaker slant: God rest *thy* soul.

Then it was over.

The Reverend held up his hands to keep them in place.

"We've laid on a little refreshment in the rectory if you'd like to join us. . . . "

He looked brightly around the group at the graveside.

"Some cookies, and sherry, I believe. . . . "

Myra must have supplied the sherry for the occasion, some rare and wonderful Amontillado at eighty bucks a bottle.

And the cookies too, Reed thought, her very own butter cookies, best on earth.

The sherry and cookies were fabulous, with some equally fabulous slices of nut cake baked by Mrs. Bodgett. She was in her sixties with one of those superdelicate faces that had probably been pretty when she was young, but had faded and sagged, leaving her nose, mouth, and chin too small for the rest of her face.

She had sparse gray-blond hair and was wearing a scrap of a hat such as Reed remembered his mother wearing when he was a kid.

She knew everyone but Reed and smiled archly when they were introduced.

"It's a privilege to meet you, Dr. Lerner. I've been hearing about you for years."

As the town's only shrink, or only Jew? he wondered.

The extra bodies raised the room temperature; Mrs. Bodgett invited the men to take off their jackets . . . and all declined. Don because he never took his jacket off except to go to bed, and Bernie because his shirt probably had stains under the arms. Bodgett still had on vestments, if that's what they were called, and Reed couldn't take off his jacket without revealing the gun in his waistband digging into his back.

On his way back to the office, he'd detour to Gun World in Oban, get a holster that'd protect his back, and still keep the gun concealed.

It was almost two; he drained his glass and announced he had a patient at three. He made his good-byes and went out into the foyer.

Myra came out after him. "Reed . . . "

"My?"

"Don't look so wary. It's nothing bad. At least I don't think it is. I want your permission to see Belle Lambert tomorrow."

"What for?"

"To talk to her."

"Oh, My, honey . . . you might as well talk to the refrigerator."

"I know. But I thought I would anyway, if it's okay."

"Why?"

"Because I've got something to tell her that she might *hear.*"

"What?"

She shrugged. "You heard what I said to Dick Lambert yesterday."

He nodded, feeling his throat tighten. *You don't know what sorry means . . . yet.*

"I said similar things to Bill and Pastori, Reed."

"My, is he . . . "

"He's fine. I checked."

"Checked how?"

"After . . . uh . . . Dale finished in the basement this morning, I drove past Trimble's. I saw him. He was fine."

Reed looked at a wall in the direction of Goody Redman's grave, wondering if Myra had had the bones in the back of her giant Buick when she "drove past Trimble's."

"Anyway, I thought I'd see Belle even if she won't exactly see me, and tell her that her grandson's okay. That my warning didn't mean what it had meant before and he'll stay okay now that the bones're buried, and hallowed as they should have been in sixteen ninety-five."

"Better late than never," Reed said, grinning. Myra grinned back and in an impulsive gesture, put her arms around his neck and kissed him on the lips. A firm asexual kiss, tasting sweet from the sherry, and full of affection.

"What was that for, My?"

"For being on my side even when I'm bonkers. For being the best friend anyone ever had and understanding things no one else would. For taking me at my word, respecting me . . . and never, never humoring me. Not to sound like the Godfather, Reed, but I owe you. If I can ever do anything to repay—"

"Make Belle listen," he said suddenly, not sure where the words came from. "Make her hear that her grandson is safe, make her care. . . . " Tears pricked his eyes.

"You care, don't you," Myra said softly.

"More than is good for me . . . or her. And Christ, My, I don't know why. I never even heard the woman's voice."

"I did. It was long, long ago when I was just a little girl, but I remember her very well."

"Was she beautiful?"

Myra smiled. "I remember a juicy-looking woman in tight clothes, with about ten pounds of reddish-brown hair. Beautiful isn't the word I'd pick. Lush maybe . . . and nice. At least I thought she was nice. She was nice to me."

"How?"

"It was around Christmas, the shops and streets were full of people, and all the trees had those tiny white lights on them . . . like they still put up."

He nodded. Myra went on, "I was this pretty little blond kid, and I had this new coat with a white bunny-fur collar and muff, and she saw me in one of the shops. Putnam's, I think. She bent over and hugged me and exclaimed what a love of a little girl I was, and didn't I look like an angel!"

As she must have, Reed thought, with her porcelain skin flushed from the cold and her Alice-blue eyes. God knows what shade of gold her hair had been. Lots of people had probably exclaimed over Myra Fox as a child.

"I sort of fell in love with her, like little girls do," Myra was saying. "Her hair smelled like roses, her voice was deep for a woman's: low and husky, not shrill like my mother's."

"Your mother had a shrill voice?" He didn't remember that about Mary Fox.

"Like a siren," Myra said. "She must have learned to speak at the top of her lungs with her teeth clenched when they sent her to finishing school."

He saw a flash of rage in Myra's eyes that came and went so fast he could have imagined it, but knew he had not. "My?"

She looked at him. "Oh, Reed . . . they were so . . . awful. I mean my folks. So much like the people who hanged her." She nodded in the direction of the churchyard.

"No they weren't, Myra. They were Quakers, they'd've never—"

"Hanged anyone? No. But they were just as sure they knew what was right as the people who *did*."

"Well . . ." he drew the word out. This was deep stuff to talk about in an entry hall in the five minutes he had.

"No *well* about it," Myra said tightly. "They *knew* you weren't supposed to have sex out of wedlock. They *knew* you were barely fit to live if you did. They *knew* if you got pregnant, you had a baby. They *knew* my life wasn't as important as what they knew was right, and they flushed it down the toilet like a dead goldfish. . . . " She ran out of breath. Reed waited to see if she was finished.

He'd always known the rage had to be there. He remembered her at the high school graduation party even though she hadn't graduated, looking lost and older than the rest of them, even though she was younger.

They hadn't meant to be cruel, but they were on their way to Yale, Radcliffe, Dartmouth, full of plans that would take them away from Fallsbridge for years, leaving Myra behind with Bob and Bob's baby.

Of course she'd been enraged, and of course she'd never shown it . . . being Myra. Of course she had hated her parents, as gentle as they were, had probably hated Bob then, no matter how much he loved her.

"My . . . would you have done it differently?" he asked. Meaning would she have aborted the baby, walked out on Bob, told her folks to stuff it?

"I don't know," she said steadily. "But it'd have been nice to have the choice."

Clear enough, fair enough.

"Can I see her?" she asked.

She meant Belle; the change of subject was dizzying.

"Something you should know," he said and told her about Belle's snapping at him.

Myra grinned. "I'll stay out of range."

"It wasn't funny . . . if it happened."

"What do you mean if it happened?"

"I touched her, and the snapping could've been a mindless reaction to the contact. Probably was."

He fell silent and Myra waited. Then he sighed and made the most disastrous decision of his life. "Okay, My. I'll check with her doctor there, guy called Mendel. If it's okay with him, it's okay with me."

CHAPTER 20

On Friday morning, Myra drove east on narrow winding roads, taking the Connecticut shortcut natives seem addicted to even when it adds miles to the trip. But this almost *was* a shortcut, Myra thought, and it kept her off the highway. Reason enough to take it.

It had been years since volunteer work had taken her to Housatonic Valley.

"Goodness," Bonnie had said when Myra had called her this morning, "I'd almost forgotten the place existed."

Bonnie was a late riser, and Myra had apologized for getting her out of bed. "But I've been up for hours," Bonnie had insisted, ashamed of the internal clock that kept her in bed after eight.

"But why go *there?*" Bonnie had gotten a shiver in her voice.

"It's been so long since any of us showed our faces there."

"That's true."

"And there's a Fallsbridge woman there."

"Who?" Bonnie's tone had sharpened.

"Belle Lambert."

"Oh, right. I heard." Not from Upper Fallsbridge, Bonnie's tone had said. Myra waited for the other woman's permission, which she didn't need. But it was a courtesy, since Bonnie ran their little pool of volunteers, which included Lambie and Helen.

They looked after the gift shop at Fallsbridge General, made sure there was fresh coffee in the surgical and ICU lounges, and rolled the book cart up and down corridors with its rubber wheels whispering comfortingly on the tiles.

In other hospitals, they visited patients who had no other visitors, read to them, brought gifts of food to some, wrote letters for those who couldn't do it themselves.

Myra had been faithful to the little group until all *this* started. Now she'd pick up where she had left off, if she could. Starting with Belle Lambert. She waited while Bonnie appeared to consider it at the other end of the phone. Normally, Myra would be in a sweat waiting for Bonnie's say-so, but not today for some reason.

"I guess it'll be okay," Bonnie said, as if dispensing a favor, and Myra thought sharply, *Of course it'll be okay.*

Myra turned north on State 40 and the hills suddenly surrounded her. Leaves fluttered in the sun, their shadows dappled the road, and the sun snapped through holes in the foliage. The hills were solid green, and a rush of joy came over her with the warm wind blowing through the car window.

She was in the foothills of the Berkshires; Goody Redman was safely buried and Barb Potter could come home. Myra had called her yesterday afternoon and left a message on the tape she'd gotten. Just her name and number, in case the college roommate did not know the story, as she probably did not.

Myra was now twenty-five miles east of Fallsbridge and must have gained altitude, because it was much cooler, and she was glad she'd brought her blazer. The road curved, then widened, trees thinned, and she saw the ragged field that began the grounds of Housatonic Valley State Psychiatric Facility—the madhouse.

It was a ghastly place to put in this lovely spot, and her sense of well-being began to evaporate. She rounded another curve; the ten-foot-high brick walls, topped by iron spikes, started here, and the building, which was blackish-red brick with narrow windows like a fortress, appeared on a rise in the distance. The sight of it killed the last of her joy.

It was huge, with a parking lot larger than all the municipal lots of Fallsbridge put together. She had no trouble finding a space, since it was a workday, and most visitors showed up on weekends.

She parked close to the front door, mounted the wide stone steps, and stepped through a double-doored portal, out of the sun and into the cool, dim interior of Housatonic Valley.

Wrong name for it, she thought, since it was in the hills. But maybe it had been a valley . . . a hundred and forty million years ago. It was the sort of place where you'd expect to dig up dinosaurs, the small, swift, especially vicious carnivorous kind.

She felt chilled and slid her arms into the sleeves of her blazer.

Ceil Ruggles, whom Bonnie had told Myra to ask for, had snarled gray hair and was wearing a polyester blouse that had seen better days. Myra was suddenly aware of her own polyester blouse, her hair snarled from the wind blowing in the car window, and wondered if she would be as gray and dingy as this poor woman in about ten years.

Ceil smiled and looked a little livelier. "Yes, yes, Bonnie called about you. I guess your little group stopped visiting before I started work here."

"I guess . . . "

"Well, we can certainly use—"

Quickly, before the woman could get her hopes up about extra volunteers, Myra explained that she was mainly here to see a woman from Fallsbridge, but of course would see anyone else Ceil asked her to. For today, anyway. "And I've got some of our books in my tote bag." She pulled out a few. "Judith Krantz, Agatha Christie . . . and for the more . . . uh . . . alert . . . *A Tale of Two Cities*."

Reading Dickens aloud always made her think of Olivia De Havilland in *Gone With the Wind*.

Ceil smiled gently. "It's very good of you, and there've been times when we—and our patients—would be so grateful. But I'm afraid there isn't really anyone here at the moment who'll be up to Dickens. Including Mrs. Lambert, actually. But if it's all right with Dr. Mendel for you to see her . . . " Ceil Ruggles shrugged.

Myra and Mendel stepped out of the elevator on the fourth floor in front of the nursing station.

"We should talk a minute," he said, and led Myra to a small lounge with the requisite black plastic couch and dog-eared magazines. No TV, as they had in the lounges at Fallsbridge General, she noticed. She sat on the couch; Mendel pulled over a molded plastic orange chair and sat facing her, his knees almost touching hers. His eyes were large, soft brown with thick black lashes. A lock of his black, curly hair fell across his high pale forehead, giving him a Romantic-era look; Byronic, Myra thought. He was not more than an inch or so taller than she was (at only five four) and thin to the point of emaciation, yet there was something very appealing about him. She found herself smiling more than usual and wishing she had on something snazzier, like the blue paisley silk she'd worn to Arlen's funeral that was now on its way to the cleaners.

Mendel spoke softly, forcing Myra to lean forward to hear, her face close to his.

He told her about Belle's apparently snapping at Reed.

Myra countered with Reed's explanation that it was probably an involuntary response to his having touched her.

"It's possible," Mendel said. "In fact it's likely, I guess. But there's something else. . . . " and he described the scene with the bailiff, Jessica Shannon, as she had described it to him.

But Belle was supposed to be catatonic, which Myra thought meant beyond human contact, positive or negative. She said so, and Mendel nodded.

"Worse than catatonic, Mrs. Ludens. Hebephrenic."

"What's that?"

He searched for a word and came up with *unrelenting*. "At least that's the admitting diagnosis. Subject to review, of course. We've done a few neurological tests. . . . "

All within normal limits, he told her, which was still consistent with the diagnosis.

"Diagnosis is the art of psychiatry," he said, then explained how difficult, sometimes impossible it was since they didn't yet have the basic science to define the workings of the mind.

He was stalling, probably uncomfortable about her seeing Belle, she thought. She let him talk, hoping he'd reassure himself, but he just got edgier, one of those skinny men who was normally nervous.

"You're telling me you're afraid she's dangerous," she said.

He sat back in the molded chair, was quiet a moment, then chuckled. "That's what I call cutting to chase, Mrs. Ludens."

"Call me Myra."

"Myra. That's exactly what I'm telling you. But when you put it into words as you just did, it sounds ludicrous."

She gave him her most radiant smile and was gratified to see his sallow cheeks color slightly. "Then maybe it *is* ludicrous," she said.

A minute later, she was in the spotless black-and-white-tiled corridor, looking through the open door of Ward 2D at Belle Lambert, who looked nothing like the big, hearty, vivacious woman of thirty-five years ago, except for her shock of dark red hair, now shot through with gray.

Mendel left her alone with Belle, but the nurse she'd seen at the desk, who was all in white and much starchier-looking than the nurses at Fallsbridge General, kept passing the door to look in. Probably by arrangement with Mendel.

Belle Lambert was as Reed had described: blank-faced, blank-eyed. Her head had a hideous tilt that made her neck look broken, and there was a mirrorlike glisten to her eyes, as if they were capable only of reflecting what was in front of them. It was creepy, and about thirty seconds after she'd sat down in another molded plastic chair facing Belle, Myra was sorry she'd come.

But she was here to tell her about her grandson, and in a subdued voice, she described how he'd escaped the fates of Antonin Pastori and Bill Withers.

"God knows what it would have been for him," Myra found herself whispering, although the only other woman on the ward, whose face had the slick pallor of a soap carving, was obviously not listening.

"I mean what was left after bees and ticks, for God's sake," Myra said, and thought, *rats and snakes . . . spiders, lizards.* Or having to face a murderous, empty-eyed, mindless being like Belle Lambert. Like the zombies in that old horror movie they'd all gone to ages ago.

Night of the something-or-other.

She'd been afraid to close her eyes at night for weeks after that movie. Had lain in bed on her back, staring up at her ceiling where moonlight cast shadows in fantastic shapes.

It'd been the scariest movie ever, and the other girls had agreed, vowing never to see another horror movie.

Their only consolation had been that Arlen, Don, and Reed had been just as scared.

Night of the Living Dead . . . that was it, Myra thought, and Belle Lambert blinked. The movement was sudden and startling, the first movement Belle had made since Myra sat down next to her.

But of course she'd blink. Mendel had told Myra she'd blink, that her eyes would rove as they'd done a couple of times in the last few minutes. Right now they were not roving, but fixed on Myra, and for the snap of an instant Myra thought Belle *saw* her, but knew that was wishful thinking.

She spent about half an hour in the ward, which smelled of floor wax with very faint whiffs of urine. She told Belle Lambert what Dick had done to Arlen, while a long, thin thread of silver drool ran down the fold between Belle's cheek and chin, in a steady stream. That was her only reaction.

Myra told her she knew Dick was sorry about what had happened.

"Not just sorry," she amended. "I think he was devastated. That's why he came to the funeral." Where he'd bumped into Myra and received the "warning" she'd given the others, she told Belle. "But it didn't mean anything this time." She wanted to give Belle a reassuring pat, but remembered her reaction to Reed touching her. Myra would yelp if Belle snapped at her, bring the white-garbed nurse who kept passing the door rushing into the ward.

"This time it was okay," she told Belle insistently. "Was probably okay the other times too. I mean, I don't think my 'warnings' had anything to do with what happened. Just a crazy coincidence. What the cop Lemon called 'grotesquely concurrent.' Did I mention Sergeant Lemon before?" She had not, and launched into a description of him.

She spent another twenty minutes in Ward 2D, and by the time she pushed back the chair and stood up, Myra had told Belle everything she knew about what had happened, although Belle hadn't seemed to hear a word of it.

Myra had not been able to make Belle hear, listen, care as Reed had begged her to. But he'd just been throwing out wishes, like a kid putting a tooth under his pillow, Myra thought.

Mendel was waiting out in the corridor for her.

"How'd it go?"

"How'd you think it went?"

"I think it didn't," he said gently. They all spoke so gently in this place, Myra wondered where they found such a well of quiet compassion in themselves.

He rode down in the elevator with her, standing a little closer than was necessary. She got a whiff of his clean sweat under some light male cologne he had on. There was definitely something about him. . . .

She thought he felt the same about her from his flushed cheeks and bright eyes that kept darting in her direction and then away when she looked at him.

They crossed the huge, echoing lobby to the huge double front doors that led to the parking lots.

"Hope your car's not in Timbuktu," he said.

"Only Rangoon."

They laughed; two grown-ups who found each other attractive, she thought. That hadn't happened to her in a long, long time. Maybe not since she'd had Dave and never quite lost the extra weight she'd put on.

Maybe she'd lost some now; be surprising if she hadn't with all that had gone on.

They shook hands; he held hers a little longer than necessary, then let her go and stepped back. "Tell Reed hello."

"Of course." She went down the steps to the walk. Halfway to her car, she turned back to wave, but he'd gone inside. She looked up the front of the building, to the fourth story, wondering which of the windows belonged to 2D.

"It went okay," Mendel told Reed on the phone. "At least I think it did. Haven't checked back on her yet, though. I'll get to it after supper."

"Did the contact . . . you know . . . click?"

"Not according to Harris, the floor nurse. But it didn't do any harm either. I guess that could be something."

"Guess so," Reed said tightly, and Mendel knew he was hiding disappointment. Probably had let himself entertain some wild, groundless hope. Our appalling optimism rearing its ugly head again, Mendel thought.

Then, to distract Reed and just because he wanted to hear the words, Mendel said, "By the way, that's one hell of an attractive woman."

"Myra?" Reed laughed. "Time was she could put a boner on a corpse."

"On you . . . ?" Mendel found himself slightly breathless.

"God, no. Platonic to the death, Myra and I . . . and a couple of other distaff buddies you've never met."

Then Reed said he'd be by tomorrow. "Will you be around?"

"What makes you think life-in-the-fast-lane Aaron Mendel will be working on a Saturday," Mendel said lightly.

"Just a hunch." They laughed, and hung up. Still smiling, feeling that he and Reed Lerner could be friends, Mendel went down to the cafeteria in the basement and had the table d'hôte: meat loaf, mashed potatoes, and canned peas. His beeper did not go off; he dawdled over coffee until almost seven, then went back up to four.

There were five wards on the fourth floor. He looked in on 1D, on eighty-year-old Ruth Fogarty, whose Alzheimer's had reached its crescendo. Nothing to do for her, nothing to say to her.

At eight, his shift would end; he'd go home and shower and straighten up the house in preparation for Jessica. What a godsend meeting her had turned out to be. She was no fabulous golden goddess like Myra Ludens, but that made it even better, he thought. You could admire Myra, long for her, dream of her . . . no way could you actually fuck her, he thought, grinning to himself. Too lovely, too ethereal. But God, it'd be fun to try.

He finished with Mrs. Fogarty, left her meager chart with Nurse Harris, and went to 2D.

Belle Lambert, Nancy Ellis.

Dead women, he thought miserably. Dead and gone. All God had to do was let them slide into their graves and find peace.

Not God, Mendel thought with bitterness that was getting worse every day. Not the Champ who gave us glioblastoma, lethal midline granuloma, spina bifida . . . and hebephrenic schizophrenia. To save his own emotional health, Mendel would have to leave here before next year. But he didn't have anything to castigate himself for; having made it three years at Housatonic was some kind of record.

He wondered if he and Jessica would be together by the time he did leave. If she'd follow him to Seattle, Miami, West Podunk, South Dakota if that's where chance took him.

He checked Nancy's meds, looked into her empty eyes, sniffed her acid breath and sweat, typical of the biochemistry of this disease. Not as noticeable with Belle Lambert yet.

He spent exactly five minutes with Mrs. Ellis, as he did twice a day, every day, except when he took vacation, as he'd done once in the last three years. Or was laid low with flu, as he'd been last winter.

"Didn't miss you," he said to the frozen face in front of him, with eyes like aggies. "Didn't even think about you, Nance." He took her hand, which was as limp as cut string. Made himself hold it for the count of ten, then put it gently into her lap next to her other hand.

As he had a thousand times, he marveled at how well the patients were kept, at the amazingly competent and caring nursing at this facility.

"Won't be this good in West Podunk," he told Nancy Ellis. She was only fifty-five, had a husband and a daughter who'd just had another daughter that Nancy had never "seen," even though the bundled baby had been brought for her to look at. And even though her husband came faithfully two Saturdays a month, she had not "seen" him for years either.

What had happened to her . . . what had happened to Belle? What had happened to all of them? His throat was very tight, his mouth dry. Maybe he wouldn't be able to make it to the end of the year after all.

He finished with Nancy. Next week, he'd have her moved to the TV room in the afternoons again; it would not make any difference, of course, but he didn't know what else to do.

He went around the bed, down the aisle toward the window, to Belle Lambert in her wheelchair. They got them all up every day, got them bathed, into clean clothes, and at least sitting up. Nancy walked some; maybe Belle would too with a little patience and a good strong orderly like Tabert Brown, an incredibly gentle, dark-skinned giant with soft brown eyes. Tabe was about as big as Reed Lerner, who was probably the largest M.D. Mendel had ever seen.

They ought'a run a Biggest M.D. in the World contest, Mendel thought, as he took the chair next to Belle that Myra had vacated.

"Whattaya think of that, Mrs. Lambert," he said. "Give the biggest M.D.—I meant tallest and strongest—a silver trophy. How does that sound?" He was smiling into her eyes, not feeling as dismal as he usually did this time of night . . . thanks to the prospect of seeing Jessica. He'd have to concentrate on not fantasizing about Myra Ludens tonight; he could get hard just thinking about her, he realized, and was so taken with her image and the flash of heat that came with it, he didn't see Belle Lambert's hand jerk out to grab his throat so suddenly, with such immense strength, he didn't even have a chance to cry out.

This was Bev Harris's least favorite time of the day. It was almost dark, with just a faint smear of light gray in the sky over the trees. The patients who could eat had been fed, those on IV . . . stayed on IV.

Most were still awake; Tabe and Fred wouldn't be up to get them into their beds for fifteen minutes yet.

Nothing to do but wait; then they'd be tucked in, like the brain-dead babies they were. Then would come the waiting . . . and more waiting.

Until nine, when she'd check the beds, put out the lights except for those who screamed in the dark. But this floor was all female, and women were less afraid of the dark than men; their loss of reason seemed more neutral, caused fewer terrors. Still, plenty of them moaned and cried out in the dark, occasionally screamed.

She saw a flash of white out of the corner of her eye and turned her head. Nothing but empty corridor, only she thought she heard the faintest click, as of a door closing. No doors between here and the elevator, except the one to the stairs.

She should see what was going on, but couldn't leave the desk until Judy returned. Judy was at the vending machine on three getting them coffee and a bag of something salty and marginally edible: stale peanuts, stale peanut-butter crackers, stale chips or pretzels.

Same choice every night at this time, to keep their blood sugar up until quitting time and a hot meal downstairs with their buddies from the other floors. It was a nice way to end the day, a moment without pressure before they had to go home and face whatever waited for them there.

She tried to think about that hour out of time she had coming, tried to conjure up the spotless cafeteria, the sense of camaraderie around the Formica-topped table, the almost cozy atmosphere in the cafeteria in spite of its immensity. The smells of brown gravy and fresh coffee....

But there *had* been a flick of something white just down the hall, and she turned her head again and stared.

Nothing. But she had seen it; she was less sure about the click of a door closing, but sure enough to have to investigate. She hated doing it, hated walking down the hall into the rooms at this time of night, when no one else was around. But she had no choice, and before she could think any more about it, she rolled her chair back, stood, and came around the desk.

She looked to her left, hoping the elevator doors would hiss open and Judy would appear with Styrofoam cups and cellophane bags.

But the doors stayed shut, leaving Bev wondering what Judy could be doing this long on three.

Maybe she had to go to the can, Bev thought, then admonished herself for being such a baby. She had gone into these rooms alone at night a million times; tonight was no different.

But it was; she felt it. And the feeling was confirmed when she stood on the threshold of 2D, saw Belle Lambert's empty chair and bed, and smelled excrement. At first she thought Mrs. Lambert had let go in her diaper, hardly a tragedy, hardly unusual, but then she might've been embarrassed enough about it to hide, and that *was* unheard of. So where was she?

"Mrs. Lambert?" Bev called softly. Nancy Ellis stared straight ahead, but her hands gripped the end of the chair arms so hard her knuckles bulged. She looked as if she were reacting to something. That was also unheard of, and Bev's heart gave a violent thud, then settled down to pounding.

"Belle . . . " Her voice sounded shrill, which you never heard from staff here. It was absurd to respond this way to patients filling their diapers; it happened all the time, hour after hour, day after day. Thank God for the orderlies . . . but this time of night, with the orderlies busy getting people to bed, she'd have to change Mrs. Lambert herself.

"Remember, they are not going to see or hear you or be able to speak to you, even to ask to relieve themselves. You know what that means, of course." That had been Mrs. Lureen Cromwell, head of nursing, talking to rookies four years ago. "You must also know that that does not make them any less human, any less worthy of respect, and if I find you behaving as if they are . . . if there is any diminution of the dignity of the people under your care . . . "

And so on.

Pay here was good, excellent, in fact. The bulk of the building was devoted to state, but there was that precious private wing where it cost eighty thou a year to keep Aunt Selma, or Papa, or little Damian, who'd started mainlining horse at eleven and setting neighborhood cats on fire.

So, okay, Belle Lambert took a dump in her drawers . . . hardly the end of the world.

But where was she!

"Bev . . . "

Bev jumped. Literally jumped straight up in the air and came down with a thud that jarred her ankles.

Judy stood in the doorway carrying the cardboard tray with two Styrofoam cups and two bags of salt-laden something.

"What the hell . . . ?" Judy said.

"Lambert's gone."

Wrong, bad, Bev thought; it was always supposed to be *Mrs.* Lambert. Or Belle.

"Mrs. Lambert," Bev corrected herself.

Judy set the cardboard tray on the floor, then, looking as wary as Bev felt, stepped into the room.

"Gone where?" Judy asked, as she should've a good twenty seconds ago. They both knew Belle was still here . . . in the room . . . hidden, lying in wait. The horror fantasy of every staff member at Housatonic. Except maybe Tabe, who was too gigantic to fear anything except a patient with a gun or knife.

Then Judy cried, "What's that?"

Bev followed her eyes and saw two black lines on the normally immaculate rubber tile.

"What the hell," Bev breathed, but she went from scared to terrified, because she knew those thin, black, parallel tracks were heel marks that had been made by someone being dragged across the floor.

Belle Lambert.

Judy and Bev looked at each other, then at Nancy Ellis, who must know what they'd find when they followed the heel tracks.

Nancy stared at a spot on the floor a few feet from her chair, with the tip of her tongue protruding between her lips.

The marks disappeared; Bev stepped forward and saw they ended beside the bed. From there, Belle must have been rolled.

She looked back at Nancy Ellis. "Oh . . . God, Nancy, what'd you do?"

Nancy's eyes slid shut. It was late, bedtime; Nancy was sleepy after the exertion of incapacitating her roommate and rolling her under the bed.

Then Judy crouched down, looked under the bed, and made a terrible strangled noise, half grunt, half scream. Nancy didn't react. Bev leaped back a pace, then forced herself to go closer. "What? Judy, for shit's sake . . . what?"

Judy's hand covered her mouth, her eyes rolled up to look at Bev, and she moaned. Bev bent down and looked under the bed.

In his whites, Aaron Mendel lay curled on his side with his eyes open and staring, and his head twisted at an impossible angle.

"This is Dr. Lerner," Reed said when Riva handed him the phone.

"Doctor, it's Beverly Harris at Housatonic. Your patient . . . Belle Lambert . . . on four. . . . "

"I only have one patient there," he said shortly, and thought, *Spit it out, lady. If she's sick, get help; if she's dead . . . tell me. I can take it.* Only Reed was not sure he could.

"She's . . . oh, God, Dr. Lerner, she's gone."

It took an instant for the word to filter through the barrier of what he'd expected to hear.

"Gone . . . ," he repeated. It was like hearing *flat-line* from Malone about Arlen. The word had become gibberish.

"Gone, sir. We need you here."

"Gone where?" he exploded.

"We think she's still in the building. She must be, and we're hoping she'll show herself if she hears your voice."

I'm not sure she ever heard my voice, Reed wanted to screech at the woman. He said, "Put Dr. Mendel on." And Beverly Harris started to cry.

"Oh, shit," Reed groaned. "Not now, lady, please. Not now."

Real sympathetic, he thought. The kindly exurban shrink whose greatest currency was sympathy and reassurance. Only he was not bucking for sainthood, and if the woman didn't get Aaron Mendel on the phone in about seven seconds, he was really going to lose it.

Belle was in an elevator somewhere in the gigantic building, riding up and down. Lost, alone, not knowing how to make the car stop. Or she had made it as far as the basement and was trapped down there in the dark, with hulking shadows of the truck-sized boiler or water heater, and ducts sliding blackly across a low ceiling. She was cowering in a corner in the dark, dragged down by her own weight to flounder on a freezing cement floor. She must have hurt herself by now, may have broken a bone. So why didn't this fool stop blubbering and put Mendel on the phone.

Because she was upset, and all Reed had done was yell at her, upsetting her more.

He softened his voice as best he could. "Ms. Harris, I really need to talk to Dr. Mendel. Please put him on. Beep him if he's not close by—"

She sobbed, "He's dead, Dr. Lerner . . . she broke his neck."

Reed finally saw what the Porsche could do on roads that had been cut for buggies a hundred years ago and paved over as they lay to accommodate the automobile. They wound and curved, narrowed, widened out in a few places, narrowed again as they ran over bridges and under canopies of trees that touched branches overhead. He never went under fifty around curves he'd normally take at twenty, and the car held the road, bore down to the road, as if it had been waiting for him to finally *drive* it.

He made the forty-five minute drive in twenty-four minutes flat.

The building and grounds were lit up, lights were on in outbuildings that must be equipment sheds. It looked like they were giving a ball.

He raced up the drive, curved around the front to the steps, and came to a screeching stop.

A man in a gray cop uniform was waiting for him.

"Lerner?"

Reed raced up the steps to him. "What the hell happened?"

"God knows. They think she's still in there. Are convinced she's still in there. Myself, I'm not so sure. Name's Corey, by the way." He stuck out a thick hand and Reed shook it. "Reed Lerner."

"I know. I was delegated to meet you."

"She must be here . . . or on the grounds or wandering on the road. No place else she could go."

"That so?" Corey had hazel eyes, dark red lashes and brows, and a face full of freckles.

"That's so," Reed said. "She doesn't have a car . . . hasn't driven in years. Probably can't. How would she get—"

"Hitchhike?"

Reed managed a sick-sounding laugh. "D'ja ever see her?"

"Can't say that I have."

"You mean *no*, don't you, Officer?"

"Guess I do."

"Well, trust me, no one who wasn't blind or suicidal would pick up Belle Lambert."

"Got lots like that on the roads these days."

Reed drew himself out of his normal slouch to tower over the other man. "This isn't funny, Corey."

Corey was unfazed. "Never said it was. Man's dead. She, or someone— not wanting to jump to conclusions—broke his neck."

"How?" Reed asked sickly.

"Bare hands, it looks like. So the lady—if she is the doer—is dangerous. And just in case you're not infallible, Doctor, and she has gotten out, where would she go?"

Home, Reed thought. But if he said so, they'd call the locals, a bunch of swaggerers who'd show up at the house on Bowman with enough fire-power to take Omaha Beach. If Belle was there, they'd kill her . . . and probably Dick and Larry and any hapless soul out walking their dog or getting a breath of evening air.

"I don't know," he said, then remembered Myra had been here today.

Corey had turned away, was heading across the rotunda. Reed went after him. "Mrs. Lambert had a visitor today."

"Woman called Ludens. But the dead man was in the cafeteria over an hour after she was seen leaving the grounds. Think maybe she came back . . . ?"

"Christ, no."

"What makes you so sure?"

Reed said, "Because Mrs. Ludens is a five foot four wife and mother who cries easily and loves to cook."

The ghost is in her mind, Landau had said. *Myra is the ghost.*

He'd give anything to talk to Landau.

"That sound like your neck-breaker, Officer Corey?"

"It's Sergeant Corey . . . and no, it doesn't."

A second of silence, then Corey said, "Sorry, Doc. No one knows what to do here, and I'm no exception."

"I understand."

"The others think like you do. That Lambert's still gotta be in the building or on the grounds."

Housatonic Valley was enormous, with hundreds of rooms, wards, broom closets, linen closets, and examination rooms. And that was just the state section. There were fifty more rooms in the private wing, with bathrooms for each, and another full complement of closets and what have you.

It'd take a day to search just the kitchens, pantries, food lockers, storage rooms.

They called in off-duty staff and security officers, added most of the tiny police departments of the two tiny upstate towns nearby, and came up woefully short. At this rate, Reed thought, as he found himself looking in a broom closet on the first floor (which was cleaner and better organized than the ER at Fallsbridge General), they'd finish searching around Labor Day.

He turned away from the closet and found himself alone in a reception area, facing a metal desk with a phone and a computer terminal.

He hesitated, then picked up the phone, waited half a minute, then slowly, letting wordless instinct guide him, he dialed New York City information. Landau's number was unlisted, but Arlen had had it. Reed remembered Landau pushing a card into Arlen's pocket before he got into the snappy blue Dodge and drove away. That was the day Arlen had been killed.

Reed thanked New York Directory Assistance, dialed Arlen's and held his breath as it rang. He had no idea what Betty had decided to do with the house . . . if she had decided anything yet. If she, or George, or anyone were there. But they had to be, you couldn't just walk away from an antique-filled, 1840s Colonial worth about three million bucks.

George answered, sounding groggy; he was drunk or had been sleeping.

"Look, George, Arlen had a card for a Job Landau. It was with him when he . . . uh . . . was killed. It would have been in his things."

"They're here. In library . . . "

George had apparently given up using articles in his grief.

"Could you look?"

"Sure . . . look."

A gentle sound came over the line that Reed prayed was the receiver being laid down, not hung up. He waited, clutching the phone in his hand, spouting sweat, terrified of hearing clicks and the dial tone. But a moment later, George came back. "Job Landau," he said in the same bleary voice, then read off a 212 number.

"It's Sabbath," Landau said. "But when I heard you on the tape, I thought it must be important." His clear, steady voice was immensely soothing; also soothing was his saying it was the Sabbath. Friday night. Reed had not thought of Sabbath since his Grandfather Lerner died, maybe thirty years ago.

It was all Reed remembered about it.

"It's a disaster," he told Landau.

"How?"

"Arlen's dead, sir. . . . "

Silence.

"He was killed." Reed told him what had happened in oral shorthand, using one word for four. But Landau seemed to understand.

Reed ended with, "Now the madwoman's disappeared—after Myra spent an hour or so with her. Mr. Landau . . . oh, God . . . Mr. Landau."

He hoped Landau wouldn't be offended by his saying *God*.

"Mr. Landau, you said the ghost was in Myra's mind, that she was the ghost."

"I said she *could* be."

"But you meant it was possible."

"That's what I meant."

"How, Mr. Landau? How could Myra be the ghost? Did you mean . . . did you mean she made the bees . . . the ticks . . . that it was possible for her to control . . . ?"

A gray-uniformed security guard passed the door, glanced in, then stopped, and stood in the doorway, watching Reed.

Reed ignored him. "Is it possible . . . ?"

"I guess I thought so," Landau said, "or I wouldn't have said it."

"Bees and ticks are mindless creatures."

"You sound like you're in a hurry, Doctor. Get to the point."

"Could she control a *person?*"

"I don't know."

"Especially if the person was . . . mindless . . . like the bees?"

Landau said, "You talk like this is backgammon, and we all know the rules. It's not, we don't. I don't have the answer, only . . ."

"Only what." Reed felt his voice jump into the mouthpiece. The security cop took a few steps into the room; Reed covered the mouthpiece, "Be right with you."

The guard stared at him.

"Only what, Mr. Landau?"

"Only . . . I guess I'd be real worried about that kid, the one you just said killed Mr. Pinchot. Real worried."

"But the woman's his grandmother."

"Is she?" Landau asked softly. "Didn't you just say she was mindless? At least that's what I inferred—"

Reed slammed the phone down.

"I have to leave," he said, heading for the door.

"We found an orderly down in the basement." The guard spoke, tonelessly, and Reed stopped. The man's eyes were blank, his face was slick and a slightly lighter gray than his uniform shirt.

"Is the orderly okay?" Reed tried to sound gentle and matter of fact at the same time, not wanting to jar the man and send him deeper into shock.

"No . . . not okay . . ."

Dead, Reed thought.

Belle killed someone else. . . .

Then the guard said, "He's pretty banged up, but he'll be okay. Said she took his car. At least his car keys. Ford Taurus, he said. I got the number." The guard raised a spiral notebook he had in his hand and read off the license number. He had on a black name tag pin with white letters, but Reed was too far away to read it.

The guard said, "It was Tabe she got. Big mother . . . about your size. She came up behind him, smashed him into the locker head first. He shouldn't have been down in the lockers this time of day, still had hours left on his shift. But he keeps a bottle down there, takes nips. Common knowledge . . . no one blames him. This is the fuckin' pit, this place. Literally, the pit. Snake pit, get it? Ha ha." The man's eyes glittered. "She just ran smack into him. Drove his head into the steel locker, then took his car keys. She's outta here."

"Car keys . . ." Something wrong there. "How'd she know which car?" Reed asked.

"Ford key . . . license plate tag on the key ring . . ."

"That's impossible. Belle Lambert couldn't find the car from a license number . . . start it . . ."

Only *she* clearly wasn't doing it. Myra was—Myra the ghost. No more Myra the helpless, he thought, then added to himself, in a fit of silliness that almost sent him into a paroxysm of laughter, *No more Mister Nice Guy.*

"Better get back," the guard said. "They want you down there to help figure out where she's headed."

Home, Reed thought; they'd figure that out without him. He looked at the terminal on the desk next to the phone.

"Look, you go on," he told the guard. "I've got one more call to make." The guard looked doubtful. "They sent me to find you."

"I'll just be a minute, but it's . . . private."

Reed picked up the phone, held it against his chest. The guard hesitated, then moved out of the doorway and down the hall. Reed waited until his footfalls died away, then he hung up the buzzing receiver and turned to the computer keyboard.

Getting into the file turned out to be easy. No reason the names of a bunch of incurable loonies would be worth anything on a mailing list or to the IRS and her file appeared when he typed her name. He moved the cursor up to *address,* pushed the yellow delete key, then *enter,* and poof! It was gone; then her name, leaving nothing on the screen but the long lines of type spelling out Dx, and all the tests that had been done on her since she'd been admitted/committed. But they began to roll up and disappear too, having no anchor to existence without her name.

A moment later, the screen was blank; Belle Lambert had essentially, for the rest of the night, anyway, vanished.

He found his way back to the rotunda and made his way across it to the front door, afraid someone would come yelling after him, but no one did.

CHAPTER 21

Myra kept getting the taped "Yo, shithead, this is five five five," and so on at the house on Bowman. And no answer at Trimble's on Route 202. The gas station must be closed, and instead of going home, the kid had gone to the movies with his buddies or a girlfriend. Or he'd stopped for a beer. Dick Lambert looked old enough to stay out past nine (it was nine fifteen) and buy a beer in the only local gin mill.

That's probably exactly where he was, she thought. There was only one in town, a shabby roadhouse down by the river. She hung up again and stared at the phone on the kitchen wall.

She had to stop this. She didn't really think anything had happened to Dick Lambert, wasn't even sure why she kept calling except that she'd been so positive this afternoon when she'd told his grandmother he was safe, she just wanted that extra certainty.

And couldn't get it. At least not tonight.

She sighed, wanting to give up and go into the den to watch TV with Bob, then upstairs to bed with a book: the best part of the day. But she reached for the phone to try Lambert again. Maybe this time she'd leave a message, although it was futile, since she knew he wouldn't call back.

She touched the receiver, and the phone rang. She snatched it off the cradle before it bothered Bob, who'd probably fallen asleep in front of the TV.

It was Reed calling from his car phone, yelling over the static with news that was sad, frightening, and almost impossible to believe.

Belle Lambert had escaped.

"She got a car key from one of the orderlies."

"How?" She had to stop herself from yelling back.

He hesitated, or that's what it sounded like, leaving her with nothing but a crackle of static. Then he said, "He must've been careless with them."

"But can she even drive . . . ?"

"I guess she can," he yelled.

Myra remembered the guardless exit from the lot. She thought it probably cost too much for the state to have a man there all hours. Or maybe they didn't feel it was necessary. But there had been a crossbar blocking the exit with a slot device, presumably for an ID card that would raise the bar. It had been raised when she'd left, but that had been around four in the afternoon. It would be down at night, a silent guard, like the traffic bumps they called sleeping policemen.

"There was a guard bar," Myra said.

"She just drove through it, My."

Myra tried to imagine the hulking, blank-faced woman, with the strand of drool running down the crease from her mouth, ramming a stolen car through the guard bar and driving off into the night.

It was beyond her, but it apparently *had* happened. The next question was why Reed called her about it.

She waited; static crackled through the phone. Then he said, "Myra, I think she's headed back to Riverside. Home."

"Probably."

"That'll be the first place they'll look for her."

Of course, Myra thought.

"My . . . I want you to go there. Intercept her if you can."

Shock kept Myra quiet.

"You hear me," Reed said urgently. He must be closer, out of the hills; the static cleared up.

"I hear you, Reed. But why?"

"I'm afraid . . . see . . . the orderly was . . . uh . . . hurt."

"She hurt him!"

"Yes . . ."

"I can't believe—"

"Well, it happened." A shrill note of impatience she had never heard from Reed before, and she knew he was leaving out something big.

"Reed . . ."

"They'll come looking for her, My. The locals will get to her before I do. You know what they're like."

Good ol' hill boys (mostly from Oban), who clanked when they moved from all the hardware they fastened to themselves.

Men craving action, and Reed said they'd come for Belle, thinking she was dangerous.

Reed said, "My, they'll know who you are, they'll be deferential. You can stop them. I won't make it in time."

She was silent.

"My . . . will you do it? Please."

"Of course." She couldn't let anything happen to Belle Lambert if she could help it. If only for the sake of the lovely woman who had hugged Myra umpteen Christmases ago and called her a love of a child.

But she better take someone to do the talking in case an attack of shyness tied her tongue. Before she could say this, Reed came out with the oddest thing. "My, stop her." His voice was low and urgent.

"I don't understand."

"I mean . . . for you to stop her. You can, My."

"From doing what?"

A beat of silence; the static came back. He must have entered a new set of hills. He said, "From getting away again. I mean . . . so the cops don't have to go on chasing her." The static rose, and he called over it, "I'll be there as soon as I can," and his voice disappeared. She didn't know if he'd hung up or been overwhelmed by the static.

She hung up, thought for a moment, then picked up the phone again to get help. Not Bob, who would ask endless questions, and hate her having anything to do with the cops. He called them townies with utter contempt.

But Lambie would go, and be much better at pulling rank on the locals than Myra. It was after nine; Lambie was probably stuck in a sitting room with her mother-in-law, who insisted on spending evenings with "her" Evan.

Lambie would grab a chance to get away if the Jaguar was out of the shop and could make it through the rest of the night. It was the most gorgeous car on the road, when it ran. If it wasn't running, Lambie'd have to sneak Evan's big, ugly, totally reliable Mercedes.

But Lambie said the Jag was operational, and *yes* . . . she wanted out for an hour or two.

"If she coos at him one more time, I'm going to break something over her head . . . and his." Lambie spoke in a hissing whisper. They must be close by.

"Only what'll I tell them?" she asked.

"The truth?" Myra suggested.

"That I'm going to help you save a madwoman from getting strapped to the fender of a cop car like a dead deer?"

Myra laughed. "No. Tell them that I need your help, and you don't know why. But I was very . . . insistent."

"The old bitch'll call you."

"I'll leave the phone off the hook." She glanced at the wall clock. "Bob's probably nodded off soundly by now. . . . " in his big easy chair, with his head resting comfortably against the side cushion.

It was almost nine thirty. Myra said, "We've got to hurry, Lamb."

"I'm on my way."

It would take Lambie five minutes to get here, then another five to eight to get to Riverside and Bowman Street. That'd still put them at the Lamberts' house well before Reed could possibly make it, even in the Porsche.

She just hoped they'd beat the cops.

She scrawled a note. "Bob, darling. Lambie called, needed to talk. We've taken a ride . . . back soon."

Then she signed *Love, My* and drew a little happy face under her name.

* * *

Dick Lambert dropped his keys on his dresser, then checked his answering machine. Nothing.

He flopped on the bed, pulled one foot across his thigh, and started untying his shoe.

He was woozy from the beer; it took a minute to get the laces in focus.

He blinked, everything steadied down, and he pulled out the knot, yanked the laces loose, then pulled off the shoe.

Something thudded in the kitchen. Or sounded like it had. He sat still, listening. Maybe the old man was out there getting a glass of water or something to eat.

He got the other shoe untied, pried it off his foot, and it fell with a thud . . . followed by another thud from the kitchen again.

The old man wouldn't thud around like that, and Dick got to his feet. He staggered slightly, then belched, sending beer fumes up his nose. He should've passed on that last round, but the others held it down just fine.

Shit-face Loamers could drink rings around Dick; a small thing, but he hated being outdone. He'd work on his drinking, though he suspected it was one thing he'd never be good at.

He pulled his shirt out of his pants, reached up under the tail, and unbuckled his belt.

He was going at this ass backwards, he thought . . . and heard another sound. Softer this time, but insistent. It sounded like someone was dragging a chair across the kitchen floor.

He opened his door; the hall was dark, no light under the old man's door.

No light in the kitchen either.

The old man wouldn't try finding his way in the dark . . . someone else was out there.

He stepped back into the room, slid open the upper drawer of his bureau, and scrabbled around in it until his hand closed around the butt of the old man's S&W 422 that he had "liberated" long ago.

He took it out of the drawer, checked that it was loaded, then sallied out into the hall in his stocking feet.

Here I come, ready or not, he thought. He should be a little nervous about this, and was joyous to find he was not. Mostly, he suspected, because he didn't believe there was a thief in the kitchen. He'd get there, snap on the light, and see some problem with a fixture or appliance, or a small animal—cat, mouse . . . bat—trying to find its way out.

He slid along the worn carpeting that the old man had actually vacuumed last Saturday, getting rid of the musty smell for the first time in living memory, got to the doorway and stopped, listening hard.

No more thumping or thudding; nothing but a very faint whoosh that sounded like breathing. Cats and mice don't breathe that loud, he thought; then he got a faint whiff of excrement and thought, *Holy shit, "Nana come home."* Like the collie. All the way from Housatonic Valley. It couldn't have been easy, and he wondered if she was wounded and emaciated, like Lassie had been.

Not emaciated, since she'd only been gone a few days. Only been here a few minutes, and already crapped in her drawers. Or maybe she'd done it before she got here.

He flicked the light switch, and there she was, her faintly gleaming eyes watching him. Looking at him, or at anything else, was something she hadn't done in years.

The fluorescents glowed green and grim, making everything uglier than it was.

She was as hideous as ever, except maybe not entirely, since her hair was still clean and still had that stupid blue ribbon in it that had been there when he'd taken his father to see her.

"Oh, shit, Nana," he said, putting the gun on the counter, "now what."

Now he'd call them to come and get her . . . or try to keep her, since this was clearly where she wanted to be. Who'd have the heart to send Lassie back after all she'd gone through to get home?

He could keep her, the money would flow again.

Only he wasn't sure he wanted the ugliest, fattest, smelliest human on earth rooted back in the kitchen like some disgusting growth.

Maybe it wasn't worth it after all; maybe he didn't give enough of a shit about the money. The fresh air was already warring with the smell of her . . . and losing.

He needed advice, and after a moment's reflection he turned his back

on the woman who sat across the room, with her blank eyes fixed on nothing, and he picked up the phone, and dialed Bart Loamers's number. Bart
also had his own phone, so Dick wouldn't wake his old lady or his killer of
a little sister, who had the attitude of a Great White with brains.

Bart answered on the first ring, sounding more than a little out of it.
Maybe he'd gotten a little pickled too.

"Whattaya want," he groaned into the phone, and Dick laughed.

"You'll never guess who's sitting in my kitchen."

"Goldilocks."

"How'd you know?" Dick said, and the old woman grabbed his arm in a
grip that felt like steel claws.

"Hey," he yelped, meaning to follow up with, "What goes!" But before
he could, she lifted and wrenched, and his feet left the floor. He heard a
loud, sickening pop, like a pistol with a worn-out silencer, and something
in his shoulder gave. He looked down, saw his arm dangling at an angle it
was never meant to, and realized his grandmother had ripped his arm out
of its socket. Pain hit at the same instant, but before he could scream, her
claws hooked the meat in front of his throat and ripped, then let go, and
hot thick blood gushed down his body and pooled around his feet.

"Dick!" Bart yelled into the phone. He got back a sound like an animal
gnawing, followed by whooshing silence. "Dick!" Bart wailed, knowing
Dick Lambert was doing a class-A number on him. That if he jammed on
his shoes, grabbed Ma's car, and raced the three blocks to Bowman, he'd
find Dickie Lambert laughing his ass off in the kitchen. "Dick!" he shouted
furiously into the phone, then heard something like heavy cloth—sailcloth
or canvas—ripping, followed by a gurgle like something thick running
down the drain . . . then nothing but that whooshing silence again.

"Dick, you cocksucking fuck!"

Whoosh-whooooosh . . . a crackle, then dead air. The deepest silence he
had ever heard.

He slammed the phone down, yanked on his sneakers, and raced for the
key rack. He hesitated and looked back at the phone. He could call the
cops and just say there was trouble at 81 Bowman without giving his name.

But calling the cops out could open Dick and maybe Bart to a whole lot
more trouble than they could handle.

Lambie killed the Jag's motor; they looked up at the house.

"Not exactly Sandringham."

"Not exactly." Myra raised her voice over what sounded like a billion
peepers in the marsh. Even in the soft light of the half moon, the house
looked shabby.

"Now what?" Lambie asked.

Myra didn't know; she had spent all her concentration getting here. "I
thought everything would be clear."

"Well, guess what."

They climbed out of the car and started up the walk to the swaybacked
front steps. "What a dump!" Lambie gave a whispered imitation of Bette
Davis.

"I guess we just wait, and try to reassure the police when they show up,"
Myra said.

"Reassure them of what?"

"That pros are on their way, and she's harmless—"

At that, the glass inset in the front door shattered, the door came out of
the frame and crashed forward, and Belle Lambert waddled out on the
porch dragging something. Myra and Lambie clutched each other's hands;
the peepers' croaks rose in volume and intensity. Belle came to the edge of
the porch and pulled whatever it was—a pile of rags, it looked like—
around in front of her and let it go. It sank to the porch floor, rolled, and
stopped, and Myra saw what was left of Dick Lambert's face.

One eye bulged out of his head; the other was gone, leaving behind a
deep red hole out of which trickled blood that looked black in the moonlight. Belle put her foot under the body and heaved; it rolled down two
steps, then one arm got hung up on a porch rail. The other arm was
missing.

Lambie gobbled and tried to scream. Her mouth opened in an oval, her
tongue froze to her palate, and she couldn't make a sound. Myra clutched
Lambie's arm, also wanting to scream, but all she could do was gasp in air

and keep gasping until she knew she was going to faint.

Breathe out, Reed once told her. Get rid of carbon dioxide . . . breathe out. . . .

She forced out air in a long, vulgar-sounding snort and let go of Lambie, who was backing toward the Jag, making little mewing noises. Myra came forward a step, then another, then she looked at the blood-covered boy on the steps, praying for some sign of life. She didn't know what she'd do if she saw one, though, because she'd never have the guts to try to wrest the body from the bulk of Belle Lambert waiting treacherously at the edge of the porch. Only Myra suddenly knew she *would*; if the kid were alive, she'd grab some part of him—the rag of his shirt, one of his legs—and pull him away.

Belle might come after them and Lambie was still backpedaling. But Lambie would rush back to help and between them they'd get the kid to the car.

But the blood was only trickling, not pumping out of the eye socket; the other eye stared fixedly at the chipped, splintered wooden step next to the cement walk. The boy was dead.

She looked up at Belle Lambert, who stared at something over Myra's head.

At Lambie?

Myra backed up. "Don't move," she hissed at Lambie. "Stand still, don't move."

Lambie froze; Myra edged back toward her. Belle Lambert took a step down and Myra moved back until her heel stepped hard on Lambie's foot. Lambie grunted in pain; Belle seemed to tense at the sound . . . then came a distraction. A vehicle pulled up, and another boy, about Dick Lambert's age, jumped out of it.

Myra knew him from the market and the garage: Bart Loamers, who had confessed to Reed two nights ago.

He moaned at what he saw and Belle turned, homing in on the sound of distress like a shark on the thrashing of a wounded fish. But the boy wasn't aware of her or of anything but the body on the second-to-last step. He raced to it, screaming the dead boy's name, then must have taken in the extent of the ruin, and came to a sudden, flailing, almost comical stop. But he was too close; and too late he looked up at the shapeless bulk of the woman above him. He reared back, she lashed out, grabbed the front of his sweatshirt, and lifted. The shirt strained under his arms, Myra saw his bare back with the indent of his spine. The sweatshirt material tautened, and she prayed it would tear, but it held. Belle shook him like a dog worrying a sock, then pitched him forward; his body sailed through the air, clipped a lamppost with a thunk, and fell. Myra started toward him, but that would leave Lambie unprotected, and the faint, dead gleam of Belle Lambert's eyes was already tracking back to fix on her. Myra slid back to shield her friend.

Then everything happened at once. The boy rolled over and tried to sit up, making Myra yell at him not to move—as much from the danger of dismantling his spine if it was injured as from Belle getting him. At the same time, a man came out of the house in his underwear, and Reed's Porsche snarled up to the house and double-parked between the boy's car and the Jag. Reed sprang out of the car, still doubled over in a sitting posture, and smashed right into the side of the car.

He reared back, and groaned dazedly.

"Christ, Myra, stop her!"

Myra looked at him, then at the woman coming down the stairs, stepping smartly over the body on them. Now Belle had her choice of Myra, Lambie, or the boy, pulling himself groggily into a sitting position. And finally Reed, trying to find his way between the boy's car and the Jag. They were too close, he leaped up on the car bumpers to come through to the sidewalk, but his foot sank into the slight space between them, leaving one leg bent, foot resting on the Jag bumper and the other foot on the ground between the cars.

He tried to dredge the foot out, but it wouldn't come; he tried to get his other foot down so he'd be balanced, but he couldn't do that either . . . while Belle's faintly gleaming eyes watched.

He could not move back or forward, was trapped, easy prey. But Belle went for the boy still trying to roll over and sit up.

Myra yelled and raised her arms to distract her. The empty eyes shifted to her, then away; she didn't want Myra. Myra shrieked, "Belle . . . over here . . . Belle . . . " until her neck tendons bulged, but Belle didn't even pause in her forward roll toward the groggy boy.

Then Reed reached under his jacket and drew a neat-looking gun that gleamed dully in the streetlight.

"Stop her!" Reed was looking at Myra.

"Reed . . ."

He trained the gun on Belle. "Stop her," he yelled at Myra.

Belle was getting closer. The boy shook his head as if to clear it. Reed pulled on his trapped foot and his pant leg tore, exposing bare skin. He pulled again, skin scraped away, blood started to soak the trousers. Reed wailed, "Myra . . . please, honey, I can't . . . can't . . . " The hulking woman approached the kid, flesh quivering under the long hospital robe.

"Stop her," Reed cried. "I can't shoot her . . . for God's sake, Myra . . . "

Myra tried to distract her again; she jigged up and down, screeching, "Belle . . . Belle . . . please . . . Belle . . . "

Reed aimed the gun dead center at Belle Lambert and sobbed, "Jesus, Myra . . . stop her." He really believed she could, seemed to *know* she could.

You don't know what sorry means yet, she'd told the kid. Well, he did now, but only after she'd gone to see Belle: Somehow set her going? And now she was supposed to stop her. Reed sobbed wordlessly, gun on target. No way could he miss blowing a hole in the woman he'd tried so hard to help for so long.

"Stop her," Reed wailed.

Belle was a few feet from the boy. Reed babbled, "Landau said it was you . . . that it's in your mind, Myra. That you started it, you can stop it. You are the ghost. You understand, Myra . . . *you are the ghost.*"

Myra gasped; Lambie huddled against the car.

"Do you hear me? Stop her . . . now." Reed cocked the gun; the solid click was audible over the peepers, and the noise of people coming out of their houses to see what was happening.

Belle kept coming, stolidly, inexorably. The boy had managed to raise his head a little and blearily watched death in the form of a fat lady in a hospital robe close in on him.

"Please . . . " sobbed Reed. Tears shone on his face in the lamplight. Myra had not seen him cry since his father died years ago. Dear, generous, funny, coarse Sol Lerner, who must have bought the gun Reed now aimed at Belle Lambert's puff-pouter chest. He was a few feet from Myra, but she could see his finger tense on the trigger.

He was going to shoot Belle to save the boy. As he should, since the kid was innocent, had not hurt anyone, and that was exactly what she had warned Goody Redman—the ghost of Goody Redman, she corrected herself—might happen. Only Reed was right. There was no ghost. Goody Redman had been rotting quietly in the basement for three hundred years like the demure corpse she had always been. There was no specter, spirit, ghost, or wraith. Nothing but what Don had enumerated as dead mice and millipedes, old sweating stone, and sour dirt.

Myra had invented the flicker-tinkle in the basement the night of the sleet storm to escape knowing what she could do. But she was stuck now, because running under her bumpy thoughts about the basement and the ghost that wasn't there was a sure, silky stream of knowledge that she *could* stop Belle Lambert.

"Myra . . . " Reed wailed, and Belle's finger hooked the boy's shirt.

Myra filled her lungs with air and said in a carrying voice that sounded crazily conversational, "Stop, Belle."

Her heart leaped with hope that Reed was wrong, because Belle kept on dragging the boy away from the lamppost to give herself more room. But she let go of him a second later. Her hand fell to her side, her body sagged, then settled slowly to the sidewalk, with her legs splayed out in front of her and her head bent back into that broken-doll tilt.

"Myra?" Reed whispered her name. Out of the corner of his eye, he saw Lambie lean against the Jag. Sirens were screaming from the direction of the river, drowning out the peepers.

"Myra . . . "

Belle canted over on her side; Bart Loamers had given up and lay flat on his back next to the lamppost, his chest rising and falling with his breath. He was okay, Belle was okay.

"Myra . . ." Reed's voice came out hoarsely.

They looked at each other.

It was over, time for him to disengage the safety, stuff the gun back in his belt, wait for the cops to show up with the paramedics or with orderlies from Housatonic, to collect the empty hulk Belle had turned back into.

But he swung the gun toward Myra and, without knowing he was going to, drew a bead on the space between her breasts.

He had to do it. He knew the interest he'd see in Lambie's eyes if he turned to look at her. Lambie was almost as quick on the uptake as My; would already be calculating what Myra might do about Joan the Bitch for her best friend Lambie.

The others' calculations wouldn't be much slower, and while there wasn't much they'd ask of their dear friend at the moment, there would be. They had been eight spoiled, scared, isolated rich kids. Would now be seven spoiled, scared, isolated, *invincible* rich adults. It was the most poisonous combination he could imagine. He could not let it come together.

His finger tightened on the trigger. Myra looked at the gun but did not flinch, and he remembered her running at a solid line of kids years ago . . .

Red rover, red rover, let Myra come over. Over she raced with her long yellow hair shining in the sun, and she would hit the line full speed, without flinching or squinching her eyes shut the way the other girls did.

They stared at each other for what felt like a long time, Myra waiting in her accepting way while he tried vainly to get rid of the vision of her as a little girl on a sunny day. He finally gave up, disengaged the safety, and let his hand with the gun in it fall to his side.

CHAPTER 22

"How?" Don sounded like the head Injun in a trash western from the forties, Myra thought. She was at the shut kitchen door, straining to hear over the gurgle of the coffee maker. She missed most of what was said, but had come out here and taken five times longer than necessary to make a pot of coffee so Reed could tell them what had happened without Myra there.

She tried to hear Reed's answer to Don's *how*. He had told her about psychokinesis, PK. (They had an acronym for everything.) But Myra didn't buy it. Don either, from what she could hear, but he didn't have an alternate explanation, and there probably wasn't one.

They were all talking back and forth now; their voices rose and fell, half hushed, half strident. They sounded shocked, angry, awed, and mostly horrified—couldn't believe Myra—their Myra—their good, dear, decent ... blah, blah, blah.

She couldn't believe it either.

But she was getting used to the idea; so were Reed and Lambie. Especially Lambie.

As soon as they had been told four days ago that Bart Loamers would be

324

okay, a gauging look had come into Lambie's eyes. Myra knew she was thinking that if Myra could take care of Pastori, who had insulted her; of Bill, who'd beaten up Angie; and the kid who had killed Arlen . . . couldn't she do something about Joan Folger, the mother-in-law from hell?

It would occur to the others as well if they gave it time. If they didn't just tell Reed they could not possibly go on having lunch and playing bridge with . . . a monster. No matter how long they had known her or how close they had been.

Their rejection would be the worst thing that ever happened to her.

She bent her head close to the door, waiting.

The coffee pot shut up. Quickly, to get back to the door as fast as possible, she poured the coffee into her mother's silver pot, put it on a tray with the orange frosted cakes she'd made, and went back to the door. It was very quiet out there . . . they might have gotten up and left while she was pouring coffee, putting the little cakes on her good Spode cake plate.

Then she heard knitting needles click. Helen was knitting! Myra clutched the tray handles; her hands were sweating and the handles started to slip. She balanced the tray on the counter and got a firmer grip on it, then went back to the door.

There was so much she could do for them. For instance, there were those delinquents from Oban who had been speeding across Don and Irene's place, trashing shrubs and flowers. Irene was also sure they sneaked back at night and used the pool, which was too far from the house for them to hear and surrounded by trees and the requisite fencing so kids or small animals couldn't fall in and drown.

They could be seven people it would be very dangerous to tamper with from now on, thanks to Myra.

It was silent again. Helen had stopped knitting, and Myra imagined her looking up from her work while the others looked back at her, waiting for her to speak. Reed, with his mouth open a fraction, and that little line of worry between his eyes because no matter now much he cared for Myra (Myra never doubted his love for her), he was a torn man. They must all be torn right now . . . except Lambie, who knew just how she felt about this, Myra thought.

C'mon, Helen, she rooted silently, say something.

Then Helen's clear, young-sounding voice said, "Whatever she can or can't do, she's still *Myra*."

Silence again, then clicking needles as Helen resumed knitting.

Irene said, "That's right, and I don't see what difference anything else makes."

"Me either," said Lambie, being a bit of a snake in the grass, Myra thought, because Lambie had her own agenda. But Myra was stupendously grateful to her anyway. Silence again. No one scraped back their chair to leave, and Myra knew they would have by now if they were going to.

She got a good grip on the tray handles, pushed her hip against the swinging door, and levered herself out into the breakfast room.

"Coffee and dessert, everyone?" she said, and was rewarded with six shy, slightly awestruck smiles of affection.